DYNASTY 30

The Measure of Days

Also in the *Dynasty* series:

THE FOUNDING
THE DARK ROSE
THE PRINCELING
THE OAK APPLE
THE BLACK PEARL
THE LONG SHADOW
THE CHEVALIER
THE MAIDEN
THE FLOOD-TIDE
THE TANGLED THREAD
THE EMPEROR
THE VICTORY
THE REGENCY
THE CAMPAIGNERS
THE RECKONING
THE DEVIL'S HORSE
THE POISON TREE
THE ABYSS
THE HIDDEN SHORE
THE WINTER JOURNEY
THE OUTCAST
THE MIRAGE
THE CAUSE
THE HOMECOMING
THE QUESTION
THE DREAM KINGDOM
THE RESTLESS SEA
THE WHITE ROAD
THE BURNING ROSES

The Measure of Days

Cynthia Harrod-Eagles

SPHERE

First published in Great Britain in 2007 by Sphere
Reprinted 2008

A CIP catalogue record for this book is available from the British Library.

ISBN: 978-1-84744-151-5

Typeset in Plantin by
Palimpsest Book Production Limited,
Grangemouth, Stirlingshire
Printed and bound in Great Britain by
Mackays of Chatham plc, Chatham, Kent

Sphere
An imprint of
Little, Brown Book Group
100 Victoria Embankment
London EC4Y 0DY

An Hachette Livre UK Company
www.hachettelivre.co.uk

www.littlebrown.co.uk

For Tony, with love and thanks – I couldn't do it without you.

THE MORLANDS OF MORLAND PLACE

James

Benedict
1812–1870
m. (1) Rosalind
Fleetham

m. (2) Sibella
Mayhew

Lucy

THE LONDON MORLANDS (*qv*)

George
1849–1885

TEDDY
b. 1850

m. (1)
Charlotte Byng

m. (2)
Alice Meynell

m. (1) Edgar
Fortescue

HENRIETTA
b. 1853
m. (2) Jerome
Compton

Regina
1857–1907
m. Sir Peregrine
Parke, Bt

NED
b. 1885
m. 1911
Jessie
Compton

POLLY
b. 1900

JAMES
WILLIAM
b. 1910

LIZZIE
b. 1872
m. 1897
Ashley
Morland

JACK
b. 1886
m. 1915
Helen
Ormerod

ROBBIE
b. 1887
m. 1909
Ethel
Cornleigh

FRANK
b. 1889

JESSIE
b. 1890
m. 1911
Ned Morland

BERTIE
b. 1876
m. 1909
Maud
Puddephat

MARTIAL
b. 1898

RUPERT
b. 1899

ROSE
b. 1909

ROBERTA
b. 1911

JEREMY
b. 1912

HARRIET
b. 1915

RICHARD
b. 1912

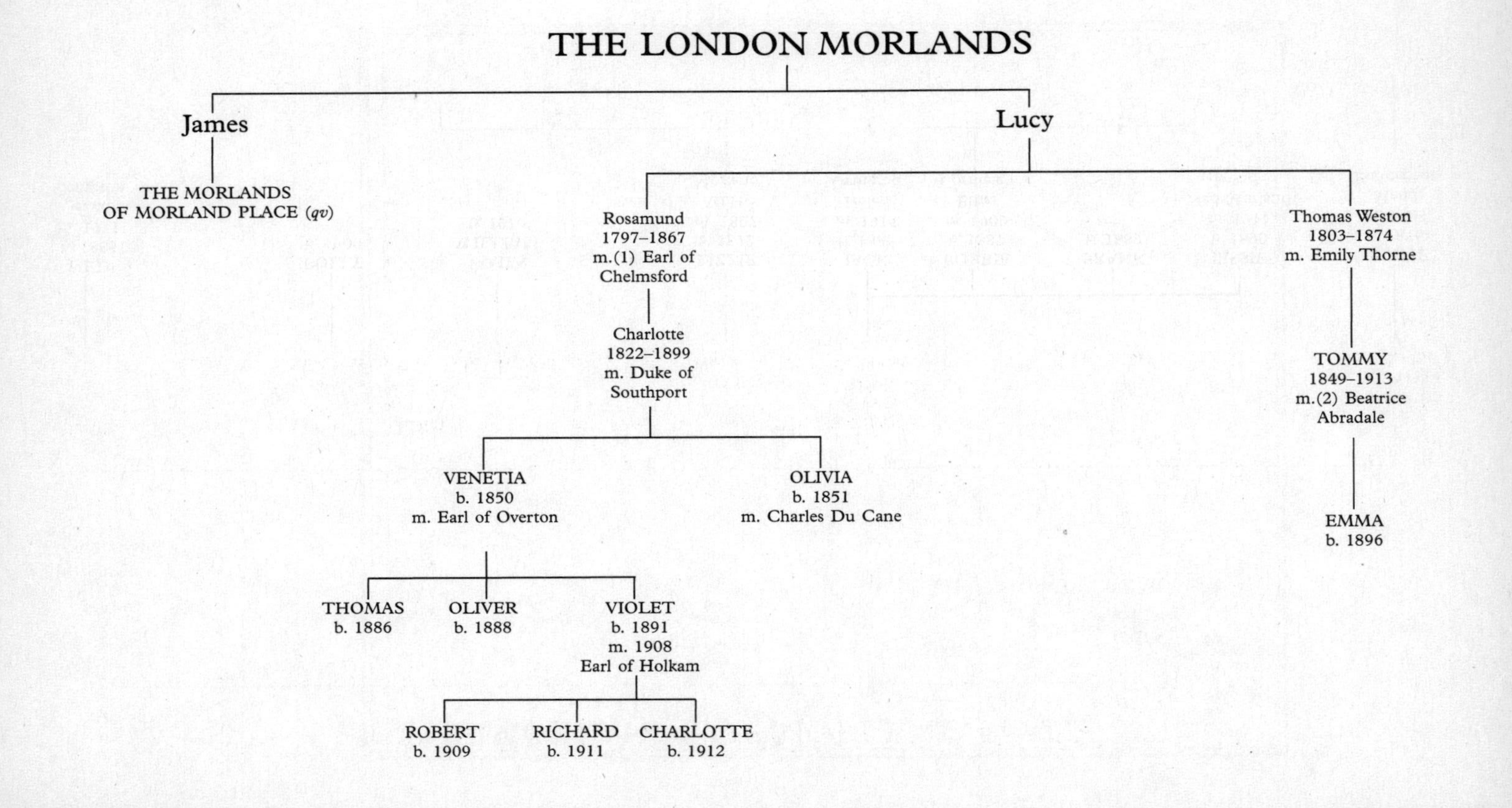
THE LONDON MORLANDS
James
Lucy
THE MORLANDS OF MORLAND PLACE (qv)
Rosamund 1797–1867 m.(1) Earl of Chelmsford
Thomas Weston 1803–1874 m. Emily Thorne
Charlotte 1822–1899 m. Duke of Southport
TOMMY 1849–1913 m.(2) Beatrice Abradale
VENETIA b. 1850 m. Earl of Overton
OLIVIA b. 1851 m. Charles Du Cane
EMMA b. 1896
THOMAS b. 1886
OLIVER b. 1888
VIOLET b. 1891 m. 1908 Earl of Holkam
ROBERT b. 1909
RICHARD b. 1911
CHARLOTTE b. 1912

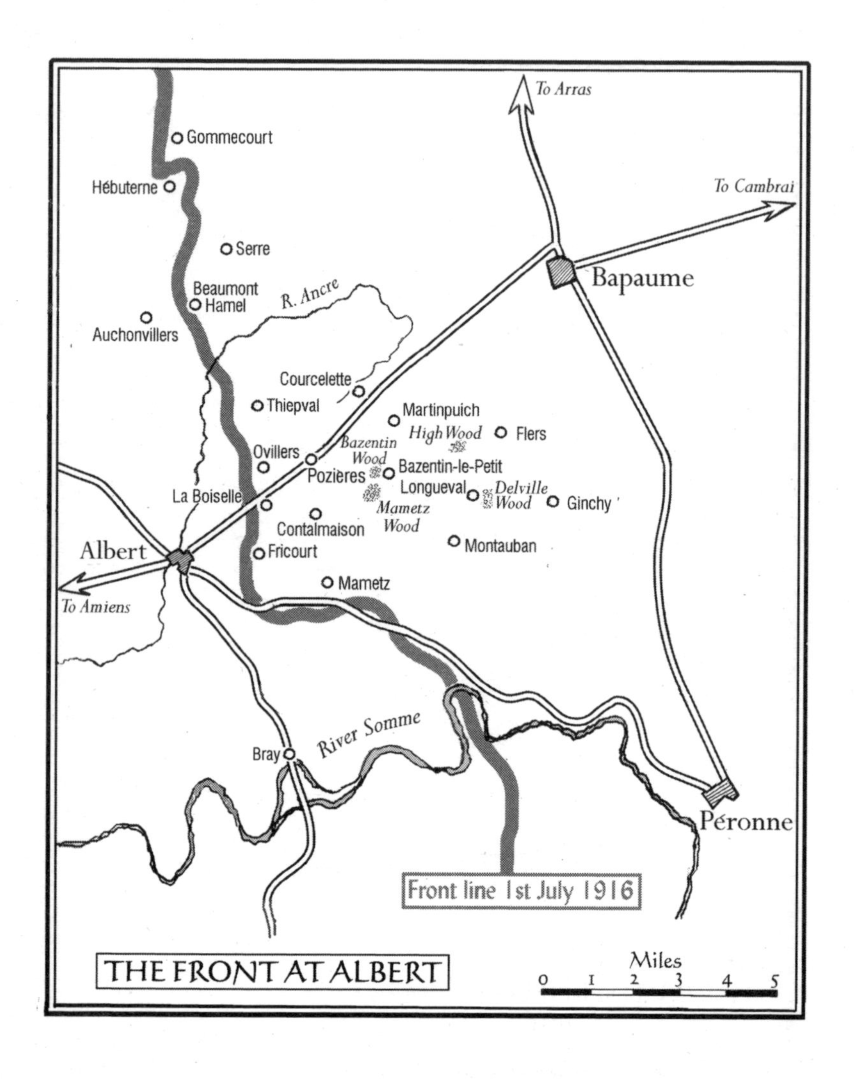
To Arras
To Cambrai
Gommecourt
Hébuterne
Serre
Beaumont Hamel
Auchonvillers
R. Ancre
Bapaume
Courcelette
Thiepval
Martinpuich
High Wood
Flers
Ovillers
Bazentin Wood
Pozières
Bazentin-le-Petit
Longueval
Delville Wood
Ginchy
La Boiselle
Mametz Wood
Contalmaison
Albert
Fricourt
Montauban
To Amiens
Mametz
River Somme
Bray
Péronne
Front line 1st July 1916
THE FRONT AT ALBERT
Miles
0 1 2 3 4 5

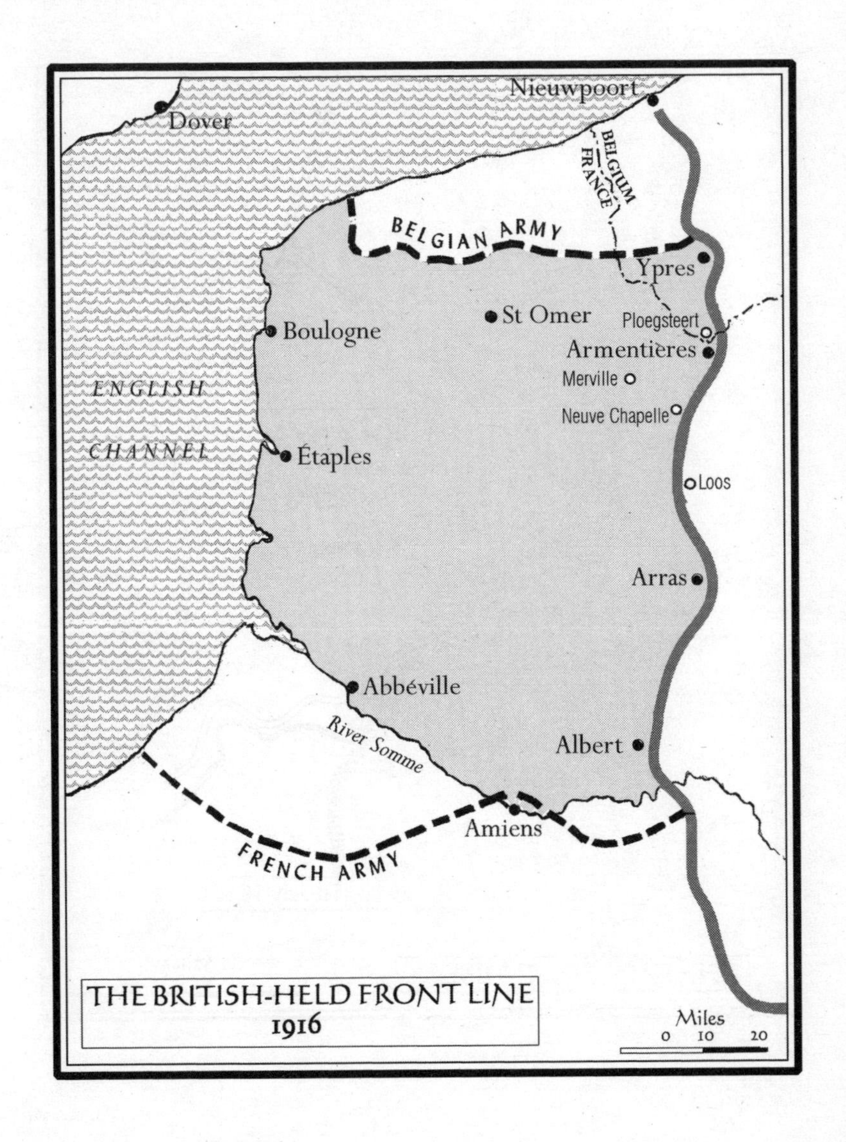

Nieuwpoort
Dover
BELGIUM
FRANCE
BELGIAN ARMY
Ypres
St Omer
Ploegsteert
Boulogne
Armentières
Merville
ENGLISH
CHANNEL
Neuve Chapelle
Étaples
Loos
Arras
Abbéville
River Somme
Albert
Amiens
FRENCH ARMY
THE BRITISH-HELD FRONT LINE
1916
Miles
0 10 20

BOOK ONE

Changes

The anguish of the earth absolves our eyes
Till beauty shines in all that we can see.
War is our scourge; yet war has made us wise,
And, fighting for our freedom, we are free.

Horror of wounds and anger at the foe,
And loss of things desired; all these must pass.
We are the happy legion, for we know
Time's but a golden wind that shakes the grass.

Siegfried Sassoon, 'Absolution'

Lord, let me know my end,
and what is the measure of my days

Psalm 39 v4

CHAPTER ONE

30th September 1915

The first post arrived early at Morland Place. Eddoes, the stable boy, lived next door to the postmaster and was given the early delivery to bring with him when he came in to work. So when Jessie came down at seven, the butler Sawry had already sorted the letters and placed them on the table in the great hall. But there was nothing for her, nothing from the Front. Her disappointment was acute. The battle at Loos had been fought on the 25th and 26th of September, and she had calculated that there could be a letter today. She turned away, pushing down disappointment and worry.

It was one of her hospital mornings, and she had to be at Clifton at a quarter to eight. The house was quiet, and the small dining-room seemed dark and a little chill. She sat alone at the long, polished table, with her dog Brach lying across her feet. Her mother Henrietta would not be up for another half-hour – since Jessie had moved back to her childhood home, it had been an object to get her mother to rest a little more. Uncle Teddy, the master of Morland Place, had already been and gone. He took his first breakfast at half past six before going off round the estate, and would return for a second at nine when the rest of the family came down. But Morland Place routine rose above all variations, and eggs and bacon were waiting for Jessie under the covers. There was fresh coffee in the pot, and as she sat down Sawry came in with toast.

He knew, of course, that there had been no letter for her. His silence brimmed with sympathy as he placed the toast-rack on the table and laid the newspaper beside her. In most households it was a cardinal sin for anyone to open the paper before the master had had it, but Sawry's gesture told Jessie that if she wanted to read it, he would see it was refolded properly before Uncle Teddy returned.

Jessie left it unopened. In her state of suspended anxiety she had no interest in the military situation. She knew what the paper would be full of. The Loos action had been hailed excitedly as the first real victory of the war. The German defences had been smashed, the line advanced and held. Without opening it, she knew there would be pages of triumphant analysis, diagrams of advances, maps showing where the front line had been and where it was now, with the area in between impressively shaded.

One day she might be able to be pleased about all that. For now, she wanted only to know that her men were safe. They were her cousins, both, and dear to her: Ned, whom she had married, and Bertie, with whom – oh, helplessly! and since they were both married, hopelessly – she had fallen in love. Bertie had been in France from the beginning; Ned had fought for the first time at Neuve Chapelle, then at Ypres. Loos was his third major action, and Bertie's . . . No, she had lost count of how many Bertie had seen. They had come through so far with only minor wounds. But it didn't make the waiting any easier each time. She chewed and swallowed bacon, eggs and toast to fuel herself for the day ahead, but they might have been cardboard for all she tasted them. All she wanted was the pencilled scrawl on a scrap of grubby paper that said, 'I am well', the life-line flung out from the Front.

At a quarter to eight she set off in the little Austin. Ned had bought it to replace their pre-war Arno when he left her to join up. He'd always said the Arno was too big for a woman to drive – a point of contention between them. He didn't really approve of women driving at all. There had been many of those little, uneasy differences between them. It seemed that you could not know what a man was really like before you married him. She and Ned had grown up together, and he had been as an indulgent and admiring elder brother. But as a husband he had what she felt were old-fashioned ideas about what she should and shouldn't do. Perhaps they shouldn't have married . . . She shook that thought away, and replaced it with an urgent prayer: *Let him be safe! Please, God, let them both be safe!*

It was a fine day, full of soft, late sunshine, a little hazy, with the smoky autumn tang of blackberries and dying leaves. As she drove along her eye took note of things – the autumn colours just beginning in the elms and chestnuts, the hawthorn berries reddening in the hedges, the sudden emptiness where the summer madness of martins had gone. The oats were ripe up at White House Farm; the potatoes wanted a week or so more. At Woodhouse, where the wheat had been cut, they would be fleet-ploughing this week. The natural world, the farming year went on in their massive immutability, as though there were no bloody struggle in France, laying waste to women's hearts.

At the hospital she was greeted by Sister Morgan with the usual snarl: like many professional nurses, she resented the volunteers the war had thrust upon her. She began with an accusation about a bottle of disinfectant broken and the pieces hidden in the dustbin. Jessie was not guilty, but she did not bother to protest. Sin was always attributed to the lowest and least nurse on the ward. Whoever really had done it would not dream of sacrificing herself to save 'the VAD' – as Jessie was called, though she was not one. 'VAD' was a pejorative term to Sister Morgan, who finished her dressing-down by giving Jessie all the toilsome and disagreeable jobs to do. First there were bed-pans to clean; then the floors to be scrubbed. After the dressing round she was given the bloody bandages to wash, and when she had finished that, there were the bed-wheels to clean and oil – anything to keep her away from the patients.

But she was glad of the hard work, which blanked out her thoughts. Besides, propriety demanded that she maintain a cheerful mien. 'Chin up' and 'There's a war on' were the phrases now commonly used in response to any hardship or privation. In peacetime any show of emotion had been regarded as not quite the done thing; in wartime it had become positively unpatriotic. Waiting for news from a man at the Front? So were ten thousand others. Grin and bear it. Don't you know there's a war on?

Her day's work finished at nine in the evening, and by then she was in a state of physical exhaustion beyond thought. She drove herself home, where her mother, knowing she could not have borne either company or conversation, silently helped her out of her coat, saw that she had her supper – mutton stew and a baked apple – then sent her straight up to bed. Her maid Tomlinson had a bath ready for her beside the fire; helped her undress, dried her afterwards and put her into a warmed nightgown, as if she were a child. Jessie was grateful both for the attention and the restraint. How hard it must be for her fellow nurses on Maitland Ward, who would not be so petted at the end of a hard day! She got into bed, and was asleep before Tomlinson had finished folding her clothes. She wasn't even wakened by the inevitable noise and bustle of removing the bath.

The 30th had been the last of her three hospital days that week, and on the next morning she slept late and went down to breakfast at ten to nine. Uncle Teddy was already there, seated at the end of the table with the newspaper open. He looked up and smiled as Jessie came in. 'Something for you from France,' he said, nodding to the letter by her plate.

It was from Bertie – she knew as soon as she saw it. He and Ned had both been taught in the same style, but his handwriting was smaller and firmer. Relief flooded her. He had written – he was safe! But, oh, it was an envelope that had seen hard times! The corners were battered, there were muddy marks on it, and the direction was smeared where water had dripped on it. Inside, the notepaper was no better – a cheap sheet to begin with, rough and porous, with what seemed to be a coffee stain on one corner, and dirty finger-marks here and there. It hurt her in a strange way, to think of Bertie's having dirty hands, when he had always been so particular about his appearance. It brought home to her the privations of the Front in a starkly simple way. Bertie was in a place where even washing your hands was not to be taken for granted.

The letter was a brief one.

28th September, near Houchin

My dearest Jessie,

I am snatching a moment from duties to let you know I am all right. We came out of the line early yesterday morning and were all day getting back to our billets, as the roads were choked. We did not get here until after ten last night. We had hard fighting but acquitted ourselves with honour. My untried men never flinched, though the German fire was hot as Hades. We are counting the cost today – around 400 of the battalion not at roll-call, though we hope many more stragglers will come in. The fighting goes on, but we are out of it for now. I came through without a scratch – Fenniman too – but Pennyfather was wounded, I don't know yet how seriously. More later, but a thousand duties call me now. God bless you.

Your loving cousin,

Bertie

She read it again for the joy of knowing he had come through. Uncle Teddy was watching her. Bertie's letters to Morland Place were always addressed to her, but everyone was interested in his welfare. She got up and took the letter to her uncle, then went to serve herself with breakfast while he read it, finding herself suddenly hungry. The sausages smelled wonderful, and there were mushrooms – the benison of autumn.

'Well, that is good news!' Teddy exclaimed. 'Now we only have to hear from Ned.' Ned was his adopted son, the bastard child of his late brother, but he had given him his name and a fortune, and could not have loved him more if he had been the child of his body. It had been a cause of great joy to him when Ned had married Jessie. He liked to keep those he loved close about him. 'So they had fierce fighting of it?' he went on. 'Shame about his friend Pennyfather. Is Fenniman the one you met in London, who took a fancy to our little Emma?'

Jessie chatted to him lightly until the others came down – her mother, Teddy's wife Alice and his daughter Polly, and Jessie's brother Robert and his wife Ethel. Teddy announced the good news, and Henrietta threw him a look of silent relief. Bertie was the son of their late sister Regina. In his rather turbulent youth he had often been at outs with his father, and had taken refuge at Morland Place, where Henrietta had mothered him. She sometimes called him her 'extra son'.

Ethel, who was not distinguished for her tact, immediately wondered why, if Bertie had written, nothing had come from Ned.

'We shall hear tomorrow, mark my words,' Teddy said at once, in a cheerful, confident tone. However worried he was, it was necessary for the master of Morland Place not to show it at a time like this. He was looked up to by so many people, from the servants and tenants to the townspeople of York and the volunteers in the York Commercials, the 'Kitchener' battalion he had helped to found. Morale must be kept up.

The next day there was no letter from Ned. Early news from the Front was good news; each day that passed made good news less likely. Of course, his unit might not have come out of the line as early as Bertie's – there was always that. And the first of the officer casualty lists appeared in *The Times* that day, and Ned's name was not there.

'He's all right, I tell you,' Teddy told the uncertain faces round the breakfast table. 'I feel it in my bones.'

Rob took up the cause. 'His letter might have gone astray. It happens all the time at the bank. I had a very angry customer the other day, who'd sent an instruction by post, which we never received. Ned could have sent a message and it got lost.'

'That's a likely explanation,' Teddy agreed. 'But he'll have had my letter by now, and he'll write again. We'll hear tomorrow for sure. Tomorrow, or the next day.'

Jessie wrote another note to Ned, and replied to Bertie's letter, asking if he knew anything. 'If you have seen him, do let us know. Or if you see him, ask him to send us a note to say he is well. We are all anxious until we hear from him.'

Another day with no letter. There were men, now, back in England, wounded, and talking to their relatives. Rumours began to circulate. There had been a lack of organisation in the aftermath. The casualties had been heavier than anticipated, and insufficient hospital trains had been provided to move the wounded to the base hospitals. The casualty clearing stations were clogged, and problems had backed up all the way down the line. Men were still lying untreated in the fields around the medical tents, their names not even having been taken.

'He could be wounded, then, and we wouldn't know about it,' said Henrietta at dinner.

Jessie ate soup without answering. She saw that her mother had stopped hoping he was completely unhurt. She was settling for his being wounded rather than dead – the latter was unthinkable. But Jessie knew a little of what machine-gun bullets and shrapnel could do. She was not willing yet to bargain. She could not bear to imagine such damage to the smooth body she had slept beside and taken such pleasure of during their marriage. He must be alive and he must be unhurt.

Still no letter came. Bertie's reply to Jessie arrived, and she knew from the length of it that it was not simple good news.

6th October 1915. Near Houchin
My dearest Jessie,
I am sorry that you have had nothing yet from Ned – though you may have heard by the time you receive this letter. I hope so. I have made enquiries of my own but have nothing definite to report. The Kents were in very fierce fighting, both on Hill 70 and at Chalk Pit Wood, and were very much cut up. I believe fewer than a hundred of them came back, but that is only hearsay. Their colonel and all the staff were among the casualties, so there is no-one left in the battalion to make arrangements and take names, etc. I understand someone from Brigade staff is to take over for the time being.

I cannot hold out much hope that he is entirely unharmed – I think my enquiries would have found him if he had been on his feet and with the survivors – but there is every hope that he will be found among the wounded. You cannot imagine the confusion and muddle here, and it is perfectly possible for a man not to be on any list. I am still having men turn up, having been 'lost' the best part of two weeks. Perhaps he is even now on his way home in a hospital ship without any idea that you do not know his fate. Once he is in England you will be sure to hear from him. I shall keep making enquiries, and let you know at once if I hear anything more.

As ever,
Bertie

There was enough here to keep hope going at Morland Place. Official notification generally took weeks to arrive, but in normal circumstances one could expect a letter from the battalion's commanding officer quite soon after the event. In this case, there was no commanding officer to perform the service, as Teddy pointed out with minor triumph. Ned's name still did not appear on any of the casualty lists, and that gave support to his hopes. Jessie would not talk about it at all. Her only defence was to blank out her thoughts with hard work. At the hospital, at her stables at Twelvetrees, where she bred horses for the army, she flung herself into the most exhausting tasks to try to keep out the fears that were knocking always at her mind, demanding admission.

So things stood on the day the telephone call came. The apparatus was fixed to the wall in the kitchen passage, on the family side of the green-baize door. Sawry came out from his room to answer it.

A woman's voice said, 'Am I connected with Morland Place?'

'Yes, madam. To whom did you wish to speak?'

'I'm not quite sure. This is Sister Wheatley of the Waterloo Ward in St George's Hospital. To whom am I speaking?'

'I am the butler, madam.'

'Ah. Then perhaps I had better speak to your master.'

'I will bring Mr Morland to the instrument, madam, if you will be so kind as to wait.'

Sawry went away, ascertained that Mr Morland was in the steward's room with his secretary, Baskin, and delivered his message. The mixture of hope and anxiety in the master's eyes was painful to see. Behind the green-baize door the same arguments and anxieties had been rehearsed as among the family. Sawry went back to the telephone in the hall, made sure that the call was connected – and then hesitated. He was a good servant and it had never in his life before even *occurred* to him to eavesdrop on a Family conversation; but if this were – as surely it must be? – something to do with Mr Ned . . . Sawry's struggle lasted one fierce second before in shame and defiance he put the receiver to his ear.

'What can I do for you, Sister Wheatley?' There was the faintest discernible tremor in the master's voice.

She explained. 'I am in charge of an acute military ward and we have recently had an intake of wounded "other ranks" from Loos. There is a soldier here, a private, who is quite seriously ill, and he keeps talking about Morland Place. At first my nurses thought he was just raving, because he *is* feverish, but then a lady visitor heard him and said there *was* a Morland Place, in Yorkshire, and that she was slightly acquainted with the family. She said perhaps we ought to contact them. So that is what I'm doing. I suppose he might be a servant or some other employee of yours. I thought you should know in case you want to visit him.'

She sounded as if she didn't think a man with a telephone and a butler to answer it would be likely to want to travel all the way to London for the sake of an employee, but that it was her Christian and professional duty to make it possible.

Teddy's feelings had seesawed wildly as she spoke, from the disappointment that it could not be Ned to the hope that it was someone with news of Ned. Perhaps he was wounded and in another hospital, somehow unable to communicate. 'What is the man's name?' he asked.

'Daltry,' Sister Wheatley said. 'Private Daltry of the North Kent regiment.'

Sawry drew in a breath at the name. Daltry was Mr Ned's manservant, who had volunteered with him and gone to France as his batman. It *must* be news of Mr Ned, then!

Teddy's voice came after a pause. 'I know him. Is he badly hurt?'

'His wounds are severe, and his condition has been complicated by pneumonia. But he is a little better this morning. If you wished to visit him, I think he would be able to talk to you.'

'Yes,' said Teddy. 'Yes, I will visit him. I will come up at once. Tell him that Mr Morland is coming to see him today.'

'I will certainly do so,' she replied, sounding much more gracious after this compassionate response. 'Does he have any relatives who ought to be told? He has not been able to give us an answer to that question.'

'As far as I know, he has no-one. He has been with our family for many years. But I will make enquiries.'

'Thank you.'

'Thank *you*, Sister, for letting me know about him. Is there anything I can bring for him? Does he need anything?'

'All our boys need everything, Mr Morland. They leave their kit behind when they're brought out. If it weren't for the volunteer ladies they wouldn't have a pair of pyjamas between them.'

'Pyjamas. What else?' Teddy was businesslike, now there was something he could do.

'Facecloth. Shaving tackle. Soap. Those would all be useful. And, of course, they always want cigarettes and chocolate, and things to read.'

'I'll see to it. Thank you, Sister, with all my heart.'

Simmons, the chauffeur, went off in the motor to fetch Jessie from Twelvetrees, while Teddy, with Henrietta's help, assembled such necessaries as could be found around the house. Soap and shaving soap were easy enough, as were a clean facecloth from the linen cupboard, and an unbroached tin of cigarettes from Teddy's own store. Henrietta sensibly suggested that matches would probably also be needed. Teddy telephoned to Makepeace's, the draper's shop he owned in York, to have them pack new pyjamas and a dressing-gown ready for collection. He told them to put in a dozen handkerchiefs, too, and asked them to send an employee along the road to Toynbee's to buy a razor and shaving-brush. Teddy's elderly manservant, Brown, meanwhile packed an overnight bag in case a stay in London should be indicated, while Tomlinson did the same for Jessie. So when Jessie arrived back from Twelvetrees – in a state of some agitation, since Simmons had not been able to tell her what the summons was all about – she had only to wash and change and they were off.

They drove into York, collected the package from Makepeace's and stopped at the newsagent on the corner for a tin of chocolate and some light reading matter. Jessie, remembering something Bertie had said in a letter, suggested boy's comic papers, and they took a selection of twopenny magazines and a couple of fourpenny 'adventure' novelettes.

Simmons dropped them off at the station, and they were able to catch an express just after noon. After the bustle of getting away, sitting still in the train left them at the mercy of their thoughts and anxieties.

'I wonder what it is he wants to tell us,' Jessie said uselessly, as the train took the beautiful curve just past Chaloner's Whin, which her engineer grandfather had laid out long ago when the railways first came to York.

'He *must* know something about Ned,' Teddy said. 'A soldier-servant stays near his master at all times.'

Jessie met his look. 'Part of me doesn't want to know. Suppose—'

'Better not,' Teddy said. He managed a smile. 'We should have bought something to read for ourselves.'

'Would you like to try the *Boy's Own Paper*?'

'No. Let's go to the dining-car and have luncheon.'

'I couldn't eat a thing.'

'Yes, you could,' Teddy said firmly. 'You've been out since breakfast, and we may not have another chance to eat for hours. Besides, it will keep us occupied.'

The train had moved into the straight and was picking up speed, and they could hear the steward coming down the corridor saying, 'First service for luncheon, madam. First service for luncheon, sir.' Jessie realised that she really was hungry, and followed her uncle meekly from the compartment.

* * *

Sister Wheatley was a very different proposition from Jessie's nemesis, Sister Morgan. Morgan was a desiccated wasp of a woman who looked for trouble and found it. Sister Wheatley was tall, well-built, handsome, with warm brown eyes and an air of calm behind her efficient briskness. She made Jessie think of a well-fed, well-schooled horse – and she always liked people who reminded her of horses.

'Private Daltry has shrapnel wounds in both legs,' she told them, when they were brought to her in her room on arrival. 'He also received a grazing wound to the head; and he was lying out on the battlefield for two days before they brought him in, which complicated matters and led to pneumonia. We did think at one time we were going to lose him, but he is fighting his way back, and the surgeon hopes we can save the legs.'

'Is he well enough to see us?' Teddy asked.

'He's very weak, but it may ease his mind to see someone from Morland Place. He's been quite agitated about it.'

They found Daltry halfway down the ward on the right. He had been a background figure in Jessie's life for many years, coming to Morland Place to valet Ned when he first reached a man's estate. Then, when she and Ned had married, he had come with them to Maystone, their neat villa in Clifton. There, he had become so much more than a gentleman's gentleman. He had acted as butler, footman and major-domo, steering the household through such crises as drunken cooks, financial recessions, the coming of the war and the consequent depletion of staff. Quietly and efficiently he had filled gaps, anticipated needs, and kept the other servants cheerful. He was a tall, good-looking man, calm and capable, and Jessie always thought of him faintly smiling.

Just for a moment she didn't recognise him. How could this be Daltry, this unshaven scarecrow, hair dishevelled, gaunt face waxy with fever? His head was bandaged, his arms stuck out of the sleeves of a hideous pair of pyjamas that were too small for him, and his fingers twitched restlessly at the bedcovers, which were stretched over a cradle protecting his legs. When they stood at the foot of his bed he stared at them with bright, hot, blank eyes for a long moment before recognition dawned. Then, to Jessie's horror, he began to cry. It was the worst thing of all, to see capable, rock-like Daltry cry. The tears rolled helplessly and he put up a feeble hand to wipe at them. 'I'm so sorry,' he moaned. 'I'm so sorry.'

Teddy had snatched out his handkerchief, but hesitated, fearing for the man's dignity. Jessie took it from him and went to minister. She drew Daltry's hand away from his face, wiped his cheeks, stroked the hair from his forehead, and murmured, 'It's all right. We've come to help you. Sister says you're going to be all right.'

After a few gasping sobs he fumbled the handkerchief out of her hand and blew his nose. She poured some water into his glass, and helped him to sip it.

'We've brought you some things,' Jessie went on. 'Shaving tackle and so on. Pyjamas, handkerchiefs. And some cigarettes and chocolate for when you're feeling better. You mustn't worry about anything except getting well.'

He looked from one to the other with a humble wonder that hurt Jessie all over again. 'You came all the way down here to see me?' he said.

'You're one of the family,' Jessie said. 'Of course we would come.'

Tears welled again, but he made an effort to hold them back. 'I don't deserve it,' he said. 'I've let you down. I failed him.'

So they had come to Ned at last, Jessie thought, and it didn't sound hopeful. 'I'm sure you haven't let anyone down,' she said. He was still feverish, she could see, and his breathing was laboured. He ought not to talk too much. Questions could wait until he was stronger. 'Why don't you rest now, try to sleep a little? We'll leave you in peace and come back another time.'

Daltry reached out to her. 'No,' he said. 'I must tell you about Mr Ned.' He looked at Teddy. 'You ought to know. I must tell you now.'

There seemed nothing for it but to let him talk.

The fighting had been fierce on the way to Hill 70. All the officers had been lost, except Ned. Eventually he had found himself in charge of about half a company of survivors, just north of Bois Hugo.

'We were in the air,' Daltry said, and then translated. 'I mean, we were ahead of our line, isolated. Far out in front, stuck there in a trench on our own, with the enemy advancing. We fought them off, but they kept coming. We had to fall back. So Mr Ned sent the men off with the sergeant. He stayed with the rearguard to lay cover. The Boche were coming up through the woods, outflanking us. And they were shelling ahead of them. There was only seven of us left. We made a run for the woods. Mr Ned was coming last with Acres and the machine-gun. Then a shell burst, and he got caught in the blast. Broke his legs, I think. They were all bloody, his trousers torn to shreds. He couldn't walk. He told me to go on. I wanted to stay with him but he ordered me. I swore I'd go back for him. I looked back when I got to the trees and he'd managed to crawl into a shell-hole.'

His voice had grown fainter, more breathless as he spoke. His interlocutors listened in silence, Jessie staring at him, not seeing him, seeing instead the scene he was describing, trying to understand it. Teddy was looking fixedly at his hands.

Daltry went on: 'That's the last time I saw him. I promised I'd go back for him, but that place, where he was – that shell-hole – it was the furthest any of us advanced that day. Everyone'd fallen back, and the Germans kept coming on. By the end of the day they'd overrun it. It's behind the German line now. So I couldn't get to him. I tried, sir, I really tried.'

'I know you did,' said Teddy. 'I believe you.'

'I shouldn't have left him,' Daltry mourned. 'I keep thinking of him, lying there, waiting, all alone. I failed him.'

'You didn't fail him. Good God, man! You had to obey orders,' said Teddy. 'There was nothing else you could do.'

Daltry only shook his head.

Sister Wheatley paused behind them, then walked round to take Daltry's pulse. 'I think that's enough for now,' she said quietly. 'His temperature is going up again. You must rest now.' She addressed the patient. 'Your visitors can come again another time.'

Daltry tried to protest, and fell into a racking spasm of coughing that left him flattened and gasping. Sister waved Teddy and Jessie back and began to draw the curtains round the bed.

Teddy said, 'Don't worry about anything, Daltry. We're going to take care of you.' But he didn't know if the man heard him, or understood.

They stood awkwardly outside the drawn curtains for a moment, then turned away down the ward. Jessie was still holding the parcel from Makepeace's, and Teddy the one containing the other items. A nurse came towards them and they gave the things to her and asked her to see Daltry got them.

'I will. Don't worry.' She looked towards the screens. 'Perhaps you'd like to come back tomorrow?'

'Yes,' said Teddy. 'We'll do that.'

Someone called out something, and the nurse looked, and said, 'Does that patient want to speak to you?'

A man a few beds down, with his arm in a splint and his head hugely bandaged, was waving, pointing at them and beckoning. They went over to him. He looked up at them anxiously. 'Are you friends of Private Daltry's, sir, miss?'

Teddy said, 'I'm the father of his officer.'

'You mean Lieutenant Morland, sir?'

'That's right. And this is Mr Morland's wife.'

'Oh, I see. Sorry, ma'am. Sir, Daltry's been that cut up. Raving, he's been, about Mr Morland, and how he never went back for him. But, sir, you ought to know, he tried to get him, he really tried. Three times he went out across no man's land, sir, I tell you no lie, and ole Fritz still chucking whiz-bangs and strafing anything that moved. That's when he got wounded. I wasn't in the action meself. I was in the cooks' party, back behind the line, but o' course we was all brought into it afterwards as stretcher-bearers. Daltry, he'd come back first off with the survivors – hardly none of *them*, sir, I give you my word. About a hundred, no more – that's all as came back. And that Daltry, he said as how Mr Morland was out there, wounded, and he was going back to get him. Well, there wasn't no CO nor no-one to tell him he could or he couldn't, so off he went. But that part o' the battlefield – where he'd been with Mr Morland, sir – well, ole Fritz had retaken that, so he couldn't get through. Fust time, he got hit in the leg with shrapnel, but he come back with some wounded Jock he'd picked up on the way, helping him along, like. And he says he's going back to try again. I says to him, "Mate, you'll never make it." Blood all running down his leg, and limping, he was, but he says, "I got to," and orf he goes again. Comes back with another wounded man, goes back again. And he never come back that time. I thought he'd bought it, till I saw him on the 'ospital ship. Shell got him, both legs, that last time, and he lay out there two days before they got to him. I copped my packet the same day they found him, so we was on the same ship, sir, the *Anglia*. But he keeps going on about Mr Morland, and how he let him down. I wisht you could make his mind easy, sir. He done everything he could. It weren't his fault. No-one couldn't have got through, I sweartergod.'

Teddy nodded. 'I've told him so already, and I'll tell him again when we visit tomorrow. Thank you for telling me what happened. It's plain that Daltry has nothing to reproach himself for. In fact, he was extremely brave.'

The man nodded anxiously. 'Didn't want you to think no-one tried, sir. I'm very sorry about Mr Morland, sir. He wasn't my officer – I was in A Company, sir – but I know everyone liked him. New to the battalion last year, he was, but he was highly thought of.'

Teddy cleared his throat. 'So, as far as you are aware, nothing is known of Mr Morland's fate?'

'Well, sir, no, sir. Where he was, up by Bois Hugo,' he pronounced it Boys You-go, 'ended up behind the German line. When I come away there was still fighting going on, but we hadn't pushed Jerry back from there, and as far as I know, we never did.' He glanced at Jessie's set face, then looked urgently at Teddy again. 'But if he didn't get back, sir, the Jerries'll take care of him, sir, like we take care o' theirs.'

'Yes,' said Teddy. 'Thank you.' He nodded a farewell and was turning away, when a thought struck him. He turned back. 'Cigarette?'

'Thank you, sir. Don't mind if I do. Always short o' fags. Left all my gear back in France.'

Teddy proffered his cigarette case, then with an impatient shake of his head at himself, scooped out the contents and laid them all on the bed between the man's hands.

'Thank you, sir. Thank you, sir. Much obliged, I'm sure.'

Teddy and Jessie did not speak until they were walking down the stairs, their feet loud on the stone in the echoing stairwell.

'He's alive,' Teddy said. Jessie looked at him, startled out of her thoughts. 'I'm sure he's alive. Daltry said he was sheltering in a shell-hole.'

'He was wounded. Badly, by the sound of it.'

'But the Germans overran the position almost immediately, from what Daltry's saying. So they'll have taken him back and given him medical treatment.'

'Then – what? He'd be a prisoner-of-war?'

'That's right. An unhappy fate, but better that than—' He didn't finish it, but she knew what he meant. *Better that than dead.*

It was a painful hope. Jessie felt exhausted with emotion. How could she bear any more uncertainty, wondering and waiting for confirmation that never came? 'How would we find out?' she asked wearily.

'I don't know, but there must be ways. The Red Cross, I suppose. Or the War Office – they must keep in touch with their opposite numbers about prisoners-of-war.' He brightened. 'There might be an exchange. Look how Jack was exchanged after only a couple of days.'

Jack, Jessie's favourite brother, was an RFC pilot who had been shot down during the first battle of Ypres. He had been captured by German flyers, and they had exchanged him for one of theirs because they did not have the medical facilities to treat him. Jack's injuries meant he hadn't flown since, but he was still hoping to get fit enough to go back. However, Jessie suspected that flyers were rather a different breed, more gentlemanly towards each other than soldiers in the line had time or space to be.

Teddy's spirits were rising, buoyed by hope and the prospect of action. 'Do you suppose Cousin Venetia would know who to contact about a prisoner-of-war? After all, her husband's in the War Office. He must know the right strings to pull. And, by the by, we must keep an eye on Daltry, and make sure he knows there's a home with us when the war's over, or when he's discharged, whichever it turns out to be. We must come back tomorrow and make sure he knows he's not to blame for anything. I don't like to think of him fretting over it.'

Jessie was swept along by his energy and optimism, and tried to think like him, but she felt too tired. She could not offer him any encouragement, only a lack of resistance.

* * *

Cousin Venetia – Lady Overton – was not at home when they called at her house in Manchester Square. The butler, Burton, informed them that she was operating at the Southport Hospital but was expected back shortly, and invited them to wait. They were glad to rest after the strains of the day, and even more glad when tea was brought and laid for them beside the fire in the drawing-room. There was always a good tea at Manchester Square. Today there were watercress sandwiches, anchovy-paste sandwiches, Viennese fingers, and Battenberg cake, to which Teddy was particularly partial. Jessie poured the tea, and they sipped and ate in silence, staring at the fire.

Venetia came in just as Jessie was pouring the second cup, closely followed by the maid with fresh crockery and hot water. 'What a pleasant surprise,' she said cheerfully. Jessie thought she looked tired, and would probably have been glad to find her hearth unoccupied. She kissed the thin cheek, which was cold from the outer air, and caught the faint antiseptic smell about her.

'Do sit down again,' Venetia said, shaking hands with Teddy. 'Don't let me disturb your tea. Jessie, will you pour me a cup?'

The tea tray had been ample and they had not made great inroads into it. Jessie handed the cup and Venetia helped herself to sandwiches. She was always hungry after finishing a list. She had been one of the first lady-doctors to qualify, and though she had given up her general practice, surgery still held a fascination for her. There was a continual demand for female surgeons, who were scarce. Retirement, she and her husband had agreed, had ceased to be an option when the war broke out. He went daily to the War Office and she operated weekly lists at the New Hospital for Women and at the Southport.

'I can see from your faces that this is not a social call,' she said, when neither of them spoke. 'You had better tell me what has happened.'

It was Jessie who spoke. 'Ned was at Loos,' she said.

'He's – missing.' It seemed a horrid word as she said it – worse in its way than 'dead'. At least there was a nobility in that – a right to grieve and be comforted. With 'missing', one was left in limbo.

'We've not been told yet that he is,' Teddy broke in quickly. 'But we can't get any news of him.' And in a businesslike manner, which was easier for him to sustain, he told Venetia the story.

She was not the sort of person to deal in platitudes or mouth false hopes. She asked one or two brisk questions, then said only, 'I will see what I can do for you. Overton is still at the War Office. He will know the right channels to try. Excuse me, and I will go and telephone him.'

She rose and went out, leaving her tea hardly touched. Jessie felt guilty; but she was grateful for the immediate response. After only a quarter-hour Venetia came back and told them that her husband was putting an enquiry in train, and asked them what their plans were. When they said they had promised to go back to the hospital the next day, she would not hear of their going to an hotel. 'You must stay here, of course. I'll have rooms prepared for you – if you will just push the bell, Jessie. I expect you'd like to have a bath and a rest before dinner. Fortunately we are not engaged tonight, so it will be just us and Oliver. We won't dress.'

Oliver, Venetia's younger son, was also a doctor. He and Jessie had known each other since childhood: Venetia's and Henrietta's children had all played together during regular summer holidays in Yorkshire; and in adulthood Oliver and Jessie had become close during her visits to London to stay with his sister Violet. He was a lively, witty young man, and it was thanks to him that what might otherwise have been a heavy evening passed pleasantly. No purpose would be served, he felt, in dwelling fruitlessly on the possibilities. At dinner they talked of everything but Loos and Ned, and Jessie was glad of the respite from her own thoughts.

When they went into the drawing-room afterwards for coffee, Lord Overton was called away to the telephone. An awkward silence seemed to threaten, and Venetia said, 'Play something for us, Oliver. It has been a difficult day and I need music.'

Oliver went obligingly to the piano, took out the first piece he came upon and put it up. It was the Brahms Variations, Opus 118. 'I think this may be rather beyond my skill as a performer,' he said, 'but I'll give it a try. Nothing venture, nothing gain, as they say. Jessie, will you turn for me?'

He was a practised if not an inspired musician, and managed well enough to keep them occupied until his father came back into the room.

'I haven't much to tell you yet,' Overton said, as he crossed to his chair. Oliver moved up on the piano stool and gestured to Jessie to sit beside him. He took her hand – it was icy cold. 'That was Lattery at the War Office telephoning me. He confirmed what you've been told – that the North Kents were very heavily cut up. I'm sorry to have to say this, but only ninety-eight of them came back unwounded, and there were no officers among them.'

Oliver felt Jessie's hand tighten, and pressed it in return.

'Someone from Brigade staff has had to take charge of them for the time being,' Overton went on. 'Lattery is going to put through an enquiry to Brigade Headquarters in France. Of course, as soon as I hear anything, I will pass it on to you, but it may be a day or two – perhaps more, given the situation out there.'

'Thank you,' said Teddy, blankly.

Overton went on, 'Lattery emphasises that there's a great deal of confusion on the ground which they're only now managing to sort out. Hundreds of people go "missing" and turn up again afterwards, not even realising that no-one knew where they were.' He paused, looking at Teddy searchingly. 'Lattery did confirm that the area around Bois Hugo is still in German hands. However, it's possible that Ned managed to get back, or was brought back, before the Germans retook the position. You shouldn't give up hope on that account.'

Teddy seemed to shake himself. 'Of course not. Give up hope? I *know* he's alive. I feel it. We'll find him all right. I'm grateful to you for doing this for us.'

'Not at all,' Overton said politely. He exchanged a brief but speaking glance with his wife, and she understood that Lattery had been much less sanguine than her husband was admitting. She felt for Jessie, but there was nothing she could say to bring her comfort. Poor Jessie had had a hard time of it since her marriage, with two miscarriages, and then Ned being transferred from his 'Pals' battalion – still in training in Yorkshire – straight to the Front.

They did not sit long that evening, everyone being ready for an early night. The following day, after visiting Daltry again, and finding him exhausted from the emotions of the previous day, but calmer in his mind, Teddy and Jessie went home to Morland Place, to wait.

CHAPTER TWO

Polite society, on the whole, did not care much about fine art. Of course, no-one would have missed the opening day of the Summer Exhibition, but that was a social occasion along the lines of Ascot or Henley. And if there was a special show of important paintings, naturally one would not have liked to miss it: it would be a bore to have to say one had not gone when everyone else was talking about it. But the paintings themselves were secondary considerations, compared with seeing one's acquaintances and being seen by them.

The National Portrait Exhibition, however, was a different matter. Pictures of people were much more interesting than bowls of fruit, plough horses, fishing-boats and thatched cottages; and there was always amusing gossip to be exchanged about the subjects. It was probably the only exhibition the *ton* attended where the painted faces were as much looked at as those present in the flesh.

Venetia's preferred art form was music, and in her busy life she had little time to keep up with the rest. She was surprised to receive an invitation to the private viewing, but in the same envelope there was a note from Violet pressing her to accept it. It was a novelty to find her daughter so interested in paintings – such a novelty, in fact, that she would have supposed there was an ulterior motive, if sweet, straightforward Violet had ever had a devious breath in her body. She decided to make the effort and go.

When she entered the gallery, she found that her chronic punctuality had presented her ahead of the crowd. She was not sorry to look at the paintings undisturbed. They were, she thought, a mixed bunch, some adequately skilled, some frankly clumsy. The only interest for her was in recognising some of the sitters.

But then she came upon it, in a favoured position at eye level in the middle of the south wall. The first shock was electric, and she felt the hair stand up on her scalp as Violet gazed down at her from within a gilt frame. *So that was why she wanted me to come*, was her first thought; the second was to wonder why Violet hadn't told her she was sitting. And then, belatedly, the reason for the shock reached her consciousness.

The painting was brilliant, there was no doubt about it. It was in a different class from everything else in the room. The light was superb, the likeness haunting; but there was about it a quality of sensuousness that seemed almost improper in this public surrounding. Violet reclined on a chaise-longue, dressed in a flowing, colourful, Rossetti-ish gown, her feet bare, her hair loose and tumbling over her shoulders. There was a fur draped over the end of the chaise – Venetia recognised Violet's sable wrap – and her soft white forearm resting against the stiff black guard-hairs of the fur seemed the essence of sensuality. Most disturbing of all was her expression. She gazed out – her eyes, through the painter's skill, looking right into those of the viewer – with a faint smile on her lips, and an almost slumberous air of utter relaxation about her. She looked as though – Venetia found the thought in her head unbidden – as though she had just been made love to.

In all the other portraits on display the subject sat up straight in formal pose, with a kind of rigid propriety, which was the expected mode. Violet's picture was as different as a fresh, dew-pearled rose from dusty wooden flower carvings. Venetia had been staring at it so long that she realised, suddenly, the gallery was filling up. She moved hastily away, anxious not to draw attention to the picture, and stationed herself solidly in front of Lady Parker, a portrait whose artist had so little grasped the principle of perspective that the pug on her lap seemed to be a two-dimensional cut-out floating in mid-air in front of her.

Alone for the moment with her thoughts, she asked herself how Violet, *her* Violet, could look like that on canvas. Why had she kept the sittings secret? Who was the artist? She had been too taken aback to look at the signature or the card on the wall. She fumbled through the catalogue now and found it. *Violet, Countess of Holkam, by Octavian Laidislaw.* Laidislaw: she had heard of him – just. He was a new and upcoming painter, rather a darling of the arty set. He had painted Lady Verney earlier that year, she remembered – Laura Verney, who had been one of the beautiful Somerset Mellis sisters, brilliant but impoverished, before she had married her wealthy young baron. Laidislaw must be one of the Verney set. But how had he come to paint Violet?

Then she remembered Violet's telling her, back in the spring, that she had gone to a *soirée* at the Verneys'. She had been surprised at the time, since they were not Violet's set, but the matter had been of too little importance for her to remember it until now. She must have met him there. But that barely answered the questions raised by the remarkable picture.

Venetia had never met Laidislaw, but she assumed him young, of an age with the Verneys. She knew nothing else about him. What was he to Violet? Now she came to think of it, there had been something different about her lately, an extra glow. It had made the mother in Venetia wonder if she might be with child again – Holkam had visited from the Front in August. She had had an air both of happiness and distraction, as though she had a secret—

Venetia stopped herself, but the thought concluded itself despite her. *As though she had a secret lover.*

It was not possible. It was not possible because it was Violet, sweet, polite, obedient, *good* Violet, who had never caused her parents a moment of anxiety in all her life. She had never wanted anything but to marry and have children and, having done so, had led a life of blameless propriety as the leader of the young marrieds of the *ton*, the sort of young matron so approved of by the high sticklers that they nodded and smiled over her, and said she gave them hope that the younger generation were not all gone to the dogs.

It was not possible. But, then, how had Laidislaw got her to look like that? Was it all his imagination? It was hard to believe even the most talented painter could conjure an expression so warm, tender and *real* if he had never seen it in life.

She shook the thought away. It hardly mattered, at least in social terms, whether he had or he hadn't. Society was going to see that painting and assume the rest. There was going to be a scandal.

She remembered how Sargent's painting *Madame X* had caused a sensation in the year before her marriage, back in the eighties. *That* painting was only guilty of showing Madame Gautreau in a rather *décolleté* black dress with the strap slipping off the shoulder, but the strap had been enough to have the portrait condemned as louche and obscene. It had ruined both sitter and painter. Sargent had had to spirit the picture away before the exhibition closed and hide it, to prevent its being destroyed by the lady's irate family. Next to *Madame X*, the painting *Violet, Countess of Holkam* (her name was given, so even those who had never met her would know!) was a barrel of gunpowder with a lit fuse.

Hearing the background noise of a throng, Venetia knew it was impossible that she would be left much longer on her own. She turned cautiously to look round, and saw that already there was a crowd around Laidislaw's painting, which was growing as the excited murmuring drew those from other parts of the room. She saw people she knew, and she caught some curious glances as well as polite nods. There was Laura Verney, with whom she was only acquainted, throwing her an agonised look that she could not interpret. Mrs Danbury and Mrs Worsley nodded and smiled to her, then put their heads together, talking while still looking at her. Lord and Lady Yearmouth – friends of Holkam's – were just turning away from the picture with a shocked look, caught her eye, and gave her a stiff bow apiece before moving away, talking in low voices. And here was Lady Egerton, the first to reach her.

'My dear, what a piece of work!' she exclaimed, smiling, but with a keenly searching eye. Venetia tried hastily to rearrange her expression to neutrality, knowing she must look as shocked as she felt. 'I must congratulate you. Violet is a very handsome young woman, and the artist has captured her beauty perfectly. Did Holkam commission it?'

She could hardly have asked a more awkward question, for to confess ignorance would be to add fuel to the flames. Instead Venetia asked, 'How is John? Have you heard from him lately? I believe his battalion wasn't at Loos – isn't that the case?'

If Lady Egerton was startled by the change of direction, she was beguiled by the subject, for there was nothing she liked to talk about more than her son. 'No, he was safe at Armentières, thank God – though it doesn't do to talk about safety, but one can't help a mother's feelings, can one? Of course he wished he had been there, but so many officers were killed. You're so lucky, my dear, not to have a son in uniform – or, I should say, at the Front, because of course your eldest boy is in uniform, isn't he, but safe in Russia.'

At that awkward moment rescue arrived in the shape of her old friends the Sandowns, who performed a neat cutting-out exercise and, flanking her so that no-one else could get to her, walked her away.

'Thank you,' Venetia said, when they were clear. 'Though

I doubt I can escape persecution for long. You've seen the picture?'

'It's a wonderful likeness of Violet,' said Lady Sandown, 'but a little – well, startling. Such an *intimate* feeling, it gives one, as if one were alone in the room with her. The painter must have quite a talent.'

Lord Sandown said, 'Do I take it you hadn't seen the work before today?'

'I didn't even know it existed,' she said. No danger in admitting as much to her close friends.

'Ah,' he said; and, after a moment, 'There'll be some who'll have plenty to say about it, I've no doubt. Pity Holkam's abroad. Would have been better if he'd been here.'

'There's the artist now,' said Lady Sandown. 'Just coming in, with Humphreys.'

'How do you know him?' Venetia asked in surprise.

'Oh, I met him at the Royal Academy dinner last year. My, he looks pleased with himself, doesn't he?'

He did. He was young, and a handsome man, in a Bohemian sort of way: his hair, Venetia thought, could do with trimming. It was black and curly, and went with an olive skin, dark eyes and white teeth to give a Byronic look; and he had about him an air of energy and health, like a high-fed horse. Attractive, yes, she could see that – but to Violet? Philip Humphreys, the gallery's director, led him into the centre of a group of benefactors and art critics, who fell on him hungrily. The fact that the director had entered with him suggested strongly that the prize was a foregone conclusion.

'Venetia?'

She realised Lady Sandown had been saying something. 'I'm sorry?'

'Shall we go? Have you seen enough? We can share a taxi-cab.' The Sandowns lived in Portman Square.

'I'm waiting for Violet. She asked me most particularly to come. Of course I understand why, now. She isn't usually interested in paintings.'

Lady Sandown looked back at the crowd around Laidislaw's picture. 'I think perhaps it would be wiser if she didn't appear. Perhaps we can intercept her if we go now.'

But it was too late. As they eased their way through the crowds towards the door, Violet came in, and stood in the doorway scanning the room. She looked so absolutely and normally herself that Venetia at once felt guilty for having supposed she could have changed. She was wearing a dress and short jacket of lavender bouclé silk, a small glazed grey hat with a black hackle, several ropes of pearls, and her silvery fox fur draped round her shoulders. Her lovely face, porcelain-delicate and framed by waves of dark hair, looked serene and gently smiling. Her usual attendant, Freddie Copthall, was at her elbow. He escorted her everywhere that Holkam didn't care to go, and was so much an accepted part of her *ensemble* that he sometimes went unnoticed for whole evenings together.

Venetia could see her daughter, but she couldn't get to her, there being an obdurate knot of close-linked backs directly in her way. She waved discreetly, trying to catch her attention; but at that moment Violet saw Laidislaw and he saw her.

They didn't *quite* run into each other's arms, but Laidislaw evidently left the director in mid-sentence at the sight of her. They met in the middle of the room, he took both her hands and kissed them, and they looked at each other in a way that could have melted granite.

'Oh *dear*,' breathed Lady Sandown.

A little space seemed to have cleared around Violet and Laidislaw. They plainly had eyes for no-one but each other; everyone else seemed to be staring at them, and whispering urgently among themselves. And then he led her ceremoniously by the hand to the picture. A way opened before them, and as Violet stood and looked at her own image, a hush fell, so that her words, though quietly spoken, could be heard by most people. 'Oh, Octavian, it's *wonderful*!'

Now the buzz rose again, excited, scandalised, knowing, malicious, or haughtily disapproving. A few of the stuffier people left, making sure that they were seen to do so. Some men, presumably representatives from the newspapers, were frantically scribbling in notebooks. Kitty Sandown pressed her friend's arm and said, 'Well, there's nothing to do now but stand fast. Shall we go and join them?'

Venetia gave her a grateful look. 'Thank you, Kitty dear. Perhaps we can still get her away.'

As they approached from one side, Lord and Lady Verney came up on the other, equally bent on rescue. Violet greeted them with excited warmth, then turned a vivid face to her mother and said, 'Oh, Mama, you came! I'm so glad. Isn't the painting *wonderful*? I had no idea, because he wouldn't let me see it until now but, oh, I never thought a painting could be so beautiful and so *real*. But forgive me – please allow me to present Octavian Laidislaw, the artist.'

'*Painter*,' Laidislaw corrected her in an underbreath, unable to help himself.

'Octavian, my mother, Lady Overton. And this is Lady Sandown and Lord Sandown – how nice of you to come,' she added, as though this were her drawing-room.

Lady Sandown leaned forward to kiss her cheek, but tried firmly to bring her down a notch. 'We came by invitation, my dear. We're trustees. We had no idea there would be a picture of *you* here.' Violet had the grace to blush, and she turned to Laidislaw. 'A remarkable piece of work, Mr Laidislaw. It quite seems to live and breathe.'

'Thank you,' he beamed. 'It is the best thing I have done. I knew from the first brushstroke that it would be.'

Lady Verney broke in, trying to recover ground, and stop Laidislaw and Violet from holding court in quite that settled, proprietary way. 'I'm afraid the mischief was done at my house, Lady Sandown. Violet came to the unveiling of my own portrait, and of course she's so beautiful Laidislaw at once wanted to paint her. It's a very fine work, Laddie. And now do you suppose we could steal you away? Verney and I are having a luncheon party at the Savoy and we've more or less promised everyone that we would bring you.' She made it sound as flattering as possible, as if his presence were the only reason for the party; but she flung an impassioned glance at Venetia, who took the cue and her daughter's arm, turning her a little one way as Laura Verney turned the painter the other.

'Yes, and we must go, too,' Venetia said. 'You're coming with us, Violet? Lady Sandown is going to drop us off at home.' Freddie Copthall had just struggled up through the throng to join them, and she smiled at him. 'Freddie, you and Violet are coming to lunch with us at home, aren't you?'

Freddie was not of the very brightest, but he had heard a lot as he wriggled through the crowd, and would have had to be blind to miss Venetia's look. 'Oh, yes, rather! Delighted. Lunch. Top hole! Very jolly, eh, what, Violet?'

It might have worked, given the determination of the elder matrons, and the habit of deference of Violet herself; but Laidislaw merely looked astonished. He spoke decidedly. 'Oh, no. That's nonsense! I beg your pardon, Lady Overton, but we can't break up the party like that. It would be very poor sport. You must all come and join us at the Savoy,' he went on largely, playing fast and loose with Laura's hospitality. 'It's by way of being a celebration, you know. Just between us,' he lowered his voice theatrically, 'I have an idea that Violet's portrait is going to win the prize.' He beamed and resumed a normal pitch. 'So everyone must come and drink champagne with us. You too, Copthall. Now, do say yes, dear Lady Overton!' He caught her hand and smiled at her beguilingly, and she felt for an instant the full force of his charm. 'It won't feel right at all if you don't come.'

Venetia looked at Laura Verney, who said, 'Very well, Laddie, we'll all go, but we must leave now.'

'Things are only just beginning to warm up,' he objected.

'And I've hardly spoken to anyone. I want to hear what people think of the picture.'

'There's the rest of the run to do that,' Laura said firmly. 'They're not going to announce the prize today, you know. Besides, you don't want to be hanging on people's sleeves like a dog begging for sugar. Much better disappear early and maintain an air of confidence and mystery.' Venetia saw the young man was struck by that, and thought Lady Verney knew her Laidislaw well. 'Besides, it's intolerably hot in here,' Laura went on. 'Poor Violet is drooping.'

Violet was not precisely drooping, but she was looking uncomfortable: she was just realising that this was an attempt to get them out of the gallery, but not understanding why.

Laidislaw looked at her in concern, and said, 'Very well, we'll go now. It *is* rather crowded.'

'That's right,' Lady Verney said, the relief just apparent in her voice as she tried to usher him away.

But though Laidislaw had given in graciously, he had one last grenade to let off. Instead of falling in at Laura's side, he offered his arm to Violet, and led the procession towards the door like royalty, smiling to this side and that, while his retinue, with glances of despair, fell in behind him, and felt the burning eyes of the entire room making of this what they would – which was precisely what Violet's protectors had hoped they wouldn't.

At the restaurant, Laidislaw held court. Venetia had joined the party purely to cover her daughter's presence there, and had expected the occasion to be tiresome in the extreme; but after a few initial moments of irritation, she found herself falling under Laidislaw's spell. He talked continuously, with a flowing facility of language, and though she could not decide that he actually said anything of importance, he was undoubtedly amusing to listen to. His quickness and high spirits gave the impression of intelligence, and he had been well educated, but as time passed she began to decide that he was not particularly clever. In fact, there was something rather childlike about him, an eager innocence, which, despite herself, she began to find endearing. There was no harm in him – and, indeed, little conceit: he seemed to have no personal vanity, did not play on his looks, and seemed not to care about fame or fortune. He was in love with his talent – which, given that it was a significant one, was forgivable, or at least understandable. His work was everything to him.

Venetia acquitted him of meaning her daughter any harm. She had been like him, in many ways, in her youth, when she was struggling to be a doctor and sacrificing everything else – reputation, family ties, even love – along the way. She knew now, with the wisdom of age, that she had caused her family – and poor Overton – a great deal of grief in the headlong process. So she understood Laidislaw, and would have applauded his single-mindedness, had her child not been caught up in its backwash.

The luncheon party was, as Lady Verney had said, a small one, with only four other guests: the Arbuthnots – a harmless country squire and his plain but obviously loved wife, who were as fascinated by Laidislaw as snakes by a charmer – and Lord and Lady Gresham. They were respectable young members of the *ton*, known to the Overtons and the Sandowns; intimates of the Verneys, and as committed to the cause of the arts as them. In such company Violet's presence became unexceptional. Venetia concluded that Laura Verney had planned the whole thing with forethought, and was grateful to her – even if it was Laidislaw's reputation she wanted to save. But it occurred to Venetia to wonder why Lady Verney had thought saving was necessary. Had she seen the painting beforehand, when Violet had not? Or did she know something else?

When it was time for the party to break up, Lady Verney murmured something urgently to Laidislaw, to which he listened with a frown, but eventual acceptance. When the intervening guests stood up, he leaned across to Violet and whispered something that made her blush, then the Verneys, Laidislaw and the Arbuthnots walked off together. The Sandowns and Greshams made their farewells, and Venetia said to her daughter, 'I'll drop you at home from my taxi-cab.' Violet, who seemed to be in a reverie, smiled vaguely and said thank you. A meaning glance at Freddie Copthall was enough to send him away, and Venetia and Violet took the taxi alone.

Violet did not seem likely to initiate any conversation. She sat, smiling faintly, looking out of the window in a happy dream. Venetia knew she must tread carefully. What the portrait suggested could not be the case. Given Violet's character, it was impossible that she had entered into an illicit relationship, however attractive Laidislaw might be. Perhaps there had been passionate feelings, but Violet was so innocent she would hardly know what to do with them. And in spite of his flamboyance, Laidislaw had that childlike quality too. A romantic infatuation between artist and sitter must be all there was to it. To hint at anything more would probably shock poor Violet dreadfully – and it was important not to shock her, if one wanted to be able to influence her actions.

So Venetia began, 'I didn't know you were sitting for your portrait. Why didn't you tell me?'

Violet came out of her reverie and said, 'I didn't tell anyone. I had it done as a birthday present for Holkam – a surprise for him. He's been talking for a long time about wanting a portrait of me.'

'A present for Holkam?' Venetia said. This was better! A good, acceptable reason. 'But then – why allow Laidislaw to exhibit it?'

Violet smiled at her mother. 'It wasn't for me to allow or not allow. Laidislaw decided. He said it was so good it must be shown to the world.'

'It is a remarkable piece of work,' Venetia said evenly. 'Had you really never seen it before?'

'No, he never would show me what he'd done.'

'How odd. Didn't he show anyone? Lady Verney, for instance?'

Violet looked surprised. 'Why would he show her?'

'They are obviously good friends. I just had the impression she had seen it before.'

'I don't think so,' Violet said. 'He said he wanted it to burst onto the world at the exhibition.'

'It will certainly do that.'

'You sound as though you don't like it. Is something wrong?'

'My love, it's a beautiful thing, a wonderful likeness, but I'm afraid there is going to be a lot of fuss about it.'

'What sort of fuss? I don't understand.'

Venetia chose her words carefully. 'It shows you *en déshabille*, and in a very informal pose. A married woman of your position is not usually seen like that by anyone but her husband. I'm afraid there will be those who say it should never have been painted – certainly that it should never have been exhibited. It does rather expose you, my love.'

Violet looked troubled, and a little hurt. 'Laidislaw says that beauty and art transcend all rules. Surely people wouldn't be so – so narrow-minded about it.'

Venetia almost laughed at such naïveté. 'Most of the world is narrow-minded, darling. And people like nothing better than condemning the behaviour of others. It makes them feel so much better about themselves. I don't want to upset you but I overheard comments along those lines in the gallery, and I'm afraid there will be many more once the general public gets to see it. And in attacking the painting they will be attacking *you* – and Laidislaw. I strongly advise you to withdraw the picture from the exhibition straight away.'

Violet's eyebrows went up. 'But I can't do that. Laidislaw would never agree.'

'He doesn't have to agree. You commissioned the work, darling. You paid for it. The painting belongs to you, not to him.'

'I did ask him to do it in the first place,' Violet said, colouring a little, 'but it soon went beyond that. He wouldn't take any money from me. He says it's his masterpiece and belongs to the world. I was worried when he wouldn't let me pay him, because he isn't a rich man, but he says it will win the prize, and then it's to go to New York and win another prize there.'

This was worse than ever. 'New York? That must never happen. You must persuade him to withdraw it. I'm quite serious about this, Violet. There is going to be a scandal if the painting goes on public view. How do you think Holkam will feel about his wife's likeness being displayed for everyone to stare at and comment on?'

For the first time in her life, Venetia saw stubbornness in her daughter's lovely face. 'I expect he'll see what a wonderful work of art it is, and be pleased,' she said. 'And I don't see at all why there should be a scandal. People have their portraits taken every day – goodness, the gallery's full of them! In any case, Mama,' she went on firmly, as Venetia was about to speak, 'there's nothing I can do about it. Laidislaw wouldn't hear of its being withdrawn, and I couldn't persuade him even if I wanted to.'

The short cab-ride was over; they were pulling up in front of the house in St James's Square. Venetia did not renew her argument. It was evidently no use – and the one thing she could take comfort from was that if Violet did not think she had enough influence with the artist to make him withdraw the painting, it was unlikely that there was any intimate relationship between them. The way forward would be to tackle Laidislaw himself.

She kissed her daughter's offered cheek. 'What do you do this afternoon?' she asked.

'Oh, nothing in particular,' Violet said, and then, hastily, with another blush, 'Oh – that is, I have a committee to go to. I'd forgotten. I shall have to hurry or I shall be late.'

Venetia was already thinking about her proposed interview

of the painter, otherwise she might have noticed how unlike Violet this confusion was.

Violet entered the tall, cold house in its afternoon quiet, calling for her maid, hardly noticing that she had had to open the door for herself – another footman had left to volunteer in the wake of the battle of Loos. Her mother's words had disturbed her and she needed a comfort she could only get in one place. Her Pekingeses, Lapsang and Souchong, reached her first, dashing across the marble floor of the hall with a skidding of paws, pink mouths wide in their sooty faces in smiles of welcome. She scooped them up and hugged them, and then, as Sanders appeared, headed for the stairs, saying, 'I need to change quickly. I'm going out at once.'

Sanders followed her upstairs. 'How was the exhibition, my lady?'

'Very exciting. The painting is quite wonderful.' Sanders was the only person in the world who had known she was having it taken. Indeed, it would have been impossible to keep it from her, given that Violet had had to let down her hair for the sittings.

'Will it win the prize, do you think, my lady?'

'It was the best thing there by *miles*. There was nothing to touch it.'

They entered the bedchamber and Violet put down the dogs and threw her fur on to the bed. 'The grey grosgrain suit, and the blouse with the pearl buttons,' she said. Sanders knew at once where her lady was going. The grey grosgrain was the plainest thing she owned, and the blouse buttoned down the front. 'And you'll have to dress my hair again, simply.'

'Yes, my lady,' said Sanders. When her mistress had first come home with her hair pinned clumsily, having evidently been undone somewhere else, she had not known what to think. And even when she knew exactly what to think, she had not known what to feel. Her mistress and master had lived more or less separate lives since the birth of their third child, as was quite common in their rank of society; and there was no doubt that whatever my lady was doing, it made her very happy. But Sanders could not help worrying that the earl was not going to be as indifferent to it as my lady thought – and now there was this portrait, on public display, which he had never even been told about. All Sanders could do was to say, 'Be careful,' and having actually said it aloud once, she did not dare say any more. But she worried none the less.

The door of the house in Ebury Street was opened by Laidislaw's landlady, Mrs Hudson, whose hard, flat eyes raked Violet with a contempt that was wasted on her, since her thoughts were very much elsewhere.

'Is Mr Laidislaw back?'

'Upstairs,' said Mrs Hudson, stepping aside reluctantly to let her in. And then, almost despite herself, she added, 'You'd better watch your step, my *lady*.' The honorific was entirely satirical. 'There's been one of them reporters hanging round outside.'

Violet heard, but did not absorb what she said. 'Thank you, Mrs Hudson,' she answered, already at the stairs.

As she reached the first landing, Laidislaw's door opened. 'I thought I heard a taxi. You've been so long!'

'I came as quickly as I could. I had to change.'

She went in and he closed the door behind her, and then they were in each other's arms. She could feel his excitement like a vibration that ran through his body. He was elated from the morning's triumph, and raised to a pinnacle by the celebratory lunch – though little of the champagne drunk there had passed his lips. There were other stimulants more effective with him. When he had kissed her, long and passionately, he raised his head to look at her, and said, 'My inspiration! My lovely muse! So beautiful, my Violet. Without you, today's triumph would not have happened.'

She gazed up into his dark eyes, and said, 'It's your talent, nothing to do with me. The picture is *wonderful*. I've never seen anything like it! I wish you'd shown it to me before.'

He laughed. 'No, I wanted the great unveiling – and I wouldn't have missed your expression for the world! If you'd seen it here first, it wouldn't have had the same effect. Darling, darling, it is going to take the world by storm! Come, come with me, I can't wait any longer.' He drew her by the hand towards the bedroom. 'You want me too?'

'So much!' she said. In the bedroom he pulled off his clothes and then helped her with hers. When they were naked she stopped him a moment, before they lay down on the bed, and said, 'There's never been anyone but you, Octavian – you know that, don't you? I've never loved anyone but you.'

'I know,' he said, his bright eyes serious. 'And I've never loved anyone but you. You are everything I've ever dreamed of.'

They lay down, then, and met in flame. She yearned and ached for him, and was satisfied, and it seemed just then the most remarkable thing about love, that it could be both the sickness and the cure; that one could want so much, and not be disappointed.

Afterwards they lay in each other's arms and talked – or rather, at first, Laidislaw talked. He was still elated from the events of the morning, and had to tell her in detail what the director had said and the hints he had given about the prize, and what some member of the hanging committee had said, and how he had felt when he saw the painting there in pride of place, and how he had felt when Violet had come in, and how she had looked when she saw it, and what he had heard from this person and that critic.

His flow of talk was punctuated by kisses and caresses, and in any case it was what Violet liked almost best of all, to lie in his arms and listen to him. But when he wound down at last, she had to bring up her mother's concerns, because now she had had time to think about it, she realised that Laura Verney had been behaving oddly too, as though she was also not completely happy about the exhibition. And Lord and Lady Sandown had looked grave, and even Freddie – she paused, wondering what it had been about Freddie, but he was too nebulous a person to be sure of what he thought or felt about anything. But there had been *something* about him, even so. So it was clear that there might be something to be concerned about, and she wanted both to warn Octavian, and to have him reassure her.

'Mother says the painting is a remarkable piece of work,' she said, 'but she is worried that there might be some adverse comments about it. Because of painting me in such an informal pose, I think. She thinks there might be – well – a scandal.' She said the last word nervously, afraid of upsetting him, not wanting to spoil his mood of happy triumph.

She need not have worried on that score. He was too far above the earth to be brought down to it so easily.

'Oh, there was bound to be someone who said that. Great works of art always have their earthbound, petty critics—'

'My mother isn't petty,' Violet objected, hurt.

He kissed the crown of her head. 'No, darling one, of course she isn't. You didn't say *she* criticised the painting, only warned that others might. And I know that there may be some who don't like it, but we won't care about them. I told you when I was painting you that many people would never really *see* what we had done. Great art is not for everyone.'

'You said people wouldn't see, but you didn't say there would be a scandal,' she said in a small voice. She did not want to seem earthbound and petty herself.

'There won't be,' he said confidently. 'Your mother naturally worries about you, but there's no need. I had much the same sort of thing from Laura, but I told her—'

'Octavian, did you show her the picture before the exhibition?'

'No, I didn't show her,' he said, laughing, 'but she broke in like a burglar while I was at Aston Magna to look at it, the wicked creature! Although she did summon me to her house as soon as I got back to confess, so I suppose it could hardly rank as a high felony.'

'What did she say about it?'

'That it was brilliant, which I knew for myself without being told,' he said.

'But she warned you as well that there might be scandal?' Violet urged nervously.

'No, nothing like that. Don't worry so much, my rose. Nothing will spoil this moment for us.'

For once, Violet was not to be put off. 'But what *did* Laura warn you about?'

He drew back his head to look at her. 'You really are worried, aren't you?' He traced the lines of her face with a finger, making her shiver with desire. 'There's no need. Laura was worried that anyone looking at the picture would know we were lovers. But *she* only guessed it because she knows us, and because she's a particularly sensitive person. No-one else will see what she sees.'

Violet was silent. Was that what her mother was worried about? Had she seen what Laura saw? Had she guessed? Violet felt bad about keeping secrets from her mother, but this was not something she could confess. Her mother would think it wrong. She might even be ashamed of her, and Violet couldn't bear that, from the mother she loved and admired so much. And Papa – what would Papa think if he knew? He and Mother had been devoted to each other all their lives, and he wouldn't understand.

She loved Octavian so much, she did not want any shadow to fall on them. She did not want anyone to criticise them – that was why she wanted their love to be kept secret. Would the painting expose it?

'You really don't think anyone else will guess?'

'My precious girl, you saw the people at the gallery.

Animated potatoes! You only have to look at their bovine faces and their blockish expressions to know they see nothing. And the people who *are* spiritually refined enough to see will be the people who will understand and accept. Does Laura condemn us? No. So, you see, there's nothing to worry about. The world is divided into people like us, and the rest. Those like us will celebrate with us, and the rest won't ever know.'

He was caressing her in such a way as to make further conversation impossible, and she put her arms round his neck and her lips up to his; but as passion carried her away in a delicious flood, she was aware of one residual question: which category did Holkam come into?

But perhaps, she thought, he would never see the painting. The exhibition would be over before he came home again from the Front.

That the scandal did not burst full-formed, like Athene from Zeus's head, into the public sphere was a matter of chance. On the day after the private viewing, Wednesday, the 13th of October, the newspapers were full of the execution by the Germans of the nurse Edith Cavell. The outrage generated by the act consumed the public for days afterwards.

Nurse Cavell had been charged, along with thirty-five other people, with helping two hundred Allied soldiers to escape from occupied Belgium into neutral Holland. She had been matron of the Berkendael Medical Institute in Brussels since 1907, and was much respected for improving standards there. When Belgium had been occupied by Germany in 1914, the Institute was taken over by the Red Cross and became a military hospital for all nationalities. Matron Cavell and her staff had nursed them all impartially, but under her aegis the Institute had secretly sheltered British, French and Belgian soldiers fleeing the Germans, and had helped them to escape.

Through the first year of the war, the German authorities

gradually became suspicious of the comings and going at the Institute. In August 1915 Edith Cavell had been arrested by the German police. She was kept in solitary confinement for ten weeks while a confession was extracted from her: she was not even allowed to see her attorney until the day her trial by court-martial opened in October. To help enemy soldiers to escape was not a capital offence in German military law; but at the trial she was obliged to acknowledge that she knew many of them would serve again against the Germans, and even that some had written thanking her for enabling them to 'fight another day'. This, the German prosecutor contended, meant she was guilty of attempting to conduct enemy soldiers back to the front line, for which, under the German military code, the penalty was death.

America and Spain, neutral countries, joined the British and Dutch in making frantic appeals for clemency, but two days after the sentence was pronounced it was carried out. Edith Cavell and her Belgian guide, the Brussels architect Philippe Baucq, were taken at dawn to the Tir National firing range, and shot dead by firing squad. The other thirty-four who had been accused with them had their sentences remitted to hard labour. It was strongly opined by the British press that this was because they were not British: Edith Cavell, a rector's daughter from Norfolk, had been shot in retaliation for the German defeat at Loos.

Amid the shock and passion of fury against the Germans for this new 'frightfulness', the critical reaction to the National Portrait Exhibition could command little space in the papers and less attention from their readers. There was a mention of Laidislaw's picture on the arts page, which described it as remarkable, but a dangerous conceit. 'While no doubt brilliant in its execution, it is none the less disturbing for the barriers it breaks down that would better have been left intact.'

There was a report on the society page about the exhibition itself, which in the usual way of such reports was little more than a list of the important people who had been there and what they had been wearing. The little more was, however, almost as bad as it could be:

> The centrepiece of the exhibition was a picture so immodest as to be quite shocking. The distinguished company hardly knew what to make of a portrait of the lovely Lady H— in a garb at once fantastic and insufficient. Lady H—, long admired in the *ton* as the leader of the younger set, appeared as no female of fashion ever has before in a public place – or indeed anywhere outside her own boudoir. If this is a new trend in portraiture, your correspondent sincerely hopes it will not catch on.

Venetia found both reports because she was looking for them, but given the rest of the content of the newspapers that day, it seemed unlikely anyone who had not been at the exhibition would notice or read them. It was a breathing-space, she thought; and despite her own feelings of sadness and outrage over Edith Cavell – whom she had met when the younger woman was training at the London Hospital – she could only be grateful that, if such a horrible thing had had to happen at all, the news of it had broken just when it did.

CHAPTER THREE

From enquiries among the servants, Teddy had learned that Daltry had always said he had no family, having been the only son of elderly parents long since deceased. There was, however, an uncle, a half-brother of his father, who was a cobbler in Knaresborough; and though Daltry had said he had not seen him since his childhood, decency demanded he be informed of the situation. Meanwhile, Teddy had written Daltry a detailed letter about the provision he meant to make for him when he was released from the hospital and the army. There would be a home for him at Morland Place; and when he was well again, whatever work he felt capable of would be provided, along with a pension and a cottage in later life. He would never want either security or affection.

Teddy never received a reply to the letter. Instead, the news came from St George's that Daltry was dead. The family was shocked – he had seemed to be going on well. But the injuries to his legs were severe, and gangrene had set in, necessitating urgent amputation. Weakened by the pneumonia, he had not survived the operation. Teddy was as distressed by Daltry's death as Jessie was, feeling that he had given his life for Ned. He wanted Daltry to be buried at Morland Place by those who had loved him best. But the half-uncle, roused to family feeling by the story of his nephew's heroism, claimed the body, and it was released to him for burial.

Teddy and Jessie attended the funeral at the church of St John the Baptist. Jessie had been afraid that the congregation would be upsettingly small, but the story of Daltry's courage had spread quickly, and almost every soul in the little town turned out to honour Knaresborough's (adopted) son, so there was nothing but standing-room in the body of the lovely old church.

They met the cobbler, who was flushed with excitement at his sudden connection with celebrity, and now remembered many stories of the child Daltry's early promise and precociously manly ways. Jessie hoped they were true – they were, at least, the sort of things that *might* be, given what she knew of the adult Daltry. The cobbler and his closest friend, a shopkeeper, were already talking about a memorial plaque in the church, and were urgent that the Morlands should return to the 'humble abode' for funeral baked meats. In what Jessie thought a remarkable piece of diplomacy, Uncle Teddy not only pleaded them off without hurting anyone's feelings, but obtained permission to choose and provide the headstone for the grave. Comforted by the knowledge that that, at least, would be seemly, they departed for Morland Place to mourn in their own way a good servant and true friend.

The battle at Loos continued through October, with fresh troops being marched in, a joint Allied offensive on the 8th of October, and desultory other actions; but as General Haig complained in a letter to Lord Kitchener, the element of surprise had been lost, and the enemy proved impossible to shift from the new line. Had the reserves been immediately available to him in the opening stages, Haig said, the German second line could have been taken; but it took the reserves twelve hours to reach Loos, by which time the Germans had regrouped. The opportunity had been lost.

Lord Kitchener could be in no doubt whom Haig thought was to blame. The commander-in-chief, Sir John French, had been in charge of the reserves. Haig said there had been an intolerable delay in sending the reserves in; French said he had sent them as soon as requested. Haig complained that they had been held too far behind the line; French retorted that they were held out of range of German artillery, as was common sense. The bitterness between the two was well known in upper military circles, and Lord Kitchener was caught uneasily between them. He deplored the breach of military etiquette shown by Haig in complaining to him over the head of French, his immediate superior. But Haig was the hero of the hour, fêted in the newspapers; and, moreover, he had the ear of influential friends, most notably the King – Haig's wife was a lady-in-waiting to Queen Mary.

The fact was, as Lord Overton said to his wife, that the people were tired of getting nowhere in the war and wanted someone to blame. They wanted new, more vigorous leadership. Furthermore, the cost at Loos was beginning to be reckoned now, and it was heavy: fifty thousand casualties, and of those twenty-five thousand were killed or missing. The number of the missing was particularly high, for countless thousands had died on Hill 70, which was now behind the German line, so the bodies were irrecoverable. They would probably never be accounted for. All over the country families waited for news that would never come.

Major Calcott, the Brigade officer who had taken temporary charge of the Kents, wrote fully and courteously to Teddy at Morland Place, but the information was all negative. Lieutenant Morland's name did not appear on any list of the wounded or the dead. Enquiries among the survivors of the battalion had yielded only that no-one could say they had seen Ned since he had stayed behind to cover the retreat from the trench at Bois Hugo.

And on the 17th of October, when things had quietened down again at Loos, a further piece of unwelcome information came from Calcott:

It is our unofficial custom after a battle to make a list of the names of German officers captured and brought back by us, and to have it dropped over the enemy trenches by one of our aircraft. The Germans reciprocate with a list of captured British officers. I am sorry to have to say that Lieutenant Morland's name was not on the list we received in this way.

Though Teddy had not hoped that Ned had been taken prisoner – he still wanted to find him on the right side of the Front – it was another closed door. The worst seemed confirmed when Bertie wrote to Jessie soon afterwards.

My own questions have met with much the same response as the official enquiry. By the way, Calcott is a very good fellow and you may be sure he is doing everything he can. Tell Uncle Teddy that no stone is being left unturned. But there is nothing to be found out. I would do anything rather than hurt you, but I think it would be worse for you in the long run to be harbouring false hopes. So I have to tell you that Ned is almost certainly dead. The place where he was last seen was heavily shelled by the Germans ahead of their advance, and under shelling of that order he could hardly have survived. I am sorry to say this, my dearest Jessie, but I think you must be brave and face the fact that he is not coming back – and face even more bravely the knowledge that you will probably never know where he lies. There will be many, many people in your position after this battle, and countless thousands more before the war ends. Take what comfort you can from the fact that his courage was never in doubt. His last action was bravely to risk his life for his men, taking the rearguard so that they could fall back and fight on. I am proud that he was my cousin and I shall honour his memory always.

But Teddy remained unconvinced. 'I don't think much of that. We heard from Daltry that he was sheltering in a shell-hole, and everyone knows shells don't fall in the same place twice. I'm still wagering that he got back. He's lying in a hospital somewhere, injured. His name doesn't appear on any list, that's all. It's nothing but an administrative error. It happens all the time,' he added stubbornly, as his wife looked at him reproachfully.

Henrietta felt she had to speak. 'But if he was in a hospital somewhere, we'd have heard by now,' she said hesitantly. 'He'd have written to us.'

'He might be too ill to send us word,' said Teddy. 'Look how long it was before we heard about Daltry – and that was only because someone happened to know the name of Morland Place. Suppose he can't talk, or – or he's lost his memory? There could be any number of reasons why we haven't heard.'

Henrietta glanced at Jessie, who was sitting a little apart on one of the settles, mending a piece of harness – the only sewing she ever did voluntarily. Her attention seemed to be fixed on the needle and palm, but Henrietta knew she must be listening. How painful was it for her to have these hopes continually revived? Or would it be harder for her if everyone gave up expecting any good news? She wished she knew what was best for her daughter.

Teddy went on: 'I'm going to start enquiries of my own, find out every hospital that received casualties from Loos and ask them if they've got him – or anyone they can't account for. There's a mistake somewhere – a wrong name put down, or wrongly spelt, or *something*. We'll find him. *I*'ll find him.'

Jessie stood up. 'I think I'll just go and check on Hotspur before I go to bed. His near-fore pastern was rather warm when I came in. I don't want him going lame.' She went out without looking at anyone, Brach so close beside her that her head might have been glued to Jessie's thigh – the bitch never strayed far from her mistress, these days.

When she had gone, Henrietta said gently to Teddy, 'I'm not sure it's the best thing for Jessie, to keep raising her hopes like that.'

Teddy said, 'Raising them? What makes you think they've fallen?'

Ethel looked up from her knitting. 'The most likely thing is that Ned is dead, however much we don't want to believe it.'

'*I* don't believe it,' said Teddy. 'And I never will until I have proof. You women give up too easily. Robbie's with me on this – aren't you, Rob?'

Robbie turned a page of the newspaper he hadn't been reading, and cleared his throat awkwardly, aware of his wife's eyes on him. 'Well,' he said, 'it isn't a satisfactory situation, not knowing for sure one way or the other, I suppose. But—'

'There's no "but" about it,' Teddy broke in. 'Ned's alive. I know it. I can feel it. And I'm going to find him. That's all there is to it.'

'It's very laudable of you, Uncle,' said Ethel, 'but—'

'*Laudable?* For God's sake, what's wrong with all of you?' Teddy cried, jumping up. 'Just because some clerk made a mistake, I'm supposed to sit down meekly and believe the worst? Well, I'm not so spineless, and nor is Ned! I'm going to find him – and then you'll all be sorry you doubted.' And he stalked out.

The outburst was so unlike the normally equable Teddy that no-one spoke for a few moments. Then Ethel sighed, and said, 'He's upset.'

Robbie agreed with this remarkable insight. 'We all are,' he added.

'Shall I go after him?' Ethel made to lay aside her knitting.

Alice caught Henrietta's appalled eye and stood up. 'No, no, don't disturb yourself. I expect he's gone up to bed, and I think I'll follow. Goodnight, everyone.'

She found him in the steward's room, where she had expected him to be. He would be too restless to go to bed. He was walking back and forth across the room, and turned to her as she came in. 'Well, have you come to harangue me?' he said testily. She only raised her eyebrows, and some of the tension left him in a little, rueful laugh. 'No, when did you ever harangue anyone? I'm sorry. Did I upset you? I didn't mean to. But I can't stand the way everyone's so willing to write him off.'

'It isn't that we're willing . . .' said gentle Alice.

'*You* don't believe he's dead.' He stared at her urgently but, much as she loved him, she couldn't lie, so she said nothing. 'I remember, you see,' said Teddy, his voice trembling a little, 'when he first came to me – how he used to sit on my knee and chatter to me, tell me all his little concerns. I'd never cared about children before. But after all that had happened to him, he *trusted* me. I can't let him down.'

'I know,' she said, and her soft, faded voice sounded too loud to her in the quiet room. Still she went on, believing it was for his own good, 'But I can't help thinking if he were alive, we'd have heard something.'

He turned away from her, to hide his face until he had control of it. He spoke with his back to her, and his voice was quiet and resigned. 'Very well. I'll just have to do it alone.'

She felt the hurt of it, but she knew then, just as she had known after *Titanic*, that there was nothing she could do to comfort him. He must find his own way out. She could only wait for him on the other side.

In the stable, Jessie leaned against Hotspur's accommodating neck and wished she could cry. It might be a release from the feelings of helplessness and confusion. She didn't know how to think about Ned, whether it was worse to hope or not hope, or even what to hope for. If he was alive, how badly hurt must he be to be unable to communicate? And if he was dead, how had he died? Her mind was raw with unwanted speculation, unanswered questions.

Brach sat at her feet and licked her hand from time to time, and Hotspur sighed and touched her enquiringly with his muzzle. No tears came to relieve her; but it was good, at least, that one didn't have to keep up a brave face with animals.

Edith Cavell's martyrdom had prevented the scandal of Violet's portrait bursting upon the general public; and since the newspapers continued to run the story for all it was worth, Venetia allowed herself to hope that the crisis might have been averted. She decided, in any case, not to worry Overton about the painting just yet. The scandal might never break, and he had a great deal on his mind just then, with the difficulties facing the Dardanelles committee.

Things were going badly in Gallipoli. Nothing had been gained since the first landings: the army was still clinging to the rocky shores while the Turks sat unassailable on the heights. Though the days remained warm and sunny, the nights had begun to be very cold. Everything had to be brought in by sea, and now frequent storms were making it difficult to land cargo on the beaches.

The men were in a poor way, racked with dysentery, fever, infected insect bites, debilitating sores, and heart disease brought on by the exhausting business merely of surviving on that inhospitable ledge, where even digging latrines and burying the dead meant hours of back-breaking labour.

Just to maintain the army through the winter would need thousands of tons of stores, not only extra food, ammunition and firewood, but winter clothing and boots, timber and corrugated iron to build shelters to replace the summer tents – all of which would become ever harder to import as sea conditions worsened. Beyond mere survival, if anything military was to be achieved heavy reinforcements would be needed – and where were they to be found, and how landed and supplied?

The alternative was to evacuate, but the eastern Mediterranean was in a delicate way. Bulgaria had just entered the war on Germany's side and had invaded Serbia, Romania was wavering and neutral Greece was under threat. The Easterners on the committee were horrified at the idea of withdrawal – what sort of signal would that send to the uncommitted countries of the world? What damage would it do to Britain's military reputation? Besides, one of the reasons for attacking in the east was to give relief to Russia, and since April the Germans had driven the Russians back out of Lithuania and Poland and were threatening Latvia. If Russian resistance failed, the full might of the German army would be freed to turn on the Western Front.

Lord Overton had always been against the peninsular adventure, but his opinion had not carried, especially against such a confirmed Easterner as Lord Kitchener. Further to add to his worries, there had been severe and unjust criticism of Sir Ian Hamilton's conduct of the campaign, including a virulent attack by Mr Keith Murdoch, the Australian journalist. He had sent a corrosive letter to the prime minister of Australia, with a copy to Lloyd George, which had been put before the committee. Hamilton, who was a personal friend of Overton, had been given no opportunity to answer the accusations. He had been condemned *in absentia*, recalled in disgrace, and was to be replaced with General Sir Charles Monro. Overton felt the injustice keenly. So Venetia was glad to spare her husband any further cause for worry.

But though there was no sudden eruption of scandal about Violet, within the circle of the *ton* and its satellites word spread from person to person like a slow infection. The whisper passed from those who had seen the painting to those who had not, and the latter hurried to view it themselves and pass the hint on to yet others.

At no time before in her life had Violet been interested in the press. Her maid had collected cuttings about her during her come-out, and had proudly shown her some of the coverage of her wedding to Lord Holkam in Westminster Abbey (the *Illustrated London News* had had three full pages). But Violet had never voluntarily picked up and opened a newspaper. Now, however, she looked daily for views and comments on Laidislaw's painting, and was disappointed that the Cavell affair seemed to have pushed out the exhibition.

As the exhibition went on and more people went to see it, word of it spread, like widening ripples, out of upper society and into the realms of the middle classes. And as Cavell interest faded and a new story was needed, the newspapers picked it up at last. What Violet read was not agreeable. The painting, she learned, was not just controversial (a word she had heard used and chosen to assume was complimentary), it was actually improper. People were incensed that such a thing was displayed in public for all to see. And soon those who were the most outraged discovered that it wasn't even a very good painting. It was too bold, too crude – quite unsubtle. The merest sensational daub. No skill to it at all. Paint thrown at the canvas. The public was being imposed upon by a charlatan.

She fled to Ebury Street and wept hot tears of anger on Laidislaw's welcoming chest.

'It's so unfair! Why are people so horrible? Fanny Church said to me that she was surprised I had gone to you because everyone knew you weren't very good. Second rate, she called you. *Second rate!* How dare she?'

He kissed and soothed her, though had she looked up just then she might have seen he was rather pale. He had been hearing things too. 'It's just jealousy, darling one. Pay no attention to the cats. You and I know the painting is brilliant, and so does everyone of taste and discernment, like Laura and Verney and our friends.'

'But why do they *say* such things?'

'Great art will always have its detractors – small, ugly people who know they can never reach our heights. *We* shan't mind them, shall we?' He raised her chin and kissed the tears from her cheeks. 'We know the truth – and soon enough the ugly people will know it too. When the painting wins the prize, they won't be able to argue with that. And when it goes to New York, the whole world will unite in its praise.'

'Aren't there ugly people in New York?' she asked, in a small voice.

'Not nearly so many,' he said with a smile.

'Fanny Church *is* rather ugly,' Violet admitted, accepting his handkerchief, comforted. 'She has a snout instead of a nose, poor thing. I always felt rather sorry for her and tried to be extra kind to her on account of it – but I shan't any more.' Laidislaw began to kiss her, and soon all worries were forgotten in their wonderfully ready, always renewable passion.

Violet was maintaining this better frame of mind when Emma came back to London. Emma Weston was an orphan and a considerable heiress, the daughter of Venetia's late cousin Tommy. He had asked Venetia just before his death to keep an eye on Emma. Her guardians, Lord and Lady Abradale, were elderly and lived in a remote part of Scotland, so in order that Emma should meet people and enjoy the diversions of London, she lived with Violet for most of the year, and was chaperoned by her. Venetia felt herself too old and certainly too busy to undertake the daily care of a lively young woman 'doing' the Season, so the arrangement suited everyone.

Emma had been with her guardians during August and the first part of September. From Scotland she had gone to stay with one of her half-sisters in Surrey – Fanny led a quiet, domestic sort of life with her large family, so it was something in the way of a rest cure for Emma, to fit her for the rigours of London.

She arrived at St James's Square with her maid and a

mountain of luggage, ready to shop for new clothes: an engrossing process in which Violet had always before immersed herself with enthusiasm. But Emma found her cousin distracted, an unusual state of affairs. When the conversation came round, as it soon did, to the portrait, everything seemed explained.

'How exciting! I didn't know you were sitting,' she said. 'When did you find the time? Was it during the summer when I was away?'

'Partly – but it started earlier than that, back in April.'

'Oh! I remember now. You *were* rather mysterious, once or twice, about where you were going. Was that it? How thrilling to be having a secret portrait taken! Has Holkam seen it yet?'

Violet explained that it was no longer really hers to command, and that any question of its being a present for her husband was now ended.

'Oh, what a shame!' said Emma. 'I can see what you mean about a great work of art belonging to the world, but all the same, it wouldn't have existed if you weren't so beautiful, and I'm sure Holkam would sooner it hung here than in some gallery somewhere. I'm longing to see it,' she went on eagerly. 'When can I? Is it really, really wonderful?'

Violet took her to see it the next day, and Emma thought it *was* wonderful: not at all what she had expected, but much, much better. 'Hardly like a painting at all – it's as if it were alive, and might start moving and speaking at any moment! Quite odd, really, and – somehow unsettling. But beautiful, my goodness! I've never seen anything so beautiful in my life. You are so *lucky*, Violet, to be so lovely, and have a real artist think so as well!'

But Emma was a quick and noticing young woman, and it wasn't long before she began to realise there was something wrong. She intercepted odd looks directed at Violet, overheard whispered comments – and some not-so-whispered that she was almost sure she was meant to overhear.

. . . wear something like that for a portrait . . . practically undressed . . . alone with the painter . . . her, of all people . . . all her good works . . . heard a thing or two about the artist . . . terribly good-looking . . . not quite the thing . . . Holkam abroad . . .

The spitefulness of the comments took her aback and made her angry. If people didn't think the portrait was a good work of art, that was one thing; but to leap from that to traducing the subject was unforgivable. No wonder, she thought, that Violet was not as calm and serene as she tried to appear. She must be aware of some of the things people were saying. Emma stuck close by Violet's side, held her head up, and gave an icy look to anyone she suspected.

Things moved towards a crisis. As gossip proliferated, the director of the gallery, Philip Humphreys, came under pressure not to award Laidislaw the prize. Though there was a prize committee, the competition had been his idea in the first place and his decision had always carried in previous years. It was an unhappy situation for him: his opinion was widely known, and the painting was undeniably brilliant – so much better than anything else that had been entered that *not* to choose it would seem a blatant act of bias.

But though there were some among the gallery's patrons who could view a piece of art for what it was in itself, there was a larger number who had no real interest in painting, and supported the gallery for the sake of the status it conferred and the opportunities it provided to mingle with important people. To them the painting was now bad because it was scandalous. The aesthetic judgement could not be separated from the social one. Awarding it the prize would be condoning wrong behaviour, and that was that.

To ignore the opinion of the benefactors would be to court financial disaster, and Humphreys had to give in. But because he had spoken rather too freely to Laidislaw in the first place, he felt some explanation was due to him before the award was announced. He called, therefore, early one morning at Ebury Street to break the bad news.

A little later, Laidislaw presented himself at St James's Square demanding to speak to Lady Holkam. He had never called there before, and whatever the servants might have heard or guessed, he was not officially 'known'. Moreover, he was in a state of agitation, he had forgotten his card-case, and it was not the time for visiting – the ladies had only just come downstairs for breakfast. A newspaper reporter who had been hanging around in the street outside for the last couple of days was alerted by the raised voices at the door, and to his great satisfaction was in time to recognise Laidislaw before he gained admission.

When the butler, Varden, came into the breakfast room with the information that a Mr Laidislaw was requesting to speak to her ladyship as a matter of urgency, Violet dropped the piece of toast she had just begun buttering, and turned pale.

Varden regarded her with interest. 'I did inform the gentleman that it was not a convenient time, my lady, but he was most insistent. Should I send him away?'

'No – no, don't do that,' Violet said faintly. Emma was looking at her, too, with wide enquiring eyes. Even the Pekingeses seemed to be staring. She said, with an effort at calmness, 'I'll see him. Show him into the ante-room, and tell him I'll be there directly.' She thought she had managed rather well, but inside her thoughts churned. Why had he come here? Something terrible must have happened. She met Emma's eyes, and simply could not frame any kind of excuse for her. She stood up, laid down her napkin and walked away.

The ante-room was a large, cold chamber off the main hall, designed in Carolean days for the formal reception of large numbers of supplicants and hangers-on. It was therefore very grand and very empty, and Laidislaw, walking up and down alone, looked dwarfed by the height of the ceiling, the vast expanse of marble floor, and the massiveness of the oil paintings – they had been sold with the house, presumably because they would not fit into any normal dwelling. He turned towards her as she came in, and she met him nervously in the middle of the room, under the huge candelabrum, which seemed to hang above them threateningly like an inverted mountain of ice ready to fall and crush them.

'My darling!' he cried passionately. The crystal above him rang with soft menace in response to his voice.

She put her finger warningly to her lips. Because the room was so large, no-one could get close enough to eavesdrop, as long as they stayed in the middle and spoke quietly.

'What is it? Has something happened?' she asked.

He spoke lower, but still with urgency. 'The most terrible thing!' he said. He gripped her hands. 'I'm sorry to come here like this. Perhaps it was unwise. But I had to see you!'

'Of course, of course. I'm glad you came. But what is it?'

'I had a visit from Humphreys this morning. He says he is not going to give me the prize.'

Violet's eyes widened. 'But he *said* you had won. You told me he did. You said it was quite certain.'

'So it was,' Laidislaw said bitterly. '*He* still wants me to have it. But the small-minded hags on the committee think differently, and he daren't go against them – it's they who pay for everything. *Cherchez l'argent!* Money speaks in this base world, you see – not integrity, not beauty, not art!'

'But, Octavian, *why*?' she asked, though she had a horrid feeling she knew. 'Why don't they want you to win? Yours was the best painting by far!'

'I know that, and Humphreys knows that. But the ignorant *canaille* who pass for supporters of the arts can't see it. All that matters to them is that the subject is not dressed in their own ugly style of clothes, and not sitting up straight like an alderman! They said—' There were tears sparkling on his eyelashes, tears of anger and frustration. 'They said my painting was *indecent*.'

'Oh, my dear,' Violet said, and she bowed her head while she struggled with her own tears. She had trusted that when he won the prize the detractors would be confounded. Now it seemed that they had won.

He pulled away from her to walk up and down some more, clenching and unclenching his hands in his helpless rage. 'I could kill them all! The stupidity, the blind, block-headed ignorance and pettiness of it! How dare they pronounce judgement on my work? It's too good for them, that's the trouble. Pearls before swine – there never was a truer saying! The swine ought to be left to wallow in their midden, if that's all they can say when the greatest painting of a generation is put in front of them.' He swung back to her. 'And do you know what the worst thing of all is? Humphreys says it won't be going to America either! Some busybody of a trustee cabled somebody on the committee of the Rothschild Gallery, and they've told Humphreys not to send it. My masterpiece!'

She tried desperately to think of some way to comfort him. 'It's a wonderful painting. It's – it's ahead of its time! People will understand it one day. For now, you must be content that *we* love it and appreciate it. And you must let me pay you for it, as we intended in the first place.'

He stared at her a moment, then folded her in his arms and kissed the crown of her head. She was terrified that someone might come in, but she could not refuse him – and the touch of his body was balm to her own unhappiness. He said, 'My darling, you are so sweet. But the money doesn't matter. How can you think it? That's not why I painted you.'

'I know it wasn't, but you must let me give you the money anyway. Do let me! Even geniuses have to eat, you know.'

She essayed a little joke to make it easier for him, but he released her and said, 'No, my rose, I shall never take money from you. I must think of some way out of this – some way of showing my work to the world.' He touched her cheek and smiled, a little wanly, but it was a smile at least. 'I'm sorry, I shouldn't have come here, but I had to speak to you. I'd better go now. Don't worry, I'm not defeated yet. I shall think of something. And in the mean time –' he picked up her hand and kissed it '– we have our love. Nothing can alter that. Come to me soon. I can't be without you.'

'I can't today,' she said unhappily. 'But tomorrow – I'll come tomorrow.'

'Until then,' he said, and left her. Varden was hovering in the hall, and intercepted him to show him out. He had been frustrated in his attempt to hear anything that was said, but the very fact of his calling at all was heating the butler's brain to boiling point.

Violet returned to the breakfast room, and almost started when she saw Emma there at the table. She had forgotten her for the moment.

'Is something wrong?' Emma asked, with great concern.

'No, nothing at all,' Violet said, sitting down. And then, realising that that would not do as an answer, she said, 'Mr Laidislaw called to let me know, out of courtesy, that his painting is not going to win the prize, after all. He heard this morning from the director of the gallery. The director felt he ought to know, since he'd told him before that he was certain to win.'

'Oh,' said Emma, not knowing what to think of that. 'Is he very disappointed?'

Violet picked up her cup, sipped at the cold coffee, and put it down again with distaste, hardly knowing she had done it. 'No, not really,' she said. 'Well, a little, perhaps.'

'It was much the best painting, I thought,' Emma said; then, tentatively, 'Did he say why?'

'It wasn't in the usual style, I suppose,' Violet said vaguely. 'These things are largely a matter of fashion.' She pulled herself together. 'Now, your clothes: we have Land's in Bond Street at half past ten – dreadfully early, I know, but it was the only time they could fit us in – and then Madame

Lacoste at two thirty, so we shall have time for luncheon in between. Where would you like to go?'

Emma had to allow herself to be diverted from the subject.

The next day the prize was announced. The serious papers did no more than to reproduce the winning entry, with some added copy mentioning that Laidislaw's painting had been widely expected to win but in the end had been regarded as too *avant-garde* by the prize committee.

But the sensational papers had got all they could out of the Cavell outrage, and seized on the story with relish. The Artist and the Society Beauty: it was delicious, it had all the right elements – and particularly given it was *that* society beauty, the unassailably virtuous Lady Holkam. They dwelt in detail on the controversial nature of the painting, its intimacy and sensuality; they described how young, handsome and exciting Laidislaw was, and how every society lady wanted his services; they mentioned that Lord Holkam was away at Headquarters in France; they mentioned excitedly that Laidislaw had been seen leaving the Holkams' house in St James's Square the day before, and that Lady Holkam, heavily veiled, had been seen entering Laidislaw's lodgings in Ebury Street the week previously. Indeed, they did everything but state in so many words that an *affaire* was in progress.

The *Daily Mail* filled the middle pages with it. They even dug out reports of Violet's wedding at the Abbey in 1908, and of her triumphant come-out earlier the same year. They ran photographs of 'the Society Bride' and 'the most popular débutante of her year', together with one of Laidislaw looking raffishly handsome in evening dress at some exhibition the year before. They described his career so far, with comments from art critics about his talent and independence of style, and described Violet as coming from 'one of our most distinguished but unconventional families', resurrecting the story of Venetia's struggle to become 'one of the first lady-doctors'. The implication was clear – despite her reputation for good works, Lady Holkam was as Bohemian as he was, and what could you expect of people like that?

St James's Square was besieged with reporters, photographers and curious members of the public. Violet stayed home and refused visitors and telephone calls; she cancelled her engagements for the day, but was distressed that many of her forward engagements were also being cancelled by the hostesses. Was she becoming untouchable? The consequences of scandal became apparent to her for the first time.

She did not see why Emma should be incarcerated with her, and urged her to go out. Emma had been intending to visit a female friend at home that morning, an engagement which did not need a chaperone, and though she said she did not want to leave Violet, she was persuaded at last to go, slipping out through the servants' entrance. But it was an awkward occasion, with odd looks, and silences caused by all the questions everyone wanted to ask her but did not like to. She returned home determined not to venture out again until the storm had passed.

'And it will, I know it will,' she tried to comfort Violet. 'All this horrid nonsense will be forgotten, and they'll run after something else.'

Violet hoped so too. She missed Octavian badly, longed to go to him, and knew it was, for the moment, the one thing she must not do.

The next day Oliver called and was admitted, and looked at his sister askance. 'Well, this is a pretty pickle! Mama sends her love, but says she won't visit you just yet, in case it inflames the papers even more. She saw the parts about her, of course.'

'Oh dear. Is she very angry?'

'Not with you – with the press. Papa is raging, too. He's out now, trying to bring pressure to bear on the editors to stop the nonsense. Of course, it's all innuendo, so he can't threaten legal action. But I think they'll pay him attention. They know he has friends in a lot of high places.'

'I'm sorry to cause everyone so much trouble,' Violet said.

'Not *your* fault,' Oliver said at once; but after a small pause, 'Though we did all think it was odd that you didn't tell any of us you were sitting for this portrait.'

'It was a secret,' Violet said awkwardly.

'Well, it isn't one now. I haven't seen the picture – is it any good? Mother seems to think it is.'

'It's a wonderful piece of work,' Violet said passionately. 'That's what's so unfair.'

'Hmm. Well, the sooner it's withdrawn from the exhibition, the better.'

'He'll never agree to that.'

'What, Humphreys? I don't think he's a match for the Aged Ps.'

'No, I meant Laidislaw. The painting belongs to him, not to me, and he wants it to be exhibited.'

'Oh, does he? We shall see about that. Now, don't cry, please, Vi! Everything will be all right. We'll all support you.'

'Thank you,' Violet said, for the comfort and the handkerchief he gave her.

'That's what family is for. You just sit tight here for a day or two, and everything will blow over.'

Freddie Copthall arrived in the afternoon and Violet was glad to see him. She asked eagerly if he had seen Laidislaw.

'Found him in Piccadilly, bein' hunted by reporters,' Freddie said. 'Practically spent. Had to take him to earth in my club. Dashed hounds couldn't follow him there – porter would have had something to say if they'd tried. Some of the members didn't like it but, dash it, I couldn't leave him out there, could I?'

'How is he? How did he look?'

'Oh, he's holdin' up all right. Worried about you, though.'

Freddie agreed to take him a note, and slipped out with it late in the afternoon, promising to return to dinner. After some enquiry and a little thought, he found Laidislaw sheltering with the Verneys, delivered the note and received one to bring back. Laidislaw, he thought, was looking flushed and excited, enjoying the fuss more now that he was safe with friends. Of course, Freddie reflected, notoriety did no harm to an artist – indeed, might positively enhance his reputation. It was different for a lady. He wished he was on such terms with Laidislaw as to point this out; but he noted that the fellow did at least sit down quietly and write a longish letter to Violet, and he liked him better for it.

He delivered it to Violet in the drawing-room before dinner, and she took it out of the room to read, returning after a while seeming composed, though with damp eyelashes. He and Emma did their best to keep the evening cheerful. Conversation was full of pitfalls, so after dinner they played three-handed whist with Violet to keep her mind off things. From time to time they both assured her that the fuss would die away soon. The difficulty, of course, Violet thought, was that neither of them had any idea that the story was anything but empty speculation.

Lord Overton's heroic efforts were successful: the following day there was nothing in any of the newspapers about Violet or Laidislaw, which was a huge relief – though, of course, Violet reflected, it would not stop the gossip. Evidence that it was thriving came by the post and telephone, with more cancellations, and refusals of invitations. For the first time in her adult life there were gaps in Violet's diary that were not of her own designing.

A crowd began to gather outside, but at mid-morning a large policeman appeared and moved them all away, and took up position before the steps to prevent further coagulation.

Venetia telephoned. 'How are things this morning?'

'Better. There's a policeman outside.'

'Ah, good, he's arrived, has he? I had a word with my

friends at Marylebone police station and they said they'd arrange it. Have you seen the newspapers?'

'Yes. Did Papa arrange that?'

'He did. It took him all day. I've never seen him so angry – you know how genial he always is.'

What would he say, Violet thought unhappily, when he knew the truth? 'I'm very grateful. Please thank him for me,' she said, in a small voice.

'I think it best if you avoid public places for a day or two,' Venetia said, 'but would you like to come here for a change of scene?'

'No, thank you, Mama. I'd rather stay home, if you don't mind.'

'If you're sure – but don't brood too much, will you? These things seem important at the time, but they pass over and are forgotten. You acted unwisely in keeping the sittings secret, but you didn't do anything wrong. It's important to remember that.'

Violet understood so well just then the expression 'coals of fire'. 'I was thinking,' she said quickly, 'that perhaps Emma ought to have a change of scene.'

'I was just going to suggest that,' said Venetia. 'Even if you won't come, there's no need for her to be cooped up. Have Sanders pack a bag for her and send her over in a taxi-cab.'

Emma did not want to abandon Violet, but was persuaded in the end. 'I'm not very good company just now. And there's no need to cancel all your engagements. Sanders can take you to your fittings, and there's the theatre tonight and the opera on Saturday. Mama or Oliver can use my ticket.'

'Will you really be all right on your own?' Emma said doubtfully. The house seemed so empty, and Violet looked so small and fragile in its indifferent spaces.

'It's only for a few days,' Violet said, and hoped desperately that that was true. She needed so much to see Laidislaw, but until the fuss died down it was impossible.

Freddie came again, sat through luncheon with her, and went off afterwards with another note to look for Laidislaw. He returned with the reply and stayed for dinner. They were sitting in the drawing-room with their sherry, waiting to be called, when there was the sound of violent knocking at the street door, raised voices, and then, alarmingly, someone being admitted. There was low but agitated conversation, and the unmistakable ring of footsteps across the hall. The dogs looked up from their curled position by the fire; Violet's fingers whitened on her glass-stem; Freddie rose to his feet, ready to protect his goddess against marauding pressmen.

The door opened, and Lord Holkam stood there. In uniform he looked somehow bigger, and filled the doorway with menace. He had the air and smell of travel about him, a hint of fog and cold night air, jewels of dampness on his shoulders and front hair, and the grimy pallor of railways to his cheeks. Varden, just behind him, held his cap and gloves and was hovering for his greatcoat, but Holkam ignored him. His hard eyes went straight to Violet, and she shrank from them.

'What in God's name is going on?' he demanded. He had had to shout to get them to open his own front door, which had not helped his mood. Belatedly, he took in Freddie Copthall's presence. 'Good evening, Freddie,' he said tersely. 'Just leaving?'

Freddie threw an agonised look at Violet and she made a small gesture with her hand, releasing him. Holkam stepped aside from the doorway to let him through but gave him no further acknowledgement. Varden slipped in behind his master and insistently took hold of the collar of the greatcoat. Holkam walked forward and out of it, leaving it in the butler's hands, and shoved the door closed in his face.

'How did you get here?' was all Violet could think to say. 'I wasn't expecting you.'

'I'm quite sure you weren't.' He walked towards her, and he looked so angry she stood up in self-defence. The dogs had risen and were waving their tails uncertainly, thinking they ought to greet the master, but sensing an unusual atmosphere. 'I had a most obliging letter from a colleague at Horseguards hinting I know not what, and then I saw the newspapers this morning – along with just about everyone at Headquarters, I might add! Haig let me go at once – urgent compassionate leave – and I've been travelling all day. Can you imagine what it's like, having my chief being tactful with me?'

'I'm sorry,' she began automatically.

'*Sorry?* I repeat my question – what the devil is going on? What is all this nonsense about a portrait? Someone said you posed in the nude for it.'

'I didn't!' she said indignantly.

'Good God, I know that! The point is, that's what people are saying. Once people start talking, it doesn't matter whether what they say is true or not. Why wasn't I told about this damned picture?'

'I was having it done as a surprise for you – a birthday present, only it wasn't ready in time for your birthday.'

'Then what the deuce is it doing hanging in a public gallery for all the world to ogle?'

Tears rose, and she tried hard to blink them back. This was not the time to lose control – and she sensed that it would make him angrier if she cried. 'It wasn't meant that way in the beginning,' she said. 'I wanted it as a present for you, but then things changed. Laidislaw says it's his masterpiece. He says a work of art of that sort belongs to the world, not to any one person.'

'The devil he does! He who pays the piper calls the tune! He had better learn that quickly, or someone will have to teach him.' His fists clenched involuntarily.

'He wouldn't let me pay for it,' Violet said. 'The painting belongs to him. I told you, things changed after the beginning.'

'Any portrait of my wife belongs to *me*, not to the petty

workman who happens to execute it,' Holkam said furiously, and then stopped, staring at her closely. She felt herself redden. 'What do you mean,' he asked more quietly, '"*things changed*"?' She tried to keep her gaze steady, but it was hard. 'What is this – this mountebank to you? I've heard all the speculation but I assumed there was nothing in it but vicious gossip. Violet, *answer me*! What is he to you?'

She lifted her head a little. She would not lie to him – had never intended to, if it came to the direct question. And why should she? 'He is my lover,' she said. The words fell like shattering glass, leaving an appalling silence behind them. She saw Holkam's scalp shift backwards as the amazement and shock hit him, and then he seemed to her apprehensive eyes to grow even bigger in his anger.

'*How dare you?*' he cried, low but furious. 'How dare you stand there and say that to my face? Have you no shame? Have you no self-respect? I'm your husband, God damn it!'

'Would you rather I lied to you?' she said bravely.

'Don't you dare to be impertinent!' he bellowed.

'I'm not being. Oh, Holkam, please sit down and be calm, and we can talk about this. Shouting won't help, and the servants will hear.'

He did sit, rather as though the legs had been knocked out from under him. His meek and obedient little wife was actually standing up to him, rather than trembling and collapsing in helpless, feminine tears, and the shock of that was rather as if one of the Pekingeses had spoken. He went on more quietly, though with a tremor of fury in his voice: 'I should imagine the servants know all about it already. Everyone in London must do. Certainly everyone in France does, from what I've been hearing! I can't believe it of you. I can't believe you're standing there telling me in that barefaced manner that you have abused and betrayed me – and then you expect me to be calm?'

She sat too, and folded her hands together in her lap to keep them from trembling. 'I have not abused and betrayed you. I've done nothing wrong. Since Charlotte was born, our marriage has been on a different footing.'

'The devil it has!' he interrupted.

She went on, with an effort: 'After Charlotte, you no longer visited my bedroom. We had our own separate lives. You seemed quite happy with the arrangement. And I know there are many couples of our rank who do the same.'

'What other couples do is nothing to the point! Did you really think I would permit you to bed another man while you remained my wife?'

'But you have other women,' she said quietly.

His eyes widened, and for a moment he was silent. Had he really not known that she knew? she thought. That was interesting. She wondered for a moment if he would deny it.

But he said, 'What I do is my concern – and if you had any modesty you would not mention such things. My arrangements are normal and acceptable, and decent women ignore them. They are made out of consideration for you as much as anything. A man has certain requirements – needs a certain outlet. These things are understood.'

'Yes, and I do understand,' she said. 'I don't blame you for it, and I never have. I have always accepted it. Now you must accept that I have certain requirements too.'

'Don't be disgusting! You're a woman,' he said. 'It's quite different for a woman.'

'It seems that it is not,' she said quietly. 'Holkam, I did not start out to do this. I had no intention except to sit for my portrait. But things changed. Laidislaw and I—'

'Don't you dare speak his name in my presence!'

'It will be difficult to talk about this if I cannot.'

'There will be no talking about it! Never again! The thing is over, do you hear me? You will never see him again, or mention him again, to me or to anyone else.'

'I love him,' she said. 'And he loves me.'

Holkam jumped to his feet and, for a breathless instant,

she thought he was going to strike her. But he turned away and paced up and down the room, trying to regain control. She watched him, anxiously, and saw hurt in his expression as well as anger; and she felt pain for him. But if she could go back and change things, she would not do so.

He stopped his pacing at last and faced her. 'Let me get this clear. You knew about my – my visits to those women. You felt slighted, or hurt, or something of the sort. So you thought you'd strike back at me by doing the same with this artist fellow. But don't you see? My actions were natural and discreet. Yours have caused a scandal! You have not been discreet – the very opposite – and an *affaire* of this sort for a woman is a very different matter.'

He was trying so hard to be reasonable, against everything he was feeling at that moment. She ached for him. But she said, 'You have not understood. I was not trying to "strike back" at you. And I do not feel I have done wrong. *You* set the pattern.'

'It's *different* for a man. Why can't you see that?'

'I've told you – I did not intend this to happen. Laidislaw and I fell in love.'

He stared at her, breathing hard, in the throes of thought. Then his eyes narrowed. 'I will not divorce you. There will be no divorce. There's been enough scandal already, and I won't have you embroil my name in any more of it.'

She was shocked. 'I don't want a divorce. I'm happy to be your wife. I'm sorry all this has come into the newspapers. If it hadn't been for the painting it *would* all have been discreet. And when the fuss dies down it will be again.'

'What are you talking about? You are not going to see him again, ever.'

'I am. I have to.'

'I forbid it.'

'I'm sorry,' she said unhappily, feeling herself tremble at her own resoluteness, 'but you can't.'

He would have spoken, but realised at the same moment

that he could not physically prevent her. He would be going back to France, and she would not be under his control. He could not be so Gothic as to have the servants lock her in her room for the rest of the war – and he wasn't sure they would obey if he ordered them to. And she had family and friends. It would cause as much scandal again as she had caused already if he were to take draconian actions against her. If she insisted on seeing this painter-fellow, he would not be able to stop her.

'I can ruin him,' he said. 'I can destroy his name. I can make sure he never sells another painting. He'll never exhibit anywhere ever again.'

She looked sad. 'I expect you could. But it wouldn't make any difference, you see.'

He was silent. The fire crackled, the French clock ticked lightly and rapidly on the overmantel, and one of the dogs sat up and scratched his neck vigorously, making his collar rattle. The sounds seemed unbearably significant, as though they were the physical evidence of some fate being decided invisibly in those sharp-edged moments.

He said, 'You're determined, then.'

She nodded, and said with difficulty, 'I thought you wouldn't mind. After all—'

'*That's completely different!* Those women I used to see—'

'*Used* to see? Aren't there women in France?' she asked, and it stopped him. Of course there were – she had known there would be.

'You will have to go out of Town,' he said at last. 'This thing will go on being a scandal and a talking if you are seen with him anywhere in London.'

She had expected that. 'I'll go down to Brancaster.'

'You will not,' he said fiercely, surprising her, 'see that man under my roof – under any of my roofs. I won't have him anywhere near Brancaster. And remember, if I can't stop you seeing him, I *can* stop you seeing the children.'

'There's no need for that,' she said quietly. 'I don't want

us to be enemies. We can be civilised about this, can't we?'

'Civilised!' He spat the word, then took a breath. 'Then you will go somewhere you're not known, somewhere remote – and for God's sake try to be discreet! When the fuss has died down – well, perhaps then we'll talk again. By that time—' Something obviously occurred to him, and he stopped abruptly, thinking hard. She watched his face curiously. At last a faint smile crossed it, and in a moment was gone. She felt apprehensive. It had not been a pleasant smile.

'What is it?' she asked.

'Nothing,' he said. 'I've said all I mean to say.'

She sighed, feeling exhausted – and hungry. Varden had evidently not dared to interrupt them to announce dinner. She wondered how much he had managed to hear. They had not been speaking quietly all the time.

'What will you do now?' she asked.

'I have to go back tomorrow morning. Have you had dinner?' He looked at the clock, trying to make sense of the time. 'I suppose you haven't.'

'Freddie and I were waiting for it when you arrived.'

He became brisk. 'Have them put it back another half-hour while I wash and change, and I'll eat with you. It might be the last meal we share for some time.'

She didn't know if it was an observation or a threat. She was relieved that it was all out in the open between them – glad she would be able to see Laidislaw, though it meant going away, at least for the time being. But she would have to call on her mother and father and explain everything to them, and on the whole she felt *that* interview would be worse than the scene she had just survived with Holkam. So much trouble, so much pain and muddle, and when would it all be sorted out? When would life seem normal again? But behind all the anguish and anxiety there glowed a small, strong, clear flame – her love for Octavian and his for her. That was what would make it all worth while.

CHAPTER FOUR

Now it had to be faced; now Violet had to tell her mother and father how things really stood between her and Laidislaw. And she must tell them quickly, before they heard it from another source.

It was the hardest thing she had ever done – much, much harder than facing down Holkam. While in her own heart she might believe she had done nothing wrong, her parents would think differently. She hated above all the idea of 'letting them down'.

The interview was painful. Venetia, at least, had begun to have some apprehension of what it might be about. But when her lovely daughter, rather pale and clutching her little dogs as though they might be a life-belt, stood straight before her and said, 'I have something I must tell you. I am in love with Octavian Laidislaw,' she found that nothing had prepared her for the reality. Words failed her, and her mind registered nothing but a shocked disbelief.

Overton was taken completely aback. He looked at Violet with incomprehension. It was he who spoke first. 'In *love* with him? But how can you be? Especially after all this fuss he's caused, insisting on exhibiting the painting. I should have thought you'd *dis*like him, rather.'

Violet was disconcerted. 'No, Papa, you don't understand. I have been in love with him since April. All the time he's been painting me. It hasn't just happened. And

– indeed, for a long time now – we have been lovers.'

The word was out. Overton said nothing. He seemed to grey a little, and sat down abruptly, staring at Violet as he tried to rearrange the world in his head. Venetia opened her mouth to speak but could think of nothing sensible to say. The worst had been confirmed. What *was* there to say, after all?

But Violet desperately wanted something from them. She put down the dogs and held out her hands in a little, helpless gesture. 'Oh, I know it's a shock to you, but please, please try to understand. I didn't mean it to happen, but I couldn't help it. I fell in love. Papa, you must know what it means to fall in love.'

He shook his head slowly, not in negation, but as a goaded bull might. 'You fell in love? But I thought you were in love with Holkam. Otherwise—' Otherwise, he thought, I would never have let you marry him. In a flash of memory he saw all the unsatisfactoriness – Holkam's financial state, his disapproval of his wife's parents, the pain he had caused them all when he had forbidden Violet to see them, the embarrassment of being 'taken back into favour' by him, the many chilly, awkward meetings – and wondered if it had all been tolerated in vain. And he thought of the many other perfectly nice young men to whom they might have married Violet, people of their own sort, if she had not set her heart on Holkam. 'I wonder, Violet, if you really know your own mind,' he concluded painfully.

'I was in love with him at first,' Violet pleaded, 'or I thought I was. But I see now it was only a girlish crush. My feelings for Octavian are quite different. Oh, please believe me, I haven't done anything lightly.'

'Lightly!' Venetia picked up the word, then didn't know what to do with it.

Violet turned to her. 'I know that you and Papa will disapprove of – of a physical relationship outside marriage, but Holkam and I are not like you. He has always – well . . .'

She faltered at expressing it to her unworldly parents. 'There have always been – women—'

'Women? Holkam?' Overton said, startled. That was one thing he had not expected of the son-in-law he mildly disliked.

'I didn't mind,' Violet said hastily. 'I never liked – that side of things. Not until Octavian. But you do see? It isn't as though I have betrayed my husband. He and I lived separate lives, not like you and Mama. I don't feel that I have done anything wrong, and though you may feel differently, I beg you not to condemn me.' She met her mother's eyes. 'Oh, please, Mummy, don't hate me!'

She hardly ever used the childish name, and it touched Venetia unbearably. 'I don't hate you,' she said. 'How could I?' You're my child, my darling daughter, her thoughts added. She imagined what it must have been like to be Violet, married to the man she had demanded, then finding it had been a mistake. Venetia blamed herself for not taking more time before the marriage to make sure Violet's feelings were settled: she had been very young, straight out of the schoolroom. But in those days Venetia had always been so busy with her profession, hardly having time to sit down for a meal with her family, let alone pursue heart-to-heart talks with its members. And Violet had always been so good, so obedient, so placid – so little trouble!

She blamed herself, too, for not making her better acquainted with 'that side of things'. That was the judgement of hindsight, of course: it was not something women spoke about, not even mother to daughter, other than to warn the daughter that the husband would want to do certain things that it was her duty to allow. But as a doctor, she ought to have been more able to overcome the barriers. Of course, it might not have made any difference – preknowledge was not a passport to sexual compatibility, after all, and many, perhaps most, women merely put up with what they had to. Had Holkam been clumsy, or unkind?

But she didn't want to think about that. Oh, but poor little Violet, never knowing what it was to share that blessed intimacy with the person one loved, as Venetia had shared a lifetime of it with Overton! Though what Violet had done was wrong, she could not quite condemn. Apart from anything else, there had been an episode in her own past – which no-one knew about – when she had felt as Violet did, that she was doing no wrong, but which now filled her with remorse. She remembered the adage about not throwing stones . . .

While she was pursuing her thoughts, Overton had recovered his voice, had been asking questions, which Violet had answered patiently and unhappily. Now he said, 'Does Holkam know? Was that why he came to London yesterday?'

Of course, Violet thought, Papa *would* know he had been home. 'Yes,' she said. 'He was angry about it. He told me I must give up Octavian, but I said I couldn't do that.'

'So – you mean to go on with this *affaire*?'

'I love him,' Violet said. 'I can't give him up.'

Overton shook his head again. 'Well, what, then?' He said it with a sort of helplessness in his voice that upset Violet more than anger would have. It made her realise that her parents were not young any more.

'Holkam says Octavian and I must go out of Town until the fuss has died down, and that's what we mean to do. We'll go somewhere quiet in the country where we're not known. I hoped,' she faltered again, receiving no reaction, 'that you might know of somewhere suitable.'

Overton searched his daughter's face. 'But afterwards – what then? Do you mean to ask Holkam for a divorce?'

The sound of the word spoken aloud shocked Venetia, and she looked sharply at her husband. She had not been thinking along those lines. To be truthful, she had barely been thinking at all, only feeling and grieving.

Violet said quickly, 'No, no, not that. Holkam would never agree, and it isn't what I want. I am happy to be married to him, and I love my children. All I want is to be able to see Octavian – quietly and without fuss or scandal. Just to be with him when I want to. You know, like Lady Eversleigh and Sir James Goldfarb. Everyone knows about them, but no-one thinks anything of it.'

Venetia almost smiled. Lady Eversleigh was in her sixties, and though she and Jimmy Goldfarb had undoubtedly been lovers in their youth, and still saw each other daily, it was doubtful either of them now got up to anything more exceptionable than gossiping over the teacups and sharing a box at the theatre. But, still, the point was taken. These things did become acceptable through sheer longevity. She could see that a time might come in the future when Lady Holkam and Octavian Laidislaw were an accepted item and raised no eyebrows. It was getting through the years in between that was the difficulty.

It was time for something practical to be said. 'I think it is a good idea for you to go out of Town,' Venetia said. 'Especially as everyone knows Holkam is at the Front. I think you should get away as soon as possible. Don't you agree?' she asked her husband. But he, poor soul, was still too shocked to be of much help. It would take him time to assimilate all this – and he had had no shady passage in his past to help him over the first hurdle, that of having always thought Violet perfect.

She turned back to her daughter. 'The problem is, where should you go? If you stay in an hotel, the pressmen will soon find you, and it will only make things look worse. There's something *about* hotels . . . And you can hardly go and stay with relatives.'

Violet blushed at this reminder that, however much she believed she had done nothing wrong, the world in general would judge differently.

'As it happens,' Venetia said thoughtfully, 'I do know of a place – a house I own, somewhere very secluded, where you can be sure no-one will know you. The difficulty is that you might find it *too* rustic.'

Violet said eagerly, 'Oh, I don't mind how quiet it is. I just want to be alone with Octavian for a while. Where is it?'

'It's in a village in Norfolk. Actually, I don't think it's even a village, just a hamlet. But I warn you, there's nothing for miles around it but sky and fields.'

'It sounds perfect,' said the Violet who was such a Town girl she regarded Hyde Park as the country. 'How soon can we go?'

'Tomorrow, if you like,' Venetia said sadly, realising that she was just about to lose her daughter all over again. 'It will only take a telephone call.'

'I'll speak to Octavian about it,' said Violet. She had sounded happy as she said it, but now her mouth drooped, and she looked from her mother to her father. 'I know I've hurt you with this. Can you ever forgive me?'

Overton made a strange sound as speech failed him, and held out his arms. Violet fell to her knees beside him and was enveloped. Venetia watched them, her throat tight, seeing how hard it had hit her husband, who loved Violet too much to be angry with her, let alone cast her off. He pressed his cheek to her glossy hair and closed his eyes in pain. Though Venetia was glad, in an academic way, that her daughter had learned something of true love at last, at that moment she wished Laidislaw at the devil.

Violet and Laidislaw were gone, but even so, and despite the enforced silence of the newspapers, little else was talked of in society's haunts but the astonishing affair of Lady Holkam and the Artist. Lord Holkam's precipitous visit had been all the confirmation the doubters needed that there was substance in the rumours; and the absence of the protagonists from the scene left them free to discuss it openly and constantly.

The painting disappeared from the gallery, depriving the slow-off-the-mark of the pleasure of seeing it for themselves, but allowing an escalating account of its shockingness to go uncontradicted. Humphreys would not answer any questions about it, so it was not known where the picture had gone or who had secured its removal. It was popularly supposed that Lord Holkam was responsible, and a story grew up that he had hired a gang of East End 'toughs' to break into the gallery and kidnap it. In fact, Lord Overton, helped by Lady Verney, had persuaded Laidislaw before he left London to write a note authorising Humphreys to hand it over to Overton, and it was now safely hidden in an attic in Manchester Square.

But the scandal did not impinge on the family at Morland Place at all. The women of the house never read the newspapers, while Rob and Teddy read only the business and war news. Teddy, besides, had been too busy with his enquiries after Ned to do more than scan the headlines. Though he had been up to London, to pay a visit to Harrington House in Craig's Court – one of those dark, secret closes off Whitehall – where information on 'the missing' was collated, he had not, of course, met anyone likely to be talking about the scandal, and certainly not to a man looking for his lost son.

But in the servants' hall, where they regularly took the *Daily Mail*, and other newspapers of the sensational sort, the coverage of Lady Holkam's portrait and the subsequent uproar was marvelled over. Mrs Stark, the cook, asked Sawry if he was going to show it to the Family. After an earnest discussion – expanded to include Alice's maid Miss Sweetlove, Teddy's valet Brown, and Jessie's Tomlinson – it was decided that unless one of the Family brought up the subject, it was not to be mentioned.

Sawry gathered all the servants together and sternly forbade them to discuss it outside the servants' hall. In the event, Lord Overton's prompt actions meant that nothing appeared in the papers on subsequent days, and Sawry felt he had made the right choice. The relevant pages disappeared into Mrs Stark's scrapbook, and it was largely assumed that it had all been lies in the first place. *You couldn't believe anything that was written in the papers,* was the commonly expressed view, while those expressing it devoured every new sensation as it burst upon them, and believed it fervently – at least until the next one came along.

So the first Jessie knew about it was when she received a most disconcerting letter from Violet. It was written, Violet said, in the motor, so begged excuse for any unevenness of writing.

> I dare say you know all about my scandal by now, so I won't weary you with details. Laidislaw and I are on the way to Norfolk where we will rusticate for a few weeks until things are quieter. I am sorry I had to deceive you when you stayed with me in London in May. Let me assure you the deception was innocent then. I was having the portrait done secretly only as a surprise present for Holkam. It was later that things changed. Then, of course, secrecy was necessary.
>
> How I have longed to be able to talk to you about it! Let me say at once that, though there is a horrid scandal, I do not feel I have done anything wrong. You know that Holkam's and my marriage has been on a different footing from yours and Ned's. I was quite content as I was, but I fell in love with L, and everything is different now. I have not done anything lightly, and I hope and pray you will understand and not hate me for it. I never meant to hurt anyone, but I cannot live without him now. Please, please understand.
>
> I have written already of my anxiety for you in your present uncertainty, but please don't think you are ever out of my thoughts, whatever is happening to me. I pray with all my heart that you will have better news of him soon. But if the news should not be good, you will always have the memory of his love for you, and

the knowledge that he gave his life in the most noble of causes, and with the utmost courage. Will that be a comfort? I don't know. Dearest, I wish I could see you and talk to you properly, but that is not possible at the moment. I will write to you again when we are settled in – I don't even know the direction at the moment – and perhaps then you will write to me. Oh, I hope you will – and won't condemn me! And I hope by then you will have the best of all news to tell me.

Your loving cousin and friend,
Violet

It was a strange letter, not in Violet's usual style, more expansive than her normally rather formal communications: their intimate exchanges had always taken place face to face. It was strange, too, because Jessie began with no idea what she was talking about, though by the end of it she had pieced together the clues and come to the astonishing conclusion. She remembered the visit she had paid to London in May and the mysterious absences of her hostess, who was deliberately vague about where she was going, and returned with a different look about her, glowing with a strange, silent bliss. Remembering it, Jessie concluded that she had been falling in love even then, though she had said in her letter that the sittings were innocent at that time. She was sure Violet was telling the truth as she knew it, but evidently she had been in danger from the beginning.

And what were her own feelings about it? Shock and disbelief aside, what she felt most was a sense of betrayal. Jessie had felt she knew her friend inside out, yet she would never have anticipated this. She couldn't hate her for it – how could anyone hate gentle Violet? Besides, she knew what it was to fall in love with the wrong person. She had never told Violet – or anyone – of her love for Bertie. She and Bertie were both married to other people, people who did not deserve to suffer. Since they could never be together as they wished, they had sworn only to be cousins to each other. Now Jessie felt hurt and almost resentful that Violet had taken with such seeming ease what Jessie had denied herself. She could not blame her for falling in love, and she envied her in a sad, sidelong way for being able to be with the man she loved. And yet what Violet had done was wrong, and there was no getting away from it. Her thoughts revolved restlessly, from wounded affection to worry for Violet's welfare, from guilt to wistful envy, and every thought was overlaid with perplexity that her friend should ever have come to this.

She was reading the letter at the breakfast table, and her mother's natural question, 'What does Violet have to say? Anything interesting?' made her wonder what she should say. Violet might feel she had done nothing wrong, but Jessie's elders would not feel like that about the breaking of marriage vows. But if there was a scandal in London about it, secrecy would be impossible. She felt suddenly that she could not cope with concealment. Worrying about Ned had left her heart bankrupt of the energy such deception would need.

'She's left London,' she said abruptly. 'She seems to think we will know all about it. Oh, you had better read it for yourself.'

She passed the letter to her mother, but Henrietta managed only a few lines before laying it down and putting her hands to her face in shock, so Ethel took it over and read it aloud. When she got to the second paragraph she stopped, and said, 'I don't think Polly ought to hear any more of this.'

Polly, who had been listening avidly, looked cross. 'Oh, really, that's too unfair! I'm fifteen, you know! Besides, you've gone too far now. You can't put the cat back in the bag. I've guessed what, anyway – she's run away with this Laid Low fellow. Only think of its being Cousin Violet, though!' she marvelled. 'The very last person!'

Teddy looked at Alice, who said, 'She will have to know sooner or later.'

Ethel finished reading the letter, and they all looked at each other in silence a moment. Then Henrietta said hesitantly, 'I understand things are done differently among the aristocracy. If she and her husband have come to an arrangement, perhaps we ought not to judge.'

'I can't agree with that,' Robbie said. 'There are certain standards.'

'A marriage vow is a marriage vow,' Ethel said.

'Poor Violet,' Alice said. 'It must be dreadful to be at the middle of a scandal.'

'Exciting, I'd call it. And running off with an artist!' said Polly.

'She's not *running*,' Jessie said.

'Driving, then. It's still more exciting than staying put.'

'That's a very improper thing to say,' Alice rebuked her, and Polly lowered her eyes, though without contrition.

'But I thought it was supposed to be a love match with her and Lord Holkam?' Teddy said complainingly to Jessie. He didn't like change and upset of this sort. 'Didn't you say as much when she married?'

'Yes,' Jessie said. 'It was. I suppose things changed.'

'But you didn't see anything of this when you visited her?'

'She and Lord Holkam always had a very – oh, *detached* relationship. They didn't seem to see each other very often. But they seemed happy together. Like good friends.'

'Oh, well,' Teddy said, 'I suppose as Hen says, they do things differently. Not our business to judge.'

'I hope Venetia's not terribly unhappy,' Henrietta said. 'I must write to her.'

But before the day was out, Venetia had telephoned, and she had learned all the details of the affair and discussed at length what her old friend felt about it. There had been a further development: Lord Abradale, hearing about the scandal, had telegraphed demanding that his niece be got out of London before it could taint her and spoil her prospects. He had said at first that Emma must go to

Aberlarich, but Emma had protested to Venetia about the unfairness of that. Venetia agreed that Aberlarich at that time of year was not the place for a young and sociable girl, and undertook the rigours of a telephone call to Scotland to try to negotiate with Abradale for a lighter sentence.

He was not inclined to yield, especially not to Venetia, who had, after all, put his precious ward into Violet's care in the first place. She did her best to quiet his apprehensions, and to make him see that scandals of this sort were of no lasting importance and blew over very quickly, however distressing they were to those involved. He remained adamant that Emma must be got out of London; but at last Venetia secured the compromise that Emma could go to Morland Place instead.

So Venetia was telephoning Henrietta to see if it was acceptable to them, and to make the arrangements for Emma's arrival. Teddy was delighted and, breathing down Henrietta's neck, repeated loudly enough for Venetia to hear at the other end that Emma could stay as long as she liked . . . for ever, if she wanted . . . it was no trouble at all . . . tell Venetia she could make her home there with them . . . he would happily stand *in loco parentis*. Henrietta pushed him gently away and, in an unexpected flash of sympathetic imagination, she had the clearest vision of what was in Teddy's mind at that moment: a vignette of himself standing with a radiant and white-clad Emma in church, giving her away at her wedding some day in the future.

Jessie was as pleased as she could be about anything just then, because she liked Emma and any agreeable visitor made a diversion from the weariness of grief and worry. And Polly was perhaps the most pleased of all because she had long had a 'crush' for Emma, and also had the thought – though she wisely did not express it aloud – that Emma would be bound to know all the grisly details of Cousin Violet's disgrace and that she, Polly, would be able to worm them out of her.

* * *

Emma was not loath to tell what she knew about the business, though it was to Jessie she revealed it: when Polly pressed her, she remained infuriatingly vague, which led Polly to haunt her and Jessie, convinced they would start 'telling' as soon as she was out of earshot. But finally she was confined indoors at the piano for her music lesson, and Jessie and Emma went out to take the air. Confidences, as Polly had feared, were exchanged.

Jessie was glad to learn that Laidislaw was a man of genuine and unusual talent – she hadn't liked to think Violet was throwing herself away on a second-rate painter. Emma had not been allowed to meet Laidislaw on the one occasion he had come to the house in Manchester Square, before he and Violet left London; but she was able to tell Jessie that Oliver had met him, and had told her he liked the fellow, even if a little in spite of himself, and believed that he was genuinely devoted to Violet.

'And he seems to think that in a few weeks they'll be able to come back to London,' Emma said.

'Will Lord Holkam accept the situation?' Jessie said doubtfully. Violet had long had her 'court' of young men who escorted her to parties and the theatre. But that had all been so patently innocent.

'I don't know about accepting it,' Emma said. 'There's not much he can do about it at the moment, being in France. But Oliver says that as long as they're discreet it will be all right. I'm not sure what "being discreet" means, whether they'll have to go about in disguise or only meet in country hotels or something. That wouldn't be much fun.'

'No, I don't suppose Violet would care for that,' Jessie said. Violet liked the life she had always led. Resuming it with the added joy of an accepted lover would be one thing; secrecy and subterfuge, let alone exile and disgrace, quite another.

'But Oliver seems to think it will all be forgotten by Christmas anyway. He says that as the war goes on longer, people won't make a fuss about things in the same way. I'm not sure what the war's got to do with it, really, but that's what he says.' She looked at Jessie cautiously. 'No news yet of Ned?'

'Nothing,' said Jessie. She remembered suddenly the first time Emma had seen him, how she had blushed and hero-worshipped, and told Jessie how *lucky* she was to have a lovely husband and a darling house to live with him in. House and husband, she had lost both now. And Bertie she could never have . . .

They were walking round the moat, followed hopefully by the swans, who kept pace with them, but casually, looking in every direction but at them, and pausing to investigate crannies in the bank as if they just happened to be going in the same direction. The six dogs had all followed them out when they left the house, and while Brach stayed close to Jessie, the others wandered about, pursuing interesting smells and occasionally tussling with each other over sticks and leaves. Morland Place: the moat, swans, dogs and walk were all so familiar to Jessie that she felt as though she had never gone away, as though she were a maid still in her maiden home, with her adulthood and marriage still ahead of her. Perhaps she would wake up and find all the strangeness of the last year only a dream. Ah, but the war – she couldn't have imagined that! Oliver was right: the war did change things.

Emma was still waiting receptively, and she forced herself to go on. 'Uncle Teddy is making his own enquiries. He's perfectly certain there's some mistake and that Ned is alive in a hospital somewhere, and that he'll find him.'

'But you don't think that?' Emma asked quietly.

'I don't know,' Jessie said. 'It seems unlikely that we wouldn't have heard by now. I think he probably is—' She still found it hard to say the word 'dead'. Emma's warm hand took hers for a moment and squeezed it, and let it go. Jessie was grateful both for the gesture and for its brevity.

'It's possible,' she went on, 'that we shall never know what happened to him. Perhaps that's the worst thing.'

It was hard for Venetia and Lord Overton to accept the situation: bad enough to have their dear, pretty daughter go away from them; but to hear her gossiped about, to have her life and character at the mercy of idle minds and tongues, was even more painful. It was impossible not to speculate on what had brought her to this point. She was plainly in love with Laidislaw, claimed to be happy; but they had thought her happy and in love before and had been mistaken. Neither said as much to the other, but the deep fear of each was that this might be the beginning of a pattern. They had both known people who were so fundamentally unhappy that their life became a series of bolts away from whatever present circumstance they felt they could pin their unhappiness on. That lovely Violet might become a 'bolter' was too horrible to be spoken of.

Venetia felt guilty, too, about the disruption to Emma's life. It had been painful to have Lord Abradale talk as if Violet were an infection from which Emma must be saved. She would be happy enough at Morland Place for a time, but would Abradale ever allow her to come back to London? If she returned, but was put under the charge of someone else, it would be such a snub to Venetia that it would be bound to cause talk.

Lord Overton at least had the benefit of a counter-irritant to take his mind off his daughter's fall from grace. General Sir Charles Monro took over Hamilton's command in Gallipoli at the end of October. He had no sooner arrived than he followed up his instructions from Lord Kitchener, which were to report 'fully and frankly' on the situation.

His report was not comfortable reading. His tour of inspection had left him shocked at the hand-to-mouth way in which the soldiers were subsisting, compared with the well-ordered and well-supplied arrangements in France.

Their suffering appalled him, and he reported that the officers on the ground were adamant that they were in no condition to mount an offensive of any sort: it was only because the Turks were short of ammunition that they were able to hold on to their position at all. When he asked them whether a breakthrough *could* be made, they advised him that nothing might be done before spring, and even then it would take four hundred thousand fresh men, and all the arms, ammunition and supplies such a number entailed.

Evacuation, Monro concluded, was the only feasible action. But it must be carried out very soon. Now that Bulgaria had joined the war on Germany's side, it would be possible to send heavy guns and ammunition to the Turks overland. Once they arrived, the Turks would be able to pulverise the Allies into submission with siege artillery and drive them into the sea, which would mean heavy losses. Only a voluntary and well-planned withdrawal – and an immediate one, before the winter storms set in – could save the lives of the men who clung so desperately to that rocky foothold.

When the report was laid before the Dardanelles committee, Overton spoke up at once for evacuation, and most of the others reluctantly agreed. Lord Kitchener, unfortunately, was not among them. 'I absolutely refuse to sign an order for evacuation,' he said, staring round the table with his hard blue eyes, his moustaches bristling with his outrage. 'The humiliation of it, the ignominy, would deal a terrible blow to British prestige! It would set the Near East in uproar!' They had only just got the Suez situation settled, he said, and Mesopotamia was a melting-pot. To abandon the peninsula would encourage every malcontent to view the Empire as weakened, and attack it.

Overton said, 'My lord, how much more humiliating will it be if the Turks force us off the peninsula with heavy losses – something we can hardly prevent without massive reinforcements that we cannot possibly provide?'

'You speak of heavy losses – but evacuation would be just as expensive,' Kitchener said. 'You see in his report Sir Charles estimates losses of thirty or forty per cent, and I have no doubt it would be worse than that. To fall in battle is one thing, but I won't condemn half my men to death or imprisonment – imprisonment in Turkish gaols, gentlemen! – for nothing more than a shameful retreat. Now Keyes, here, has an alternative suggestion, which I think we should consider.'

Admiral Keyes presented a new plan to use the navy to force the strait, which would enable men to be landed further up the coast and attack the Turks across the high ground. Kitchener was eager for anything that would prevent the shame of a retreat, and still clung to his belief that the Eastern theatre was where the war would be won; but since no-one except Admiral Keyes agreed with him, he was gradually forced onto the back foot.

At last, to break the stalemate, Overton said, 'My lord, should you not at least see the situation out there with your own eyes, before you make a decision? Your considerable experience will allow you to make a fresh evaluation. Reports are very well in their own way, but nothing beats first-hand evidence.' He was thinking in particular of the reports from Hamilton's enemies that had condemned him *in absentia*, though he did not say so, of course.

For a moment he thought Kitchener was going to refuse to consider it, but as he stared at Overton, a gleam suddenly came into his eyes. 'You're right,' he said. 'I *should* go myself. Gentlemen, I believe we should hold off from making a decision until I have done so.' There was an eager murmur of agreement from men who were tired, now, of hitting their heads against a wall. Overton was a little surprised at having won so easily; but the gleam in Kitchener's eye was explained when he added, 'Overton, *you* will accompany me. As the principal sponsor of the evacuation scheme, you, too, should see with your own eyes whether things are as bad as you fear.'

So Overton had to leave his distressed wife to cope alone with the situation at home, while he, Kitchener, their servants and a small staff took train for Marseilles. There, a naval destroyer would call for them to take them to Headquarters, on the Greek island of Lemnos, before crossing to the peninsula. Venetia clung to Overton a moment as they said goodbye. She mistrusted the sea, and the eastern Mediterranean was a hazardous place, these days. She resented his being taken away from her for no better reason than Kitchener's stubbornness, and thought again ruefully of how before the war they had planned a rural retirement where they would have nothing to do but tend their garden and enjoy each other's company. Given her restless character it would probably not have worked out quite like that, but this was going too far in the opposite direction. However, as she and Kitchener were exact contemporaries – and Overton only two years older – she could not reasonably talk to him about retirement.

'Take care of yourself,' she said, laying her lips a moment against her husband's.

'I'll keep my feet dry and always wear flannel next to the skin,' he said teasingly.

'See that you do,' she said, letting him go. They both knew that mines, U-boats, torpedoes, German warships, enemy aeroplanes and violent storms were the real threats to his health and well-being, but there was no point in talking about those.

On the 8th of November, General Haig pronounced the battle of Loos officially over. On the same day, Teddy received a letter from Harrington House. It said that the War Office was now satisfied that Lieutenant Morland was not among the living, while the Red Cross had confirmed that his name was not on any of the lists of prisoners-of-war sent by the German military authorities under the reciprocal arrangement. All lines of enquiry were now exhausted.

Lieutenant Morland would be listed as 'missing, believed killed', and the War Office would be officially communicating the same to Mrs Morland in due course.

The letter-form arrived, addressed to Jessie, the next day. She received it without much emotion, for it only confirmed what she had accepted now for some time. For once, Teddy forbore to say anything, but, official notification notwithstanding, he did not accept it, and never would.

The following day he was out, about the estate, when the post was delivered. Emma brought his letters to him later in the steward's room, accompanied by Henrietta, who wanted to ask him something about the pheasants. But before she could speak, he held up his hand, saying, 'Ah, I know this handwriting. This is from Major Calcott. Now we may learn something.' They waited in silence while he opened the envelope and began reading. 'They're sending back Ned's kit,' he said in surprise.

Henrietta said, 'Oh, yes. Ethel's mother says they always send the men's things if they can. Her neighbour Mrs Enderby lost her son and she got his things two weeks later. I suppose if Daltry hadn't been wounded, Ned's would have got here sooner.'

'But I thought it had all been lost,' Teddy says. 'Listen. He says, "The action, as you may know by now, has been declared over, and I have been able at last to locate his kit. It was put away before the battle, but there were so few of the battalion left no-one knew exactly where. Brigade thought it would be in Vermelles, but it transpired everything was stowed where they were last billeted before the battle, in a village called Nœux-les-Mines" – however you pronounce that. He says it should arrive in the next day or two, and he apologises for the delay.'

'That's kind of him,' said Henrietta. 'But – oh dear – I do hope it won't upset Jessie too much.'

But Teddy was reading on, and now his eyebrows went up, and he exclaimed, 'Good gracious me! Listen to this!'

'And now to happier news. I am more pleased than I can say to be able to tell you that Lieutenant Morland's name has been sent in with a recommendation that he receive the posthumous award of the Military Cross for his actions at Bois Hugo. Mrs Morland will receive official notification of this in due course, but I thought perhaps that it might afford you some measure of comfort at this sad time to know that your son's courage and gallantry are to be acknowledged in this way. The survivors of the action speak most highly of him and believe that it is no more than he deserved. I have no doubt the decoration will give pleasure to many here in France.

You might also perhaps like to know that his servant, Private Daltry, has been recommended for the Military Medal, also posthumously, for his courage in crossing the battlefield three times in his attempts to find Lieutenant Morland.

If there is anything else I can do for you or for Mrs Morland, I trust and hope that you will command me, and believe me,

Your obedient servant
Charles Calcott.'

'But that's wonderful!' cried Henrietta.

'The MC?' said Emma. 'I'm so pleased for you.'

'And how nice that poor Daltry is to be decorated too,' said Henrietta. 'We must write to his uncle. I wonder if it can be added on to the gravestone? Would there be room for it, do you think?'

'It's no more than Ned deserves,' Teddy said. 'I'm sure he did wonderful things at Neuve Chapelle and Ypres that we never heard about. But they're talking about it as a posthumous award. I don't want it called that. I know he's not dead.'

Emma and Henrietta exchanged a swift glance of consternation. 'But, Teddy, dear,' said Henrietta, 'we've had the official notification now. Can't you accept it?'

'No! Never! I know he's alive.'

'But for Jessie's sake,' Henrietta urged. 'Let her mourn him and have it over with. She's still young – let her get on with her life. It will hurt her so to have false hopes continually raised, and then dashed.'

Teddy looked hurt. 'You want to forget him, as if he never existed.'

'None of us will ever forget him,' Henrietta said. 'And I can't make you stop trying to find him, if that's what you want to do. All I ask is that you do it privately, and don't talk about it. Let Jessie's wounds heal. Doesn't she deserve that much from you?'

'And when I find him, what then?' Teddy asked defiantly.

'Then we'll all rejoice with you,' Henrietta said. She felt exhausted by his granite resistance.

He saw her weariness, and was afraid. He could not let go of his belief that Ned was alive because he dared not look into the void of loss. But he saw that she could take no more. 'Very well,' he said. 'I shall go on doing what I have to do, but we won't talk about it any more.'

'That's all I ask,' said Henrietta, and went away.

After a moment, Emma broke the silence, and he started, having forgotten she was there. 'I'll help you,' she said.

'What?'

'With letters and telephone calls and so on. I'd be glad to help you.'

'Thank you,' he said awkwardly. 'You do believe he's alive?'

'I don't know. I don't think it's likely,' Emma said frankly, 'but I think to myself, What if it was me? What if I was alive, and everyone had given *me* up?'

* * *

A few days later Jessie arrived home from Twelvetrees to find her mother, Alice and Ethel gathered in the hall round Ned's luggage. At the sight of his trunk and valise, her heart contracted so painfully that for a moment she thought she was going to faint. She felt her face turn cold and her hands grow damp, and had to sit down on the nearest hard little hall chair.

Henrietta reached her first, and made her put her head down. At last her ears stopped ringing, and after a few deep breaths she straightened up. 'I thought for a moment—' she began, but she did not need to finish the sentence. Her mother knew. She had thought for a moment that he had come home, after all. 'I'm all right now,' she said. 'It was just the shock.'

Brach was sniffing round the luggage with puzzled interest. Jessie would have liked to order it taken away at once, but she knew the others would have been hurt if she did. There seemed nothing to be done but to open it. On the top was a book, shabby and worn, the page ends grubby: *La Porte Étroite* by André Gide. It was in French. Why was he reading a book in French? He had learned the language at school, she knew, but she had never heard him try to speak it, or seen him try to read it. It made her realise that he had had a whole new life over there, for those few short months – a life she knew nothing about.

Under the book was his housewife, folded up, containing his shaving tackle, tooth powder, hairbrushes and so on. The cloth smelled faintly of the bay rum Daltry used to soothe his skin after shaving him. Underneath again were his folded night-things, and a shirt he had worn, which had not been washed yet. Even after all this time, they smelled faintly of him. Her hands were shaking badly. This was too personal, too real. She couldn't bear it. She grabbed blindly at the next thing – a bundle of what she recognised as her own letters to him. Such a meagre bundle, as she saw it now, and it reproached her. She should have written to him more often, and longer, much longer letters. She had never been a very good correspondent, and his letters to her had always been painfully formal and stiff. They had not known, of course, that it would ever matter. Oh, Ned, Ned, I'm sorry! She remembered suddenly, vividly, the time she had taken him to the station, to see him off for the Front, and he had asked her to have a photograph of herself taken to send to him, so that he could have it with him always. It was not here, of course. He would have had it with him, in his pocket book, and wherever he was, it would be also. If anything was left of it. The place where he had last been seen had been heavily shelled, so Bertie said. Jessie knew what that meant. It was most likely that he, his pocket book and the photograph had all been blown to unidentifiable shreds.

She got to her feet, walked blindly away, and only halted when the hearthstone of the great fireplace stopped her. After a moment Brach's cold nose was pushed into her palm. She heard someone – Ethel, she thought – ask if she was all right.

'I can't look at any more,' she said. She knew what was there: his life, locked up in that leather valise and the leather-bound trunk, as he had left it aside on the last day he marched up to the Front; the faint smell of him, trapped among his leavings like a ghost.

Ethel began to say something and Alice hushed her; and Henrietta came up close behind Jessie and said, 'Shall I have them sent up to your room?'

Jessie said, 'Burn them. Get rid of them. I don't care. I don't want to see anything of his ever again.'

Henrietta laid a hand on Jessie's rigid shoulder. She could not order them burned – it would hurt Teddy terribly. She would have them hidden away somewhere. One day, when the shock had passed, Jessie might want to see them herself, and be glad they had been kept.

'Go up and get changed for luncheon,' she said. 'When you come back they'll be gone.'

Jessie nodded, her back still to her mother. Then she said, 'Thank you,' and moved away, crossed the hall and disappeared into the staircase hall without looking back.

That night, in bed, Jessie lay wakeful, staring into the dark and thinking. Ned's kit had been a horrible shock, a left-over from the land of the living. But it was Calcott's news about the recommendation for an MC that convinced her he was dead. They would give *her* his medal, because he was dead. Posthumous: the word said everything. He was dead and she was now, in the eyes of the law and the world at large, a widow. Her marriage was ended, and all that part of her life that had included Ned was over. He would never come home again. She would never live with him again, or sleep beside him, dine with him, talk to him, or walk into a room with her hand on his arm. All that was finished, gone.

She remembered the words of Bertie's wife, Maud, earlier that year, when she had spoken of her gladness that she and Bertie had a son. *If Ned should fall,* she had said (not meaning to be cruel, it was just her way), *you would have nothing.* It was true: she had nothing to show for having been his wife; there was nothing left to show he had ever existed. She wished, more than ever, that she had been able to give him a child. She remembered her last conversation with him, back in the summer, when he had come home briefly on leave. He had been strange and awkward with her; he had asked if she ever thought they should not have married. It was bitter now to think that she might somehow have made him feel she did not care for him. She hoped and prayed that he had not gone into battle that last day believing himself unloved.

When they had given up Maystone Villa, their marital home, Ned had tried to comfort her by saying they would get it back after the war. She had known even then that she would never live there again. It had become something that no longer related to her. And now all of her life with him was like that, like a stream whose flow is blocked, and becomes an ox-bow. He was a place she would never revisit; and with the finality of it, now at last the tears came. She turned onto her face and wept into her pillow so that no-one should hear. Brach came from her place by the fire and sat anxiously by the bed; then put her paws on it; and finally eased the rest of her body up so that she could lie close to her mistress and lick the salt wetness from her cheek. It was a long time before the tears stopped and they both slept.

CHAPTER FIVE

The government had known for some time that it would not be possible to raise enough men to win the war by voluntary means alone. On the continent, it was the practice for every young man to be required to do military service at a certain age, so there was a huge pool of trained soldiers to be called on. Britain was unusual because it had never had more than a small professional army, plus civilian volunteers in time of need. It had always relied first on its island status and the might of the Royal Navy to protect its borders.

In the first year of the war, hundreds of thousands of volunteers had flocked eagerly to the colours to do their bit for their country; but losses had been greater than had ever been envisaged. The war was turning out to be a far heavier commitment than the glorious dash to victory – 'all over by Christmas' – that was originally anticipated. It was evident now that it going to be a long, hard grind, and that millions, not hundreds of thousands, were going to have to bear arms. The battalions at the Front were all under strength, and even the routine work of holding the line drained away manpower in a constant flow of some five thousand casualties a week.

To mount a successful offensive would require large numbers of new recruits, and they must be delivered in a systematic, reliable way – in a word, conscription. But

England hated the very idea of conscription: it might be acceptable to slave-minded foreigners with militaristic leaders, who gloried in war and its paraphernalia, but it was anathema to a proud, freedom-loving nation of peaceful traders and explorers. Some way had to be found to make it palatable.

The Earl of Derby had already proved his worth in the area of recruitment when in 1914 he had initiated the 'Pals' system, where friends and colleagues could enlist with the certainty of serving together. Comradeship and friendly rivalry had made the system popular: men from the same club, the same factory, the same street had rushed to volunteer together. A village might supply a platoon, a football team a section; whole battalions of Pals had been raised by some towns, like Manchester, Leeds and Bradford.

On the 11th of October 1915, Asquith had made Lord Derby Director-General of Recruitment, and a mere five days later he put forward his compromise, known from the beginning as the Derby Scheme. Under it, men between the ages of nineteen and forty-one could register for military service, and either volunteer immediately and have their choice of service and regiment, or 'attest' with an obligation to come if called up, and go where they were sent. In this way, an element of free will seemed to be retained, which it was hoped would soften the blow.

Each man was paid two and ninepence on attesting, and was given an armband to wear, to save him from the attentions of the ladies with white feathers. Men who were physically unable, or who were performing a job deemed essential to the country or the war effort, could apply to be exempted. It was further promised that single men would be called before the married. The government also introduced a War Pension to ease the concerns of those with dependants. It was calculated that five million men would come into the category covered by the scheme.

Several of the servants at Morland Place attested, and one of the grooms, Blean, volunteered so that he could get into the same regiment as his brother. Robbie did not see any reason to register. His work at the bank he considered essential, and he didn't need a tribunal to tell him so. Besides – as he said several times at the dining-table when the subject arose – married men *with children* ought to be in a different category from both single men and married men. To be expecting a man with young children to go off and leave his wife to care for them all alone was quite wrong. What were they fighting for, if not a better world for their offspring – which must surely include a father's being on hand to discipline and guide them?

With these hints, some of the family were not surprised to learn in November that Ethel was pregnant again, with her fourth child. Everyone was delighted: it seemed the most welcome antithesis to war that a new baby should be coming to the house. A happy evening was passed discussing dates, names, who the child was likely to take after and – lifted by the fumes of champagne into the realms of airy speculation – possible future careers.

Later, in the privacy of their bedroom, Ethel expressed anxiety about the Derby Scheme, worrying whether Robbie was right about his job being a reserved occupation, whether he ought to attest, whether the rumours were true that if attestation did not produce sufficient numbers, general conscription would be brought in. He calmed her fears by reminding her that the government was pledged to take single men first. The war could not possibly last so long that married men would ever be called on: she had nothing to worry about.

The Derby Scheme had also been on Oliver's mind. He was assisting Mark Darroway with an operation at the free clinic in Dean Street. Darroway had been a medical student at the same time as Venetia had been trying to become a doctor. During the time when she was barred from the medical schools, he had helped her by giving her lessons, passing on what he learned day by day – he had been poor and needed the money, so it helped both of them. They had remained friends ever since, and when Oliver followed his mother into the profession, Darroway had taken him under his wing.

The St James and St Ann Benevolent Dispensary, conveniently round the corner from Darroway's home in Soho Square, had long provided free medical treatment to the poor of Soho and St Giles, but the operating theatre was a recent addition. Originally the dispensary had occupied the basement and ground floor of the house, and the upper floors had been let as cheap rooms. When the leasehold fell in, Darroway feared that the clinic would have to close. But a secret benefactor had bought the new leasehold of the whole house and donated it to the neighbourhood; and had provided the funds to turn the first floor into an operating theatre where the poor could receive surgical treatment in aseptic conditions.

It was a small, plain room, with the long windows of the original drawing-room to let in as much daylight as was possible in that narrow, sooty street. The floor was covered with linoleum, and there was an operating table in the centre of the room (rather rickety because of its folding legs, which tended to discover their primary vocation at awkward moments) with two enamel slop buckets underneath it. A stand of hand-bowls stood beside it, which opened out on hinges like the cake-stands in Gunter's restaurant, and held surgical instruments in a solution of carbolic. There was a wide sink in the corner, and a white-painted dresser against the wall was stacked with containers and bottles, antiseptics and dishes of swabs, dressings and sutures. A new partition wall had created a small preparation and recovery room next door. Only minor surgery was performed here. For major cutting, requiring a long stay, the poor had to go to the great free hospitals, most of them originally endowed in mediaeval times – and some of them hardly less primitive, to Oliver's mind.

The patient was wheeled in on a trolley, wide awake and looking terrified. Darroway went over to her and patted her hand, smiled and said, 'Don't worry, my dear. It will all be quite quick, and you won't feel a thing.'

She was young and very pretty, apart from a large and disfiguring mole on her cheek, dark-pigmented and sprouting coarse hairs. It was that which Darroway was intending to remove. Normally surgery of that sort was out of the reach of the poor, but when the girl had come to him originally at the dispensary, for a septic toenail, he had decided on the spot that the mole was an abomination on someone so young and pretty, and had asked her if she would like it removed.

'It will change her life entirely,' he told Oliver later, when he asked him to assist. 'She's very conscious of it, walks about with her hand to her face to hide it. It's holding her back. She's quite a bright little thing, and could do much better for herself if she had the confidence. I'd like to give her the chance – and it'll be good practice for you, if you'll help me.'

Oliver was happy to agree, for he shared with Darroway an interest in reparative or what was known as 'plastic' surgery. He had treated some terrible burn cases; and now the war was producing many more and different mutilations. It pained him to leave the victims with life but not much more. This young woman, whose terrified eyes were flitting from one face to another, was not suffering physically, but it would be good to send her out into the world equipped for a better and more rewarding life.

Oliver draped the girl's shoulders, neck and upper face with sterile towels, then handed the syringe of local anaesthetic to Darroway.

'I wish we could get more of our paying patients to have

their operations done in proper conditions,' he said, as he ran the needle into the firm cheek. The patient winced, but made no sound – the poor rarely complained, no matter what was done to them. 'But they will insist on the comfort of their own homes, no matter what we tell them about sepsis.'

While he excised the mole, he talked only of the operation. Oliver steadied the table, handed instruments and swabbed away the trickling blood. Soon the offending object was detached and lying like a bloody wad in a kidney dish. Then Darroway said, 'I was speaking to young David Tenby yesterday at the Middlesex. He was passing gas for me for that neck tumour—'

'Oh, yes. How did it go?'

'Very well. No complications, and it looks completely benign. The man should make a complete recovery – if he stays off the drink. But, as I was saying, Tenby said he'd been talking to you about going to the Front. Have you made up your mind about it?'

'Not absolutely, but I did think that it would be better to go in my own time than to be called up and have no say in the matter. He rather agreed with me.'

'Evidently. He told me he's decided to go after Christmas.' He looked up from dressing the wound. 'What about you?'

Oliver hesitated. 'I had been thinking along the same lines, but things are rather strained at home at the moment.'

'Yes, I heard. I'm sorry,' said Darroway. He finished the dressing, removed the towels, and smiled at the patient, whose face was as white as wax. 'All over, my dear. You were very brave. And you'll be much better off without it. You'll have a little rest next door and then you can go home. Nurse will give you a drink of water, and some aspirin to take away with you, because it will hurt a bit when the anaesthetic wears off.'

Alone again, they washed their hands at the sink side by

side. Oliver said, 'I would have talked to you about it, of course, before I decided anything. I wouldn't want you to think me ungrateful.'

'I don't think you need worry about being called up, you know,' Darroway said. 'They can't denude the country of doctors, and you do so much work with the poor I'm sure they'll leave you be.'

Oliver shook his head. 'But I'm not married, and they're bound to leave the married doctors until last. And besides . . .' He hesitated. 'I hope you don't take this amiss, but I'd really like to go. Not just because one has one's duty to do. You see, at the Front I'd do more surgery in a week than I do in six months back here. And it'd be vital work. I'd be saving lives. That sort of experience – well, it doesn't come to most people in a lifetime.'

'Thank God for it,' said Darroway, drily.

'Yes, of course,' said Oliver, subdued. He thought Darroway was angry that he wanted to leave him.

'I were your age and unmarried, I'd want to go too. Oh, don't look so surprised. I wasn't always dull and grey-headed, you know.'

'I know that, sir,' Oliver said, smiling with relief.

'Have you thought where you want to go, if you're given the choice?'

'I thought I'd rather like to go and join the same unit as Kit Westhoven. I suppose the doctoring will be much the same anywhere on the Front, and it would be good to have a friend to work with.'

'Quite so. And David Tenby too?'

'Yes, we thought we'd go and sign up together. I like him very much, and I know Westhoven will too. There's just the matter of leaving my mother.'

'If I were you,' Darroway said, 'I'd talk to her about it straight away. She won't want to stand in the way of your doing your duty, and I suspect she'd resent the implication that she might, if you hold back on her.'

'Do you think so? But with my father away, it would mean leaving her quite alone.'

'How long will your father be abroad?'

'I've no idea. But I don't suppose Kitchener will linger too long over there. Weeks rather than months.'

'A few weeks? Well, then, my dear boy, I suggest you treat her like an adult and talk to her. From what I know of her, she'll be too busy to notice you're gone.'

It was not quite true to say that Venetia was indifferent to Oliver's going. Despite what he had said on other occasions about feeling he would have to go 'sooner or later', she had assumed his work at home was too important and that he would never be called up. That he would volunteer had not occurred to her. But she understood perfectly his point about the experience, and listened to all he had to say without allowing any dismay to show. Though she was busy during the daytime, her evenings would be lonely until Overton came home; and she was worried about Violet. It would have been such a support to both of them to have Oliver there when she and Laidislaw came back to London. But those considerations had no weight compared with her son's going to save lives at the Front, and she kept them to herself.

What she said was, 'Of course you must go, if it's what you want. You'll come back a better doctor for it – and a better man, I dare say. Before this war ends, they'll need every doctor they can lay hands on. I may end up having to go myself.'

Oliver laughed affectionately. 'I wouldn't put it past you, Mum.'

Venetia, who had visited a medical facility at the Front, was not joking, but she said nothing more. She was glad, at least, that he would be going to a friend, if he got his way. She liked Westhoven, and had been very glad to see the friendship growing between him and Oliver, for Oliver's life had always struck her as rather a lonely one. He didn't seem to have many friends. Medicine as a profession did not conduce much to friendship.

'When do you think of going?' she asked him.

'Well, now I know you don't mind, as soon as possible. I'll have a talk to Tenby and we'll go and sign up right away. I suppose it will take a couple of weeks for them to put us through the books, that's all.'

On the 10th of November Kitchener's party crossed from Lemnos to the peninsula, and saw for themselves a little of what the eastern Mediterranean was capable of. It was blowing hard, and the sea was grey and hostile, with white-caps as far as the eye could see. The destroyer ploughed through the steep waves, sticking her nose down and shipping buckets of spray, rearing up again like a horse as the swell passed under her, until she was almost standing on her tail. The sailors put on their most stoical faces, as they always did when they had the army on board, but several of the staff were rather pale about the gills and one or two had to excuse themselves hastily. Even Overton, who was a good sailor, felt it; and he could not think what Kitchener was going through, for he knew the Old Man was susceptible – though his iron discipline over himself allowed nothing to show.

Things got worse when the destroyer hove-to. The violence of the seesaw motion relented when she stopped trying to fight the sea, but the relief was short-lived: the captain told them cheerfully that he could not get any further in, and they would have to transfer into a lighter. The smaller vessel leaped about in a way that defied reason, spun about like a cork in the currents, and seemed ready to dash itself on the rocks, which were visible like teeth through the foam. It was, Overton thought, concentrating hard on the horizon, the best possible way to teach them how hard it would be to supply the army through the winter.

And the condition of the army was worse even than

Overton had imagined. How they had managed to hold on at all was a miracle – and yet their spirits remained undaunted. They visited each of the beaches in turn, and more than once he saw Kitchener almost in tears at the courage and resilience of those beleaguered men.

On the 13th, from a calmer sea, they landed at Anzac, where the Australian and New Zealand troops were holding the line. They were received by General Sir William 'Birdie' Birdwood, the British commander of the Anzac forces. As the party walked up the North Beach pier, it seemed that word had got out of the illustrious visitor, for men came running from every direction to form a solid crowd and cheer the arrival. Kitchener, tall and distinguished in field marshal's uniform, was at his best, acknowledging the cheers, slowing his pace to a stroll as he went through the crowds, stopping to chat to one man and another in a pleasant, friendly way. Overton saw the grins of appreciation, and knew they were thinking, *He's a soldier, like us*. Here and there, where his words would carry best, he said, 'The King has asked me to tell you how splendidly he thinks you have done. You have all done splendidly, better even than I thought you would.' There was no doubting the sincerity of his words, and the cheers redoubled.

When they had cleared the 'reception committee', as Birdwood called it, Kitchener was introduced to some of the officers, and then he asked to see some of the front-line positions. Birdwood led the way. He was a tall, lean man with a high, bald head that made him look as if he were always reaching upwards to be taller yet. He was an immensely popular soldier, as was proved by the fact that the Australians and New Zealanders, famously bloody-minded and independent, had accepted him as one of their own. It was he who had promoted the name 'Anzac', suggested to him by a staff lieutenant, which had been greatly instrumental in building the spirit of the corps. He understood the temper of his men, and he shared their dangers, walked about the trenches daily, and had his own dugout close to the line, where it was in danger of Turkish shelling. When he went up to the front line, he would never accept a drink of water, however hot it was, because he knew how much labour it took the ordinary soldiers to haul even a pint of the precious stuff up from the valleys.

The value of this gesture was brought home to them all as they toiled up the dusty, precipitous road towards Walker's Ridge. It was not a particularly hot day, but after ten minutes Overton was sweating and his dry throat cried out for water. This was a place of naked rock, barren, inhospitable: towering crags and steep, narrow gullies; rough tracks carved along the edges of precipices; loose stones underfoot and dust rising at every step. It was an awful place, a landscape that rejected man, and the sheer labour involved in simply subsisting there became very apparent to the visitors.

They toiled on up to Chunuk Bair, and inspected the positions at Bully Beef Sap, Pope's Hill, Quinn's Post and Lone Pine. And then, standing on a high point looking out towards the sea, Kitchener laid his hand on Birdwood's arm and said, 'Thank God I came to see this for myself, Birdie. I had no idea of the difficulties you were up against. You've all done wonders.'

Overton, standing just behind him, thanked God too. The thought of what the men would suffer if they remained through the winter was not to be borne.

Kitchener said he had seen enough, and they turned away and began their walk back down. An Australian chaplain, one of Birdwood's party, fell in beside Overton and pointed out things of interest to him on the way. And then he lowered his voice and said, 'Will the Old Man go for evacuation now, do you think?'

'I think so.'

'Thank God,' he said. 'I'm an army chaplain, I'm a soldier

and I minister to soldiers, but what I've seen here isn't war, not the sort of war any of us signed up for. Every day when I get up, I look around me in astonishment and say, "What in the name of reason are we doing here?"'

'And yet the men have wonderful spirit,' Overton remarked.

'Oh, you won't break an Aussie's heart that way,' said the chaplain. He paused, and added softly, 'Not that way.' He pointed over to the right, where a small pocket of earth formed by the interaction of slopes bore a profusion of rough wooden crosses. 'See there?' he said. 'One of the cemeteries. When I have an hour to myself, I walk around the graveyards and up the gullies and I scatter silver wattle seed wherever I go. Whatever happens, I want there to be a bit of Australia left, to show we've been here.'

Overton could think of nothing to say, and could only bow his head in acknowledgement.

The chaplain went on, but in a normal, cheerful voice: 'I soak the seeds for about twenty hours beforehand, to give them a start. It seems to be working. I've seen some shoots already. I think they'll thrive.'

Overton hoped that when Kitchener said he had seen enough, it meant they were on their way home. But first the general wanted to visit Salonika, where two brigades had been landed in October to help the Serbs against Bulgarian aggression and another front had opened up. Matters there were very complicated, and it was the 24th of November before Kitchener was ready to set sail to England. Two days before, on the 22nd, he cabled his report on Gallipoli to the Cabinet in London, recommending evacuation, and sent his orders to the commanders on the ground to make preliminary preparations.

Two days after they had left, a violent storm swept down on the peninsula. In the hurricane winds, trees were uprooted and carried hundreds of feet, corrugated-iron roofs were ripped off, equipment and meagre possessions simply disappeared. The laboriously built piers in the harbours were snatched away, and boats and lighters were smashed to matchwood on the rocks. Sheeting rain fell for twenty-four hours, the dry gullies turned into raging torrents and many men were drowned. Dugouts and trenches were flooded, stores were washed away, sandbags disintegrated, every shelter was flattened, until there was nothing left but a sea of mud and debris, with the soldiers crouched, shivering, in the open in their sodden clothes. Hundreds died of exposure. If the Turks had not been in the same position, they could have inflicted slaughter unopposed; as it was, an unofficial armistice prevailed.

Had the decision not already been made to evacuate, it would have been forced now. The question remaining was how many of the men could be got away alive. Munro had estimated 30 or 40 per cent losses; Kitchener expected even more and, having read the report of the storm damage, Overton tended to agree with him.

Heath Cottage, in the Norfolk village of Chetton Farthing, was a small, square house standing right on the edge of the marsh, with nothing but a hedge and a low bank separating its scrap of garden from the wild. It was a plain and simple building of straight lines, rather like a child's drawing, with the air of having its roof pulled down hard against the prevailing winds. But inside it was snug, and surprisingly comfortable, with four rooms downstairs, four bedrooms upstairs, and two rooms for servants in the attic.

Venetia had told her daughter, 'It belonged to my mother – she grew up there, in fact. She kept it out of sentiment, and left it to me with the rest of her estate. It's rented out in the summer, usually to artists – the light, apparently, is rather special, and they rave about it – but it's generally empty at this time of year.'

It was extremely remote: the village was tiny, a handful

of cottages, and the agricultural slump had denuded the locality of carriage-families, so there was no-one to call, or be inquisitive about the new arrivals. And there were other advantages: it was kept always in a state of readiness by a resident housekeeper, who as an employee of the family would know how to hold her tongue; and it was designed and arranged for the comfort of people of refinement, which might not always be the case with rented cottages.

Violet had needed no persuasion. She had much rather stay in her grandmother's house than a stranger's: she was fascinated by the idea of seeing where that almost mythical figure from her childhood had grown up. Besides, there was her mother's mention of artists. If *they* raved about it, Laidislaw would like it, and she determined that he should have it.

So now here they were, installed in this homelike little house like a pair of newly-weds. Violet could not have been happier. The housekeeper was rather aloof, but she was a good cook, and she knew how to run the house. Given instructions from Venetia, via the agent, she had ordered in food, coals and wood, and hired extra staff, a daily house-maid and scullery-maid, and put a reliable local laundress on notice.

There could not have been a place more perfect for two lovers, driven out of London by scandal, to hide away unnoticed. To be with Octavian all day and sleep with him all night was the summit of bliss for Violet. She woke beside him in the morning, and often found him leaning up on one elbow, gazing at her.

'I've been waiting ages for you to wake,' he would say.

And she would say, 'You should have woken me.' She did not like to think of any minute they could be together being wasted.

'No, no, I couldn't do that. You looked so peaceful.'

'But I wouldn't have minded.' They outdid each other in tenderness.

They breakfasted together in the morning-room, which seemed always full of sunlight. Mrs Brisely made good coffee, and Violet was amused at her own appetite. Usually a small breakfaster, she found herself hungry for country eggs – which tasted so different from London ones – and Norfolk-cured bacon, and mushrooms freshly picked from the fields around.

'I think love makes you hungry,' Laidislaw would say, laughing. It must be that, she thought. Love had turned out to be a very energetic business, once it was let off the leash.

The only odd thing about breakfast was not having any post, no sheaf of invitations to sift through – and therefore no letters to write and no telephone calls to return. The cottage did not even have the telephone.

After breakfast they went for a walk together. Laidislaw could not wait to get out into the fresh air, and hurried her into her warm overcoat as soon as she had drained her cup. The Pekingeses loved the walks, too. They had become different characters altogether. Suddenly their Town-bred noses were assailed by a torrent of new and exciting smells; every ditch, hedgerow, bush, virtually every tussock of grass, quivered with sounds and movements that demanded urgent investigation. The previously polite little dogs raced about, their ears turned inside out, their sooty faces split with pink grins of delight, their silky fur gathering mud and knots and burrs that would have made their imperial ancestors faint with shame. They jumped ditches, investigated drains, anointed gateposts, barked at cows and chased crows, and their mistress, her arm through that of her lover, only smiled indulgently.

Laidislaw had brought his paints with him, and he painted every day, for hours on end. Violet had been worried when she first saw the place that it would not please him, for there seemed nothing to paint. 'It's all flat,' she said, disappointed, as they stood in the garden looking out over the marsh. 'Not a hill, not a wood – hardly a tree. No buildings, no people.'

But Laidislaw raved, as others had before him. 'But the sky, my darling! The light! It's *wonderful*! It changes every minute. Look at that silver ray sweeping across the grass,' he cried, as a cloud shadow passed. 'I must paint it! The sky most of all! There's so much of it!'

There was, Violet thought – and not much of anything else. But she was glad that he was pleased, and more than glad to see him rushing eagerly to paint every day. She wanted him only to be happy. Soon he cast aside his oil paints and declared them too coarse for the subject. He must have water-colours. It required a trip into the nearest town, which he undertook alone. It was long since he had expressed himself in that medium, so it took many days before he was satisfied with what he had done. But the challenge pleased him and, watching him work, Violet began to see a little of what he saw. Perhaps the place was not so dull and ugly after all; she learned to watch the great bowl of the sky with something like his wonder.

They were lucky that the weather remained benign, cold and sometimes with a sharp wind, but dry. They were outside a great deal, and came home tired and happy to the pleasure of a good fire, a simple, well-cooked dinner, and an evening together of utter peace. They talked a great deal. Violet loved to listen to Octavian, who seemed to her to make poetry of the simplest conversation; and she, who had always been a listener, talked to him far more than to anyone ever in her whole life. She felt he knew her, *really* knew her, and that she could tell him anything without fear that he would misunderstand or disapprove.

Sometimes he drew her, liking the effect of lamplight – for there was no electricity or even gas in the cottage, just lamps downstairs and candles up. He loved the shadows it made, and the curves and lines it revealed. He drew her, loving every part of her, her head resting on her hand, the shadow of her eyelashes on her cheek, the tender curves of her mouth, the elegant line of her shoulder and arm. She reminded him of a cat, in that no posture or movement of hers was ever less than graceful. She fascinated him endlessly.

For all his apparent sophistication and his enormous talent, Laidislaw was at the core a simple man. His requirements were old-fashioned. A clever woman like Laura Verney would never have suited him, nor an independent woman like Jessie. He wanted to cherish, inform and impress his lover; and at the same time to worship her. Violet seemed to him everything that was lovely and good; and she thought him clever, and admired him. All was well. He had never been in love before, and he took love seriously. He adored her, and knew himself captured for ever.

When he had had enough, temporarily, of drawing her, he read to her. She would recline on the sofa, her head in his lap, or they would sit on cushions on the floor, entwined together, with the dogs curled between them and the fire, their pale fur rosy, snoring a little in contented sleep. Laidislaw liked to read aloud: he had an actor's talent for and pleasure in it. For Violet, it was almost like being back in the nursery: the warmth, comfort and safety, the sense of being unconditionally loved, and the story unfolding for her, effortlessly, from the pages. The only difference was that, when the loved reader said it was time for bed, that was not the end of the pleasure.

She had not brought her maid with her. Venetia had advised against it: Sanders was not a country woman, and there would be nothing in the world for her to do. Violet was glad she had accepted the advice. Sanders would indeed have been delirious with boredom – and very much in the way. Mrs Brisely took herself to her own room when she had served dinner and never troubled them again, and they felt that the cottage was all theirs. When they went to bed, Octavian saw to her buttons and hooks and helped her undress. Having to do it herself, she had to arrange her hair simply, but that was suitable to the place and the time; and when she took out her pins he loved to brush it out for her, lingering over it, so that she felt it was part of their love-making.

And when they came together in the privacy of the big old-fashioned bed, it was as wonderful as ever – more wonderful, indeed, now that there was no hurry, no secrecy, no subterfuge. There was no need to part. Nightly they lay together in passion, exploring each other, giving and receiving tenderness. Once the sad little thought crossed her mind that it should always be like this for a man and a woman, and so obviously wasn't; that it should have been like this for her and her husband. But she pushed the thought away. She had what she had, and she was glad of it. She loved Octavian, and he loved her, and it seemed a miraculous piece of luck that they had found each other, and that, being in love, there was so much they could do about it.

By day the house and the wide countryside that lay around it seemed always lapped in quiet, and she welcomed it after the noise and bustle of London. It seemed an intimate part of their time together, as though it were generated by their love. But at night there were always sounds, and she often woke in the dark to listen to them with pleasure. There were the creaks and whispers of the house itself, easing its bones in the darkness; the hooning of the wind in the chimney, and the branch of the old mulberry tree scratching the window-pane; and outside the soft cry of the tawny owl, the sharp bark of the vixen, the little starts and rustlings of other night creatures. Sleep was lovely, but it seemed also very good to be awake, so as to be aware of the comfort and safety of the bed, the nearness of Octavian and the smell of his skin, the simple miracle of his presence there beside her. In those moments of wakefulness, it seemed as though the whole world were centred on her. She felt it all around, cradling her like loving arms; and drifting back into sleep, she felt the universe, warm and benign, turning slowly round her like a great, peaceful humming-top

Bereavement, Jessie found, was not a sudden event, but an accumulation: a series of blows, some sharp, some dull, falling at expected and unexpected moments, as memory dictated. Waking in the morning was the hardest of them, after the warm oblivion of sleep. There was a moment's respite as night's cobwebs melted away, and then the weight of realisation came, like a stone rolling onto her chest. The stone she carried all day, sometimes forgotten for a little while – work was the best thing for that – but making her ache all the same with the weariness of it.

She came to recognise it in the faces of other women she spoke to who had suffered a loss. There would be interest, even animation, in what was being said, and then at some point would come that sudden blank look, as the dull inevitability of realisation returned. Made sensitive, Jessie had become aware of how many others in and around York had suffered a loss. Everywhere she went, she now saw the women in mourning, the children in black bands. Before, they had been an indistinguishable part of the crowd; now she realised how many families she knew who had lost a husband, a son, a brother.

Well, she was one of them now, and like everyone else she put on a brave face and tried to behave as if nothing had happened. It was not done to parade one's grief at a time when so many had men facing death at the Front. For that reason, the extravagant mourning of the pre-war period had been abandoned: plain drab clothes for women, black bands for men and children were as far as anyone went. No door knockers were taken off or pictures and looking-glasses covered, no wreaths hung on street doors, no servants put into mourning livery, no crape round hats, no veils, no weeping, no black-bordered handkerchiefs. Victorian and Edwardian rituals and customs were regarded as in bad taste now.

With the numbers of dead steadily rising after a year of war, the government had ordered that there were to be no more private memorials put up. It had been decided quite early in the conflict that no bodies would be brought back and, cheated of a funeral, one or two wealthy families had spared no expense in the early months in erecting extravagant monuments. Clearly a halt must be called if the country was not to be littered with elaborate columns, statues and mausoleums.

A memorial service in the local church was deemed acceptable, and Jessie felt she might have liked that, but Uncle Teddy would not consider it, convinced as he was that Ned would still be found. He no longer talked openly about it, and carried on his enquiries with discretion, but he remained staunchly cheerful, and viewed any expression of sorrow as an affront. People who called had to pay their condolences to Henrietta, for Teddy would not be condoled, and if they happened to meet him they found themselves baffled at every turn by the agility with which he could change the subject.

It made it harder for Jessie to come to terms with Ned's death. And along with the sorrow for someone she had loved dearly and known all her life, there were the feelings of guilt to deal with. Bertie had survived and Ned had died. Perhaps Ned had died because she had not loved him enough. Perhaps her gladness and relief that Bertie had come through safely had somehow condemned Ned to die. She knew it was irrational, but she couldn't shake it away. She went over and over Ned's last visit home, what he had said and how he had seemed, and felt wretched that she had not made him happier.

She had dozens of letters: from her brother Jack and his wife Helen in Wiltshire, expecting their first child very soon;

from her brother Frank with the Rifles in Malta, hoping hard to be transferred to the Front; from Frank's young lady Maria Stanhope in London; from her half-sister Lizzie in America. Family and friends, neighbours and other connections wrote their condolences. Many of the workers of Ned's factory wrote letters, touching in their warmth. She had not realised he had been so much admired as an employer. And there was a joint letter, signed by his former colleagues in the York Commercials, the Pals battalion from which he had been transferred to the Front because of a shortage of junior officers. The battalion had moved that summer to Ripon for brigade training, and now an accompanying letter from the commanding officer, dear old Colonel 'Hound' Bassett, mentioned that they were on alert to go abroad at last, expecting orders any day for Egypt. The Hound would not be going with them: he had come out of retirement to form the battalion, but was considered too old to lead them in action. He would be returning to Black Brow to train another battalion, and the almost palpable regret about this that came through in his letter made Jessie smile. She must never forget that Ned had volunteered to go to the Front. Men saw these things differently: the Hound's condolences were outweighed by congratulations for Ned's medal, and his pride that he had had the training of him. She might tell herself that if Ned had not left the Commercials he would still be alive and heading for nothing more hazardous than the heat and flies of Port Said, but there probably wasn't a single man in his former battalion who would not have changed places with him, and the Hound expected her, as a soldier's wife, to feel that too.

She had a letter from Bertie's wife, Maud, who, after formal expressions of sympathy, turned to her own news.

> Ned's medal will be a great comfort to you, so I know you will be pleased for me when I tell you that Bertie has been Mentioned in Dispatches for meritorious

conduct. It is his second MID, of course – he was mentioned after the first battle of Ypres. I expect he would have been decorated on that occasion except that they did not give out medals as freely in the early months as they do now. Little Richard will grow up very proud of his papa. When a recent visitor asked him what his daddy did, he replied at once, 'Papa is a soldier hero,' which delighted everyone. My father Richard asks to be included in my condolences, and begs to be forgiven for not writing himself, but he is confined to bed with an attack of bronchitis. My respects to all your family.

Your sincere friend,
Maud Parke

Jessie was never entirely sure what Maud meant by the things she said – how far it was unkindness and how far simply the insensitivity in a woman of few emotions. The remark about giving away medals freely, for instance: was that meant to be a slight to Ned? But even if it were true, did it not devalue Bertie's MID just as much? Jessie reflected that if it were a conscious slight, Maud would surely have realised that. No, it was just Maud being Maud, after all.

The letters that gave Jessie most comfort were from Bertie. He wrote as though he were in the same room, speaking to her, and she felt the sense of his presence through them. He had promised her at the beginning that he would not deal in platitudes in his letters but tell her everything just as it was. She found that more than ever a comfort now because it made the Front seem real to her, just when it was slipping into unreality, taking Ned with it.

After fine warm days in October that seemed as if they would never end, the winter weather has set in. No snow yet – just dark November skies and endless, dreary rain. We are back in the trenches after our rest period, and the view is uninspiring. Loos was not an attractive spot at the best of times, with its mines and spoil heaps and cranes, but the battle did not improve it. Everything is smashed and ruined. Between us and the Germans lie the dead – impossible to bring them in. In places they fell in ranks, and so they lie, as if they were being drilled in death. They are a constant presence, our silent companions. There's a saying I hear a lot now – 'quiet as the Loos dead'. But they do at least provide cover for listening-parties. The patrols creep out and lie among them, and as long as they keep still, the Huns don't know they're there.

Trench routine, at a quiet time like this, is boredom punctuated by sharp moments of danger. We stand-to at dawn, in case of a surprise attack, but for the rest of the day there's nothing to do, except when Fritz sends over some hate or a sniper manages to get the range of us. One longs for something – anything – to read. The most miserable, thumbed, torn and grimy bits of paper are passed about like holy relics if they have printed words on them!

When it rains, the mud is the hardest thing to bear. It gets absolutely everywhere, not the clean mud of home fields but a filthy, rank stuff that leaves its stink long after you've cleaned it off. And the nights are getting very cold now. When it doesn't rain there is often a sharp frost. You know how on clear, frosty nights every sound seems to travel for miles? The men get jittery and there are scares all the time. They hear something rustling, they think they see something move in the darkness, and they loose off a burst of gunfire. Fritz, equally nervous, fires back. Usually it's nothing but nerves, but it has us up and down all night. On moonlit nights it's worse in some ways. The dead lying out there seem to move sometimes – unnerving.

You ask why I didn't tell you about my MID: I didn't want to boast, of course, especially in the face of Ned's decoration. Did Maud also tell you I've been promoted to major? Fenniman too. He is being made second in command to the battalion, and no-one deserves it more. I am staying with my company for the time being. There is such a shortage of experienced officers I am wanted where I am.

We are getting the new men out slowly, a score here and a score there, and many of our wounded have recovered and returned, but the battalion is still under strength. The new boys are very keen but wet behind the ears. It's amusing to see my 'veterans' of a few weeks lording it over them as if they know it all! Some of the sights are very hard on the new men. There was a body that had fallen into the trench during the battle. Earth had been thrown over it, but the rain gradually washed it away. One of the new men suddenly saw a face in the mud in front of him, the instant before his foot went through some part of the body. There was no way to get the body out. We just had to cover it up again.

Thank God we are moving soon! I have heard unofficially that we are rotating out to Picardy – a nice, quiet sector where we can train the newcomers in peace. Best of all, it is chalk downland, so we shall get away from this everlasting mud!

Let me finally pass on to you a pleasant philosophy that is doing the rounds at the moment.

When you are a soldier, you are either at the Front or behind the lines. If you are behind the lines you needn't worry. If you are at the Front you are either in a dangerous sector or a cushy sector. If you are in a cushy sector you needn't worry. If you are in a dangerous sector you are either wounded or not wounded. If you are not wounded you needn't worry. If you are wounded you are either seriously wounded or slightly wounded. If you are slightly wounded you needn't worry. If you are seriously wounded you will either die or get well. If you get well you needn't worry. If you die you can't worry. So, you see, there's no need to worry at all.

I hope you find this profound thought comforting. We all do!

Your loving cousin,
Bertie

So Jessie finished the reading with laughter, and went to find Emma to show the letter to her.

CHAPTER SIX

The *Britannic*, sister ship to *Olympic* and *Titanic*, had had her keel laid on the 30th of November 1911, with the intention that she should enter passenger service in the summer of 1914. But the loss of *Titanic* meant that extensive safety alterations had to be made, which delayed her completion. She was launched at Belfast on the 26th of February 1914 and was towed to the fitting-out dock.

She was to be even more luxurious than *Titanic*, with all the same beautiful fittings and amenities, and the addition of a ladies' hairdressing salon, a manicurist's shop, a playroom for children, a separate mail room for passengers, and a gymnasium for second-class passengers as well as for first. There was also to be a grand two-hundred-and-fifty-pipe organ on the landing of the Grand Staircase, ordered from the German company Welte & Sons.

Then the war intervened. Admiralty shipping contracts were given priority over all raw materials and labour. *Britannic*'s fitting-out continued only intermittently; and because of U-boat danger, *Olympic* was taken out of service and languished in dock beside her sister.

Many ships were requisitioned by the government for war work, but the smaller vessels were taken first. However, the Gallipoli campaign created a need for larger capacity. First the Cunarders were requisitioned as troop carriers; then, in August 1915, Cunard's *Aquitania* was transferred into hospital service, and *Olympic* was called on to take her place.

The Gallipoli situation worsened, casualties mounted, and the government decided at last that *Britannic* could not be left to lie idle and useless in the dock in Belfast. On the 13th of November 1915 she was officially requisitioned as a hospital ship.

Teddy heard the news with approval. His contract to provide the linens and soft furnishings for *Britannic* had so far been profitless; but though there would be no luxurious draperies on a hospital ship, it would want large numbers of sheets and towels, and possibly materials for the staff quarters. Even before he received an official letter, he hurried to Belfast to see the requisitioning officer and find out what would be needed.

In the Harland & Wolff yard, the scene around *Britannic* had been transformed. Officially sanctioned urgency had replaced the listless silence. Dozens of men hanging over the side in cradles were painting the hull white: this, with a green band from stem to sternpost, punctuated in three places on either side by red crosses, was the internationally agreed livery of a hospital ship. As this was the first war in which aeroplanes might play a part, there was also a party busy painting two large red crosses on the boat deck.

With her yellow funnels and red keel-stripe, she looked very smart, Teddy thought. The effect was only spoiled by the massive, ugly gantry davits – especially as only five of the eight had yet been installed, leaving her asymmetrical. But he understood the reason for them. After *Titanic* had foundered, the new rules said every ship must carry enough lifeboat places for all. *Olympic* had had more lifeboats installed, but with the old launching system, it meant the boat deck was completely lined on either side with lifeboats and Wellin davits, severely limiting the space for passengers to promenade, and entirely blocking their view.

However, *Britannic* was then still under construction, so

she could be fitted with a new system. The lifeboats – forty-six of them, plus two motor launches – were stacked up at eight points, leaving the rest of the deck clear and the view unimpeded. The boats could be boarded from the deck, and then the gantries, which were powered by motor, lifted them out and lowered them a safe distance from the hull. Two of the gantries, those sited away from the funnels, could even lift a boat from one side of the ship to the other.

Teddy thought of that terrible night on *Titanic*: the agonising slowness of lowering the boats by hand winch, the difficulty of keeping them level, the danger as the ship listed and the boats scraped against her flanks, the desperate haste to get the launched boats far enough away from the ship's side. On *Britannic*, if evacuation should ever be needed, there would be an effortless, mechanised ballet, the boats swung out in a graceful arc and placed gently well out on the water. One of the engineers he spoke to told him they could all be launched within twenty minutes. It seemed a miraculous claim to Teddy, and well worth the awkward look of the things.

He met the requisitioning officer, a Captain Hardacre, and was invited aboard to see how the ship would be arranged. The fittings already installed had been removed and put into storage, and the public rooms were being altered. Teddy followed the captain, listening with interest; but at the head of the Grand Staircase, with its rich panelling and lantern dome, he stopped dead. The similarity with *Titanic* made him feel hot and light-headed. In a lightning flash of memory he saw again the great, doomed ship in her luxury: the lamps and carpets and upholstery, mirrors and chandeliers, the glittering crowds slowly promenading from one grand room to another, the white-jacketed stewards serving champagne. He heard the gay music, the conversation and laughter. He closed his eyes against it, but he could still smell the newness of the carpets and the hint of wax polish in the air. He grabbed the banister rail as remembered visions swung vertiginously around him. The grandeur, the unheeding passengers, his lonely foreknowledge of onrushing death, all came back to him, sickeningly. He felt again the agony of despair, and terror, and sorrow.

Hardacre, who had started down, stopped and looked back, and at the sight of Teddy's pallor his face creased with concern. 'Are you all right, sir?'

Teddy opened his eyes, shook his head, took hold of reality. 'Yes,' he said weakly. 'Yes, I'm all right. It was just – memories.' She had been the most beautiful artefact ever to grace the sea, and his heart still ached for her loss. He would not – dared not – remember those who had perished. Sometimes in his dreams he heard their dying cries across the dark water . . .

Hardacre's eyebrows shot up as he suddenly remembered what he knew about Mr Edward Morland. 'I'm so sorry. I'd forgotten. It must be—' In fact, he couldn't think what it must be like.

But Teddy's colour was returning. 'I'm quite all right now. Shall we continue?'

He walked on with the captain and looked into the various public spaces and asked about the hospital arrangements. He was himself again, a level-headed businessman, feet firmly on the ground. It was just that every now and then he would catch a glimpse of the old ship overlying the new one like a mist: images of lost luxury in the emptiness; ghosts of the perished in their finery walking, unseen but to him, among the carpenters and electricians and labourers.

They went back to Captain Hardacre's dockside office and discussed the linens that would be required. Captain Hardacre gave him rough figures and told him he would be sent exact specifications very soon.

'When will you want delivery?' Teddy asked, offering a cigar. The captain refused, but he put one between his own lips and felt for his matches.

'We are going ahead with all speed. We hope to have the

sea trials early next month, and to have her fully equipped and ready for service by the middle of December.'

Teddy almost bit right through his cigar. 'That's only a month away!'

Hardacre shrugged. 'The situation in the eastern Mediterranean is bad and likely to get worse. We can't spare more than a month. But if you can't supply us within that time . . .'

Teddy raised his hands. 'Of course I can supply you. It's just rather short notice.'

'There's a war on,' Hardacre pointed out, as everyone always did when anything was out of the ordinary.

Departing the office, Teddy took one last look at the magnificent ship, gleaming in her white livery, and took his leave. He had no time to waste. He must get over to Manchester at once and see his mill managers. A sense of purpose and vigour filled him. There was nothing like an emergency for giving relief from long-term, grinding concerns.

If Venetia had hoped to see more of her husband when he returned from Salonika, she was disappointed. There were urgent meetings of the Dardanelles Committee concerning the evacuation; he was called to Cabinet conferences for his advice; and then the War Committee had to review the events of the past year and form a strategy for the continuation of the war.

In the early part of December, Overton's man, Ash, had to pack again for his master, though the trip this time was shorter: to Chantilly, for another Anglo-French conference. Asquith, Sir Edward Grey and Lloyd George all went, as well as Kitchener and the leading lights of the War Office. At least they travelled in comfort, in their own private train, and were housed at the best hotel with all possible luxury; but Overton hoped this would be the last time he was called away.

The weather in France was vile, horribly cold and with driving sleet. Most of the time Overton was dry and warm inside, but he could not help thinking of the men in the trenches and their discomfort. It was quiet along the line now, which meant just the routine amount of shelling and sniping, the routine number of casualties. Nothing more could be attempted until spring, except to hold the line where it was.

In the train on the journey home, Overton was called again to give his opinion to the Big Three – prime minister, foreign secretary and minister of munitions – on the continuing hostility between Haig and Sir John French. Their arguments over the degree of failure at Loos, and whose fault it really was, had rumbled away like distant thunder since September. The train was a small one – only two carriages – and, travelling slowly on the congested lines, it did not make much noise. But the Cabinet ministers did not bother to lower their voices. After returning to his seat, Overton, like everyone else around him, heard their frank discussion – and their decision that Sir John French was to be replaced as commander-in-chief of the BEF by Sir Douglas Haig.

Overton was sad – French was an old friend – and he did not personally like Haig; though he had no specific doubts about his competency. But he had known for some time that a change was likely: politicians were always attracted to it. They liked to appear to be doing something when things were not going well. Parliament, like the general public, could not be expected to understand *why* victory had proved elusive so far, or what the unique military difficulties of the situation were. A new year, a new campaign, a new commander: these would sound good in the newspapers and raise the government in the public's eyes.

Well, for all Overton knew, they might yield results. For the rest of their conclusions, Overton could not fault them. Gallipoli had been a disaster, and there must be no more improvisations. Thorough planning, realistic goals and experienced leadership were required. Officers must be appointed on the basis of ability, not seniority. Egypt and the Suez Canal must, of course, be defended, but otherwise the Eastern campaign should be abandoned and efforts concentrated on the Western Front, where Loos had shown that a breakthrough was possible. But a far greater supply of heavy guns and shells was needed to achieve it, and far more men. The quality of the British soldiers was beyond criticism – the courage and endurance of the Terriers and the Kitchener units so far used had astonished the professionals on the field. With sound planning and a great deal more artillery support, 1916 might show marked advances over 1915.

But, the leaders concluded, there could be no new offensive until a sufficient force of the New Army had been brought out. The men must be trained and armed, and accustomed to trench life, before being pitched into battle, and that could not be before the autumn of 1916 at the earliest. Until then, the British Army must simply hold fast – under Haig.

The Channel crossing was rough and unpleasant. Once safely in the train on the other side, Overton allowed himself to relax and, feeling very tired, thought of home, of Venetia, even of Christmas. They had originally planned to go down to Wolvercote, to stay with Venetia's Aylesbury cousins, where a large family gathering, much tradition and unpretentious comfort always meant an enjoyable stay. But this year the question of Violet hung over everything.

She had written from Chetton Farthing of her happiness there, and to Overton's surprise showed no sign of wanting to come back to London: he had expected her to be restless and bored away from the capital. He thought it worrying that she was *not* longing for reinstatement. It had been hard for him to bear his darling daughter's fall; it troubled him that she had absorbed, somehow, a different set of rules from those he had assumed she shared. It would be terrible if she had to live the rest of her life in exile with Laidislaw, and that he might therefore see little of her.

He wondered, though, if it wouldn't be worse if the thing blew over, if it was not grand, lasting love but a passing fancy. What would that say about his daughter? To be overmastered once and for all by love had a sort of nobility to it, but to fall prey to a whim – well, men did it all the time, of course, but somehow one couldn't like it in women.

But if she did stay with the painter, what then? Would Holkam tolerate it? *What if there were a divorce?* Contemplating this last, horrifying possibility, he fell at last victim to the rhythm of the wheels, and sank into sleep.

It was going to be a quiet Christmas at Morland Place, with Frank in Malta and Jack and Helen unable to come because of the advanced stage of Helen's pregnancy – she was due to deliver early in January. And over everything hung Ned's death, and Teddy's refusal to acknowledge it. Henrietta felt it would have been easier to have a Christmas in mourning, for at least everything would have been clear, to them, their tenants and neighbours. As it was, any attempt to mute the celebrations was taken by Teddy as 'giving up on Ned'; yet full-blooded celebration felt awkward and wrong to everyone else. A compromise was eventually secured by Henrietta, who persuaded Teddy that quiet cheerfulness would be better suited to wartime, and the fact that many in the neighbourhood had men who had died or been wounded.

So there were to be no loud revels, just the 'good old traditions', as Teddy put it: fetching in the Yule log, carols on Christmas Eve, a tree in the hall, presents for the tenants on Christmas morning, and the Boxing Day hunt. Christmas Day fell on a Saturday, so at least there would be no prolonged holiday to get through.

There was one more trip to London for Teddy in December, this time accompanied by Jessie and Henrietta, when they went to Buckingham Palace to receive Ned's medal from the King. Henrietta spoke firmly to Teddy beforehand about not making any fuss before His Majesty about the award's being called posthumous, and Teddy looked wounded and said he hoped he knew better than to embarrass anyone in a public place. But in any case, the presentation was made to Jessie, as Ned's wife, and her mother and uncle, her guests, were never in a position to say anything, had they wanted.

Afterwards they went to Manchester Square, where Venetia had invited them for a 'medal tea' after the custom of her youth. Henrietta was glad to meet her old friend face to face after such a long time, and they had plenty to talk about. Oliver made a fuss of Jessie, made her laugh with various medical anecdotes and told her about the latest plays and shows; and Lord Overton chatted comfortably with Teddy about the war, *Britannic*'s fitting-out, and the Gallipoli situation. They didn't talk about Ned, and they didn't talk about Violet. Each family had its sadness, and the other knew about it, but it seemed best to everyone to leave them unspoken.

The closest Venetia got to the forbidden topics was to ask after Emma, and Henrietta told her that by some means or other, Emma had managed to persuade her guardians to let her stay at Morland Place for Christmas.

'She wouldn't tell me what arguments she used – she just laughed when I asked her – but I must say I'm very glad she'll be with us,' said Henrietta. 'She has already made herself invaluable by escorting Polly about, and getting her interested in war work. There's no difficulty in keeping her occupied in summer, what with tennis parties, boating, picnics and so on, but she has so much energy she needs to be about something all the time.'

'I know the age,' said Venetia.

'She and Emma have joined a first-aid class, and they visit wounded officers and read to them, the way Jessie used to before she started nursing. And they help on a soldiers' relief committee – they're collecting for Christmas parcels for the men at the Front at the moment. And then there's the knitting.' She laughed suddenly. 'If I were to tell you about the knitting!'

Venetia laughed too. 'Winter setting in on the Front?' she suggested. 'Socks and gloves and balaclavas needed?' Appeals were in all the newspapers.

'Polly prefers scarves,' said Henrietta. 'They work off quickly. Everyone in the house is doing it, even me when I have a moment. Balls of khaki wool everywhere, and you daren't sit down without checking the chair for knitting-needles!'

'But it's serious work,' Venetia said. 'They'll need all the warm clothing they can get this winter. Overton said it was bitterly cold over there last week. The army is going to issue the men with fur waistcoats, but it will take time to get enough of them together.'

'Fur?' Henrietta queried.

'Rabbit and pony-skin and the like.' Venetia corrected her evident misapprehension.'

'They'll make a motley sight,' said Henrietta. 'But I suppose they probably already do.' She sighed a little. 'I can't believe the war's only been going on a year and a bit. It seems to have been with us for ever.'

It was getting too close to sad things. Venetia said, 'Have another piece of cake and tell me about my godson. Dear Jack! He never forgets my birthday, you know. Will he be flying again soon? And when is Helen's baby due?'

On the 12th of December HMHS *Britannic* sailed from Belfast to Liverpool under heavily armed escort, there to receive her final fitting-out as a hospital ship. Teddy hurried to Liverpool to oversee the delivery of the goods he was providing. The ship had been handed over to her operational commander, Captain Charles A. Bartlett. He was an experienced White Star master, nicknamed 'Iceberg Charlie' for his uncanny ability to detect ice, and known as a safe hand and popular with the passengers. Teddy had met him once during his association with White Star. When he arrived in Liverpool and presented himself to Bartlett, the captain greeted him in a friendly way and offered to show him over the ship.

The Grand Reception Room had become the main operating theatre, and the first-class dining-room next door was the intensive-care ward, for the most seriously wounded. The public rooms on the upper decks were laid out as wards, where the patients would be closest to the lifeboats if there were an emergency, and there were also beds on the promenade decks, so that the wounded could get the benefit of fresh air. The first-class staterooms were to be cabins for the doctors, the matron, the RAMC officers and the chaplains; the nurses and orderlies would have the second- and third-class cabins.

Bartlett showed Teddy about, and cheerfully quoted figures to him: 2034 beds, she would carry, and 1035 cots. In all she could transport well over three thousand wounded – only the giant *Aquitania* could take more – and she would have almost 350 medical staff, doctors, nurses and orderlies, and a ship's crew of 52 officers and 675 men.

'My ship's surgeon says she's the most wonderful hospital ship ever to sail the seas,' said Bartlett, 'and I'm sure he's right. Her only drawback is that she is so big she has to anchor in deep water, so we won't be able to get close in to shore. It's no fun for the wounded to have to be ferried out to us in small boats and then transferred. But once aboard they'll have the best of care. I don't think I'm betraying any secrets when I tell you we shall be doing the Dardanelles run.'

'No,' Teddy said. 'I was quite sure that's where you'd be going. Lemnos, isn't it?'

'Yes, that's the collection point for the wounded. We coal at Naples on the way out so that we can come back non-stop once the wounded are on board, give them the best run possible. It'll be a queer old thing to have such undemanding passengers,' he added, with a laugh. 'I shan't be receiving many complaints from those poor fellows as I do my rounds. I'm sure most of the people aboard will never have travelled in such luxury. We'll be empty going out to the Med, so I mean to let the medical staff use those passenger facilities we *haven't* removed, like the gymnasium and the swimming-pool.'

'I don't suppose they'll have much to do without any patients.'

'And one wants to keep the nurses occupied and out of trouble,' Bartlett grinned. 'Good job they'll all be under strict discipline. There's nothing like a cruise for raising the amorous temperature. But I've met the matron, and she's a Tartar!'

Shortly before Christmas, Morland Place received a visitor. Lennox Manning, a Morland cousin from America, had been staying with them in 1914 when the war broke out, and had volunteered at once, even though it meant losing his American citizenship. Recently he had been stationed out in Egypt; now he wrote that his battalion was going to the Front, and that he would have leave. Polly was wild with excitement. Ever since he had volunteered, she had half fancied herself in love with him; now that he had actually served abroad and been shot at, she was sure she was.

She was affronted that Henrietta would not hear of giving him a room in the guest wing. Emma persuaded her that a grand reception would embarrass Lennie, and that he would be happier in the bachelors' wing where he had always slept before. Polly took personal charge of preparing his room, commandeering the nicest candle-holder (the one with the glass chimney and the automatic snuffer), sheets without any mends in them, and the thickest bedside rug. She swapped the washstand with the one from her own room, which was nicer, and laid out a new cake of soap and one of the best towels. She arranged some evergreen sprays and stems with berries in a vase for the windowsill, put two of her favourite books on the nightstand, and personally filled the biscuit-barrel – which she took out of one of the guest rooms – then set it on the mantelpiece.

On the day on which he was to arrive she dashed about, unable to sit still, driving the dogs wild and asking every few minutes if it wasn't time to go to the station yet. 'We don't want to be late. Suppose the train is early?'

'Troop trains are never early,' Ethel pointed out. 'Much more likely to be late, and then you'd be standing about in the cold for hours.'

Alice took pity on her, and helped her choose what to wear. No-one else had the patience.

'Do you think my plaid frock or the blue velvet? The plaid goes better with my red coat, but I've got that beautiful blue ribbon, and blue goes better with my hair. Or is hair ribbon too childish? You can't see the ribbon anyway under my tam o'shanter. Should I wear the tam or the black hat? If I wear the plaid it should be the tam, but the black goes with my new boots . . .'

By the time Teddy was ready to depart for the station, Polly was nearly sick with excitement. She didn't speak on the short drive, and her father was also silent, thinking about Ned, and how it would be if it were him they were going to meet instead of Lennie. Oh, hasten the day! How would a prisoner-of-war spend Christmas? The Red Cross arranged for parcels to be sent. Would he get his share? If he was in hospital, was he in pain? Was he being taken care of? The Germans were civilised people – on the whole. One read of 'atrocities', but that was in the heat of battle. Back home, in their cities and towns, they would take care of prisoners properly – wouldn't they?

The train was late, as Ethel had predicted. Finally it steamed slowly in, the carriage windows crowded with khaki figures straining for a first glimpse of one face in the throngs waiting for them. As the train sighed and shuddered to a halt, nurses and orderlies began to unload stretcher-cases from the hospital carriages. The walking wounded climbed down, with their bandaged heads, faces and limbs, crutches and slings and empty sleeves. A VAD trolley trundled up with mugs of tea, and helpers lit cigarettes for those who had difficulty. Soldiers with armbands and officers with lists directed the human traffic; policemen and Boy Scouts kept passage open for them.

With the rest of the train, matters were less orderly: it was jostle and shove, stand a-tiptoe, crane and wave along with everyone else.

Teddy spotted Lennie first. 'There he is!'

'Where?' Polly scanned the torrent of men descending from the carriages and pouring along the platform, discovering in a practical way the point of a uniform. In their khaki and peaked caps, they all looked the same to her.

'There, just getting out of the next carriage – second door along. Now he's hidden by that kitbag. Stay still, he'll be by in a second.'

Here he was. A grin split his face at the sight of them. He shook Teddy's hand and reached for Polly's. 'You came to meet me! I never expected that. Thanks a heap!'

Polly stared at him in perplexity. Surely her Lennie had been taller? And definitely far more handsome. This weather-tanned man was quite ordinary-looking. He had a nice face, but he was no Greek god. He was grimy from travelling, his uniform was shabby, his boots were dusty and he smelled sooty from the train. She had expected his glory to shine all about him. This was just a soldier like any other.

'I've had terrific news,' he said, beaming at them, unable to keep it to himself. 'I had a letter from Granny. She says her campaign worked, and Congress is going to revoke the law – you know, the one that says Americans who fight for foreign armies have to lose their citizenship. Can you believe it? Good old Granny Ruth! I knew the United States government would be no match for her! I'm going to get my citizenship back! Isn't that grand? She says Dad's as pleased as a dog with two tails!'

Teddy wrung his hand and congratulated him, but the significance of the news passed Polly by. She could not get to grips with this stranger who had taken the place of the Lennie of her imaginings. She felt cold, disappointed and slightly cross. She had looked forward so much to this moment and now it all seemed to be going wrong. In the motor going home, Lennie and Teddy talked about Egypt and the war and American citizenship. Each assumed that Polly was feeling shy, and was kindly letting her alone; but on top of everything else, now she felt left out, and wondered why she had bothered to come to meet the train at all.

At home, in the general warmth and excitement of greeting, the talk and movement and smiles, Polly began to get over her reaction. Lennie looked at her with admiration and noticed the care she had taken over her appearance. He asked her about her new mare, Vesper, proving he remembered that she had written about her in her letters. And when he saw his room, he at once attributed the little touches of comfort in it to Polly. She began to feel better.

There was much about him, after all, that had not changed: his character, the eager, open, friendly manner that she had always found attractive, so different from the tongue-tied dullness of many English lads. He was in uniform, which was a point in his favour; and he was off to France – a great many more points. It gave her an interesting pang to think of him going to the proper Front, like a real soldier.

But by the end of his visit, she had come to the conclusion that although he was really nice, and she liked him very much, she didn't think she was in love with him after all. That was sad, in a way – she had liked being in love – but in another way it was exciting, because it left a vacancy for someone else. And not being in love with him allowed her to enjoy his company as a cousin, to do more talking, laughing and arguing, and less silent anguished gazing – and Polly was a girl who liked to take the active part.

By the time his departure came round she was perfectly natural with him. She was not going to the station – she and Emma had a bandaging class to go to – so it was in the great hall that she said goodbye, rather briskly and quite cheerfully. Lennie, however, in the one moment they were alone, took her hand in both of his and said, 'I've hardly had a chance to talk to you properly. Leave is so short. It seems like yesterday I got here, and now I'm going again.'

'I'm sorry I can't come and see you off,' Polly said, though she wasn't, not really. To stand about on the platform waiting for trains to leave was a tedious business – especially these days when they never left on time.

'Partings are hard in wartime. It's better like this,' he said. 'You will write to me?'

'Of course,' she said. She looked down at her hand, still captured, and wished he would let it go.

He lowered his voice. 'I'll be thinking of you every day, Polly. And every night before I go to sleep, I'll think of you then, most of all.'

He hesitated, seeking words. He'd never been interested in a female in this way before. When he'd left last time, Polly had been just a girl, rather like a kid sister. But he had come back and found her transformed into a woman. She was so pretty – dainty and ladylike – but underneath still the same grand girl as before. It seemed to him the perfect combination. Being shut up for months on end in all-male company had prepared the ground; her frank, affectionate letters, which he had so looked forward to and treasured, had warmed it; and now her new maturity planted the seed. He was going to France; he was ready to give his heart away.

'What I'm trying to say,' he went on, 'is that I guess your father wouldn't want us to get engaged yet, what with me being away, and the war and all, and you still being so young, but when it's over, the war, I mean – well, then maybe, when I come back, we could do it then. What do you think?'

He looked down at her tenderly and hopefully. A girl of fifteen would have to have a heart of stone not to be moved by what was effectively her first proposal of marriage. She was very fond of Lennie, and in his uniform cap she thought, actually, he did look quite handsome after all. He was off to the Front: for a moment she came close to 'fancying' him again. Looking up at him, she began to smile.

Fortunately her father came up at that point and said, 'All ready? Time to go,' so she did not have to answer Lennie's question. He released her hand and was urged away to the car without the chance of further words. Polly stood on the steps with the rest of the family and waved goodbye as the motor drove out of the yard, and when it was out of sight she heaved a sigh of considerable satisfaction as she went indoors. It was really a nice position to be in, to have a proposal in the bag, so to speak – and a secret one at that, which was something pleasant to think about in bed at night, but which in no way committed her, so would not get in the way of any other nice young man who showed interest in her. When the war ended and Lennie came back – who knew? The end of the war seemed a long way off just then, and not worth worrying about.

Emma had been keeping up a correspondence with Maria Stanhope, whom she had met when Jessie had been in London in May and introduced them. The two young women had taken a liking to each other, and had met whenever time and a chaperon were available. Just before Christmas, Maria wrote to Emma to say that her father had died, suddenly, of a heart-attack. He had been quite elderly – much older than her mother – and had scarcely left the house for many months, but he had not exhibited any particular symptoms of ill health, so his death was still a shock. Both Emma and Jessie wrote with their condolences, and

Jessie forwarded Maria's letter to Frank in Malta, feeling that at such a time it would not be a breach of etiquette for him to write to Maria direct.

Frank was not to have any leave before Christmas, and the family had been assembling a parcel for him. By the time it was sent off from the post office in York, it was a wonderful thing of smoked ham, potted shrimps, home-made jam, Mrs Stark's plum cake, shortbread, pickled peaches, nuts, oranges, cigarettes, chocolate, a bottle of port and one of whisky, knitted things from the women, cigars from Teddy, books from Rob, and a dozen handkerchiefs from Henrietta. Malta was not, in fact, a place of shortages and deprivation, but no-one let that spoil the fun.

On Christmas Eve they fetched in the Yule log, which had been drying out under a tarpaulin for a couple of months ever since Teddy and his steward Maltby had identified it. With only Rob home, there were not enough men of the family to drag the log, so Jessie fixed up a harness for her Bhutia pony Mouse to do the work. Once they got it home, the log was installed and set alight with the usual prayers, and there was lamb's wool – hot, spiced cider with fluffy pulped apple floating on the top – to drink for all. After tea the choir from the village church came to sing carols in the Great Hall. The candles on the Christmas tree were lit, while two footmen stood by with wet sponges on poles in case of accidents, and the other servants crowded in with the family to listen. The choristers were regaled with hot punch and spiced biscuits for their return journey, and went off in good humour, knowing that Teddy had given the choirmaster a fistful of silver to distribute to them for their trouble. Christmas Eve had always been the part Jessie liked best: the glittering, shining tree, the sweet voices, the familiar old carols, the quiet darkness outside and the sense of wonder and waiting seemed to her the essence of the season.

Christmas Day began with prayers in the chapel, and then the tenants and pensioners came up to the house and there were presents for all of them, and for the servants. Christmas dinner was the usual goose and plum pudding, and all the nursery children were allowed down for it, round-eyed to see the pudding brought in, wreathed in blue flames of burning brandy. Port and nuts followed, and after the loyal toast, Teddy made his usual Christmas speech, and proposed a toast to 'absent friends'. It was a perilous moment as everyone thought about Ned. No-one knew what to say or think in the face of Teddy's defiance.

But afterwards, in the drawing-room, Emma proved a genius at improvising games and driving everyone to join in, no matter what their protests. When the company flagged at last, she persuaded Ethel to go to the piano and play ragtime tunes and popular songs, the sillier the better. Traditional airs might have made them melancholy, but to hear Uncle Teddy solemnly singing about chimpanzees and pickled cucumbers reduced them all to tears of mirth. So the day ended happily.

On the official Boxing Day on Monday there was the traditional hunt. Polly was hunting Vesper for the first time. Teddy and Jessie were also going out, and since Emma, whose riding was much improved, had expressed a wistful desire to join them, Teddy had found time in all his other concerns to scour the countryside for a suitable horse for her. The army had taken so many there was little left that was not too old, too young, or too small, but he managed at the last moment to borrow a lady's ride from Mrs Chubb of Bootham Park, who had sprained her wrist and so would not be hunting. It was a fifteen-hand bay mare, whom Mrs Chubb said jumped like a stag but was as gentle as a lamb. Jessie tried her out briefly before Emma came down to make sure she would not get their guest into trouble, and thought her a slug with a poor mouth, but she supposed beggars could not be choosers, and Emma seemed delighted with her, stroked her neck extravagantly and called her a 'beautiful creature'.

The meet was a lawner at Healaugh Manor, and the turn-out was impressive, though the majority of the field was on foot. Everyone was talking about the desperate shortage of horses, and predicting that this might be the last season until the war ended. Polly was surrounded by an admiring crowd of both sexes: all the young women – and most of the young men – were deeply envious of Vesper. Teddy looked on with pride, thinking what a picture she was in her neat habit, top hat and veil, while he chatted genially to friends and neighbours, pooh-poohed the death of the hunt, and promised a lawn meet at Morland Place before the season ended.

To Jessie's surprise, she enjoyed the meet too. Those people who came up to her with condolences spoke warmly of Ned's fine qualities and congratulated her on his decoration, rather than dwelling on his death, and then went on to talk about hunting and horses. It was all much easier to bear, now that the custom had evolved of *not* mourning, of being proud of one's lost ones, rather than weeping for them. Whatever was going on inside you, you were expected to behave outwardly with dignified cheerfulness, and that was so much easier to maintain in public.

When hounds arrived, Emma's mount, who had been dozing with one hoof cocked, suddenly woke up and began dancing about in a very lively manner. Perhaps Mrs Chubb had not been exaggerating, Jessie thought, noting this change of character as the mare walked backwards into Hotspur, offending him deeply.

'Are you all right? Will you be able to hold her?' she asked Emma.

Emma turned a beaming face. 'Oh, I think so. Isn't she lovely? I'm so looking forward to this.'

'Stay near the back until you see how she goes,' Jessie advised. She looked around to see how Polly was doing. Vesper was too astonished by the sight of hounds to misbehave yet. She goggled at them, snorting like a dragon when any came near, and turning on the spot to keep them in view as they mingled with the crowd begging shamelessly for sausage rolls. Polly had been riding almost since birth and wasn't the least troubled, merely turning her again so that she could carry on her conversation. Jessie wasn't worried: Vesper hadn't an ounce of vice in her, and had a great deal of courage. She might get excited, but was unlikely to 'spook' or bolt.

The Master came up, touching his hat, and stopped to talk to her. She commiserated with him on the shortage of horses and the fact that both his whippers-in had lately volunteered so he was having to rely on boys of sixteen and seventeen respectively.

He deplored the situation volubly. 'Then there's this damned conscription coming in. Un-English, I call it. My huntsman is within the age group. What if they take him? And both my hunters are getting on – that's why the army left me them. What happens when I have to retire them?'

'I suppose you could hunt hounds on foot,' Jessie said, trying to be helpful.

He shook his head. 'The old ways are passing. Wouldn't be surprised if the hunt folds. Enjoy it while you can, m'dear. By the by, that's a nice sort of mare Miss Morland has there.' There was naked greed in his voice as he eyed Vesper. 'Youngster, isn't she? Where did she get her?'

'I bred her myself,' said Jessie.

'Wish you could breed something for me. But if you did the army would probably take it. Well, must go and do the rounds, if you'll excuse me. Have to jolly the field along.' He touched his hat again and moved on. Jessie was amused by the idea of his 'jollying' anyone in his present mood, especially when she overheard him a few moments later saying gloomily, 'I suppose next they'll be expecting me to use *female* whips. I'll knock hounds on the head if ever it comes to that. And you can knock me on the head at the same time!'

* * *

The Overtons had withdrawn from the Christmas invitation to Wolvercote, and were staying in Manchester Square, hoping that Violet would join them. Venetia was preparing to part with Oliver: conscription would begin in February, and he had volunteered himself ready to go at once. She had not expected to mind so much, but in fact she was dreading his leaving. She had got used to having him about the house, and enjoyed their long, frank conversations. Thomas would not be home for Christmas – he would not have leave until the summer, when the imperial family, whom he served as military liaison, went to Livadia – but she had thought to have two of her children together for what might be the last time for several years.

But Violet did not want to leave Chetton. She wrote to say she was happy there, and saw no reason ever to leave. Venetia doubted the frame of mind would last, or that Laidislaw entirely shared it, but for the moment they were steeped in the rural idyll, and Violet wrote that she would visit Brancaster for Christmas itself, for the children's sake, then return to Chetton.

'Perhaps *we* should go *there*,' Oliver suggested, when she showed him the letter. 'There's obviously some powerful attraction about the place.'

'Nonsensical boy! Oh, but why wouldn't she come here? She could bring the children. If she's going to be apart from her painter anyway . . . And your aunt Olivia and Charlie are going to Wolvercote, so we shan't see them. Oh dear. We shall be a glum party here on our own.'

'Nonsense! How can you be glum with me around? We'll make our own amusement. It's only two days, in any case. I have a list at the clinic on Monday.'

'How on earth are they going to manage without you when you go to France?'

'Oh, didn't I tell you? Darroway has a new young assistant just out of medical school, penniless and keen, like him at the same age. He says the boy is the most talented doctor he's met in an age, far better than me in every respect. He won't even notice I'm gone.'

'Poor darling. To be *vieux jeux* at your age!'

Overton was glad enough just to stay at home and enjoy his wife's company. As Christmas Day was a Saturday, the government had made Monday the official Boxing Day so, barring any military emergency, he had three days to rest, with no need to leave the house except to go to church. It suited him perfectly.

He was not best pleased, therefore, to be roused from a post-prandial doze on the Sunday afternoon to be told that Laidislaw was on the doorstep and demanding to see him.

It had not occurred to any of them to wonder what Laidislaw would do when Violet went to Brancaster. On her other trips to see the children, who lived all the time at Brancaster, he had been content to stay at the cottage, painting. They had been short visits in any case, there and back on the same day – she could not bear to be long away from him. But she felt guilty about the children's Christmas. Their father would be in France and, in the circumstances, she told Laidislaw, she felt she could not just visit them on Christmas Day. She would go to Brancaster on Christmas Eve and come back on the Monday.

Laidislaw had been noble about it, but by the evening of Christmas Day he had been alone for long enough to start thinking, and by Sunday morning his thinking had driven him impatiently to action. He was shown into the drawing-room and wasted no time on polite nothings. 'You still have the painting safe?' he asked his startled audience.

'The painting?' Overton said. He had been having a pleasant half-dream, half-daydream, and was not quite ready for reality yet.

'The portrait,' Laidislaw said impatiently, with the air of being about to walk up and down the room.

While Overton had been dozing, Venetia had been in another room writing letters and Oliver had gone to the library in search of a book, but they both came hurrying back when they heard who had called.

'Is Violet ill?' Venetia asked urgently, as she came in. She was unable to think of any other reason he might be here.

'Violet?' He looked surprised. 'Of course not. At least, I suppose not. She went to Brancaster. She was quite well when she left. Why do you ask?'

Oliver stepped in as interpreter. 'Laidislaw, just tell us why you are here.'

'I came to see the painting, to make sure it's all right.'

'Of course it's all right,' Overton said.

'The place you're keeping it – it's not damp? Are there mice? Mice will eat canvases, you know. Or birds – if you have starlings in the attic, their lime will destroy it.' No-one answered him for a moment and he cut to the core of the matter. 'I want it back. All day yesterday I kept thinking about it. It's my greatest work. I must have it.'

'What do you want to do with it?' Overton managed to ask.

'Exhibit it. Show it to the world.'

'No,' said Venetia decisively. 'Never.'

'You don't understand—!'

'*You* don't understand. You cannot be allowed to make a scandal of our daughter.'

He waved that away with a distracted hand. 'It was a fuss over nothing. Small-minded people, that's all. They'll soon forget and jabber about something else. They don't matter. But the picture is important. My painting belongs to the world, for all time. Art must not, cannot, be suppressed by petty human concerns that will be blown away like dust by the great winds of eternity. It endures, when all else fades and fails.'

It was not the first time Venetia had seen him in full flood on the subject of Art, but she was impressed none the less. There was no doubting his energy and conviction. His eyes sparked, his hair seemed almost to wave with passion. She could see why Violet found him attractive. She tried to speak more gently. 'One day, perhaps, the world will catch up with you. For the moment it is what it is, and we have to live in it, small-minded people included. When the scandal dies down, then we can talk about what to do with the painting.'

'Then you'll give it back to me?' he asked eagerly. She didn't answer and he looked at Lord Overton.

'I'll consider it,' said Overton.

Laidislaw was dejected. Like a child, he knew the value of a grown-up's *I'll think about it.* 'You don't appreciate it,' he said. 'You don't see the beauty. If you did, you could never bear to leave it mouldering in an attic.'

'It isn't mouldering.' Overton now took pity on him – Venetia saw he was being charmed too by this volatile young man. 'The attic is perfectly dry and there are no mice or birds. Do you think I'd let anything happen to such a fine picture of my daughter? She is beautiful – and your work is brilliant.'

'You think so?' He seemed cheered by this.

Venetia did not want a discussion of his talent. She had more important concerns. 'What are you and Violet going to do? How long will you be staying in Chetton?'

He turned to her. 'I don't know. Violet says she never wants to leave. We are very happy there, and I'm doing some extraordinary work. Perhaps we'll make it our home.'

'Do you really think Violet will be happy to live in a cottage in the middle of nowhere for the rest of her life?' Oliver asked, fascinated by the painter's mental processes.

'Why not?' Laidislaw said. He was a creature of the present, and the future seemed too far off to be worried about. 'We have everything we need there: peace and quiet to work, and the light is wonderful. Of course, I would have to come up to Town sometimes, to exhibit.' He looked around their bemused faces, aware that they were waiting for something more. He didn't know what it was. He went on, 'We might go to New York one day. They are a tremendous people, the

New Yorkers – passionate about art. Open-minded, generous – nothing petty about them. With such a public, I could do great work.'

'I can see that's what you want,' said Oliver, 'but what does Violet want?'

Laidislaw looked puzzled. 'We love each other. We want the same things.'

'I'm sure you think so. But I would rather hear it from Violet herself,' said Venetia.

'Then you shall,' said Laidislaw.

He must have passed on the substance of the conversation to Violet as soon as they were together again, for a letter arrived from her on the Wednesday.

> All I want is to be with him, and to help him in his work. He is a brilliant artist and if I can be his inspiration, I am content. It doesn't matter to me where we are, as long as we are together. We are happy here at Chetton. Eventually, perhaps, we might come back to London – that depends on Holkam as much as anyone. Or we might travel. Europe will have to wait until after the war, I suppose, but we could visit America. Don't worry about me, Mother. As long as I can be with him, I am happy. I have never been as happy as this. He is my Great Love, and I am his.

Venetia thought sadly that it did not seem likely Holkam would ever agree to their living together in London. The war was a blessing in a way, for if he had been at home the whole situation would have had to be dealt with, and he would probably have made sure they were kept apart. A life in exile seemed to lie ahead of her daughter. She hoped it really was Violet's Great Love, for anything less would make the pain and sacrifice too high a price.

Perhaps one day Holkam would agree to a divorce. Divorced people were accepted in some circles; they could make *some* sort of a life, though not the life for which Violet was bred, and which she had enjoyed until now. Venetia sighed. It was not what one would have expected or hoped for the lovely Lady Violet Winchmore, the Overtons' exquisite daughter.

And, on a selfish note, whatever Violet's future with Laidislaw, it would mean that she, Venetia, would not see her half as much as before. Thomas in Russia (and, from what he said in his letters, he saw his life out there rather than in England), Violet gone and now Oliver going. It was a good job she had her work to keep her busy. The war was a blessing in that respect, too.

CHAPTER SEVEN

The evacuation of Gallipoli was a triumph of organisation. After the terrible storm in late November, which had ripped through the camps, trenches and harbours with such destruction, a period of fine but cold weather had set in: still and frosty at night, chilly and sunny by day, and with calm seas. The good weather and the tremendous discipline of the troops allowed the implementation of a plan to get away without the Turks becoming aware of it. The soldiers withdrew in batches, taking off their boots to creep away on stockinged feet in the night, assembling in absolute silence on the beaches, being ferried by lighters across the dark sea to the waiting ships, which had lowered their anchors by hand so that the sound of chains would not give them away.

As the numbers thinned, the men left behind had to make the Turks believe nothing had changed, for if the enemy suspected and attacked it would be a disaster. So they dashed back and forth from one part of the line to another, sending up flares here and firing rifles there, setting off mines and passing back and forth along the roads that were under observation. Ingenious commanders set up devices of all sorts to help the deception – for instance, a series of fixed rifles in a trench that could be fired by jerking a single cord, and a grenade-tossing machine. One lieutenant left behind his treasured gramophone so that music could be played loudly at night.

On the final day of evacuation, it was especially important for the last few men to put on a show. At Anzac, one group was ordered to hang around on Artillery Road where the Turks would be able to observe them 'obviously loafing and smoking', as they had always done at a certain hour. Another group had a cricket match on Shell Green – a place that lived up to its name, as enemy shells whistled over the players' heads. By nightfall there was nothing but a small rearguard left, who ran around in the dark firing rifles and making enough noise for a whole garrison; and then in the early hours they, too, slipped down to the beach and were taken off, leaving the place to the Turks.

The Turks had been worthy enemies and clean fighters, and in the satisfaction of having at last stolen a march on them, many of the departing warriors left little friendly notes for them to find when they should finally come and investigate: 'So long, Johnny. It's all yours now,' attached to some treasure left behind; and 'See you in Australia, mate!'

On the night of the 20th of December the last man left Gallipoli, except for the 29th Division, which was to remain to garrison Cape Helles for seventeen days more. In contrast to the gloomy estimates of Munro and Kitchener, not a single man was lost in the evacuation. It was the one part of the Gallipoli campaign that was an undoubted success.

Contrary to the rule that first babies generally arrive in the middle of the night, throwing their parents into a panic, Helen Compton went into labour on a Sunday morning in January when her husband was at home and at leisure. She had woken up with backache, but didn't think too much of it. In the late stages of pregnancy backache is rather the rule than otherwise. Jack got up and went off to wash and shave while she had the cup of tea in bed that had become customary. By the time he returned, the dull ache had developed a spike in the middle of it.

'Perhaps it's the baby coming,' Helen suggested tentatively.

'Do you think so?'

'I don't know. I've never had a baby before.'

Jack looked perplexed. 'Neither have I. Perhaps we should ask Mrs Binny.'

Helen said, 'I think the "Mrs" is a courtesy title. I don't think she's ever been married.'

'Still, she's older than us, and she can't know less than we do. Darling!' He started as his wife's face compressed with pain.

'It's all right,' she said, through gritted teeth.

Jack flung on his clothes, and hurried out to the kitchen where the cook, Mrs Binny, was leisurely cutting the rinds off bacon rashers. She came at once, seeming flattered by the call, and having closeted herself with Helen for five minutes, called Jack in and said the baby was definitely on its way. Jack wanted to ask her how she knew, but didn't want to upset Helen, who seemed distracted and a little anxious.

'Don't worry, sir,' Mrs Binny went on. 'First babies take hours and hours. I remember my sister was near-on two days about it with her first. Plenty of time to get the doctor in. Give him a ring and I dessay he'll tell you the same.'

She proved right in that, at least. Jack telephoned Dr Harper, who said that he would be along in an hour, and meanwhile would alert the midwife they had booked.

There was time, therefore, for Jack to have breakfast, which Helen insisted on. 'I couldn't eat a thing, but you're going to need to keep your strength up. From the stories one hears, it will be nearly as hard for you as for me.'

So Jack had breakfast with Helen's sister Molly, who had been staying since just after the New Year with the purpose of helping Helen with the baby. She was seventeen, a lively, energetic girl, and the anxiety of her mother. Mrs Ormerod had produced Molly unexpectedly and late in life, and simply hadn't the energy to cope with the demands of another daughter at a time when her principal interests had become playing bridge and embroidering teacloths.

'We ought to be planning her come-out,' she had said despairingly to Helen before Christmas, 'but I don't believe anything of that sort is going on any more, what with the war and shortages and everything, and if we don't bring her out, what on earth are we to do with her? We can't send her to finishing school, either, with those dreadful Germans everywhere all over Europe, and she makes such a noise in the house, it makes my head ache. She ought to be going to dances and getting married, that would use up her energy, but who is there for her to marry? There isn't a single man within miles – they're all in uniform and going off to the Front. I can't bear to think of having another old maid on my hands. Not that you're an old maid, dear, after all, but it was hard enough getting you off – twenty-six before you even got engaged! I was sure I was going to have you at home for ever. You were so *difficult*, Helen, no-one was good enough for you. That nice Fulleylove boy asked for you at least twice, and hung around the house for months like a sick spaniel, but you wouldn't have him, and in the end he married the Peterson girl with the freckles and the gap in her teeth and that dreadful, vulgar mother, always pushing herself forward at church on Sundays – so embarrassing for the vicar, because he can hardly be uncivil in his position. I simply had to *avoid* Mrs Fulleylove after the engagement was announced, because I'd have had to congratulate her and, really, it was such a come-down for her it would have been a downright lie to say I was pleased for her, especially when I felt partly to blame because I'd encouraged the boy, which she knew quite well.' She faltered, having lost her thread. 'What was I talking of?'

'Not bringing Molly out,' Helen prompted her patiently. There was never any use in trying to short-circuit her mother – it only confused her more.

'Oh, of course. Well, what *am* I to do with her? She hasn't the least interest in her appearance. All she does is rush about with the dogs and make a noise or sit reading trashy novels all day. Not even love stories,' Mrs Ormerod concluded, as if it was the last straw, 'but lurid things about spies and prisoners-of-war escaping and aeroplane pilots shooting at each other. I think the gardener must get them for her. Your father certainly never reads that sort of thing.'

'She's full of energy, Mother,' Helen began.

'I *know* that. I told you so just now. Never walks when she can run. Up and down the stairs all day. Your father says she's like a herd of elephants – five years of ballet lessons simply *wasted*.'

'You ought to let her be trained for something – secretarial lessons, perhaps.'

'Darling,' said Mrs Ormerod, shocked, 'your father would never allow her to take a *job*.'

'He might have to,' Helen said. 'There's a war on, you know, and we all have to do our bit. Before long, women will have to take over most of the jobs that men do.'

Mrs Ormerod shuddered. 'Oh, I've read that sort of thing in the newspapers but, really, it can't mean people like us. Daddy was upset enough when you took that job delivering aeroplanes, but at least hardly anyone knew about it – not anyone who mattered, anyway. And you were already married. And you've given it up now, thank heaven.'

Helen knew how bored her sister was with doing nothing, and struck a blow for her. 'Well, you'd better talk to Daddy and try to change his mind, because Molly's been talking about joining a VAD and taking up nursing, and if you want to deflect her from *that*, you'll need something else to offer her. Secretarial training is better than nursing, surely?'

Mrs Ormerod needed considerable convincing, and ended by saying that she would think about it. 'In the mean time you had better have Molly to stay with you for a few weeks. She can be useful to you around the house when the baby comes, and you don't seem to mind her noise as much as I do. And she's always liked puppies and so on,' she added vaguely, 'so I expect she'll like helping with a baby.'

When Jack told Molly that Helen was probably in labour, she exhibited her excitement by becoming very practical and organising. 'I expect you're worried, because fathers always are the first time,' she said kindly, 'but there's no need. I know Helen's a bit old for babies, but she's very healthy, and Mother's last-dachshund-but-one, Melisande, had puppies for the first time when she was eight, which is jolly old for a dog, and she was perfectly all right.'

'I'll try not to worry,' Jack assured her solemnly.

'Good. Then the first thing is for us to have a good breakfast, because nothing will happen for ages, and it would be a shame to waste it all. I don't suppose Helen wants anything.'

'No.'

'I thought not. It must be a bit like having a tremendous tummy-ache, mustn't it?'

Dr Harper came at half past nine and confirmed that labour had started, accepted a cup of coffee, which he drank at a gulp, and hurried away to another confinement, saying he'd return later. The midwife arrived at ten, swept everything and everyone out of the way, and 'got busy' behind closed doors; but once the expectant mother and the bedchamber were arranged to her satisfaction she relented and allowed Jack in for a moment. Helen looked pale and too tidy in the unfamiliarly bare room, as if she'd been subdued and chastened by a professional hand.

'It's not too bad. Comes and goes, you know,' she replied, to his tender question. She glanced almost nervously at the midwife, kissed him and dismissed him. 'You go off and do something. Don't worry about me.'

'You wouldn't rather I sat with you?'

She smiled faintly. 'Absolutely not. Besides, Nurse Beesely wouldn't hear of it,' she added, in a whisper.

Molly managed to make herself fetcher-and-carrier for the midwife, which gave her a role and an importance. Jack had to pass the hours somehow, with nothing useful to do to mitigate his anxiety. He read the papers, smoked his pipe, and walked up and down the small strip of garden, ignoring Rug's blandishments and imploring looks at the gate that led to the wider downs. He did not want to go out of earshot of the house.

He walked with barely a limp now, using only a stick, and that more from habit than necessity. Fourteen months after he was shot down at Ypres, his ankle was healed at last. He was to see the sawbones in two weeks' time for what ought to be the last examination, and then he hoped he would be given exercises to strengthen it, and be able to start flying by the end of February. He longed for the wide sky again. It had been a frustrating time for him, with ground-based teaching of the new RFC intake at the flying school – where he could see that the fresh-faced youngsters already looked on him as an old man past his flying years – alternating with research and design work in the Royal Aircraft Factory. The Allied flyers in France were taking a terrible beating from the Germans since the latter had developed a 'fighter' aeroplane, which could fire forwards through the propellor. The Fokker Eindecker, despite being neither fast nor manoeuvrable, could inflict terrible losses by dropping from a height directly behind an Allied machine, where it could not defend itself. Over the last three months, more than fifty pilots had been shot down, in what was being called the 'Fokker Scourge'. RFC flyers were begging for a 'proper fighter' like the enemy's. The only forward-firing machines they had were slow, clumsy 'pushers', where the engine and propellor were behind the pilot, out of the way: the Vickers 'airbus' and the RE8, known (in rhyming slang) as the 'Harry Tate' after the music-hall performer.

The theory behind the interrupter gear that the Germans had fitted was well known to Jack and his colleagues: an additional cam, attached to the camshaft of the engine, connected to a rod, fixed to the breech block of the machine-gun and held by a spring, which intermittently tripped the trigger, allowing the machine-gun to fire only when the propellor blade had passed the muzzle. Since the engine turned at least 1000 revolutions per minute, with two opportunities to fire in each revolution, this allowed 2000 shots per minute. The rate of fire of the average machine-gun was only 500 or 600 shots per minute. The gun could therefore work at full speed regardless of the ordinary variations in revolutions of the engine.

But putting the theory into practice was the difficulty, especially within the confines of the RAF, with its cumbersome processes, restrictions and protocols imposed by government-department clerks. Jack had heard that at his old firm, Sopwiths, which provided exclusively for the more go-ahead Royal Naval Air Service, they had got much further ahead with the interrupter gear, and were poised to test a forward-firing one-seater based on the dear old Tabloid of fond memory. It was another of the difficulties caused by the refusal of the services even to consider a separate air force. The army and the navy hated each other and were locked in an historic and unending rivalry, but the one thing they agreed on was that there should be only two services, not three, and that air power should be attached separately to each of them for their particular uses. Meanwhile, RFC pilots were at the mercy of the likes of Immelmann and Boelcke in their Eindeckers: they were 'Fokker fodder'.

Molly came out of the bedroom and gave him progress reports from time to time – or, rather, lack-of-progress reports – and managed to seem very busy about what little she was given to do. The doctor returned at twelve, pronounced nothing doing, and went away to his dinner. Mrs Binny produced 'a light lunch, because I didn't think you'd want to be doing with a big dinner, in the circs', to which the midwife came and sat down, and ate extensively.

Jack had no appetite, thinking of Helen starving in the bedroom. He left the midwife to her second plateful and went in to see his wife, and to send Molly, who had been sitting with Helen, for her luncheon. Helen was looking strained about the eyes, but was quite calm, and assured him that no-one was keeping any secrets from him. Nurse really did think everything was going on quite normally.

Shortly after Nurse Beesely returned to duty, Molly came scuttling out to say things were moving at last, and to bid Jack telephone the doctor. Harper was already on his way back, and after his arrival there was a period of brisk activity. Just after half past two, the wail of a new baby, clearly heard through the house, made Rug lay back his ears and bark sharply. There was an anguished wait, and then Molly came out of the bedroom with a white bundle in her arms and a transformed expression on her face.

'It's a boy,' she said, placing him in Jack's arms. 'Helen's fine, you can see her in a minute, they're just tidying her up. It was amazing! I'm glad I was there, but I'm not sure I'd want to do it myself. Dogs are much better at it. But I have to say the baby's a perfect darling, much nicer-looking than I expected. More interesting than a puppy, after all.'

The baby was small, rather red and scrunched about the face, but with a beautifully shaped head covered with black hair, and delicate fingers that might have been carved out of ivory by China's most skilled master craftsman. Jack stared and stared, enchanted, trying to make himself understand that this was the creature that had been inside Helen until minutes ago, the amorphous lump that had sometimes kicked his back in the night. Already he looked so complete, so detached from them. This was his son, their son, but a quite separate human being, who would grow up to be a man in his own right, with his own character and beliefs and desires, someone impossible for Jack to imagine now, here at this beginning.

Molly's thoughts were perhaps running on similar lines.

'I can hardly believe I'm his auntie,' she said. 'It's so amazing to see him there and alive and separate and everything. Can I have him back? You'll want to go and see Helen. Dr Harper said she came through like a trouper. Look, Ruggy darling, here's your little brother! What d'you think?'

Harper came out. 'All's well. Everything was straightforward and Mrs Compton had no difficulties at all. You can come in now for a moment, and then she ought to be let sleep for an hour or two.'

Helen was sitting up in bed, propped on the pillows, the bedclothes pulled tight around her amazingly flat front, and with a soft shine in her eyes that Jack had never seen before.

'How was it?' he asked.

'Oh, not too bad. More like hard work than anything. I know now why they call it "labour".'

'But are you really all right?'

She grinned her urchin grin, so that he knew she really was. 'Yes, darling. A bit sore and rather tired, but otherwise fit to go a country mile.'

He took her hand and kissed it, too moved for words.

'I'm glad it's a boy,' Helen said. 'I wanted you to have a boy.'

'I wouldn't have minded either way. But I'm glad too. He's a fine baby.'

'*Fine?* Is that the best you can do? I want superlatives.'

'He's a superlative baby,' said Jack. 'Supremely superlative.'

'I love his hands. He has the hands of a pilot.'

'Or a pianist.'

Nurse Beesely, who had been hovering, put a stop to this nonsense. 'My patient needs to rest now,' she said possessively. 'You can come back later, when she's had a little sleep.'

Jack was expelled, and since the baby and Molly disappeared too, he took Rug out for the walk on the downs he had been longing for all day. The sharp wind turned the dog's ears inside out, and blew the cobwebs from Jack's head. It filled him with vigour and purpose. He not only had an adored wife now, he had a son too, and it was imperative that he got back into the war and did his bit to make the world safe for them. He was a man, and had a man's duty to do.

When he got back, Helen was awake, sitting up and tucking into a large boiled-egg tea – 'Just like after hunting,' Molly said – and looking so much like her old self it was a surprise all over again to see the baby tight asleep in the crib in the corner.

That evening, following long debate, they decided to call him George Edward Basil, after Helen's father, Uncle Teddy and Helen's second cousin, a wealthy bachelor who, she hoped, would be a generous godfather. Molly, however, seized on the last name, saying it suited him best, and called him 'Little Baby Basil' all evening. The name stuck and within days had become a habit.

The Derby Scheme had not been an unqualified success. Around two hundred thousand men had volunteered, and just over two million had attested, but from a census taken the previous year the War Office knew how many men fell within the age group and it was clear that vast numbers were not coming forward. So the Derby Scheme was closed, all voluntary enlistment was stopped, and on the 27th of January 1916, the Military Service Act was brought in. All British men between nineteen and forty-one were deemed to have enlisted if they resided in Great Britain and were unmarried or a widower on the 2nd of November 1915. They would have to go when called, and would have no choice in what unit they joined – though if they expressed a preference for the navy, the senior service would still have first call. A series of tribunals was set up to hear the cases of those who believed they should be exempt by reason of ill-health or occupation. The first intake would be called on the 10th of February; and those close to the government knew that the Act was to be extended in the near future to cover married men as well. There were already nearly one and a half million men whose names were 'starred' on the lists, meaning they were exempt, and it was anticipated that a great many more of those called would join them. There would simply not be enough fit unmarried men to fill the need: the married would have to bear arms too.

At Morland Place Robbie read about the Act in the newspapers, and felt justified in his decision not to 'attest' three months ago. They were only going to call unmarried men – as it should have been all along. The talk about extending conscription to married men later did not worry him. There was still his occupation to consider. Banking was essential to the nation, in war or peace. In the unlikely event that he was ever called, he reassured Ethel firmly, he would of course appeal at once, and the tribunal would soon discover the mistake.

At the beginning of February Oliver received a letter telling him he was made a second lieutenant in the RAMC, and went at once to his tailor, Henry Poole's of Savile Row, to be measured for his uniform – only to be told, to his chagrin, that there was no possibility of making anything for him within three months.

'So many of our gentlemen are going out to France,' said Meeker, who always made for him, apologetically. The Hon. Oliver Winchmore had been a customer since his father brought him to be fitted for his first suit – not as particular as his lordship, Meeker thought, nor as free-spending as his brother, Lord Hazelmere, when he was in London, but a very nice gentleman all the same, always very affable, and it pained Meeker to have to disappoint him. 'If you had only let us know sooner that a uniform was likely to be wanted,' he hinted, with a touch of reproach.

'It didn't cross my mind,' Oliver admitted. There was no

use his hoping for special treatment. Poole's would have dropped everything for his father, but Oliver was nothing of a dandy. He only went to old Meeker because his father always had and he was too lazy to change – though there was no doubt Poole's were the best, if you wanted old-fashioned quality and didn't care about the latest fashions and quirks. Chastened, he took himself off to Gorringe's where they sold uniforms ready-made.

'I think I must have very ordinary proportions,' he told his mother later, 'because everything seems to fit very well. Really, I wonder actually whether I need Meeker at all.'

'Don't say that in front of your father,' Venetia said. 'It fits quite nicely, but it doesn't have that finished look about it.' She tweaked the jacket straighter across the shoulders as he revolved in front of her. He looked heartbreakingly handsome, she thought, even in a ready-made uniform. She stroked with one finger the proud badge with its serpent-and-staff enclosed in a laurel wreath.

'I'm sure it's quite good enough for the mud and gore of Ypres,' said Oliver. 'It's not as if I'll just be toddling from parade-ground to mess and back. My illustrious brother-in-law at Headquarters might need bespoke tailoring, but this will do for me.'

'Are you sure you're going to Ypres?' Venetia asked. She remembered her brief visit there earlier in the year, the noise of constant shelling, and the continuous stream of wounded men through the aid stations. It would certainly not be a 'cushy billet'.

'That's what I asked for,' said Oliver. 'I'm just waiting for confirmation, and my departure date. They won't keep me hanging around.'

But instead of a departure date, he was sent an instruction to attend for interview at the RAMC headquarters at Millbank. On the appointed morning he was not kept long waiting in an ante-room before being admitted into the office of the Director General himself, Sir Alfred Keogh, who had been largely responsible for the reorganisation of the army medical services after the Boer War, and had been recalled from retirement in 1914 to take over his old post. He greeted Oliver warmly. He was a handsome man, with a kindly, intelligent face behind his large white moustache, and a humorous look in his eyes, as though nothing much in life could disturb him.

'How are you, my dear young man? And how is your mother? It's some years since we last met, but I hear she's doing sterling work.'

'She's very well, sir, thank you. Still operating at the Southport and the New Hospital for Women.'

'Indeed, indeed. And her research into tuberculosis? Any advance there?'

'I'm afraid not,' Oliver said.

'Ah, it's a slow business,' Keogh said, gesturing Oliver to a comfortable leather armchair beside the fire. It was a raw day outside, and the bright blaze was welcome. 'I know from my own interest in typhoid how much time and patience it takes to see any results at all. But your mother won't be put off by that. I remember her excellent report into the camps in South Africa – no detail omitted, every piece of evidence weighed meticulously. Kitchener always used to say to me that a brain like hers was wasted on a woman. You'll forgive me – he meant it as a compliment, and so do I!'

'I'm sure she would see it that way too.'

'And now you've followed her into the profession. Have you a particular field of interest?'

'Oh, I'm still making my way, sir. But when the war's over, I have a fancy to look into plastics.'

Keogh's white eyebrows rose. 'Have you indeed? Well, now, that's a surprise – though it's a young man's speciality, all right – in so far as it's anything at all. But rather the poor cousin, don't you think? What does your mother say about that? If you want to make a name for yourself in surgery, you need to delve about in the abdomen, my boy – that's where the gold is hidden. Plenty of organs to play with, and quite a few you can take out without killing the patient.'

Oliver grinned. 'I haven't got as far as thinking about making a name, sir. I've treated a lot of burn injuries, including an airman who was shot down, and I'd like to be able to do more to reconstruct what the fire took away. The pilot lived, but his hands are useless claws and his face would give his mother nightmares.'

Keogh nodded thoughtfully. 'It's an interesting notion. Hold onto the dream, my boy, if it's what you really want to do. But for the next year or so, until the war's over, it'll be saving lives that matters. There'll be no time for refinements.'

'Do you think it will be over next year, as they're saying, sir?'

'It may be,' said Keogh, cautiously. 'I'm a physician, not a soldier. But one thing I know, war always goes on longer than predicted. We thought we'd the Boer War wrapped up in 1900, but it went on another two years after that. So, now,' he reached for some papers from the table beside him, 'I see you've requested to be attached to the Leicestershire Fusiliers.'

'Yes, sir. I have a friend in the RAMC who's with them.'

'And naturally you'd like to serve with a friend. Nothing wrong with that at all. But I wonder if I can change your mind.'

Oliver felt a lowering of spirits. He had been looking forward to seeing Kit Westhoven again, and to having a friend to share his off-duty hours with. It would not be so much fun to be the new boy among strangers. But Keogh was watching his face, with one eyebrow raised and a faintly amused smile, so he swallowed his disappointment and said, 'Of course, sir, I'll serve wherever I'm needed, wherever I'll be of the most use.'

Keogh sat forward. 'Do you really mean that? It's a fine attitude, and no more than I'd expect from your mother's son. The difficulty is this, you see: since the war began, we've had a large number of young men come forward to join us – an excellent response altogether – but naturally enough, they want to go to France. That's where the excitement is. Can't blame them at all. But we've a need back here in England, too. I expect you know we've taken over certain buildings for war hospitals – and earmarked a good many more, by the by, for when they're needed – and the fact is that we're desperately short of doctors for them. Now, you can send a soldier where he's needed, but you can't make a doctor go somewhere he doesn't want to go. Physicians serve with the RAMC under quite different conditions. And, of course, we need them at the Front too. But finding a young man who'll forgo the glamour and stay in England – that's the hardest bit. Will ye do it?'

The earnest face, the warm eyes, the eager look – Oliver could no more have refused him than have kicked a puppy. 'If it's what you want, sir, of course I will.'

Keogh sat back again with a sigh of relief. 'Ah, you're a good fellow! I knew you would be. And I promise you this – you'll have your turn at the Front. You sign on for a year at a time, as you know. Give me a year in England, and I promise you you'll have your free choice for the second year – assuming you sign on again. And if I have a sudden influx of surgeons wanting to stay home, you'll be the first to be offered an overseas posting. How's that?'

Oliver smiled. 'Thank you, sir. I appreciate it. Where will I be sent, do you know?'

'I do indeed. To the Number Two General at Chelsea. We've lately lost two of our surgeons there – gone off to France. I'll have your orders made out and you'll hear in a day or two.'

He stood up and offered his hand, and Oliver stood, too, ready to take his departure. Keogh walked him courteously to the door, and said, 'My respects to your mother, if you please. She'll be busy with war work, I've no doubt, as well as her usual lists?'

'Yes, sir. She's on a number of committees, but her most pressing interest is in trying to raise mobile X-ray units for the Front.'

'Ah, yes! I've read something about that. Or was it Lord Kitchener spoke to me about it? I think it was the latter. Yes, that's it, he mentioned she'd written to him asking for his support. No official money forthcoming, I suppose? No, I didn't think so. Too many calls on the military attention just at present. But tell her not to give up – not that she would anyway. Things will change.'

Outside it had come on to sleet, and Oliver couldn't get a taxi, so he turned up his coat collar and started walking. After all that preparation, he thought, and his mother's being brave and pretending not to mind that he was going to France, it turned out that he was going no further than Chelsea! He could even continue to live at home. He wondered if she'd be pleased for her own sake, or sorry for his. But there was a war on, after all, and it was his duty to go where he was most needed. And Keogh had said he could have his choice after a year, and he was obviously a decent sort who would keep his word. He wondered how well his mother had known him. With his head down against the weather and his thoughts revolving busily, he didn't notice one cab and then another pass him with their flags up, and in the end he walked all the way home.

The Queen Hotel in Aldershot was grand and Victorian, grown a little shabby in late years but enjoying a revival of fortune since the war began. Its lounge was not the sort of place Violet had ever expected to find herself, but she was calmed during her otherwise impatient wait by watching a respectable-looking gentleman and his wife taking what was evidently a farewell tea with their subaltern son. He was a blue-eyed, rosy-cheeked young man whose embryo moustache did nothing to make him look old enough to be going. The father talked earnestly and seriously to the boy, who nodded gravely over what was surely good Christian advice; the mother kept making a curious gesture, her hand going out involuntarily to touch her boy, then being drawn back as she remembered his new dignity, and the fact that he was not her boy now, but a grown man in command of other grown men. Violet, in her new circumstances, felt an almost affectionate interest in them.

She did not recognise Laidislaw at first. He had come right up to her table and she had begun to frown at a potential impertinence before she saw who it was, and made her own involuntary gesture. The dogs stood up on their chairs and waggled their bottoms in greeting. He sat down beside her and took off his cap, and her first words were, 'Octavian! Your hair!'

He put up a self-conscious hand to touch it. 'It's regulation. They do it to everyone, almost the moment you get there. Does it look very bad?'

'No! No, not at all. It's just – different.' But she stared all the same. 'You look tired. And thinner.'

'I am tired. I've never lived such a strenuous life. Dragged from bed at some unearthly hour, marching, digging trenches, cross-country running, and then to cap it all PT lessons, as if we weren't exhausted enough. Swedish drill, they call it.'

'My poor darling!'

'And never a moment to ourselves. They don't encourage you to go off on your own, even in what's supposed to be free time. Reading is very much frowned on. They always want you to "join in" something or other. Yesterday afternoon it was a football match. I told them I wasn't interested in football but they didn't take that awfully well. Insisted I went along to cheer. *Esprit de corps*, I suppose, but I'd banked on getting out to see you. I'm so sorry I couldn't come.'

'I'm just glad you're here now,' she said, feasting her eyes on him. Now she was used to the hair, she thought the stern glamour of the uniform only enhanced his beauty. She felt the familiar stirring in her stomach of that longing for him, which seemed only to increase with the time she knew him. 'I've been thinking about you all week.'

His face creased with sympathy. 'Oh, my love, I hate to think of your waiting here all alone in the hope of my getting away.'

She knew where that line tended and tried to divert it. 'I don't mind the waiting. It's worth it just to see you. It must be worse for you. Is it really terrible?'

He shrugged, trying to make light of it. 'It's like being back at school: uncomfortable uniform, sleeping in a dormitory, cold water, shouting, peculiar rules. Only the food's rather better here,' he concluded.

'Food!' she remembered. 'I'll have them bring tea.'

The waiter had been hovering at a distance for some time and needed only a glance from her. Despite Violet's plain attire, everyone on the hotel staff had recognised quality when they saw it, and during the week the knowledge of her identity and the scandal of the previous autumn had spread among them. They were not censorious. The female employees thought the whole thing wonderfully romantic: they were accustomed to view the upper classes as existing purely for their entertainment, and did not expect them to live by the same rules as themselves. The male employees were keen that such a wealthy client should stay as long as possible and tip as freely as possible, to which end she needed to be convinced not only of their good service but of their discretion. So everyone was in league to make Violet comfortable, and if they tended rather to lurk and stare at her whenever they had the chance, that was not something she would notice in the normal course of events, having been stared at ever since she came out.

It only needed the hot water to be poured into the pot, so the waiter and a maid were soon back with the tray and the stand. There were sandwiches on the bottom level, scones on the next, and fancy cakes on top. In addition there was a plate of thin brown bread-and-butter and another of shortbread – a Scottish regiment was newly arrived in town. Violet poured the tea, Laidislaw did not wait for his cup before beginning on the sandwiches. He ate fast and furiously, and she wondered at his appetite, while thinking wistfully of the tiny delicacies he had plied her with in the early days of their relationship. She had always thought of him as too spiritual to be a great eater, and it upset her to think of his having been brought down to earth in this way, subject to the coarseness of the soldier's life. She nibbled at a piece of bread-and-butter, and listened to his description of his new regimen.

Despite having done nothing all week but wait and hope, she felt tired herself. Things seemed to have moved so quickly. One minute they were living happily at Heath Cottage, and the next they had packed up and left, to drive from the rural silence of Norfolk to this teeming military town. A letter had come, forwarded by Mrs Hudson, informing Laidislaw that he was being 'called up' and instructing him to present himself at the depot of a regular foot regiment the very next day. It was all so sudden that Violet had found it bewildering. She had heard about the Act, and known in theory that every man within the age range was potentially liable to be called; but she had never thought of its applying to her lover. Gentlemen were not conscripted, they volunteered. Perhaps at some point in the future Laidislaw would volunteer, as Holkam had – though it was impossible to think of Laidislaw carrying a gun. Unless there were some particular use for an artist at the Front, he would surely not need to go. But if ever he did, it would be as an officer, and he would depart in an orderly and dignified manner at a time of his own choosing, once his tailor had made up his uniforms; not be dragged away without warning to serve as a common soldier. Yet the letter was quite specific, and spoke harshly of the penalties of law for anyone who did not comply. There had been no choice but for Laidislaw to go. The letter had arrived on the 10th of February, the very day conscription had come into force. What species of random chance or ill luck had settled on him as one of the very first to be called? In theory she was proud that he was going to do his duty; but she was deeply in love, and in practice would have been just as proud and infinitely happier if the call had come a year from now, or two years, or indeed if the war had ended first.

They drove to Aldershot and spent their last night together in the Queen Hotel's best bedroom, and in the morning he had tried to persuade her to go back to London, to her own house, where she could be near her mother and her usual amusements.

But she had been adamant. 'I shall stay here. I must be near you. You're bound to have some free time, and then you can come and see me, but if I'm in London it would be too far if you had only an hour or two.'

'I don't know whether soldiers *have* any free time,' he said doubtfully.

'Of course they do,' she had said robustly. 'You see them all the time walking about the streets and sitting in cafés and queuing at the cinema.'

Laidislaw could not argue on that point, knowing as little about it as she did. 'But even if I can get out, it isn't likely to be very often. And this hotel isn't a suitable place for you.'

'It seems quite comfortable to me. Not exactly what I'm used to, but then neither was Heath Cottage.'

He had to admit that was true, and so he had left her there, promising to write or telephone as soon as he knew when he could come. The week had passed slowly for her. She had nothing to do but walk the dogs and look in the shop windows. She was not a reader, but by the time Saturday came round she had read every illustrated in the lounge, and had even taken to flicking through the newspapers. She sustained herself with her memories and longings; and then on Saturday he had not come. But now he was here at last. The longueurs of the week fled away, forgotten, and she was happy just to be with him, to look at him and listen as he told her what he'd been doing.

'I'm the newest of the new boys. The others have been doing everything longer than me so I've had to catch up. Fortunately, most of it isn't too difficult, just a matter of following the man in front. I must say, the parade-ground stuff does seem rather bizarre sometimes. Finding oneself in the middle of a mass of men all dressed alike and doing the same thing at the same time – it's like a strange dream. But it's satisfying, in an odd way – wheel and turn and stamp, click, click, click, like a giant machine. There's a queer sort of power to it – an excitement, if you like.'

Violet frowned. 'But weren't you in OTC at Oxford? I know Oliver and Thomas were.'

He smiled. 'Dearest, I didn't go to university. I went to art school. And if I *had* gone to Oxford, I shouldn't have joined an OTC. Not my sort of thing at all.'

'But you will be an officer?'

'Eventually, I suppose. I haven't been able to ask anyone about that yet, but some of the fellows seem to think that you have to do the basic training first, and then you are taken out for officer training.'

'And when will that be?'

'I really don't know. Several weeks at least, I should think. I'm going to be doing rifle training next week.'

'But I know you can shoot! You shoot at Aston Magna.'

'Of course, but this is a different sort of shooting. You have to learn to do it as a drill, by commands. And then there'll be other things, grenades and so on, to learn about. I suppose that takes time. Two or three weeks, anyway. They say – some of the fellows say – that it takes six months to train to be a soldier, but I can't believe that. It all seems fairly simple to me. I suppose it may be a case of going at the speed of the slowest.'

Violet refilled his cup. He had emptied the lower tiers of the stand and now began on the cakes. They were the usual teatime 'fancies' and each one was only a mouthful for him. When they were gone, only the shortbread would be left. She wondered if she should have ordered something more substantial for him. 'So, do you think you'll be here for the whole time – several weeks?'

'I don't know. I wish I did. Darling, I wish you would go back to London. I can't bear to think of you waiting here with nothing to do and no-one to talk to. You see how it's been this week. Another week I might not even be able to get out on Sunday. And what if they move me away somewhere else?'

'Then I'll follow,' she said. 'I must be near you for as long as I can. There are bound to be hotels wherever you go.'

'Like this?'

'It's comfortable enough. I have a nice sitting-room, and the staff seem very attentive.'

'But you have no friends here.'

'I can always go up to Town on the train for the day if I want to see someone. It isn't a long journey. Don't send me away, Octavian,' she concluded pathetically. 'My only joy is to be near you.'

He took her hand under the table. 'Mine, too. Oh, my darling, this damned war! If it weren't for that . . .'

'When it's over,' she said, 'what shall we do then?'

'Be together always,' he said quickly, pressing her fingers. 'We'll go abroad. You shall be my muse, and I shall paint for you. The world is full of beauty, and I want to show it all to you. And one day, perhaps, we'll tire of travelling and find a place where we'll settle down for good – the South of France, Ireland, Italy. A small house, a beautiful view, a friend or two – that's all we'll need. The west of Ireland has sunsets like the breath of God – *le pourpre d'empire*, you know. Or there's Tuscany – those hot landscapes, the cypresses, the crumbling hill towns, all the shades of fawn and gold! Wonderful Tuscan wines, and dark churches full of gilded madonnas . . .'

'Holkam will never agree to a divorce,' she said, then wished she hadn't, because he had been on a flight and she had brought him back to reality.

He looked at her then, not with his wild and shining look, his artist's look as she thought of it, but with a real, earthly tenderness that saw her as a person, not an icon. It made her feel quite hollow with love; and a little awed, because she knew absolutely that he loved her as much as she loved him, and cared for her and about her.

'It doesn't matter,' he said. 'Does it? It would make me happy if I could marry you and claim you before the world, but it won't make me unhappy if I can't. Only losing you could do that. I hope you feel the same.'

'I do,' she said, and it was like a vow, promising herself to him, for richer or for poorer.

BOOK TWO

Preparation

We're in billets again now and, barring alarms,
There'll be no occasion for standing to arms,
And you'll find if you'd many night-watches to keep
That the hour before daylight's the best hour for sleep.

We're feasting on chocolate, cake, currant buns,
To a faint, German-band obbligato of guns,
For I've noticed, wherever the regiment may go,
That we always end up pretty close to the foe.

Charles Scott-Moncrieff, 'Back in Billets'

CHAPTER EIGHT

Frank's battalion was going to the Front at last. After a whole year in what they regarded as the backwater of Malta, they were being relieved of garrison duties by a Kitchener unit coming out fresh from England. Everyone was in a ferment of excitement. The routine of square-bashing around Imtarfa Barracks, route-marching along the Mediterranean coast roads, and sampling the mild delights of Valletta on weekend passes would soon be forgotten. They were going to France, to real trenches to kill real Germans.

Packing up was a mammoth task. Kit had to be inspected, and missing items indented for. Previously lost items, already logged and replaced, reappeared in the general turning out, and caused no end of administrative confusion. Platoon officers had to inspect every inch of the camp and record any damage – a cracked window here, furtively carved initials there, a mysterious accumulation of rubbish under Hut C, which featured a detached bootsole, a sodden half-loaf of bread and a crumpled newspaper, which had apparently been used to clean a frying-pan. Soldiers had to take leave of Valletta ladies to whom they had become attached – or who had become attached to them – and there were many tears and one hastily arranged marriage.

The battalion had had a good relationship with the islanders – leaving aside one or two minor frictions, such as the Valletta Christian Ladies' Committee objecting to the soldiers' bathing in the nude, a regrettable spillage on the carpet at the Floriana Soldiers' Club, and a disputed one and sixpence allegedly owed to a vociferous fruit-seller. On departure day the governor of the island paid the Rifles the compliment of inspecting them, and made an emotional speech of farewell and praise. The whole town turned out to cheer them on their way as they marched down to the Custom House Quay. In the harbour the ships had dressed overall in their honour, giving an air of festivity to the occasion. There were two bands playing, and the Barracas were packed with people cheering and waving flags. When the SS *Amazon* finally steamed out of harbour, she was escorted by a bobbing mass of local boats, and sent off to a cacophony of ships' hooters, with the conflicting strains of 'Auld Lang Syne' and 'Rule Britannia' blaring from the two bands, who hadn't been able to agree on which was the more appropriate.

After the excitement of the send-off, the sea journey was something to be endured. The men had comfortable berths on the ship and ample food was provided, but the weather was wet and windy and the seas rough, and many of them were not in a condition to enjoy the cruise. But at Marseilles, despite the rain, another crowd waited to cheer their arrival, which raised their spirits for the long train journey north. The men were packed into the usual cattle trucks, furnished with fresh straw – they had heard about them, but it was the first time they had experienced them, and their reaction was divided between indignation and raucous amusement. The officers were assigned two proper coaches, and while the long process of loading the baggage and horses was going on, they were allowed off in batches to get a meal. Frank and his particular friend Prendergast went off with Freddie Mascall and 'Jock' Langley to a restaurant in a narrow street beside the Hôtel Bristol, where they dined well, and astonishingly cheaply, on mussels in garlic, ham hock cooked with lentils, and cheese, accompanied by a rough but delicious local wine. Then they shopped for supplies for the journey, and went back to the train laden with biscuits, jam, cheese, sardines, chocolate, bread, bottles of wine and beer, and a two-foot-long garlic sausage. The latter was *sotto voce* enough out in the cold of the evening, but began to sing rather noticeably when the confines of the compartment were warmed by the heat of their bodies.

There was no other heat: the heating-pipe had not been connected, and as they travelled further north and the rain turned to sleet, the cold began to creep up on them. It was a long journey: it took thirty-six hours to reach Paris, broken only by a fifty-minute stop at lunchtime the next day and an hour stop for dinner, at both of which the officers were allowed to dash out for a quick meal. The men had been issued with their rations in Marseilles, but at the stops they were provided with hot coffee, and there were various vendors trundling up and down the station platforms to supply hot pies, buns and chocolate to those who had money.

The next morning when they woke there was snow on the ground. As the train steamed with agonising slowness through the flat countryside everyone was stiff and cold, missing the Mediterranean mildness and the comforts of the island. But they cheered themselves with the thought that at least they were going to the Front. In the late afternoon they reached their destination, detrained, and marched as best they could through the slippery sleet and mud to the transit camp at Étaples.

It was not a pretty place. The grey and moody sea beat on the empty shore. Sand dunes separated it from a flat, bleak landscape of salt-marsh and spoiled farmland, across which was pitched a forest of tents that bulged and shrank under the onslaught of the bitter wind. They were miles from the Front, and the word began to filter round that they would not be travelling on tomorrow, or any day soon. They were to remain here for 'further training', which might go on for weeks or even months.

The general degree of fed-upness was thicker than a marsh fog, as the battalion settled down and tried to sleep. All night the wind banged the canvas above them and hooned about the tent poles, sending searching icy fingers down the least crack between neck and blanket. But the cooks were up early the next day, and the issue of hot tea and a hot breakfast did something to restore spirits. A sack of mail continued the process; and there was better news from the CO – first, that they were to be issued with cold-weather kit (for they were still in their Mediterranean drills), and second, that while the period of further training continued, every man and officer in the battalion was to be allowed off in rotation for the long-promised leave.

As soon as Frank learned the date of his release, he dashed off notes to the family at home and a letter to Maria. He was worried about her. He had written his condolence to her after hearing the news about her father, and had received a stilted and formal note from her mother in return. Since then, Jessie said she had not heard any more from Maria, and Emma's letter to her in January had not received a reply. Frank wanted to know that everything was all right with her, that she was not grieving too much for her father, that her mother was coping with her sudden widowhood. He felt in the circumstances, and having set the precedent with his letter of condolence, that it would not be too forward of him to write to her direct. He worked hard over the wording, trying to make it formal enough not to upset the mother's ideas of propriety, but warm enough to give some comfort and reassurance to Maria. In it, he proposed to call on them as soon as he arrived in England.

No reply came, and Frank's anxiety grew. Was she too grieved to write, or was her mother forbidding it? Did Mrs Stanhope think him an unsuitable suitor, or had Maria changed her mind about him? Perhaps she had met someone else and didn't know how to tell him. Perhaps the strain of her father's death had made her ill. With nothing to go on, his imagination took free rein. Perhaps she had caught pneumonia at the funeral and died. Perhaps there had been a Zeppelin raid on Wimbledon and the bodies of Maria and her mother lay crushed under the rubble of 21 Ruskin Avenue.

He fretted all through the journey home, by train to Boulogne, on the boat across to Dover, on the train up to London. London seemed full of soldiers – there was so much khaki in every direction he felt as if he had never left camp – but on the District Railway to Wimbledon he found himself among civilians again, going home from work. It was not as cold as it had been in France, but it was wet, the rain falling steadily, blown in gusts by a fitful wind, blattering against the windows. At the station everyone turned up his or her collar against the cheerless evening and scurried off into the darkness, eager for home and supper.

Frank walked fast through the rain, glad to note there was no sign of bomb damage in the identical streets of neat villas. The exertion warmed him and his natural optimism rose a little. There must be some simple explanation for why she hadn't written – a letter gone astray, most likely, he thought. But when he reached the house, it stood in darkness; and when he walked up the path towards the front door, he could see through the bay window that the room beyond it was empty, not just of people but of furniture. It seemed as though they had gone away without telling him.

He went to the house next door, and rang the bell. After a prolonged wait the door was answered by a small man with a grey cardigan under his jacket and a trace of something on his moustache. Given the penetrating odour of haddock wafting out behind him from the region of the dining-room, Frank guessed that he had interrupted the household's supper, and began with an apology. 'I came to see Mrs and Miss Stanhope, next door, but there's no-one there, and I wondered if you knew where they were.'

The little man answered him in an accent of strained

gentility. 'I'm afraid I don't. We weren't really on *intimate* terms with them, you see. Kept themselves very much to themselves, the Stanhopes,' he added, rather sniffily. 'We didn't even know Mr Stanhope had died until the day of the funeral when the hearse drew up outside. Then the next thing we knew they were gone, and that was that. Thirteen years we've lived next door to them, and not so much as a goodbye. So where they've gone I couldn't tell you.' He eyed Frank curiously but with respect.

Frank guessed that his uniform was responsible for the civility's outweighing the indignation. 'How long ago did they leave?' he asked.

'Ooh, must be a month at least, maybe more.'

'And they didn't leave a forwarding address?'

'Never said a word. Whether they left one with the estate agent or the post office I couldn't tell you.' His pique overcame him, and he said, 'Thirteen years, and never even the courtesy to say they were going. Thought themselves a cut above, that's the truth of it. I'm very sorry for their bereavement, but it has to be said they weren't what you'd call neighbourly. The new people come next week and it's to be hoped they'll be friendlier.'

Frank thanked him and departed. He tried the house on the other side, where his reception was more kindly. A servant answered the door, he was shown in, and the lady of the house received him; but she had little more to add. While obviously longing to ask him what his connection with the family was, she could only repeat that the Stanhopes had gone away without saying where. She did mention that Mrs Stanhope had been devastated by her husband's death, poor soul, *quite* gone to pieces, refused to see anyone and never left the house. She, the neighbour, had called several times to offer her condolences but the servant had always said her mistress wasn't receiving.

She tried in a sidelong manner to ply Frank with questions, but he extricated himself politely and left. Outside in the street he concluded there was nothing more he could do that night, and retraced his steps to the station. He would go up to Town, find himself lodgings for the night, and – most urgently, for he hadn't eaten since breakfast – have dinner. Tomorrow he would go to Maria's place of work and find her. She was assistant librarian at University College. Old Benson, her chief, didn't like anyone talking to his staff during working hours, but Old Benson – in the vernacular of soldiers, which had by now attached itself to Frank's academic vocabulary – could jolly well lump it.

It was strange to be back at University College after all this time. The building looked at once familiar and unreal, homelike and yet nothing to do with him. Winters was the beadle on duty in the lodge, and saluted him smartly. 'Mr Compton, sir. Very nice to see you back here, sir. On leave, is it?'

'Yes, Winters. I left Étaples yesterday.'

'Eat Apples, sir? I got a nephew passed through there only last month, on his way to the Front. Reg'lars. He'll be banging away at Jerry by now. Heard you was in Malta, sir, with the Terriers. Not seen any action yet, I suppose?'

'Not yet, I'm afraid,' Frank admitted, admiring the economy of Winters's style. In just a few words he had elevated his nephew and demolished any pretence Frank might have to being a soldier.

'You'll get your turn, sir, one o' these days,' Winters said kindly. 'Plenty for everyone before this lot's finished. Come to do some research?'

'I've come to see Miss Stanhope,' Frank said, perfectly sure the beadles knew everything about his romance.

Winters looked surprised. 'Miss Stanhope from the lib'ry? You're too late, arencha?'

'Too late?' Frank's blood ran cold.

'Gorn, sir,' said Winters, smartly.

'Gone?'

'Left. Don't work here no more.' He lowered his head towards Frank's and added sepulchrally, 'Heard she'd been sacked, sir, between you and me. Taking days off, coming in late, not attending to her work properly, that sort o' thing. What with her father dying, was what *we* heard.' *We* signifying the fraternity of beadles. 'But Mr Benson, you know what he's like. Wouldn't take an excuse from a corpse, he wouldn't, and he never did hold with females anyway.' He straightened up and looked at Frank with the satisfaction of having been the harbinger of ill.

Frank collected himself. 'You don't know where she went, I suppose, do you?' He allowed his hand to stray towards his pocket, to signify the seriousness of the matter.

Winters eyed the hand with regret. 'Well, sir, no, I don't. I never heard nothing about that.' He searched about to be helpful. 'You tried her at home?'

'Yes, but she and her mother have moved away, I don't know where. There was no address left.'

Winters shook his head slowly, still thinking. 'I dunno what to say, sir. Mebbe they'd have gone to stay with some relative or other?'

'Very likely. But I don't know anything about her relatives.'

'Wasn't there an aunt, sir, lived out Hammersmith way?'

'Yes, of course! Why didn't I think of that? Not an aunt, but a cousin of her mother's, Mrs Wilberforce. I met her once when she chaperoned Miss Stanhope. But I don't know her address.'

'I do know it was Riverside Mansions, sir, them big flats next the bridge. I heard Miss Stanhope mention it once to young Ballins – you know, the front-hall beadle – because he lives out that way himself, and the lady what his mum worked for lived there. Riverside Mansions,' he repeated, pleased with himself. 'I dunno what number, sir, but they'd know there all right. Oh, thank you, sir, thank you very much! Glad I could 'elp, sir.' He pocketed the coin and saluted again.

'Bad case o' love there,' he murmured to himself, as he

watched Frank hurry away. 'I hope he finds her all right. Nice young lady.'

Frank walked down Gower Street to Euston Square station and took the underground railway to Hammersmith. Mrs Wilberforce, Riverside Mansions. Surely she would know where Maria was. Maria had lost her job, and she and her mother had left the house; the neighbour said Mrs Stanhope had been distraught. Added together it suggested some trouble beyond the death of her father. Why hadn't she written to him? Or to Jessie or Emma? The train clamoured its way across north Paddington and then southward on the Metropolitan Railway Extension through Shepherd's Bush to Hammersmith. It ran above ground all the way, and the rain lashed drearily against the windows from a lowering sky, while Frank fretted to the rhythm of the wheels.

It was not far from the station to the bridge, and he found the mansions easily, a tall, square block of Victorian flats in smoke-stained red brick with dirty white trim, which sat beside the river, overshadowed by the span of the bridge. There was no porter in the hall, but a legend on the wall gave the names of the residents, and Mrs Wilberforce's was there, thank God. The lift was somewhere up above and, impatient now, he didn't wait for it but ran up the stairs two at a time to the fourth floor.

Mrs Wilberforce herself answered the door, blinking at him in a puzzled way. He said, 'Mrs Wilberforce, I'm Frank Compton. We met last year when I escorted you and Miss Stanhope to the exhibition at the Royal Academy.'

Recognition spread over her face, and she fluttered, moving her hands ineffectually, and half glancing back over her shoulder as if she feared being overheard. 'Oh! Mr Compton! Of course, I recognise you now. It was the uniform. How – how did you know . . . ? I mean, what brings you here?'

'I'm looking for Miss Stanhope and her mother. I hoped you might know where they are,' he said simply.

She looked at him for a moment, seeming to debate internally, then sighed and said, 'I *told* her it would be no good. You had better come in – but quietly, if you please. Sadie – Mrs Stanhope – is asleep. I've only just managed to get her off.'

'They're here?' Frank said, with lifting joy in his voice.

'Sadie is. Maria's at work. Come in, and I'll tell you about it.'

The flat seemed dark and stuffy, with tall but narrow windows that let in little of the day's poor light. There was brown linoleum on the floor, brown paint on the doors, brown wallpaper and a faint brown smell of soup and dust and shoes and tea leaves. Mrs Wilberforce conducted him into a parlour, overstuffed with furniture and knick-knacks, and dark from the heavy velvet drapes at the window. There was no fire lit in the grate, but there was so little moving air in the flat that it did not seem particularly cold. She invited him to sit down, and took an armchair herself. He perched on the slippery curve of a black horsehair sofa, and begged her to begin.

'Sadie told me about your letter of condolence after Ronald died, so I know you know about that,' she said. 'It was very sudden, though of course to be expected, given his age, and he had never been in what I'd call *robust* health. But it was a shock all the same. Sadie didn't take it too well, and Maria had to stay at home with her for a few days – well, that was the beginning of it. But then as things emerged . . .'

She paused, looking at Frank speculatively. She was a stout, elderly woman with a front of grey curls in the style made fashionable by Queen Alexandra, which, combined with her brown eyes and long nose, gave her rather the look of a poodle. But the eyes were sharp and her expression sensible. She clasped her hands in her lap and went on, 'I'm not sure Maria would want me to tell you all this. But on the other hand, you *have* come here looking for her, which suggests . . . May I ask, what is your intention towards Maria?' She watched his face keenly for his reaction.

'I love her, and I hope to marry her,' he said. 'I hope she feels the same way about me. But I have to admit that there is no engagement between us. And, of course, I'm in the army now for the duration of the war, which makes things a little awkward. I have no establishment to offer her.'

She nodded, as though he had confirmed something she knew. 'I think I understand. I guessed it from what Maria said – and things she didn't say, too. I think, in the circumstances, you ought to know. You see, when Ronald died, he left matters in a poor way for Sadie and Maria. I hope you won't be offended if I talk about money?'

'Please go ahead,' Frank said, though his heart sank a little. He hoped she hadn't got the wrong idea about him from his relationship with Morland Place and the fact that Jessie was Violet Holkam's intimate friend. He had once had to scold Maria for saying she was not of his station in life. If this was a revival of that old nonsense . . .!

'Very well,' said Mrs Wilberforce. 'Ronald, you see, had a pension from his time as a schoolmaster, and that was pretty much what the family lived on, along with Maria's wages. Sadie has very little of her own. But the pension died with him, and when Maria came to look into it, there were hardly any savings. She and Sadie had always assumed he had been putting something away for them, but it turned out that there was nothing. Sadie took it very badly. Her nerves went and she took to her bed, and Maria had to stay home and look after her. Well, Maria's wages were hardly enough for them to get by on as it was, and when she lost her job . . .'

'I'm so sorry. I had no idea,' Frank said abjectly. He couldn't bear to think of the worry Maria must have gone through.

'No. She would never have told you, silly girl. Well, there was nothing for it but to give up the house. Fortunately I have a spare bedroom, and I was able to take them in. Sadie and I grew up together, almost like sisters, and I'd always said to her that if ever the day came when she was on her own – because, of course, Ronald was much older than her – she could come and live with me. But she's still suffering from her nerves, and hardly gets out of bed.'

'But why didn't Maria tell me?' Frank asked. 'I wrote saying I was coming home on leave and that I wanted to see her, and she didn't reply. I didn't even know where she was. Perhaps she didn't get the letter?'

Mrs Wilberforce shook her head. 'Oh, she had it – they have their letters forwarded by the post office. But poor Sadie said she'd be ashamed for you to know how badly they were left, and Maria agreed with her. "Better he forgets about us," she said.' A sudden qualm seemed to come over her. 'I hope I'm doing right by telling you?'

'God, yes!' Frank said. 'What can she have been thinking? Did she imagine I wouldn't love her just because her father left no money?'

Mrs Wilberforce said slowly, 'Sadie was ashamed because they had to sell the furniture to pay for the funeral. Well, to be frank with you, there wouldn't have been room for it here, so they'd have had to sell it anyway. But something like that is never easy for a person to admit, even to herself. I think Maria didn't want you to feel sorry for them. And then there's the job. Ronald and Sadie never liked her having to go out to work, but at least it was at the university, which was respectable, and Maria liked it. She'd always wanted to go to university herself, but that wasn't possible. The library job was the next best thing. But now she's working at the café—'

'The café? What café?'

'She had to have a job of some sort, and the only thing she could get nearby was at the Kardomah in King Street.' Mrs Wilberforce looked at him pleadingly, and Frank saw that, despite what she had said, she was afraid he might feel after all that he couldn't love a waitress and it would be her fault for telling him.

'Is she there now?' Frank asked.

'Yes, of course.'

He stood up. 'Would you forgive me? I must go and see her straight away.'

Mrs Wilberforce stood too, smiling with relief. 'I'm so glad. I knew I was right about you. As soon as I saw you, I knew you wouldn't – well, they've both been so upset lately, they're probably not thinking clearly. But I knew you were a real gentleman.'

Frank took her hand and pressed it. 'Thank you for telling me everything. You did the right thing.'

'Oh, goodness, I do hope so. But I'm afraid Maria will be angry. She's very strong-headed.'

The Kardomah café was busy with its mid-morning trade, ladies in hats having coffee together, a lone soldier in khaki reading the newspaper over a poached egg on toast, elderly people of both sexes eking out a pot of tea for the sake of the warmth and the company it bought them. Frank looked around impatiently. A thin waitress with a chronic sniff approached him and said, 'Can I show you to a table, sir?'

He gestured her away with his hand. 'No, thank you. I'm looking for—' He saw her at that moment, coming through the swing door from the kitchen with a tray. His heart lurched at the sight of her, and then lurched again with pity as he took in the black dress and white apron and cap. That his lovely Maria should be brought to this! He went after her as she turned towards the back of the café, brushing past the thin girl without hearing what she said.

He reached Maria as she stopped at a table and began to unload teapot, milk, sugar and a plate of Scotch pancakes before two middle-aged women in woollen coats and last year's hats. He had just enough sense not to speak to her or grab her arm until she had completed the task; but as she turned round and found him standing there the shock was so great that she dropped the empty tray and went quite white. For a moment as her hand faltered at her throat he thought she might actually faint; but she steadied almost at once, and said in a low voice, 'What are you doing here?'

He bent to pick up the tray. 'Why did you go away without telling me?' he countered.

'How did you find me?'

'I went to your cousin's to see if she knew where you were, and she told me you were here.'

'But how did you—?'

'Excuse *me*, miss! Would you mind awfully not standing there right in front of our table?' said one of the women, in a tone of deep affront. She added to her friend, with no attempt at lowering her voice, 'Carrying on with a soldier like that, quite shameless. These modern girls!'

Maria's face now flushed painfully, and she brushed past Frank and walked briskly away. He hurried after her, hearing the tutting going on behind him. He caught her arm, and she turned on him, her eyes angry. 'Doesn't it occur to you that if I didn't tell you where I was it was because I didn't want to see you?'

'I don't believe it. That isn't like you. If you'd stopped caring for me you'd have told me so.'

'Perhaps you don't know me as well as you think you do,' she said, and then, glancing over her shoulder, 'You must go. The manageress is looking, and I can't afford to lose this job. *Please* go away.'

He shook his head firmly. 'It's no good, I have to talk to you. Can you get out for five minutes?'

'Not possibly.'

'Please!'

'Oh—!' An exasperated sigh. 'Go round to the back, then – there's an alley to the side – and wait for me by the kitchen door. I'll try to slip out. Go now – quickly.' She shrugged herself free and turned away, walking towards the swing door with her head up. Frank saw the manageress on the far side start towards him with eviction in her eye. He hurried out onto the street.

He found the alley, and went down it to an area behind the café's back door where there were dustbins and collections of empty crates, and a pig bucket full of crusts and vegetable peelings. Cabbage-smelling steam issued from the vent of a frosted window, and the sooty back wall of the building in the next street blocked out the light. It was a depressing place, and it hurt him to think it must already be familiar to Maria. He waited five minutes, ten, and began to think she wasn't coming; fifteen minutes, and then the door opened and she stepped out, and at once shivered in her thin waitress uniform.

'I couldn't get away. She's watching me – Miss Hayman. I don't want to lose this job. The tips are good. So be quick. Say what you want to say and then go.'

'Maria, I don't deserve this. What have I done?'

'*Nothing*. But it's impossible between us. You don't understand.'

'I do. Your aunt told me everything.'

That gave her pause. She scanned his face. He wanted to rip the foolish muslin and ribbon from her hallowed head, sweep her into his arms, kiss her into submission. She spoke now in a lower voice. 'Then you know how impossible it is.'

'Do you really think I care about that? I know it must have been very hard for your mother to find herself penniless. But the idea that I should think less of you because of it is frankly insulting. I love you, Maria. Tell me you don't love me and I'll go away, but don't expect me to swallow nonsense about the difference in our stations, or whatever it is that's bothering you.'

'There *is* a difference in our stations,' she insisted.

He couldn't help smiling. 'You are *so* stubborn! Listen to me, my beloved idiot: you are a gentlewoman and I am a gentleman, and neither of us has any money or expectations. So we are absolutely even. You've had such a hard few months, and I blame myself for not leaving things in better order with you before I went abroad. But I'm going to sort everything out now. Unless you *really* don't love me any more?' he finished, with sudden trepidation.

She sighed, and the tension went out of her shoulders. 'I love you,' she said, 'so much it hurts.'

He took the last step towards her and enfolded her in his arms, and felt her yield softly against him. He kissed the top of her head tenderly. 'My darling,' he said huskily.

In a moment he felt her stir. 'I must go back.'

He wanted to protest, but he saw the sense of it. He could not yet urge her to quit, when he had nothing immediately to give her.

She released herself and looked up at him. 'What now?'

He had been thinking rapidly. If he got engaged to her, it would leave her with assurance, but nothing else. More drastic action was needed.

'Will you marry me?' he said.

She almost laughed. 'Is that a proposal?'

'I mean now – at once. I have two weeks' leave before I go back to France. We can get a special licence. Listen to me: if we are married, I can have half my pay sent to you, so you won't have to be a waitress. And if we're married I can ask my sister and mother to keep an eye on you, so that if anything goes wrong again when I'm overseas you'll have someone to turn to for help.'

Now she did laugh, not from amusement but relief. 'I have to go back in. Can we talk about it tonight, after work?'

'At least tell me that you'll marry me.'

'I'll marry you. But there's a lot to think about.'

'What time do you finish here?'

'Half past seven.'

'I'll be waiting for you here, on this spot,' he promised.

She was late, and looked very tired. 'I had to clear up, and Miss Hayman kept finding me more things to do. She found out I'd slipped out to see you, and she was very angry, but she hadn't actually seen me go out or come back in so she couldn't sack me. Oh, I'm so tired, and my feet hurt.'

'I went back to see your cousin – your mother was still asleep – and told her we'd decided to get married, and in the circumstances she agreed that we could go out for a meal together this evening without a chaperon.'

'Dear Cousin Sonia! Mother would never have said that.'

'So I'm taking you to the White Hart Hotel, just along the road here, which is terribly respectable but nice and quiet. I hope you're hungry.'

'Starving.'

There was nothing about the sight of a young woman eating dinner with a soldier to raise any curiosity; and in fact their waiter decided for himself that it was a farewell meal for a soldier going overseas and treated them with sentimental kindness that involved sighing a great deal whenever he was near their table, and leaving them blessedly alone for long periods. Frank never remembered what they had eaten. He was too busy relishing the sense of freedom he had, not only in being with Maria again, but in being with her as her declared suitor. Why had he not done it long before? Now there were no doubts or reservations between them, and they talked more comfortably and satisfyingly than ever.

They discussed their plans. 'I suppose you'll have to stay with your cousin while I'm away. But that flat seems so dark and depressing.'

'Oh, it's not so bad. Cousin Sonia's a dear, and she's company for Mother, especially when I'm at work. They grew up together, you know.'

'But it must be cramped there. You're sharing a room with your mother, aren't you?'

'I don't mind that, but I must confess I don't enjoy sharing the bed. Mother's so restless, she wakes me up – and then *she* falls asleep, and her snoring keeps *me* awake. But while you're away, I don't see what else there is to be done.'

Frank didn't either. An officer's pay was not much, and he had to settle his mess bills out of it, pay for his laundry, buy cigarettes and soap and so on. Even if he was frugal, and sent Maria all that was left, it would not be enough for her to set up a separate home for her and her mother. As a married woman she *could* live alone, but he didn't want her to, and knew that her mother and cousin would not approve. There seemed no alternative to her sharing the dark, musty flat at Riverside Mansions. But at least as an officer's wife she would be able to stop waitressing.

They got down to plans. 'What I propose is that we get married next week by special licence. That will give us four or five days for our honeymoon.'

She blushed at the word and the thought behind it, and covered it by saying briskly, 'And what do we do until then?'

'We have to go to Yorkshire, so we might as well have a few days there. Anyway, it would look churlish to dash up and then away again.'

'Go to Yorkshire? You mean to see your family? Go to Morland Place?' She seemed to shrink.

'Darling! You can't be scared of that!'

'But it's so old and splendid, and your family's so grand: your uncle the squire, your mother visiting the tenants and so on. I wouldn't know what to do with myself. I wouldn't fit in at all.'

'Mother and Uncle Teddy aren't the least bit grand, and you've met Jessie.'

'*She*'s grand.'

'Oh, she isn't! And Emma will be there, too, and you know Emma.'

'Emma's even grander. She's an *heiress* – fabulously rich.'

He realised she was teasing him now. 'Well, I want to show you off to them – and I couldn't possibly get married without telling them, and letting them meet you. They'd be dreadfully hurt. And, of course, they are expecting to see me, so I'll have to fit in a visit to them anyway, before I go back.'

'Go back!' She reached across the table for his hand, and her eyes were momentarily bleak.

'I know. I don't want to leave you either. But it will be better to be married and apart than to be apart the way we were before, with nothing settled between us.'

'Will it? I don't know. It's a case of having so much more to lose.'

'We won't lose it.' He didn't pretend not to know what she was thinking. 'I told Jessie at the beginning that I have a strong feeling I shall come through all right. I might get wounded, perhaps, but nothing more than that. And when the war ends we'll have our whole lives before us, to be together.'

The waiter arrived beside them just in time to hear the last words, and his sigh was so profound it stirred their hair. 'Coffee, madam, sir? Would you like to take it here, or in the lounge?' He bent a little closer and said, 'It's probably quieter here than in the lounge. More private, like.'

Frank ordered coffee and the waiter went away with a lingering glance. They looked at each other across the table and laughed. 'I think he thinks we're young people in love,' Maria said.

'Well, aren't we?'

'Much more. I feel as if we're married already,' she said.

'How shocking! But I assure you, Miss Stanhope, that being married to me will be an experience so extraordinary and wonderful that nothing in your imagination can come close.'

'I haven't the least doubt of it,' she said, and her smile made his knees feel weak.

'He wants to marry a waitress?' Henrietta said in perplexity.

'That's what he said.' Teddy was just as puzzled. 'He's bringing her to see us.'

'Oh dear. I hope he hasn't got her into trouble.'

'Not Frank, surely. He's always been so sensible and level-headed. And he's never been interested in women.'

'But that's it, you see. He's so very innocent. And he's a soldier now, and you know how some women throw themselves at soldiers. She might have trapped him.'

'Well, if she has, that won't be a way out for him, if I know Frank. He'll insist on doing the right thing.'

'I shouldn't want him to be any other way,' Henrietta said stoutly, but they looked at each other in deep gloom.

When the news was relayed to Jessie and Emma, they were even more puzzled. 'You can't have got it right,' Jessie protested.

Teddy looked defensive. 'Well, you know what public telephones are like. The line was bad and I think there were railway trains in the background. He sounded rather agitated and I couldn't catch everything he said, but he definitely said she was a waitress and he was bringing her to see us. Said something about rescuing her—'

'Oh dear!' Henrietta said, as images of fallen women rushed through her mind again.

'But this is silly,' Jessie said. 'Frank's in love with a very nice young woman who works at the university. She's a librarian. Emma and I have met her.'

'I never heard about that,' Teddy said. To Henrietta, 'Did *you* know?' She shook her head.

'He didn't want anyone to know,' Jessie said. 'He didn't have any prospect of supporting her for years, so he couldn't ask her to marry him. He told me, because he wanted me to write to her while he was overseas. And Emma met her when I was in London.'

'She was very nice,' Emma said. 'Clever and funny and – well, you could see why Frank loved her.'

'I wonder what's gone wrong,' Jessie said. 'I *told* him he ought to propose before he went to Malta. Now I suppose she's met someone else – that would explain why she didn't answer your letter, Em.'

'Heartless girl! And now poor Frank's stumbled heart-broken into the arms of an adventuress,' Emma said indignantly.

'I'm not sure an adventuress would be wise to pick on Frank. He hasn't any money,' Henrietta said, trying to keep at least one finger on reality.

'Are adventuresses wise?' Jessie asked.

'Probably she knows he's *my* nephew and assumes I'll pay up,' Teddy said. 'Well, if it's anything like *that*, we shall have to put a stop to it right away. You'll take Frank aside and talk to him, Hen, while I see the girl off.'

'Unless . . .' She nodded significantly, not wanting to say the words out loud. But if there was a child on the way . . .

Teddy closed his hand over hers. 'Don't worry. We'll sort everything out. At least he has the sense and good manners to bring her here *before* he marries her.'

After the bewilderment and anxiety of the prologue, it was such a huge relief to everyone when the betrothed turned out to be Maria after all, that she could have been much less agreeable than she was and still have been welcomed. Jessie and Emma laughed delightedly and presented her to Uncle Teddy in such terms that his remaining gravity melted away.

Knowing Jessie and Emma already helped Maria overcome her initial shyness, and once she had chatted for a while to Henrietta and Teddy, she impressed both of them with her good sense and virtue. For her part, she found Henrietta motherly and sympathetic, while Teddy was so obviously what he seemed – a big-hearted, kindly man without guile, fond of his family and his comfort, and always ready to enjoy himself – that she liked him at once.

Teddy was fascinated by her, wanted to keep her by him all day and talk and listen so that he could get to the bottom of her. He was not used to intellectual women and had always suspected they might be *lusus naturae*, awkward and prickly and rather alarming. But Maria he found womanly and delightful, even while he marvelled at the workings of her mind, and thought it a pity such mental horsepower could not be harnessed to some national problem that needed solving. His conclusion, delivered at dinner that evening, was 'You and Frank are both such brainboxes, you'll have wonderful clever children.' It made Maria blush, but said all that needed to be said about approval and acceptance.

Maria went to bed that night exhausted by the new images and information she had had to take in. The house was so big and rambling, and there were so many people to sort out, as well as a swathe of children in the nursery and what seemed like a host of servants. She liked the dogs, the big fires, the family portraits on the walls, the smell of the house – a mixture of beeswax and woodsmoke, lavender and old wood. She liked bright, sharp, pretty Polly, who examined her with such a frank lack of tact or reserve, before deciding she would do. She liked gentle, vague Aunt Alice who reminded her a little of her mother, but who, she suspected, might have more common sense than her own parent. She was worried about Ethel, who would be her sister-in-law and seemed rather standoffish, and brother Robert, who was obviously completely under Ethel's thumb, and inclined to be a little grand towards her. She was overawed by the butler, who was like something out of a twopenny novel disconcertingly come to life.

And this was only the household! Tomorrow she would be shown the estate. As she lay in the unfamiliar bed in the unfamiliar room with the strange creaking sounds of the ancient house troubling her, a large part of her wanted to creep out of bed and run away, rather than have to face the multitude of new experiences. Two familiar images came at last to steady her: Frank and the Kardomah café.

The next day serious talks had to be had about the wedding itself and the immediate arrangements for Frank's leave and his departure. Teddy wanted them to get married at Morland Place, in the chapel. 'If you're marrying by special licence it doesn't matter where it comes off, so it might as well be here so that we can make a fine "do" of it.'

Maria looked her alarm at Frank, and he said, 'I think Maria wants to be with her own people, Uncle. She wants to get married in London with her mother and her cousin.'

'Well, they can come up here, can't they? Plenty of room for everyone.'

'My mother isn't in very robust health. I don't think she could stand the railway journey,' Maria said.

'Oh, I'm sorry to hear that. Then I'll send the motor for them. Every comfort, rugs, foot-warmers, luncheon basket. Simmons is a wonderful smooth driver. It'll be like travelling in her own bed.'

Maria thought of the effect 'all this' would have on her mother, who cared so much more than Maria ever had about their poverty and the shame of a daughter going out to work. Morland Place would impress her no end. It might comfort her to know that her daughter was to be distantly connected to it; but on the other hand Maria doubted her nerves could cope with it. And Cousin Sonia would be made profoundly uncomfortable. She didn't want the shabbiness of her life placed in full juxtaposition to 'all this' so that everyone could see it. And she didn't want Mother's expectations raised: she could imagine the lifetime of querulous complaints and requests that would face her if Mother got the idea that Frank was entitled to any of it.

'No,' she said firmly. 'Thank you very much for offering, but we'd rather get married quietly in London.'

Disappointment to an epic degree buckled Teddy's face and both he and Polly were evidently going to protest, but Henrietta, though she felt it just as keenly, said, 'I expect the young people have the right idea. It must be as Maria wants, Teddy. They have little enough time together before Frank goes back and they won't want to waste it on all the fuss of a big wedding.'

Teddy subsided, though with the uncomprehending look of a hurt dog, and Jessie pinched Polly hard to stop her expressing *her* opinion.

Later that day Teddy invited the young couple into the steward's room for a 'little talk'. Maria went with uncomfortable feelings. Having snubbed him over the wedding, she expected to find him resentful and ready to raise difficulties for them. But he had evidently put aside his disappointment, for the first thing he said, with an expansive gesture of his hands, was, 'Now, you must tell me what you want for a wedding present. And don't hold back. I won't be fobbed off with some trumpery nonsense. It must be something big that you both really want or need. Frank, you know I mean what I say. Maria, my dear, you must allow me the satisfaction of seeing you excited and pleased. Name it and it's yours.'

Maria was already demurring, her cheeks hot with embarrassment at the whole situation, but Frank knew there would be no peace if they did not satisfy Uncle's generosity. And it came to him suddenly that there was something they both wanted and needed.

'Well, sir,' he said, 'you could give us the lease of a little place where Maria could live with her mother while I'm away at the war. Just a flat or tiny house with two bedrooms, and it need only be a short lease, just until the war's over. When I come back, I'll support them myself, but I can't do it on army pay.'

Teddy frowned in thought, and Maria was horrified, thinking Frank had asked for far too much. Teddy had meant a tea service or a clock or something, and now he was selecting the words to express his shock at their presumption. She began to stammer something, some retraction, but he didn't hear her, and Frank pinched her arm to make her stop. Then Teddy said, 'Of course, if that's what you want you shall have it. But, my dear child,' he looked kindly on Maria, 'why don't you come and live here until the war's over? You'd be much more comfortable.'

'Thank you, sir,' Maria said faintly, 'but I couldn't leave my mother.'

'Bring her too,' Teddy said expansively. 'Plenty of room.'

'But you see,' Maria went on uncomfortably, 'she wouldn't want to be so far from her cousin. They grew up together like sisters, and particularly at this time, my father just having died . . .'

For a moment it looked as though Teddy was going to invite Mrs Wilberforce to stay as well; but sanity intervened. 'Of course, of course, I understand,' he said. 'I expect they'll be happier in London, if that's what they're used to, and naturally you want to be near them.'

'What Frank asked for is too much, sir,' Maria began, but Teddy cut her off, his eyebrows raised in surprise.

'Too much? No, you mustn't say that. Nothing is too much for our young men at the Front, fighting to keep our country safe. Old fellows like me who can't go have to satisfy ourselves with doing our bit at home. It's a kind thing in you, my dear, to let me feel I am doing something to help in this way. And Frank is like a son to me. I expect you know that my own son—' He couldn't go on, and had to draw out his handkerchief and blow his nose.

Maria had heard about Ned. She was moved that he was considering her pride, and felt ashamed of her own smallness of spirit. If he wanted to give, the generous thing to do was to let him have his pleasure. 'Thank you,' she said warmly. 'It would be a wonderful present to give us, and I should be always grateful.'

Teddy beamed. 'Make this nevvy of mine happy and that will be thanks enough. Now then, how shall we arrange it? You won't want to waste your honeymoon looking for a house. Where will you go for it, by the by?'

'The honeymoon? We thought we might go to Brighton for a few days,' said Frank.

'Brighton? Well, I expect you can be as happy there as anywhere. So the new Mrs Compton will look for a place after you've gone back, then? Do you feel able to do that, my dear?'

'I expect I shall be glad of something to keep my mind off things.'

'Yes, good thought.' Teddy knew about keeping minds off. 'How would it be if I came up to London for a day or two to help you? There are sharps everywhere and a young woman on her own might not spot their tricks. As a landlord myself, I do know what questions to ask about damp and drains and leases and such.'

'It would be very kind of you,' Maria said, 'but surely you couldn't spare the time?'

'Oh, I've business to do in London, people to see. I have a few days in Town from time to time, so I can combine your bit of business with mine.'

So it was settled. Frank was much relieved that his uncle would be overseeing the matter, for as clever as he knew Maria to be, he did not think her worldly enough for business of that sort. Maria, observing the satisfied smile on Teddy's face, concluded that she would have a struggle on her hands to have the property of her choice rather than his. But whatever it was it would be better than sharing the cramped confines of Cousin Sonia's flat, and she was suitably grateful. And the thought of never having to go back to the Kardomah made her more grateful still.

CHAPTER NINE

Venetia arrived home from another fruitless expedition to the War Office, where she had been badgering for help with her mobile X-ray cars scheme, to find a heap of luggage in the hall, which in itself was enough to account for the mild agitation of her butler, Burton. She allowed herself a moment of frivolity. 'Are you leaving us, Burton? Have we been working you too hard, or are you longing for adventure?'

Burton looked disapproving. He hadn't a humorous bone in his body – only the humerus, Venetia corrected herself inwardly.

'The luggage belongs to Lady Holkam, my lady. She has just arrived from Aldershot. Her ladyship is in the drawing-room.'

Venetia shed her coat, hat, gloves and umbrella, ordered tea to be brought at once, and climbed the stairs. In the drawing-room the fire had been freshly made up and was leaping merrily, and the little dogs were lying in front of it, staring at the flames, their fawn coats rosy with reflection. Violet rose at once and came towards her. She looked a little pale, even for Violet, and the hands she placed in her mother's were cold. Venetia kissed her cheek and stood back to examine her. She had taken off her hat, which presaged a long call. Something of her usual composure had left her, and her eyes looked tired and shadowed, as if she had been crying.

'Well, darling?' Venetia said. 'This is a sudden appearance – and with your luggage, too.'

'I wondered if I might stay here, at least for tonight. I don't want to go back to St James's Square just yet.'

'Of course you can stay, for as long as you like.' Venetia drew her to a chair by the fire, and sat near her. She was beginning to guess now what it might be. The various clues had prepared her for a story of love ending, and she sighed inwardly. 'You've left Aldershot?'

Tears welled in Violet's eyes at the question. She said, in a voice that shook a little, 'There's nothing to stay there for now. Laidislaw's gone.'

'You mean he's left you?'

Violet nodded. The tears spilled over, and she gasped as she tried to catch them back. She reached for the fragment of expensive lace that did service as her handkerchief, and Venetia, thinking it wholly inadequate, substituted her own stout and practical square. Violet disappeared into it for a moment, while Venetia sat silently rehearsing phrases of comfort and philosophy, and thinking them all hateful. She had thought poor Violet's lover more constant; but perhaps the intensity of their time together – alone in a rural village – had worn his love out the sooner. As the sword wears out the sheath, so the heart outwears the breast . . .

Violet emerged at last, carefully dried her cheeks, and managed a watery smile. 'I know one is supposed to be pleased and proud at such a time,' she said, 'and I *am* proud of him, Mummy, but I love him so much I can't bear to think of not seeing him for months, or years, or whatever it is. How long do you think it will last?'

Confused, Venetia said, 'How long *what* will last?'

'The war. It can't *really* be years, can it? If I had to be without him for years I think I should *die*.'

'Darling,' said Venetia, carefully, 'I don't understand you. You said that Laidislaw has left you?'

'For the Front. He's been sent to France,' said Violet, and

two more tears welled over. 'Oh dear, I didn't mean to cry. He seemed so excited, just like a little boy, and he made me promise not to be sad, but one can't really help something like that, can one? And though I'm pleased for *him*, I can't help wishing they'd sent someone else so that I could be near him for a while longer.'

'But he's only been in the army for a month,' Venetia said. 'Surely it's too soon to be sending him to the Front?'

'That's what I thought,' said Violet, drying her eyes again on a new corner, 'and he said to begin with that he thought the training would go on for several months. But a military gentleman I got into conversation with at the hotel said that it was because he had joined a regular unit. He said regulars did sometimes get sent out before they'd finished training, when there was a shortage of manpower in their front-line battalion. It was just the luck of the draw, he said. Very peculiar luck, was what I thought, because it was only Octavian who was sent.'

'What do you mean?'

'Well, the others who joined at the same time weren't sent. They're still in Aldershot. Octavian was sorry to leave them behind because he said they were splendid fellows and he would miss them, but of course he was terribly proud that he'd been chosen over them. He thought it was because he already knew how to shoot before he was called up, but *I* think it's because he's a gentleman, and educated, and the others are farm workers and clerks and so on. So obviously he must be better than them, mustn't he?'

Venetia assented absently. She was thinking that it did seem rather odd that he had been selected to fill a vacancy. Probably it was an administrative muddle, and they didn't know he was untrained, or they'd confused his name with someone else's – that happened all the time in the Army. Or perhaps it *was* his prowess with a rifle, after all – she had heard him spoken of as a good shot. But why only him? Vacancies in the ranks were not filled singly, but by drafts of soldiers when they were ready. But then Laidislaw, being a gentleman, would surely be applying for a commission. Perhaps it was an officer they needed and they were anticipating his gazetting. She put this last thought to Violet.

'Oh, yes, he told me that he could apply for a commission after a few weeks – though the last thing he said was that he might *not*, after all, because there was something noble in serving one's country as a common soldier.'

'Hmm,' said Venetia. Since the war began she had heard a good deal of that sort of nonsense from military-starstruck young men, overwhelmed by the romance of the khaki – and from their sentimental mothers, who had read too many twopenny novelettes about princes in disguise. She was pretty sure that for any gently born youth the impulse would not long survive the privations of the ranks, particularly in regard to food. The Tommy was very well fed, but the food was neither delicate nor varied. A couple of weeks of bully-and-biscuit monotony would be enough to have them putting their names in. 'There's more nobility in serving to the best of one's ability,' she said, 'and if one is officer material, it's a waste of it not to try for a commission.'

'Oh, I think he will,' said Violet, sensibly, 'despite what he said. I don't think he'd like to be a common soldier for ever. And I would sooner have him be an officer. Especially now, because—'

Just then Burton opened the door and came in with a maid and the tea tray, and Violet walked over to the window while they set out the table before the fire. The dogs sat up, nostrils busy, then planted themselves within full view of the sandwich plate.

'That's all, thank you, Burton,' said Venetia.

When the door closed behind the servants, Violet came back to the fire. For almost the first time that Venetia remembered, her nose and eyes were pink. She must have been crying a lot recently, she thought, with a pang. She poured her a cup of tea and handed it.

Violet drank gratefully, but did not look at the delicacies spread for her. 'Oh dear,' she said, putting her cup down, 'I don't know what's wrong with me. I don't usually cry so much. But perhaps it's my—' She stopped abruptly and, to Venetia's surprise, she blushed. She looked at her mother with a conscious, embarrassed air, and a touch of defiance.

Venetia had a feeling of foreboding. 'Darling, what is it?'

Violet sighed. 'I shall have to tell you – of course, I want to tell you – but it's all so awkward, now that he's been sent away. I don't know exactly what to do. I mean, how *are* things arranged, in circumstances like these? You see, I think I'm going to have a baby.'

'You *think*?' Venetia didn't know what else to say.

'Well, I know, really. I knew anyway, even before I saw the doctor. But I thought I ought to be sure, so I went to one in Aldershot. I didn't want to see anyone who might know me.' She made a *moue*. 'It was horrid, Mama. I had to go to his consulting-room, instead of having him come to me, and it was in a shabby street and everything looked not quite clean, and there were other women waiting to see him and they *looked* at me. And then – well, he was quite kind, but he didn't know me so I was just one more strange woman to him. He didn't seem really to *care*. But he said I definitely was *enceinte*, and the baby should come in August.'

'Three months,' Venetia calculated automatically. Early December – when she had written to say she never wanted to leave Chetton. A child conceived in love, that was certain. But what of its future? 'Does Holkam know?' she asked.

'Oh, no! You're the first person I've told.'

'Apart from Laidislaw.'

'I haven't told him, either. I didn't quite know how to. It seemed too strange. And then, when I knew he was going away, I was afraid it would make it too hard for him to go, so I didn't say anything. But I wanted to ask your advice. Because I don't know how things are arranged in cases like these. Holkam will know it can't be his. I haven't seen him since August. And –' she looked shyly at her mother '– and in any case, I don't think I would *want* him to think it was his. I love Laidislaw. It would be a betrayal to pretend. But the thing is, I don't think Holkam will like it very much.'

That, Venetia thought, was an understatement. Holkam would be furious. 'He didn't like anything about you and Laidislaw,' she reminded her daughter.

'It isn't fair, though,' Violet said, with sudden spirit. 'I'm perfectly certain he's seeing other women out there in France, and if men could get pregnant he would have been, ten times over at least.'

Venetia smiled faintly. 'My love, the whole of human civilisation has been shaped by the fact that men can't get pregnant.'

Violet nodded, the spirit fading as rapidly as it had come. Now she looked depressed, and rather scared – like a child who fears it's about to be found out. 'I don't exactly know what to do. To begin with, I don't want to go back to St James's Square, not like this. It will feel like deceiving Holkam – and Octavian, too. And the servants will soon find out, and then everyone will know.'

'Everyone will soon know anyway,' Venetia said gently.

'Yes,' said Violet, looking directly at her, 'and I'll have to face it, but not yet. That's why I came here.'

'You can stay as long as you want,' said Venetia. 'And it will seem perfectly natural that you should, with Holkam away.'

Violet said starkly, 'Everyone in London knows about me and Laidislaw. They'll know it's because *he*'s gone to the Front. There'll be whispering and looks and impertinent questions, and horrid things written in the papers.'

'You had all that before.'

'Yes – only then I had him with me, to make it all worth while.'

Venetia filled their cups again, and they drank tea in silence. The dogs sat like statues, round eyes fixed imploringly on the tea tray, pink tongues moist with desire in their dark faces.

At last Violet said, 'What do you think I had better do? Should I write to Holkam now? Or should I wait? He's going to be very angry. I'd just as soon put it off.'

There was a memory tugging at Venetia's mind, something someone had said.

Holkam? No, someone else, but in Holkam's presence. She couldn't remember what it was or why it had bearing on the situation, but it nagged at her as something she *ought* to remember. She shook it away and said, 'I think you ought to write to him at once. It will be far worse if someone else tells him and he's seen not to know about it. If you tell him first he can decide for himself whether to acknowledge the child. I imagine he will.'

'Do you think so?' said Violet, dully.

'It will keep up appearances,' Venetia said. Holkam cared about that sort of thing – and, for her daughter's sake, so did Venetia. Some fiction might be spun about a short visit home before Christmas and a reconciliation – and with Laidislaw out of the country the story might stick. Things might settle down into some semblance of normality.

After a pause, Violet said, 'What will happen to us afterwards?'

She meant after the war; and it wasn't really a question. Holkam had said he would not divorce her; but if she went to live with Octavian and their child, would he carry out his threat to stop her seeing her other children? But they, and he, seemed remote from her at the present moment. All that was real was the new life inside her, and the memory of her lover, which always lay close and warm in her mind. Even the war was unreal.

'War changes things,' Venetia said, out of a train of thought of her own; but it fitted with Violet's, and she nodded. 'War changes everything,' Venetia went on, 'and us with it.'

Venetia told Overton that night, when they were in bed. Violet had retired before he came home, so there had been no need for a confrontation, and she chose the intimacy of darkness to tell him what she knew would shock and sadden him.

But he had gone through the worst of the reaction when he first learned about Laidislaw, and the coming of a child seemed to him something of an inevitable consequence. It presented practical problems, but no new disappointment.

'Does Holkam know?' His first question was pretty much what Venetia's had been.

'She hasn't told him yet.'

'She ought to, then, as soon as possible.'

'That's what I told her.'

'The sooner he can put his own story about, the more it will be believed.'

'Yes, and though it's very sad for Violet, it's fortunate really that Laidislaw *was* sent to France, because if she was known to be still with him, no-one would believe she and Holkam had been reconciled.'

There was a pause, and then Overton's voice came quietly out of the darkness. 'I wonder if it *was* just fortune.'

Venetia felt a chill of foreboding. 'What do you mean?'

'Don't you think it's a little odd that he was called up on the very first day of conscription, and that he's been sent to the Front with the minimum of training?'

It came to her then. 'Uriah the Hittite!'

'Precisely.'

'It was something Oliver said to me when we were at the opera with Holkam and Violet. It's been in the back of my mind but I couldn't call it forward. Oh, Beauty, you don't really think Holkam can have had anything to do with it?'

'I think it very likely. You said only he, out of his intake, was sent.'

'But how could he?'

'If you mean how was it possible – he was at Horseguards, and now he's in Headquarters Staff. He will have many useful contacts. And with a helpful clerk under one's influence it's not too difficult to get someone's name put on a particular list. The practicalities are not difficult to arrange. But if you mean how could he bring himself to do it – well, you saw how angry he was. He's a young man of great pride—'

'Conceit, rather,' Venetia corrected.

'Even more reason. I must say, now that I've thought about it, and given the circumstances and particular characters involved, I'm not at all surprised that something like this has happened. The only question in my mind is whether he merely wants to remove his wife's lover from her arms, or whether he's hoping for a more permanent separation.'

'A more . . . You mean Uriah again?'

'It did occur to me,' Overton said apologetically, 'that an artist, not the most practical and down-to-earth of people, might be more vulnerable at the Front than other men. Particularly when he hasn't had much training.'

Venetia was distressed. She had hated the whole Laidislaw situation, but she loved her daughter more, and Violet was in love with him. For Violet's sake, she didn't want him to be killed. 'Can anything be done?' she asked. 'Can *you* do anything?'

'To get him out? No. I'm shocked you should ask. Every unmarried man under forty-one is liable to conscription. Why should Laidislaw be different? He has to take his chance with all the others.'

'Oh Beauty, you know I didn't mean that—'

'What did you mean, then? It seems to me that was precisely what you meant.'

'Well, I suppose it was. You must forgive me if occasionally I have a woman's reaction.'

He smiled and kissed her. 'I've always known you were a woman, darling, all evidence to the contrary.'

'But if you can't get him *out*, could you get him *back*?'

'To somewhere safe? I notice you don't worry about Holkam's safety.'

Venetia was silent, shocked at her own feelings. She had not worried in the least when Holkam went to France. Why? Did she really not mind if he was killed? But, in her favour, she had never for a moment supposed that he would be. He was not the sort. Somehow, she believed, he would always be able to look after himself. She said at last, 'He's in Headquarters Staff, practically Haig's right hand. He could hardly be more safe at home in England.'

Her long pause had given her away, but Overton did not press the point. He knew his wife would perform her own spiritual house-cleaning. He said, 'The first thing to do is to find out whether he did have any part in Laidislaw's removal. That's going to be a delicate business. I can hardly march in and ask direct questions.'

'Then you *do* mean to do something?' Venetia discovered gratefully.

'If there has been any unfairness – deliberately sending him out without the training others have had, for instance – it might be appropriate to correct the balance. I can't promise more than that. It would be very wrong to try to protect those in whom one has an interest from the dangers that everyone else faces.'

'Spoken like a man,' Venetia said. 'Women do that all the time, or try to. There's no equality in love. Do you think that if either you or Laidislaw had to die, and I could affect the outcome, I wouldn't save you? Fairness wouldn't come into it.'

'And if it were between Laidislaw and Holkam?' he asked quietly.

But she had gone past that point. She said briskly, 'Beauty, don't ask pointless questions. Will you see what you can find out?'

'I will make discreet enquiries, for my own satisfaction. Even if there's nothing to be done about it, I'd like to know what sort of a man my son-in-law is. I hope I shall find out that it is all a coincidence and he had nothing to do with it.'

'But *then* we'll have bad consciences for thinking the worst of him.'

'Oh, I'll settle for that,' said Overton, drawing her close to kiss her again.

Under her parents' urging, Violet wrote the difficult letter to her husband and posted it. There followed several days of tension when every knock at the door made her jump, and the sound of footsteps on the stairs had her watching the doorway like a prisoner in the condemned cell. She half expected Holkam to come rushing back from France to confront her; and if not that, there would be a letter so searing it might eat through the hand that held it. Oliver did his best to cheer his sister up. Just at this time he had two whole days off, and instead of spending them sleeping, bathing and eating, which would have been his choice, he talked to her, took her for walks, played silly childhood games with her in the evening, and would even have taken her to a show if she had been willing. But she still did not want to go into public.

He had to go back on duty at last, but told her, 'When I next have free time in the evening, you *shall* go out with me, even if I have to carry you.'

'I'm sorry,' she said. 'Perhaps by next time everything will have been settled and I shall feel better about it.'

He kissed her tenderly. 'Try not to worry, little sister. Whatever happens, we'll always look after you, the Aged Ps and I.'

That morning, shortly after he had left, a letter came from Holkam. Violet tore it open with trembling fingers, but it said only that she should close up the house in St James's Square, and gave some instructions. A caretaker staff was to be retained, the others were to be dismissed with pay instead of notice. Rooms were to be shut up, furniture and pictures covered, the shutters closed, certain *objets* sent to the bank. She had told him she was intending to stay with her parents, so it was logical that he should want the house closed. She was only surprised he had not ordered it earlier. She supposed, if he came home on leave, he would stay at his club.

The business of closing the house gave her something to do for a few days. She expected the letter to be followed by another, giving his reaction to the news and stating his intentions, but as the days passed, nothing happened. Violet lived in a state of taut readiness for disaster, but the human frame cannot sustain that for ever, and gradually she relaxed and fell into a new routine of life. So far only her parents and Oliver knew about the pregnancy. Eventually word would slip out – it was inevitable – and then it would be necessary for her to know what her husband wanted her to say. The matter would have to be faced with him, however dreadful that would be. But for the time being she was glad to have space simply to grow accustomed to the new life within her, and to daydream about her lover and a golden time in the future, after the war, when they would be together.

One breezy day in March Jack was walking across the airfield, with Rug at his heels, towards the hut where he gave his ground-based lessons to aspiring pilots. He generally took Rug on his training days, and the little dog seemed quite happy to lie under his desk during the lessons, and enjoyed the long walks on the perimeter in between. He was a general favourite with everyone at the school, especially the mechanics, who could always be inveigled into sharing their sandwiches with him at lunchtime.

Jack was too early for the lesson, but he had wanted a little quiet to work on a design, and the house was not in a state to provide such tranquillity. He understood now why wealthy families always had a nursery in some distant part of the mansion: it was amazing how much noise one very small baby could make. Much as he adored Little Baby Basil (he *must* stop calling him that!), Jack found the pitch of his voice distractingly unignorable.

He was walking without a stick, having been signed off by the sawbones last month, his ankle declared sound at last. It was still a new enough sensation for him to be aware of it, and as he walked he still scanned the ground ahead for fear of putting his foot down a hole or stumbling over a rock. The doctor had said he could resume all normal activities, but he had been favouring the shattered ankle so long it was hard to trust it. And, he thought with some bitterness, he was not the only one who did not trust. He had not yet been given permission to fly again. He had a dreadful feeling that he had slipped down one of those backwaters that existed everywhere in the army, where one was forgotten and left for ever.

Automatically he looked up to check the cloud ceiling, the wind strength and direction, the likelihood of rain, gauging the 'lift' with his flyer's senses. He *missed* the sky. It was like a constant low ache in him, like the longing for an absent lover. He wanted to be up there, in the clear air, feeling it buoying him up like loving arms, hearing its sweet passage over the planes and the singing of the wires. He wanted to *fly* – man's eternal longing since he first rose from all fours and saw the birds above him. How *could* the army forget him and leave him here, earthbound, teaching other lucky young men to do what they wouldn't let him do? It was a terrible thing.

He had almost reached the door of the hut when someone

called his name. It was one of the sergeant-instructors, Parry by name, hurrying towards him. 'Mr Compton! Mr Compton, sir!' Jack turned. 'The CO sent me, sir. Have you got a minute?'

'I've got almost an hour. My first lesson isn't until nine.'

Parry nodded. 'That's what the CO said.' He bent down to return Rug's greeting, scratching the dog's ruff vigorously. 'And seeing as you've got a bit of time on your hands – would you come with me, sir, please?'

'What is it?' Jack asked, falling in beside him.

'If you wouldn't mind coming down to the sheds, sir. You're wanted there.'

Jack was not surprised to be so summoned. His knowledge of engines was as great as his flying skills, and he had the pleasant habit of dropping in to chat to the mechanics. Often they would ask his advice about a problem, and he was happy to help. If he could not fly, the next best thing was to get his hands oily inside the guts of an engine.

When they reached the sheds he saw one of the trainers – an old BE2 – had been pulled out, and a couple of mechanics were leaning against the wings, chatting. They grinned at the sight of Jack, and answered his greeting call of 'What's the matter with the old bus?' with a knowing look at each other. Jack looked at Parry for enlightenment, and found he was grinning too.

'The CO thought you might like to take her up, sir,' he said. 'Get your air-legs back, so to speak.'

Jack stared. 'You mean – I'm allowed to fly again?'

'Got the paperwork sorted out at last, sir – landed on the CO's desk this morning. He thought you wouldn't want to wait.' Parry was evidently delighted with the little trick they'd played, and with the dawning pleasure on Jack's face. 'Feeling nervous, sir?' he added, as Jack still hesitated.

'Of course not,' Jack laughed. 'I can't wait!'

'We've got your flying helmet here, sir,' said one of the mechanics, 'and the little feller's too.'

Jack sprang onto the wing and inserted himself into the cockpit, for once entirely forgetting to worry about his ankle. The seat seemed to fit him like a comfortable shoe and he sighed with pleasure. Rug barked his disapproval of being left behind, but Parry fixed on his goggles and lifted him onto the wing, and he jumped into the front seat and looked about him with satisfaction.

Jack tested the controls, nodded to the mechanic, who swung the propellor for him, and as the engine caught he adjusted the throttle and tested the flaps and rudder again. Parry came close to shout up to him: 'Don't forget she needs a bit of left rudder in the air.'

'Tell your grandmother!' he shouted back.

'And don't do any loops, sir, or you'll lose the co-pilot!'

Jack stuck up his thumb, nodded to the mechanic to remove the blocks, and as they skipped out of the way he eased her forward. They went bumping over the uneven field, each springless jolt seeming to shove his spine up into his skull. He loved it. His feet touched the rudder to keep her from swinging; he increased throttle, the engine roared and the tail came off the ground. The machine bounced over the rough grass, the jolts coming harder and faster, and then there was that wonderful, sudden smoothness as she unpeeled herself from the ground, came unstuck from the grip of the earth, and they were airborne. In front of him, Jack could see Rug grinning in canine delight as the world sloped away and left them alone, and he gave her stick and throttle and climbed, climbed up the crystal air. 'My God, my God!' Jack cried out, and there was nothing of blasphemy in it. It was pure joy and thanksgiving.

Verdun was a mediaeval fortified town on the river Meuse, about 120 miles almost directly east of Paris, close to the French border with Germany. Within the town, the citadel had been built by the great Vauban himself, and it was here that French troops were garrisoned. By the end of the nineteenth century an underground complex had been built below it, housing workshops, a munitions dump, a hospital, and quarters for the soldiery, making the place virtually impregnable.

Verdun guarded the northern entrance to the plains of Champagne, and therefore, ultimately, Paris. There had been a fortress on the site since Roman times; Attila the Hun had never managed to capture it; and it had been the last stronghold to fall in the Franco-Prussian War of 1870–71. After the war it had become the centrepiece of a line of defensive fortifications built against the German threat; and in 1914 it had withstood the new German invasion, even when attacked with the massive *Dicke Bertha* – Fat Bertha – siege mortars, which hurled 370-pound explosive shells. It was, therefore, almost a holy place in the minds of the French people. As long as Verdun stood, they believed, France would survive; the idea of its falling to the Germans was intolerable.

It could be no coincidence, then, that Germany had decided to attack Verdun in February 1916. A massive nine-hour bombardment, smashing an estimated one million shells into a front of thirty miles, preceded an attack by three entire army corps. Fortunately the German plan had been postponed by bad weather from the 12th to the 21st of February, and between those dates intelligence had warned the French, who were able to rush two divisions into the area to strengthen the defences. All the same, they were heavily outnumbered by the Germans, who were evidently pouring all their resources into the action, including a regiment equipped with flamethrowers to clear trenches. By the 24th, the French had been driven back from their first and second lines of defence, and were only five miles from Verdun itself.

The French commander-in-chief, Joseph Joffre, would have preferred to let Verdun fall and concentrate his forces elsewhere, but French public opinion, and therefore the government, would not countenance it. He sent in the Second Army under General Henri-Philippe Pétain. Against their spirited defence the German frontal attack eventually ground to a halt in the sea of mud that had replaced the Meuse valley. So on the 6th of March the Germans mounted a second offensive, this time attacking the flanks, and managed to advance another two miles, before being stopped by furious French resistance. The battles raged all through the month of March, with heavy losses on both sides, and there seemed no end in sight.

There were many on the Allied side who agreed with 'Papa' Joffre that Verdun was not worth the lives it was costing, but it was politically impossible for it to be allowed to fall. And Lord Overton was not the only one who believed that the Germans knew this, and were exploiting it.

'I can't help thinking the French are playing into the Germans' hands,' he said to his son, one evening after dinner. They were alone in the drawing-room. Violet had gone early to bed, and Venetia was in her study writing letters. 'If you look at it from the German point of view, they can't really hope to make a big breakthrough in that area. The defences are too heavy. And why should they have withdrawn men from the Eastern Front just when the Russians were close to collapse? What can their object be?'

'I can never imagine what the German object can be,' said Oliver. 'Why would any sane person have started this war in the first place?'

'That's not thinking like a soldier,' said his father.

'I'm not a soldier.'

'You're in the army now.'

'True. Well, then, enlighten me, O sage Papa. What *are* the Germans doing at Verdun?'

'Wearing the French out. Making them waste all their young manhood on defending an icon. They know the French can't abandon it. If they can suck in more and more defenders and inflict heavy casualties, they can weaken France – eventually, perhaps, bleed her dry.'

'But the Germans are suffering heavy casualties themselves – according to the newspapers.'

'Obviously they will hope to lose fewer men than the French.'

'A game of who runs out of men first? My dearest Dad,' Oliver protested, 'that's not a policy, it's madness. I don't believe even the Germans are that potty.'

Overton shrugged and let it pass. 'Well, whatever their game may be, it's giving us a quieter time along the rest of the Front, and a wonderful opportunity to train the new men coming out. Solid trench and weaponry training. No chances can be taken with this autumn's big push. Everything must be done to ensure the victory.'

'And then "the boys come home", eh? On which subject, have you managed to find out anything about Laidislaw?'

'Nothing concrete yet. It seems he *was* called out of order, but I haven't been able to discover why. I have to tread carefully. The last thing we want is for any hint of what we suspect to get out.'

'Well, old Holkam seems to be playing it very close to his chest,' said Oliver. 'I quite expected him to come plunging over here to batter the door down in rage when he found out about the baby. But there's been nothing except that one letter. What can he be up to?'

Overton shook his head. 'If it's as I suspect, he already has all he wanted: Laidislaw and Violet are separated, and Laidislaw is out in France, under Holkam's eye and perhaps under his control.'

'But sooner or later Violet's condition will become known, and then he'll have to say something.'

'I'm not sure that he will. Suppose it *were* his child, what would he do?'

'Send her tender letters?'

'I mean in the public domain.'

'I see what you mean. There would be an announcement in the papers when the child was born, but nothing beforehand.'

'He may already have told his colleagues at Headquarters in a friendly way. Of course, we won't know about that until and unless the word comes back home in *their* letters to their wives.'

'And, meanwhile, poor Violet is left on tenterhooks, not knowing when or even whether the axe is going to fall?' Overton nodded, and they both contemplated the thought in silence. 'I say,' said Oliver at last, 'if you're right, that's a terrible revenge.'

Venetia was preparing to do some work in her laboratory one morning a few days later when Burton came up to tell her that Mr Asquith had called to see her.

Venetia was surprised. Though the Overtons and the Asquiths dined at each other's houses, they were not intimates. Margot Asquith called now and then, but Venetia couldn't imagine what business the prime minister might possibly have with her. 'Are you sure he asked for me, and not his lordship?' she asked.

Burton almost looked hurt at such a question. 'He asked most particularly for you, my lady. I showed him into the morning-room, as the fire has not been lit in the drawing-room.'

'Quite right,' said Venetia. 'I'll come at once.' She thought it must be some kind of emergency or bad news – what else could have drawn Asquith out of his usual circuit? – but then she could not imagine what sort of bad news the prime minister would feel only he personally could break. Had something happened to Holkam? But then he would tell Overton first, and let him break it to her. Oh, dear Lord, was there something wrong with Overton? Had he been concealing an illness? She shook that thought away with ridicule. The idea that Beauty would tell the prime minister before her . . . And, besides, he had been looking particularly well of late.

Entering the morning-room she saw at once that there was nothing to worry about. Asquith was the picture of ease. He was leaning back in one of the Voltaires by the fire, his legs crossed, the newspaper on his knee, his left hand thrust carelessly into his trouser pocket. She smiled, recognising the pose from Overton's description of him in the Cabinet Office, when once he had been called in for a talk. Some people criticised the Yorkshireman for being too relaxed about government, and wanted a bit more go-on and bustle; but Venetia's life was too complicated just then to want anything but calm, and she viewed the stocky figure, with the shock of white hair and the blunt, square face, with approval.

He stood up as she came in and put aside the newspaper.

'This is a pleasant surprise,' she said, offering her hand.

'I hope I haven't disturbed your work?' he said. 'Your man said you'd only just gone up to your laboratory.'

'That's right. I hadn't begun anything yet. May I offer you some refreshment?'

'No, no, thank you. Don't trouble yourself. I shan't keep you long.'

He eyed her with a quiet amusement, and she couldn't think what might be coming. Belatedly, she invited him to sit.

'I hear you've been making a nuisance of yourself at the War Office,' he said.

Venetia looked her indignation. 'If they have been complaining to you . . . Good heavens! To waste *your* time like this! And besides—'

'Dear lady, you can't think I've come here to scold you,' he said, smiling openly now. 'No, no, I am rather the fingers at the end of a very long arm. You thought your requests were being buried and ignored – and, I have to be honest with you, they probably were, until an old friend of yours intervened. Well,' he said, reflectively, 'it was three old friends, rather. You are a person of considerable influence, Lady Overton, and it's the greatest pity in the world you aren't a man, because you'd be invaluable to me in government.'

She laughed. 'But you have my husband, sir, and we are as one.'

'Not in every respect,' he said regretfully. 'However, to the point: your old friend Sir Alfred Keogh heard what you were up to, and thought these mobile X-ray vehicles of yours were a very good idea. He has a wonderfully elastic mind, you know. Full of innovation. It was he who brought in the Military Massage Corps, of course – a considerable innovation. I wonder you didn't go to him in the first place.'

'I wonder, too, now you have me think of it, instead of rushing headlong at the War Office like a bull at a gate – and getting nothing but a concussion for my pains.'

'I suppose you didn't get where you are today by avoiding confrontation,' said Asquith. 'However, on this occasion the indirect method has worked better. Keogh spoke to Kitchener – who has a great admiration for you, by the by – and he spoke to your friend Addison, who brought it to me. I have come here to give myself the pleasure of telling you that we have found a little money for you, and – which I understand you want more – an official position. You are to be Director of Mobile Radiological Services, if you please, with a commission from HM Government for the first four cars. Thereafter, I'm afraid I can't positively promise more money – but I understand you have been raising good sums voluntarily?'

'Indeed I have, and with official status I can always find more. Better than that, I can get things *done* at last.'

'Just so. There's nothing like a resounding title and official letter-paper for making people comply with one's wishes.'

'This will make every possible difference. I can't thank you enough, Prime Minister.'

'Oh, I had very little to do about it, you know, just nod and say yes and sign a letter or two. You will have an official notice, but don't let that hold you up. We've even managed to find you an office. It's just a corner, but you'll have a telephone, and a clerk and a typewriter. Both females, but you won't mind that.'

'No, indeed!' It was more than she had ever hoped for. 'Where is the office?'

'At the War Office – not the main building, but one of the annexes, Winchester House in St James's Square. Quite handy for you.'

'I shouldn't mind where it was,' said Venetia. 'This is everything I could want. Thank you so much.'

'Thank *you*,' he said gravely, 'on behalf of all of those in active service – and their fond families. And now,' he drew out his fob watch, glanced at it and rose, 'I shall have to take my leave. Things to do, you know. When shall Margot and I have the pleasure of your company at dinner again?'

'At any time of your choosing,' Venetia said.

'Next week, perhaps? I'll have her telephone you and arrange it. There's a very interesting Red Cross fellow coming back from Belgium I think you'd like to meet. Been trying to sort out this military-graves muddle with the French.'

'I'll be most interested to meet him.' She rang the bell. 'How is Raymond, by the way?'

Asquith smiled at the mention of his son, a brilliant scholar and lawyer like his father, now serving with the Grenadier Guards. 'Very well, I thank you. Still in Ypres. We had a letter from him the other day. I don't know if you knew, but his wife is expecting another child very soon – next month, in fact.'

'How delightful. I expect you're hoping for a boy this time?'

'It would be pleasant, of course. And we're hoping Raymond may get leave for the happy occasion.'

Burton appeared at the door and they said their goodbyes. Alone, she thought of Asquith's simple pleasure in the birth of another grandchild. *We're hoping Raymond may get leave for the happy occasion.* The coming of a baby ought always to be a happy occasion, but when Violet's came . . . She sighed; and then remembered the wonderful news Asquith had brought, and went along to her study to begin her plans and write some letters.

The army took away another batch of Jessie's horses in early February, leaving her with very little stock. But it was perhaps not entirely a bad thing that there was not so much to do at Twelvetrees, for two of her grooms were taken by conscription, one in February and one in March, leaving her very short-handed. Uncle Teddy lent her Wickes, the home groom, on a part-time basis to fill the gap, while Jessie tried to find a replacement. Young men were becoming impossible to find – and if she did find one, she wouldn't know how long he would stay. The same applied to taking on boys: two applied for the job, but boys rapidly became men, and if the war did not end this year she would be back where she started. Instead, rather surprising herself, she decided to take on the girl who had applied.

It was not that she had anything against employing females – how could she, when all her life she had railed against being prevented from doing things because she was one? She had something of a job to persuade her head man, Webster, that there was no alternative, and only managed it in the end by pretending to be offended. 'If you don't like females working with horses, what do you think of me?' After which he could only retreat with apologies.

But still Jessie found it very odd at first to have a young woman walk into her stableyard and do things like mucking-out, picking hoofs and strapping. These were all things that Jessie herself had done and thought nothing of, but she had always considered herself different, the exception to the rule.

The new girl (whom she called briskly by her surname, Field, in the hope of disguising her difference as much as possible) came to work wearing khaki breeches and puttees and heavy boots, so that from the back, except for her hair, you wouldn't have known she was not a lad. It was disconcerting; and despite what Field herself said, Webster was always trying to help her with things that she could very well manage alone.

But they settled down together eventually, once Webster could bring himself to believe what Jessie herself had found, that Field was very good with the horses. 'Ah must say, Miss Jessie, that she doesn't hang back when there's work to be done,' he said, in grudging approval. 'She could teach Mattock a thing or two – he's forever skulking in the tack room, smoking, when Ah want him about summat. Ah suppose she's trying to prove herself,' he concluded. 'But that's all right with me, as long as it lasts.'

And before the month was out, Jessie was coming to the yard and finding him deep in conversation with his new underling, who was a much more sympathetic ear than Mattock – or, indeed, his wife at home.

'I'm glad you're getting on with her,' she said one day, 'because if this war goes on much longer, girls will be all we'll be able to get when they take Mattock.'

'They won't take him,' Webster said scornfully. 'What'd they do with a great dozy dollop like him? Now, if the Germans took him, we might win the war in a fortneet!'

Polly was terribly excited at first that Jessie was to employ a female groom, and applauded the idea. 'There's no reason women shouldn't do the jobs men do,' she said. 'Goodness, when all the men are at the Front, they'll pretty well have to, won't they?' She made a point of coming, as if on impulse, to the yard on Field's first day, and hung around talking to Webster so that she could stare covertly at the freak of nature in the breeches. But she soon decided that there was nothing very exciting in it. Women doing men's jobs sounded all right, but why would any woman want to dress like that, and get herself filthy, when there was no glory in it? The men's jobs *she* liked the idea of were things like being prime minister or the captain of a great ship. When she expounded this to Jessie, Jessie said that perhaps women would have to start in a small way and work up, but Polly dismissed that out of hand. 'All very well for some people, I suppose, but I'm Miss Morland of Morland Place, and when I start it will be at the top.'

And Jessie only laughed and said, 'I don't doubt it, Pol. You'll start at the top and then go higher.'

Teddy had not immediately gone to London, when Frank went back to France, to fulfil his promise about the house. He was not able to leave his business at once, and Maria declared herself in no great hurry; but he was not idle. He engaged an agent to look for suitable properties, so that when he did come to London, his time might be most fruitfully spent. Property in London was becoming hard to find, so it was as well to have someone else do the hard work.

Towards the end of March he had a letter from Maud Parke with sad news. His old friend, her father Richard Puddephat, had died after a short illness. He had been in failing health for some months, but his death was unexpected, and Teddy was very sorry. He wrote a warm letter to Maud, and proposed to call on her when he was in London.

'I want to make sure she is all right. Poor thing, she hasn't any other family, and with Bertie in France she will feel very much alone.' Henrietta knew what the next words would be before he said them. 'I wonder if I should ask her to come and stay for a while. The country air would do her good. I can't think it's healthy to be living all the time in London.'

'But Maud likes to live in London,' Henrietta said, 'and she has a country estate of her own if she wants country air.'

'True, but if she went to Beaumont she'd still be alone.'

'Maud is very well able to look after herself, and all her friends are in London, and her committees and so on. Better she stays in the place she knows, and keeps busy.'

Teddy felt that Henrietta was being less than hospitable. 'She *is* our niece,' he said, in hurt tones. 'And with Bertie away we ought to be looking out for her.'

Henrietta yielded. 'Ask her if you want, Ted, but don't press her. She lives in London by choice, you know, and she's never cared much for Yorkshire. That's why Bertie bought Beaumont in the first place, because she wouldn't come up to the Red House.'

So Teddy took his trip to London, and made Pont Street his first call. He found Maud dressed very elegantly in full mourning blacks, which surprised him a little. The gown was new and fashionably cut, and black suited her colouring, with her blue eyes and pale skin. She looked as composed as ever, and showed no sign of the grief he knew she must be feeling. She ordered refreshments for Teddy, and sat with him in the drawing-room, telling him in calm and measured tones about her father's last illness and death. It was only when Teddy's eyes filled with tears that her voice wavered, and she turned her face away for a moment, biting her lips. Teddy liked her more for displaying some emotion. He proffered his handkerchief, and she carefully dried her eyes.

'Thank you,' she said, after a moment, when her control was once more perfect. 'It has been just the two of us for so long, since Mother died, and my poor brother Ray in South Africa, that we were very close. I shall miss him very much.'

'You will indeed,' said Teddy. 'But you have little Richard – that will be a great comfort for you.'

'Yes, I'm sure it will. He is a great blessing. Would you like to see him?'

'Very much,' said Teddy.

Maud rang the bell, and sent for the child. She said, 'It is such a pity that Jessie was not able to give Ned a son. That would have been a consolation to you in your loss. Of course you have other children – but nothing can replace him.'

Teddy nodded, paused a moment, and then said, 'But Ned is not dead, you know. I am sure of it. I feel it. I believe he was taken prisoner. We'll find him one day, and when the war's over he'll come back to us.'

Maud stared at him for a moment in surprise, then inclined her head graciously. 'I'm sure it must help you to think so,' she said.

Teddy accepted by now that no-one shared his belief, and said no more. There was no point in expecting pity from Maud when she had none for herself. He thought her very brave for the way she was facing the situation. In a warm voice he said, 'Tell me, my dear, what do you intend to do? In the immediate future, I mean. A change of scene and a change of air might do you good. You are looking rather pale. Should you not like to come to Morland Place for a few weeks? Let us feed you up with good Yorkshire food and make you rosy again.'

Maud's eyebrows went up a shade. She said, 'Thank you, you are most kind, but I have no plans to leave London. This is my home, and all my work is here. And people know where to find me here. It's convenient.'

'People?' Teddy queried. 'Oh, you mean when Bertie comes home on leave?'

'Yes – yes, of course. Bertie may have a short period of leave and not have time to travel to Yorkshire.'

'But if you knew he was coming you could come back,' said Teddy.

'He might not be able to tell me. Sometimes they have leave given them at the last minute.'

'Even if he sends a telegram when he sets off, you could be back here by the time he arrives.'

Maud did not address this point. 'There are other people, too – from abroad. Friends of my father. They may come without prior notice. It's better that I am here where they can find me.'

She seemed a little distracted as she said this. Teddy did not properly understand it, but he remembered what Henrietta had said about not pressing her, and left it alone. 'Well, if you change your mind, my dear, you know you are welcome at Morland Place at any time. A telephone call or a telegram is all the notice we need.'

Maud thanked him again, politely but indifferently, and then the nursery-maid came in with young Master Parke. He was almost four, and a well-grown boy, fair-haired and with very much a look of Bertie about him. He was out of dresses now, but Teddy was surprised to see that he, too, was all in black. It seemed excessive on a child so small; but he swallowed his comment nobly, and applied himself to winning a smile from the solemn little boy, who was evidently bewildered by the change in his household and the sudden disappearance of his grandfather. After nineteen months of war, he had probably known him much better than his absent father.

Children were always attracted to Teddy, whose simple directness and good humour made him like a large child himself, and soon little Richard was telling him all about the school he went to in the mornings, which was just round the corner, and the lessons he was doing there. There was a writing desk in the corner of the room and, furnished with pencil and paper, Richard was soon demonstrating the letters he had mastered so far, and offering to draw Uncle Teddy a boat. Teddy asked him what he liked best about school, and Richard gave it a good deal of thought before pronouncing judiciously that it was the milk and bun at eleven each morning. Teddy laughed and said that that was probably all *he* had got out of Eton and Oxford combined.

Maud intervened at this point, and said that Richard was

a very bright boy and would be an excellent scholar, and that if he had not been going to inherit his estate and title, he could no doubt have looked forward to a career in the law and a judge's seat in the House of Lords. Teddy had no quarrel with that sort of parental partiality, since he thought the same about his own little James, and so the interview came to a good-natured end.

Leaving Pont Street, he turned his thoughts to the interesting project of finding his new niece a place to live. The agent had prepared a list, and Maria was to meet them both at the agent's office. She arrived looking very well, in a neat, if not smart, dark blue jacket and skirt (Teddy had been in the business long enough now to recognise the hallmarks of department store ready-mades) with mourning bands on the sleeves, and a rather jaunty new hat with a black-and-white hackle. He beamed at her, and when she smiled back, he availed himself of an uncle's privilege and kissed her. 'Ready?' he asked her.

'Oh, yes – and excited. I can't believe I shall have a place of my own. You are so very kind, sir—'

'Uncle. You must call me Uncle Teddy.'

She looked shy. 'I'll try. It's very new to me.'

'I know, I know. But you'll get used to it. There's no harm in me, you know, not a jot. Just take my arm, won't you? That's right. And now, Plender, what have you for us?'

They took a taxi-cab. Mr Plender had a list of the properties he had identified – with some difficulty, he assured them, since London was so crowded these days. Everyone was wanting a *pied-à-terre*, more and more people were working in London because of all the new ministries and wartime establishments, and people with country estates were staying up, which was putting pressure on the market generally. But he had managed to find one or two places he thought Mr Morland might like.

The first was a flat just behind Kensington High Street, and it was plain, as they went through the door, that Plender had misunderstood his brief. It had five bedrooms, a twenty-five-foot drawing-room, dining-room, sitting-room, and servants' quarters behind the kitchen. It was beautiful, but Maria shrank back against Teddy's sheltering bulk and looked up at him with shocked eyes.

'Too big, Plender,' said Teddy, squeezing her hand against his side. 'Were you not told I was looking for something very small, and only two bedrooms?'

'Oh dear, yes, now you mention it, I was told *two*, but I assumed it was a mistake – that is, the budget seemed far too small, and I supposed, knowing a little about you, Mr Morland, and thinking—'

'Thinking is what you haven't done,' said Teddy, kindly. 'It isn't for me, it's for my niece here and her mother, while my nephew's away in France, and she wants something very small and easy to manage. Now, have you anything like that on that list of yours, or have we to come again another day?'

Looking embarrassed, he turned over the page and said, 'Well, there are one or two things my assistant suggested, but I thought he had mistaken the instruction. They're down at the bottom of the list. I put them in just in case nothing else suited, though I was sure they wouldn't do.'

'Well, then, why don't we start at the other end of your list and work up?'

'Oh dear,' said Plender again, looking round at the handsome mouldings and marble fireplace of the drawing-room, 'this is such a lovely property, and I know I can get the remainder of the lease very reasonably.'

'No.'

'But the next on the list, perhaps – a modern block in Baker Street – beautifully clean and new, just on the market, and it only has four bedrooms . . . ?'

'No. Take us to the last thing on your list, or we shall be off home.'

Unhappily, Plender submitted to their will. 'I know you won't like it,' he said, several times, as they chugged along in the taxi. 'It was Stevens's idea, but it's far too small. And it's in Brook Green!'

'Brook Green is just right.' It was only a step from Riverside Mansions.

'It isn't fashionable!'

'We don't want it to be fashionable.'

'I know you won't like it at all,' Plender moaned. 'Stevens only put it in because it has a bathroom, which is unusual in a property like this. But you'll take insult when you see it, I know you will.'

Teddy caught Maria's eye, and they both laughed.

It was a tiny cottage, sitting on its own in its long garden, a little detached from the later accretion of neat Edwardian villas of the sort Maria had grown up in. It must have been there, she thought, since Brook Green was a village. It was built of yellow London brick, which had faded to a pleasant grey, with a slate roof, and nicely proportioned windows that gave it an air of dignity. Inside there were two rooms, one either side of the entrance passage, each about fourteen feet square, with good cast-iron fireplaces. Behind them, on the garden side, were a kitchen, scullery, lavatory, and a wash-house with a copper. Upstairs there were two bedrooms at the front, over the main rooms and of the same dimensions, and a third at the back, which had been converted into a bathroom. The rear garden was unkempt and overgrown, but it was full of birds, and at the bottom of it was a small orchard – two apples, two cherries and two plums – just coming into flower.

Teddy raised his eyebrows at the furniture, which was rustic mock-Jacobean from the Tottenham Court Road, and Plender blushed and began to mumble apologies again. But Maria was not shocked by it: she had had schoolfriends whose parents deliberately furnished their houses in just such a way, and she saw only that it was all clean and well cared-for.

She turned to Teddy with her eyes sparkling like sunlight

on water. 'It's perfect! It's exactly right! If only it isn't too much—'

'It's at the bottom of his list,' said Teddy. 'How can it be too much?'

She laughed. 'But look what was at the top of his list!'

'From the sublime to the ridiculous, eh?'

'I rather think it was the other way round. *This* is sublime.'

He squeezed her hand. 'Then you shall have it, my dear, if it makes you happy. I'm sure it won't be too much. He was *very* reluctant to show it.'

They smiled at each other in perfect understanding. Teddy liked Frank's young lady more and more every minute, and was sure she would make him very happy. She was wonderfully sensible and level-headed, yet had a nice sense of humour, and warm feelings to go with it.

'Well, let's go and break his heart,' he said, turning away from the window. 'I don't think he has quite given up hope of Kensington. Why don't you have a little walk round the garden while I talk business with him? And then what do you say to my taking you to luncheon to celebrate?'

'I'd like that very much,' she said, meeting his eyes with such a warm look that Teddy felt if he had been twenty years younger he might have given young Frank a run for his money.

CHAPTER TEN

At the beginning of April, the York Commercials, who had lately been training on Salisbury Plain, at last learned they were going to France, and were given embarkation leave. York was suddenly full of khaki-clad sons and husbands. Everybody wanted to visit everybody else to display young Jim in his uniform or our Fred with his new stripe, and the to-ing and fro-ing was considerable. Any member of the Morland family out in a public place was likely to be stopped by a self-consciously grinning Commercial, with a beaming mother on one arm and an adoring sister or fiancée on the other, a proud father standing silent in the background, a gaggle of younger siblings clamouring to tell how their brother was the best in his platoon at shooting at t'target, or had been spoke to personal by the CO for his smart appearance.

The shops did a grand trade as everyone bought parting presents for the potential heroes – chocolate, cigarettes, scarves, razors, books. The cafés and restaurants were full to bursting with families showing off; and the public houses with escapees from the relentless adoration, taking a quiet pint and smoke with friends before returning to Mother and Pa and our Betty. There were queues outside the photographers' shops until late into the evening, and the churches and register offices held a constant succession of weddings.

Many of the Commercials made the trip out to Morland

Place to pay their respects to Teddy who, because of his major part in setting up the battalion, was regarded as their unofficial, honorary colonel-in-chief. They came, shy, respectful, serious; proud in their uniforms; a little awkward but determined when it came to speaking of Ned. *He* ought to have been with them on this special occasion, but he had gone ahead, volunteered, shown them the way. He had died with another regiment's badge on his cap, but to them he was a York Commercial still.

They spoke to Teddy of his death with quiet sadness, and of his medal with pride and envy. Lieutenant Morland had been the first of them to be decorated, but they were determined he would not be the last. They would follow his example and make sure his memory was never disgraced by any of their actions.

Teddy received them all kindly and listened to them with patience. Not to them would he express his conviction that Ned was still alive: it was not appropriate, and would only puzzle and embarrass them. He let them praise his son, and spoke the words of his pride in them that they wanted to hear. He had long prepared for the moment when the battalion would go overseas, and had arranged a present for everyone in it: a steel cigarette case, engraved with the battalion's badge, for each man, and a silver hip flask, similarly engraved, for each officer. The battalion had been an expensive business for him so far, but he was doing very well out of war contracts, and was glad to give something back. These farewell presents were to be distributed by the colonel. To those who called on him in person he gave a tin of chocolate; and to all of them his blessing.

This time was a trial to Jessie. When the soldiers came to the house she could avoid them, but when she passed them in the street she had to stop and talk to them, bear their condolences and the shy, inarticulate offerings of their memories of Ned at the Yorks' training camp at Black Brow. She was gracious and friendly with them but, far from being a balm, their words only stirred up memories she had tried to bury, and woke her wounds to fresh aching. She was glad when the period of leave ended. The place seemed empty without them. It was like the time in autumn when one day every telegraph wire and roof tree is thronged with twittering swallows, and the next they are suddenly gone. Their families and friends continued talking about them for weeks afterwards, but she could escape most of those conversations.

Though Emma had not wanted to leave London to begin with, she had settled down contentedly at Morland Place. There was plenty to do, and she felt herself useful. She was with Polly a good deal of the time. They did their hospital visiting and first-aid classes, and called on Polly's friends. They took part together in Uncle Teddy's home-defence drills, when the household and estate workers practised what they would do if the Germans invaded. Emma was getting to be quite a good shot, though she could not stop herself giving a little shriek every time the gun went off. Sometimes Uncle Teddy took them both up to Black Brow, where a new battalion was forming, to Ladies' Night in the mess, or to grace a concert the men were giving. To Teddy it was a compliment of the highest order to bring his daughter to them, and Emma was amused to see that the battalion agreed with him, and behaved as if they were being visited by one of the royal princesses. He would have liked to take Jessie – the equivalent of a dowager princess of Wales – but Jessie would not go. She pleaded busyness and there was no doubt that she was busy most of the time, so the excuse was fair.

Jessie gave Emma a driving lesson whenever she had the time, and Emma made a point of going riding with her as often as possible. She felt guilty that more of her time was spent with Polly than her older friend, but when she expressed this, tentatively, Jessie dismissed it. She had little time for leisure, she said; and besides, 'Polly's always restless, and everyone's grateful to you for keeping her occupied. We all dread her boredom.' It seemed to Emma that a grimness had settled on Jessie, and it hurt her to see it. It was six months since Ned's death, but Jessie showed little sign of her old spirit of fun. Emma thought the hospital work tired her too much, but there was no point in saying that. On the only occasion she hinted at it, Jessie said, 'I can't go to the Front and fight. This is something I can do. And I must do something.'

The York Commercials' embarkation leave gave everyone a lively week, and shortly after they had departed, Polly went to her father with a new request. She had been thinking about women doing men's jobs ever since Jessie took on Field, and about not wanting to start at the bottom and work up. Perhaps she couldn't *quite* begin as prime minister, but her father had a drapery store in York, Makepeace's, and department stores, also called Makepeace's, in Leeds and Manchester. Papa had said they would be hers one day – little James would have the Morland estate – so she could start there, which at least was a lot closer to the top than a stable. So, in preparation, she asked her father if she could learn how the business worked.

Teddy responded as he would have to any other fancy of hers. If she had wanted to learn archery or keep fancy bantams or take up stamp-collecting he would have indulged her, made the arrangements and spent the money with great cheerfulness and no expectation that the fad would last. So now he arranged for her to be taken to the store whenever she wanted, and told Mrs Lowe, the manager, and Mr Corvine, the book-keeper, to show her everything and answer all her questions. He expected one visit would be enough to cool her enthusiasm, but to his surprise she found it interesting enough to want to go back.

'There's so much to learn,' she said. 'Some of it's awfully confusing, especially the accounting side. I'm not sure Mr Corvine really has everything pat, because there were lots of things he couldn't explain to me properly – but I really want to understand it all. And,' she added, with a gleam in her eye, 'when I *do* understand it, I bet I shall want to change a lot of things.'

Teddy beamed at her, proud of her nascent business sense. 'I expect you will, my darling, and when the war's over we'll make all the changes you want. Trade will boom after the war.'

Polly went into the shop on two mornings a week, and soon had to have a new outfit for it, a very serious-looking tailor-made with white blouses and a supply of paper cuffs to keep her sleeves clean. Henrietta was glad that she did have a new interest and hoped she would stick at it. Polly would be sixteen in May, and a girl of that age needed something disciplined to do to keep her occupied. Had there not been a war on, Teddy would no doubt have sent her to a finishing school abroad – he had been talking about one in Vienna some years ago – and the difficult two years between school and come-out would have been used up in that way. Polly's notice of boys was still light and capricious – her object changed almost weekly – but girls of sixteen with too much time on their hands could easily fancy themselves seriously in love, and Polly was headstrong enough to make things difficult if she did. Teddy would certainly deem anyone lower than the Prince of Wales no match for his darling, and the horrid prospect of tears and tantrums, and possible threats of elopement, beckoned.

Polly's youthful fancy for Lennie seemed to have faded – Henrietta noticed that he wrote to her much more often than she replied – which was a shame, because he was safely out of the way at the Front, and that sort of distant yearning gave a girl something to think about on which she could not act. Henrietta remembered how Jessie had had a similar crush on her cousin Bertie when he was at the war in South Africa. What nobody wanted was for Polly to develop a crush on a local boy, think it was true love, and make everyone's life miserable. The more she had to keep her busy the better.

Polly's being at the shop gave Emma more time to pursue her own interests, and she enjoyed having two mornings a week to herself. She had made one or two friends of her own now, whom she liked to visit. And she was still corresponding with Maria, and was delighted when Maria wrote with an invitation to go and stay with her in London.

> Now I am a married woman, I can escort you, but if your guardians don't think my chaperonage enough, there is my mother to guarantee respectability. My little house is not grand, and you will have to share a bed with me, but we will do our best to make you comfortable. I can't take you to the fashionable balls, of course, and the opera and theatre are beyond my purse, but there are still the galleries and exhibitions (and even the kinema!) to amuse us. I think we could have a pleasant time together, and to be frank, dear friend, you would do me a kindness in coming. This is the first time since I left school that I have not had a job to use up my time, and I am finding it hangs heavily on my hands.

London! Emma's old longings sprang up. Apart from being the most exciting place on earth, it was her home, and she missed it. She didn't mind about not being part of the Season – though she hoped she might be able to call on one or two friends while she was there. She longed to see Maria's 'little house', and knew she would enjoy her company and her conversation; and having plenty of money herself, she hoped she would be allowed to pay for tickets to the plays Maria would like to see. She wrote accepting, subject to her guardians' approval, which she had no doubt would be forthcoming. Maria and her mother were quiet, decent people, and far removed from the stratum of society Uncle Bruce now viewed with suspicion.

The reply from Aberlarich was not what she had expected.

'My uncle says I'm not to go to London!' she cried in dismay, when she opened the letter at the breakfast table. 'He wants me to go to stay with him and Aunt Betty. They're taking a house in Edinburgh on purpose. Apparently they have a Season there, too.' As her eyes travelled down the page, she gave a wail of anguish. 'And after that they've arranged a series of country-house visits for me for the whole of the summer!'

'Oh dear,' said Henrietta. She knew how little Emma liked Scotland; but evidently the Abradales now viewed London as the Pit, and would do everything to keep Emma from it. She tried to find reconciling words. 'But, you know, it's natural that they should want to have you with them. They've seen very little of you in the past few years. And I'm sure you'll enjoy all the dances and so on.'

Emma looked at her in despair. 'But can you imagine what the Season will be like in Edinburgh? Dowdy girls and second-rate bands, and nothing but awkward, dull young men straight out of the highlands, who can hardly speak English, never mind know how to amuse a girl. And tartan everywhere!'

'Tartan!' Alice shuddered at that thought, and had to fortify herself with a sip of coffee.

Henrietta tried to strike a balance. 'You don't know it will be like that. I'm sure there are lots of good families in Scotland. I expect you'll find that Edinburgh's just as lively and fashionable as London, and you'll have a lovely time.'

'She won't. It won't be,' said Polly, with certainty. 'Don't go, Emma! *I* wouldn't.'

'You'd go if you were told to,' said Ethel, who often thought Polly was allowed to get away with too much.

'I wouldn't.'

'You don't understand,' said Emma. 'Uncle isn't asking me, he's ordering me to come. Everything's arranged. He says which train I have to catch, and they'll meet it. He's even telegraphed the price of the ticket to York station in case I've spent my month's allowance. I have to go.'

'Of course Emma must do what her guardians want,' Henrietta said, to forestall Polly. 'But I'm sure you'll enjoy it, Emma dear, and you can always come back here afterwards.'

'After the country houses there'll be shooting parties and hunting parties right up to Christmas, and they'll expect me to stay there for that, and for the New Year. Then it will be something else. They'll never let me go.' Emma shook her head miserably. 'It was my wanting to go to London that did the mischief. Because of Violet, Uncle thinks London is a den of iniquity. They mean to get me married off, that's what it is. They'll dangle me at every unmarried man they know, and make me be nice to them, and keep me there until I give up in despair. I'll end up marrying someone with red hair who lives in the wilds of Cromarty and thinks a visit to Inverness is enough excitement for a lifetime!'

Henrietta laughed at that, and said, 'Oh, Emma!'

'It's true! I'll have to live in some terrible damp castle and have fourteen children, and I'll never be seen again!'

'You do exaggerate! Your aunt and uncle can't make you marry anyone you don't like, you know.'

Jessie looked up from the harness catalogue she had been pretending to read. 'They can't keep you there for ever, Em. You'll be twenty-one next January, and then you'll be free to go wherever you want.'

'But I don't come into my fortune until I'm twenty-five.'

'But, still, they have to give you an allowance, don't they? You told me that was in your father's will.'

'I think it was,' Emma said. 'I don't remember much about the exact terms – I wasn't listening much when they were explained to me – thinking about Papa, you know. If there is an allowance in it, I don't know how much it would be.'

'Why don't you write to the solicitor?' Jessie said. 'What's his name? Bracey, didn't you say?'

'Yes, Peter Bracey,' said Emma. 'He was always very nice to me, and tried to explain things clearly, only I was too upset to take it in properly.'

'Write and ask him, then, what the will says. Then you'll know the worst. And, remember, even if you won't have enough to be independent, they can't stop you coming back here if you want, once you're twenty-one.'

'I suppose not,' she sighed. Little as she wanted to go to Scotland, she didn't like the thought of defying her kind uncle and aunt and making them unhappy.

'You'll have to go to them now and make the best of it,' Jessie said, 'but if you talk to them you might make them see reason and let you come back sooner. I expect they only want what they think is best for you. They can't *want* to make you unhappy.'

Emma nodded reluctantly. 'But I shall miss you all so much, and dear Morland Place. Oh dear!'

'Don't cry, or you'll make me cry,' Jessie said.

Emma sniffed back the tears. 'Not you. You never cry,' she said, feeling for her handkerchief.

Jessie felt rather like crying when Emma had gone. The house seemed empty without her. Polly was out a great deal, and in any case was too young to be much of a companion to her. Uncle Teddy was going through a busy period and was hardly ever at home, so when Jessie was in the house she usually had for company only the three matrons, who all in their way reminded her of her widowed and barren state. Work at the stables was so slack now that she wasn't needed; and work at the hospital was tiring and monotonous without being in any way fulfilling. Her thoughts were harder to escape, and as comfortless as they had been for months past.

She felt as though she had been abandoned by life. Ned was dead, and had left a cavernous hole in her life. Bertie was far away, and she tried not to think about him too often, because when the war ended things would be no better: she loved him, and she would never be able to be with him. Violet seemed just as lost to her, for different reasons. What had her life to offer? Never love again, or marriage, or children. Was she doomed to remain here, the daughter-at-home, filling the void of days with running the stables? Polly would marry and go away, James would marry and inherit, and then she would be poor Cousin Jessie, a grey old dependant tolerated by James's wife and laughed at by his children.

She caught herself back from self-pity. She need never be tolerated or laughed at. The stables were hers, and the income thereof, and after the war she would get back Ned's factory, which had been requisitioned. She would have enough to keep herself in decent style in a home of her own. She would have independence, and how many women were as blessed as that? But she saw herself in the decent home, and shivered. It looked so lonely and pointless. She *was* lonely – and she hadn't enough purpose in her life to make her forget that.

Easter approached, and relief came in the form of a visit from Jack and Helen, bringing baby Basil with them. Jessie hoped they might come by aeroplane again – it had been very enlivening last time, when Helen had flown herself and Jack in a borrowed trainer and landed in a field lovingly prepared by Uncle Teddy. Helen had taken Jessie up for a pleasure trip, and she had understood for the first time the great joy and fascination of flying.

But this time, perhaps because of the newness of the baby, they came by train. The first thing Helen said when she stepped down from it was, 'Goodness, how long it takes, travelling this way! I can't wait to get airborne again.'

'You look wonderfully well,' Jessie said, giving her a hug.

'I feel absurdly well, considering what I've been through. Childbirth is not the unmitigated joy one is led to believe, you know. One can't help feeling, while one's in the middle of it, that God didn't think it out quite carefully enough. But here's the boy himself.' She reached back for the baby, handed down to her by Jack, and plumped him into Jessie's arms. He was awake, and looked wonderingly at her, and when she smiled he gave her a gummy smile in return. He was a very attractive-looking baby, she thought, much prettier than Ethel's had been at the same age. 'We didn't bring a nurse,' Helen went on, 'because it seemed like bringing coals to Newcastle; and, besides, Jack said Nanny Emma would be mortally offended.'

'Quite true,' said Jack, getting down with two bags.

Jessie thrust the baby back at Helen to free both her arms for her darling brother. He enfolded her in a hug, and she felt the wonderful sensation of a young man's arms and strength and hard body, something she had long missed. 'Dear Jackie! I'm so glad you've come,' she whispered, and felt tears rising. She wanted to weep on his shoulder and have him make everything all right. But this was the grown-up world, and things couldn't be made right that were so very wrong. Fortunately she was distracted then by having to greet Rug, who had some passionate things to say about being on a leash, and about railway journeys generally.

Jack examined her face closely. 'How are you, Jess? You look thin. And tired.'

'I'm all right,' she said. 'But look at you! No stick, no limp – and you're flying again!'

'Oh, yes, and the ankle's holding up perfectly well. It ached a bit at first – it aches rather when it's cold, too, and the medico says it always will. But I'm fit to go. They won't let me go to the Front just yet. I'm having to practise with all the new aeroplanes they've brought in since my time. And there are lots of other skills I have to learn before I go. But I shall be going to France this summer, that's certain.'

They linked arms and walked after Uncle Teddy and Helen, who were following the porter towards the exit.

‘What does Helen think about that?’ she said.

‘What do women always think? She’s pleased for me, of course, but would rather have me at home. *I*’d rather be at home,’ he added, ‘just in case you thought otherwise, but I’m needed at the Front, and the quicker we can beat the Boche, the sooner I can come back and settle down for good.’

‘I heard things were bad out there – for the RFC, I mean.’

He looked grave. ‘Those Fokkers are simply destroying us with their forward-firing guns, and there’s nothing we can do about it.’

‘But didn’t you say in one of your letters that you’ve solved the problem of the – what was it?’

‘Interrupter gear? Yes, we’ve got a working prototype, but it takes such ages to get things through production at the RAF. Sopwith’s have already got a new bus they call the 1½ Strutter, which has interrupter gear, but the first models are going to the navy, of course, and the army won’t get any until July at the earliest. That’s a two-seater, an observation aeroplane. My old friend Harry Hawker has been testing a single-seater version they call the Pup – because it looks like the pup of the 1½ Strutter – but it will be even longer before that’s in service. The RFC probably won’t get it until the autumn. Meanwhile Trenchard has to order every observation plane to be accompanied by three or four fighters to protect it, so you can imagine how that slows things down. And in some sectors the scouts aren’t allowed to cross the front line at all – it’s simply too dangerous.’

‘Is that the Major Trenchard who’s Helen’s uncle?’

‘“Boom” Trenchard is Helen’s uncle’s brother-in-law,’ Jack corrected, ‘but he’s an old friend of her father’s too. And he’s a brigadier now. He commands the whole of the RFC on the Western Front. I must say, it’s a great help to have someone in charge who understands flying and knows how to use aircraft properly. And now with Haig we’ve got a commander-in-chief who’s air-minded, too.’

'Didn't you teach Brigadier Trenchard to fly in the first place?'

'Yes, at Sopwith's school. A long time ago that seems, now.' They stepped out into the station yard. 'Ah, there's dear old Simmons, still going strong.'

'Yes,' said Jessie vaguely. 'Jack, how do *you* feel about going out? I mean, you really want to go, don't you?'

'I've already said, I'd sooner be at home. But there's a war on, and I have to do my bit.'

'You *want* to do your bit.'

'Of course. I couldn't sit by and let the Germans get away with it. Any man would feel the same. I have to do every last thing in my power to save the dear old country, and civilisation in general.' He looked at her curiously. 'But why do you ask?' She didn't answer. 'Are you thinking about Ned, and wondering whether it was worth it?' She looked away, and he squeezed her arm. 'Look here, none of us *wants* to die, but if that's what it takes, there isn't one of us who wouldn't pay the price, and willingly, for the things and the people we love. Ned would have said the same. His life wasn't wasted. You should be proud of him.'

'I am,' she said. 'It isn't that.'

'What is it, then?' he asked, but she shook her head. They had reached the motor now, and there was no more opportunity for private talk.

Nanny Emma was delighted with the new baby. Of her own 'babies', Frank was her favourite, but she had always thought Jack the pick of the bunch. She was pleased that he had married such a 'right 'un' and was thrilled beyond measure to have his son in her arms. She didn't like the name Basil, though. George was a perfectly good English name, and it seemed a shame to be calling a poor helpless baby by a nasty foreign name when he couldn't help himself.

'The ploy didn't work, either,' Helen said. 'My cousin Basil turned out to be a snare and a delusion as a godfather. We thought he would come down with a handsome present if we named the baby after him, but all he gave was a silver spoon. Not even a set, just a single spoon! Still, we've got used to the name now, so there's nothing we can do.'

Helen didn't need Jack's quiet words when they were in bed that night to tell her Jessie was unhappy. She was sorry to see how shut-away she seemed – what Emma had described to herself as 'grim' – with the spark of joy in life dimmed. She was determined to find a way to have a good, long talk with her, and told Jack so.

'Good. Perhaps you can help her to come to terms with it. Poor Jess, it was doubly hard for her because she wasn't just losing a husband, she was losing someone like a brother.'

'And she had those miscarriages,' Helen said. 'She's been left with nothing, poor girl.'

Jack thought of how baby Basil had already enriched their lives. If he should 'go west', he would be glad to think that Helen had something of him to remember him by.

The next day, when Jack was deep in a manly conversation with Uncle Teddy and Robbie, about the war, business and finance, Helen took Jessie away on the excuse of giving Rug a walk, and they and the dogs went out and headed, pretty much at random, up the slope towards the Monument – a sort of half-ruined folly. It was a bright day, cool and rather breezy, with thin, fretful sunshine gleaming between fast-moving clouds. There were primroses showing pale in the shadows of the hedge-banks, and along the ditch edges the wild daffodils on their short stems bent and straightened, curtsying to the wind. The air smelled of spring, of the green, growing things thrusting their heads up above the damp earth at last.

The dogs romped about, getting the wind in their ears, excited to have a new playmate in Rug. The hounds were four times his size, and rolled him over like a skittle, but he was tough and could hold his own. Helen said he made up in personality what he lacked in stature and, true enough, he soon established himself as the leader of the pack and had them charging away over the rise, looking for adventure.

Jessie found Helen a good person to walk with because she strode out properly and didn't mince along and dawdle like most women – Jessie always found dawdling made her back ache. They talked about the baby, and Helen's house and what she hoped to do with it, and Jack's reviving career.

'He won't tell you, but he's terribly afraid they're going to put him onto Home Defence. With all these Zeppelin raids, the politicians are worried that they're not seen to be doing enough, so they're setting up airfields all round London – nine of them so far. The idea, as far as we gather, is to have two BE2s at each field, with two pilots to fly them. They're to be experienced instructors, so that during the day they can be training new pilots, while they're on call at night for defence flying – shooting down the Zepps if they come over. Well, obviously Jack fits the bill rather too well, and he's afraid that they'll use his ankle as an excuse to send him there rather than to France.'

'I should think *you*'d be glad if they did,' said Jessie, 'especially with what he was saying about the Fokkers.'

Helen didn't answer for a moment. Then she said, 'I would rather have a husband who was free to do what he felt he must, even at the risk of his life, than one safe at home with the fight gone out of him, like a neutered cat.' Jessie looked startled at the metaphor. Helen went on, 'I'm quite serious. I've seen what this injury has done to him, during all those long months when he thought he was never going to fly again. I've had him at home, tied by the leg. Now it's time to let him go. He's aching to go to France. He may be killed – I have to accept that. But he has to do what's in him to do. Of course,' she added, 'I pray like anything that the war ends soon and he'll come back safely to me. But I suppose God has a lot of requests like that.'

She glanced at her companion. 'He can't say yes to all of them.'

'And you,' Jessie said, her eyes fixed forward, 'will you go back to what you were doing before – delivering aeroplanes?'

'Yes, if they'll have me. Not for a few more weeks, but when Basil's six months old I shall reapply. We've got a good girl now, and I feel I can be away one or two days a week if I have to.'

'Will you be doing it for the love of flying, or for the war effort?'

'Both, of course. I love to fly – but if I couldn't, I believe I'd have to find some other way to do my bit. Molly feels the same. She's enrolled in a secretarial college now. It took some lengthy badgering to get Mother to agree – she's terrified it will turn Molly into even more of a tomboy, and she'll never see her married. I had to tell her that secretarial ladies were universally known to be the daintiest, most feminine creatures on the earth.' She laughed. 'I'm not sure she believed me. But, oddly, Father was in favour – and, of course, Molly wore Mother down. She gave in in the end because she couldn't face having the subject revived at every single meal for the rest of time!'

They reached the top of the rise as the dogs came haring back, tongues lolling, out of breath from their expedition. Just looking at them made Helen feel tired so she proposed sitting on the Monument's steps for a while, and the dogs flopped down around them. Rug rolled back and forth in the grass, his legs waving ridiculously, then slid along on his back, rubbing his muzzle along the ground until he sneezed.

Helen left a silence into which Jessie could pour her troubles if she wanted, and in a little while she did. Hesitantly at first – because she had kept everything inside for so long – but gradually with more fluency, she told of her feelings of isolation and loneliness, the sense that life had abandoned her, that she was stranded in a backwater while the main river flowed on past, bearing everything and everyone away from her.

'You have your work,' Helen said at last, when Jessie came to an end of the immediate outpouring. 'Nothing can bring Ned back, but you could make your work your purpose in life – for the time being, at least.'

'But it's stupid work,' Jessie said. 'Anyone could do it. They don't really need me at the stables. The head man knows what to do, and he can run everything. And at the hospital all I do is clean things and, if I'm very lucky, feed the men who can't feed themselves. It isn't,' she added hastily, 'that I don't want to do those things for them. It *is* an honour to do anything for the men who've given so much for us, but—'

'You are capable of so much more,' Helen finished for her. 'Your work doesn't fulfil you.'

'That sounds selfish.'

'Not at all,' said Helen, firmly. 'Waste is a sin, and your abilities are being wasted. And there's nothing wrong in enjoying your work, if it's important to the war effort. Look here, I see a clear parallel with my own case. I love to fly, I enjoy it, but there's important work to be done delivering aircraft, which frees the male pilots, who would otherwise have to do it, for the war.'

'You're lucky,' said Jessie.

'Yes, I am. But we're talking about you now. You want to do something worthwhile to help the war effort?'

'Yes.'

'And you like to nurse?'

'I think I would, very much, if I were allowed to do it properly.'

'Then *do* it properly. Join a VAD and nurse in a military hospital. Nurse the soldiers when they need it most, fresh from the Front. And let someone else scrub the bedpans and the Mackintosh sheets – someone who can't do any better.'

Jessie stared at her, thinking it through. 'Do you think I could?'

'Only you can answer that. You've seen something of nursing by now. Would you like to be doing what the proper nurses do?'

'I think so. Yes, I think I would.' She thought again. 'And it would be for the men at the Front. I'd be doing it for every one of them.' She was remembering Bertie's words when she had first gone to work at the hospital: *You are doing for those soldiers what I hope some other angel would do for me if ever I should need it.*

Fortunately Helen understood what she meant. 'Don't rush into it, but think it out carefully. It would be hard work, I don't doubt, but you'd have the satisfaction of knowing you were doing your utmost for the war effort.'

Jessie smiled. 'That's what Jack said – that he had to do every last thing in his power. Thank you, Helen. It ought to have been obvious to me, but I needed you to open my eyes. It's the answer, I know it is.'

Helen laid a hand on hers. 'Jessie, it won't cure your loneliness. But one day the war will be over, and people will take up their lives again, and then you'll meet someone else. He won't be Ned, but he'll love you and you'll love him and it will be all right. That's what happens.'

Jessie thought at once of Bertie, and her eyes grew bleak. *But not for me,* she thought.

Helen saw the expression and was saddened. Well, after all, it was only six months. God forbid she could get over losing Jack in six months, if the worst should happen. She had planted a seed in Jessie's mind, anyway, and no-one could do more. She stood up. 'I'm getting cold. Shall we walk on, or turn back? I think it might be going to rain, don't you?'

Oliver found his work at the No. 2 General rewarding, and it would have been wrong to say he did not appreciate the comforts of home. He was even able sometimes, during his hours off, to help Mark Darroway with a case or two, which relieved his conscience about not going to the Front. His friend Kit Westhoven wrote regularly from Ypres, and expressed himself as disappointed as Oliver that they would not be working together for some time. He had just 'signed on' again for another year and, as was customary at that time in the RAMC, had received a promotion to captain. 'So now when we meet you will have to call me "sir"!' he wrote jokingly.

Oliver enjoyed their correspondence. With his mother's help, he regularly sent Kit parcels. Kit's father was dead, and his stepmother had been so glad to be rid of the boys she would never have dreamed of ministering to their comfort in any way. As well as the usual soap, chocolate, cigarettes and tinned food, the parcel always included a book, something Oliver had read, which they would discuss by letter when Kit had read it too. Kit said it helped to keep his mind flexible to think about other things than war, wounds and sickness. He confessed also to writing poetry when he was not on duty, but so far had refused to let Oliver read any of it.

An interruption to the lightheartedness of the correspondence came in April when Kit wrote to say that he had received news of his brother's death. Roger, Lord Westhoven, was a Guards major and had been serving with Headquarters staff. He had been killed when inspecting a section of the line near Armentières, shot in the head by a sniper. Ironically, it was to avoid that increasingly common cause of death that the troops at the Front had just been issued with steel helmets to wear in the trenches. The tin hats, as the soldiers called them, replaced the universal soft caps, which offered no protection. Lord Westhoven had been sent by Headquarters to a recently supplied battalion to see what they thought of them, and whether they had reduced casualties.

Kit was now Captain Lord Westhoven, and the family estate near Lutterworth was his. As it was a quiet time at Ypres he was allowed a two-day special leave to visit his home, settle his stepmother and interview his solicitor. He shared a man of business with Emma Weston – like one or two other fashionable London lawyers, Bracey dealt with the estates of many of the aristocratic and wealthy.

The time left was too short for Kit to visit Manchester Square, but Oliver contrived to meet him at the railway station on his way back to the Front. They shook hands heartily and made their way to the refreshment room. 'How long have you got?' Oliver asked.

Kit looked at his watch. 'Half an hour before the train goes. No, let me – I'm the newly wealthy Lord Westhoven, remember? Brandy and soda?'

Oliver found them a small table in a quiet corner, and soon they were sitting with their drinks. All around them surged a tide of khaki, only lightly sprinkled with females: the war had been going on long enough for lengthy farewells to have fallen out of fashion.

'You're looking well,' said Kit. 'How's the new job?'

'Interesting. Long hours, but such a variety of cases it hasn't palled yet. You're looking tired.'

'There's been a lot to do in a short time.'

'I'm sorry about your brother.'

'Poor Roger! It was such a trifling way to go, after all – not falling in glorious battle, which is what I suspect he would have wanted, but picked off on his way up to the line, without even knowing it. You know how platoon officers always write to the families that such and such a man was "shot in the head and died without suffering", no matter what actually happened? Well, it really was that way for Roger. I suppose the not-suffering bit's a blessing anyway.'

'And how was your stepmother?'

Kit's face hardened. 'Oh, she's positively blithe. Why should she care about Roger? She never did before.'

'Does she stay on at the house?'

'For the time being. There is a dower house on the other side of the park, but of course it's much less grand than the "pile" so she's not eager to move. And Bracey thinks it better to have the house inhabited than left empty, and recommended I left her be, until and unless I want to live there myself.'

'You inherit the pile, of course?'

'And the estate. Apparently it's in pretty decent order. I had a long talk with Bracey. You see, Father died in 1914, and everything got sorted out then, so what with Rog having been at the Front the whole time since, there hasn't been time for any new muddles to form. Bracey knows where to lay his hand on everything. Roger wasn't extravagant – he's hardly drawn anything since he inherited, just his mess expenses – and my stepmother had her settlement when Father died and couldn't touch anything from the main estate . . . fortunately, or she'd have spent the lot! So it doesn't hurt me to let her go on living there. The servants are paid for by the estate, except her own woman, but someone has to tell them what to do. Of course, the blasted death duties will take a chunk out of the inheritance – damn the man who thought of them! – but agricultural prices always rise in wartime, and Bracey thinks, if I'm careful, the effect of them will be got over in a few years.'

'So you're a rich man?' Oliver said with a grin.

'Not *am* – will be. And only probably. And not rich, really, only comfortable. Not as rich as you, I dare say.'

'What a lot of conditionals! Anyway, I'm not rich. I don't have anything at all, except my salary.'

Kit blushed. 'Oh! Sorry. I thought—'

'I expect you're confusing me with my mother. She's immensely rich. I dare say she'll leave me a little something one day, seeing as there's no old family estate to be kept together, but I don't like to think about that since she'll have to be dead to leave it to me, and I rather like to have her alive.'

Kit recovered his colour. 'You're a lucky man. I wish she was my mother too.'

Oliver smiled benignly. 'I'll share her with you, if you like – and the pater. But luck has nothing to do with it, you know. I've put in years of careful training on the Aged Ps to get them the way they are.'

When he had seen Kit off with renewed promises to write, he walked home, to find only Violet there. She was in a state of agitation, and Oliver sat down with her in the drawing-room and set himself to calm her and hear her story.

As it was a fine day, and tiring of being so much indoors, she had gone out with her maid to look at the shops in Bond Street. There, she had had the ill-luck to encounter Mrs Desborough, whose husband Percy – always known as Des – was on General Plumer's staff at the Front.

'I was across the street from her and wearing a veil, so I didn't think she'd see me, but perhaps it was Sanders she recognised, because she gave a little wave and came straight across. I simply couldn't escape.'

'But why should you want to?' Oliver said. 'I thought Betsy Desborough was one of your "bosoms" before all this?'

'But I haven't seen anyone or spoken to anyone since I came back, and I really didn't want to yet.'

Oliver thought that in that case she should not have gone to Bond Street, but he didn't say so. 'I hope she wasn't unkind?' he said instead.

'No, not at all – at least, she didn't mean to be. In fact, she was being very nice, except that it was what she was saying . . . Oh, Oliver, she *congratulated* me!'

'Congratulated you? On what?'

'The baby, of course. She said she heard it from Des. He wrote saying he'd dined with Holkam and some other officers when General Plumer went to Headquarters, and he said – Holkam said – he *announced* to the company that I was expecting a child. Des told Betsy about it in a letter and they both seem to have assumed it was Holkam's.'

'Well, that's good, isn't it?' Oliver said. 'It must mean that Holkam didn't say anything to the contrary – or even hint at it, because Mrs Desborough would have made the most of it if she thought there was any scandal attached.'

'You can be sure of that,' Violet said bitterly. 'As it was, she put her head right up to mine and whispered how glad she was that everything was all right again and that she couldn't be more thrilled for me, and that children were always the best ambassadors, and that it was a great shame the other thing had got out of hand because there was no harm in it as long as everyone concerned was discreet.' She made a face of disgust. 'The impertinence! To think of someone like her sitting in judgement on me! And now she'll tell everyone about the baby and I'll have people calling and staring at me –'

'Dearest—'

'– and calling Octavian "that other thing" as though he were a shameful secret!'

'Well, in reason—'

'And, oh, Oliver, the worst thing of all is that Holkam's telling people I'm having a child and letting them congratulate him, but he hasn't written a word to me, not a *word*!' Tears – as much of anger, Oliver thought, as grief – spilled over from his sister's violet eyes and shone like diamonds on her magnolia cheeks. He thought distractedly that she was growing more beautiful in pregnancy even than she had been before.

He went to sit beside her and drew her against him. 'Poor darling,' he said, proffering his handkerchief. 'But, you know, you must try to grow a thicker hide. I dare say you will have a lot of pinpricks like this to bear – and living in London you were bound to come up against people you knew sooner or later. As for Holkam, it seems to me he's doing the right thing by you, allowing it to be thought the child is his; and given the circumstances, you can hardly expect him to be overjoyed about it, or be writing you tender letters.'

'I didn't say I wanted a tender letter,' Violet said, drying her eyes. 'Just a letter of any sort. Now I can feel the baby moving, it makes it all seem so much more real, and urgent. But poor Octavian doesn't even *know* yet, because I dare not tell him until I know for sure what Holkam means to do. Sometimes I think he intends to let me go to the very end in this state of suspense. He tells someone he cares as little for as Desborough, but he doesn't tell me what he wants me to say. It isn't fair. It isn't *courteous*.'

Oliver suppressed a smile. He thought courtesy was a milepost long passed; but he did think Holkam could have been kinder. But, then, Holkam had never been a kind person. Still, it would surely have been sensible to tell Violet what he meant to say so that she could say the same. Or did he hope that by keeping her in confusion and ignorance he might make it impossible for her to go out into company at all? No, that was too Machiavellian for Holkam, whom Oliver thought rather a simple brute. Probably he had not thought about her at all, until meeting Desborough presented him with an opportunity of putting out the story that did him most credit.

To take Violet's mind off things he began to tell her about his meeting with Kit Westhoven, and then had to start again when his mother came in two sentences later. Venetia listened to the story with attention, and asked a number of questions, for she had a keen and motherly interest in Kit. She seemed struck by the story in some particular way he could not identify, and when Violet went upstairs shortly afterwards he asked her, 'What was it about Kit's brother dying that gave you pause? You looked "struck all of a heap" for a moment.'

'Oh, was it obvious? Well, it was the fact that Roger Westhoven was a staff officer. I was saying to your father the other day that Holkam was as safe as houses because he was on the staff, and now here's Westhoven proving me wrong.'

'Ah, and you were hoping Violet wouldn't put two and two together?'

'I wasn't so much worried on her account as on my own,' said Venetia. 'You see, I realised I had never even thought about Holkam being killed, and I had to do some soul-searching—'

'Because it might mean you didn't care if he *was*? Oh, Mum!' Oliver shook his head in reproof. 'Perhaps you even hoped he might be?'

'Don't tease, you horrid boy. The situation is complicated enough. And I've never hoped anything of the sort!'

'I believe you – just. But now you must hear Violet's news.' He relayed to her the meeting with Mrs Desborough.

'Well, that's excellent,' Venetia said. 'Betsy Desborough will have it all over Town in no time – and she's bound to tell her mother, who will inform the older generation too. It could hardly have worked out better. The news had to come out some time, and I know Violet was fretting about having to lie. This way she won't have to say a word.'

'But what an odd sort Holkam is, not to have written to *her* on the subject,' Oliver said.

'Perhaps he's busy,' Venetia said, and frowned when Oliver laughed. 'I know it sounds silly, but I mean it! When one has so much to do, it crowds everything else out of one's mind. I haven't thought about Violet's situation all day, and I'm her mother!'

'Notwithstanding,' Oliver said, 'I beg leave to go on thinking Holkam is a callous and selfish brute.'

In her room, Violet had been persuaded by Sanders to lie down and rest. The maid removed her shoes, bathed her face in lavender-water, and helped her onto the sofa under the window. Violet told her to leave the curtains open, and asked for her satinwood box to be handed to her before Sanders departed. In the box, Violet kept her treasures, and from it she took Laidislaw's most recent letter and read it again.

He didn't write much about what life was like at the Front, only that the food was horrible, the dirt wearisome and the noise unspeakable – 'You can't imagine how loud a shell is – no-one could who hadn't heard it – it's *unendurable*!' Mostly he wrote with vivid enthusiasm about the drawing he was doing: 'Faces, faces, faces! So many of them, and so varied!' With his predilection for portraiture, he was like a child let loose in a sweet shop. In the trenches, in a quiet time, there was little to do all day, so he had ample opportunity, and his companions showed no reluctance to sit for him. His work before had been mostly of women, and gentlewomen at that, captured in the calm of their elegant drawing-rooms. Now he had only men, rough Tommies and their officers, against a background of privation and danger. He could not get enough of their physiognomies and expressions. He drew and drew obsessively in every spare moment, and it had the power to block out from his mind the real and potential horrors of his situation. He gave her a list of things that he must have sent as soon as possible, more sketching-pads, charcoal, pencils, erasers – along with the usual cigarettes, chocolate and tinned delicacies.

Violet liked to imagine him crouched in a trench and drawing his companions as frantically as he had drawn her. She did not know what a trench was like, so she imagined it rather more commodious and a great deal cleaner than reality, and generally invested him with a proper stool and drawing-board. It made her happy to think of him so occupied, rather than firing a gun; her artist still, only wearing a soldier's clothes.

But it was the last part of the letter she read and reread with the greatest pleasure.

> Though I hid it from you, I was resentful at first when I was called up, because it interrupted my work, but now I see that I was sent here by God's will. I am

recording something which has never been seen before in the world, and there is no-one but me to do it. My painting of you will always be, to me, my finest work, but what I am doing here may come to be more important. Yet if I had not met you, I would probably have gone abroad and not have been conscripted. Being here has made me realise more than ever that you and I were brought together for a purpose. It is yet another reason for me to love you.

Because I do love you, my beloved: I realise it more every day. Here at the Front, with death a close companion, I know our love is no light fancy, but a great and burning beacon lit for the whole world, and it will endure for ever. We shall be together, I promise you. You have done your duty by Holkam and need feel no guilt on his behalf. When the war is over I shall approach him man to man, and he must and shall release you. We shall marry, and set up quiet and retired, and live a life of domestic bliss, like those dear days in Norfolk. I shall paint the world for you and lay it at your feet, and History will celebrate you as my muse and inspiration. Your fame, with mine, will never die.

She read the treasured words, and thought of that time beyond the end of the war, which was like a glimpse of a distant country seen between two hills – sunlit, desirable, a little unreal. Laying the letter down, she closed her eyes, feeling the baby stir within her, and tried to imagine their life together. She loved his vision, but there were difficulties about it. Holkam had said he would not consider divorce, and she respected him for it. She felt no guilt about her relationship with Laidislaw: the dynastic marriages of the peerage were not like those of other people. But Laidislaw was from another stratum of society. He did not see that divorce was an entirely different matter, not to be contemplated; remarriage an even more unthinkable horror.

And she had serious doubts that the flamboyant Laddie, the successful artist, would be happy to live 'quiet and retired'. He loved society and public appearances and adulation, and he could have none of that with her in England. Yet how could they go abroad? It would mean leaving her children – for if she disgraced Holkam by doing something so public as fleeing the country with her lover, he would surely never let her see them again.

She let her mind turn from these intractable problems to the cherished memories of their time together in Ebury Street, and the sweeter, quieter days in Norfolk. It was to the latter she turned more often now, rather than to the kingfisher-bright moments of their first passion. Oh, how she loved him! She longed for him. In her mind she could see him so clearly, trace every line of his adored face, feel again the touch of his lips, his hands, hear the exact tone of his voice speaking love to her: *O si chère de loin et proche et blanche si délicieusement toi . . .*

Rocked on the sea of words, she drifted gently into sleep, and the child inside her – of whose existence her lover was still unaware – grew still and slept too.

CHAPTER ELEVEN

Easter Monday fell on the 24th of April, and before the day ended disturbing news was coming in about an armed uprising in Dublin. The Irish Question had long been an intractiable problem for the British political class, though it was one largely ignored and certainly not understood by the generality of the population. A partial solution had already been negotiatied by the Irish parliamentary party under John Redmond, resulting in the Home Rule Act of 1914, which granted a degree of self-government to Ireland. Unfortunately, the war had intervened, and the Act was suspended for the duration of hostilities. However, in deference to this embryo Irish independence, Ireland was exempted from conscription – although many thousands volunteered, and there was hardly a battalion that did not have Irishmen on its roll.

But this constitutional progress was too slow for the more hot-headed elements, who distinguished themselves from the mainstream by the belief that only physical force could get them what they wanted. Among them, the Irish Republican Brotherhood, a largely middle-class and educated movement, felt that an England distracted by the war against Germany was an easier target. 'England's difficulty is Ireland's opportunity,' they said, and planned the rebellion, to be carried out during Easter 1916.

It happened that a separate, smaller body, the Irish Citizen Army – a group of socialist trades-unionists – was planning its own uprising. Since they numbered only about two hundred they had little chance of success, and the IRB was afraid that a small, failed action would spoil their own chances, so they persuaded the ICA to throw in their lot with them. The rebellion was largely planned by the leader of the IRB, Joseph Mary Plunkett, but was to be carried out by their armed wing, the Irish Volunteers under Padraig Pearse – though since most of the senior members of the IRB also held the top positions in the Volunteers, the distinction was largely spurious.

The plan was to seize strategic buildings and public spaces in Dublin and cordon off the centre of the city, so as to be in a position to fight off the inevitable counter-action by the British Army. The rebellion began well, with the General Post Office being seized. There, Pearse read out a proclamation, declaring that Ireland was now a republic. This was received less than rapturously by the crowds, most of whom were indifferent, while some were downright disapproving, given the greater struggle going on against Germany. Most of the passers-by had at least one relative or friend fighting at the Front in France.

The courts, some factories, and St Stephen's Green were seized, but the rebels did not have enough forces to take Dublin Castle or Trinity College, which left their strongholds dangerously isolated from each other. The British commander at Dublin Castle, General Lowe, had only twelve hundred men under him and little idea how many he was facing, so he concentrated his first efforts on securing the castle and attacking the rebels' headquarters at the GPO.

In response to the upheaval, Dublin's slum population poured into the centre of the city and there was an orgy of looting. One Volunteers officer ordered looters to be shot, while another angrily countermanded the order. The situation was rapidly deteriorating. A policeman was shot dead outside Dublin Castle; Lowe ordered his single gunboat up the river and parts of the city were shelled; fires broke out;

and public disorder was widespread. There were many casualties, and in the confusion of running and shooting, and with the separation of the rebel units from each other, most of them were innocent civilians caught in the crossfire.

Reinforcement troops were rushed from England under General Maxwell, and for the rest of the week the rebels were hunted from place to place, gradually isolated, and captured. On Saturday the 29th, Pearse realised that the game was up and ordered all units to surrender.

While the rebels lost eighty men and the British Army suffered four hundred and fifty casualties, the real victims of the week's action were the civilians – at least two hundred killed and six hundred wounded. For this reason the rebels got little sympathy from the newspapers or the public at large.

The only rebel leader to be killed during the rising was, ironically, The O'Rahilly – Michael Joseph O'Rahilly – who had been against the armed action from the beginning, and had done everything he could to stop it. At the end, when he could not prevent the rising going ahead, he joined it out of loyalty to its cause. He was one of the unit defending the GPO, until, on the Friday, when the situation became hopeless, he led a party of volunteers to try to find a way out, and was caught in machine-gun fire. He died on the cobbles of Sackville Lane, clutching a letter to his wife which he had scribbled in his last moments on the back of an envelope:

> Written after I was shot. Darling Nancy I was shot leading a rush up Moore Street and took refuge in a doorway. While I was there I heard the men pointing out where I was and made a bolt for the laneway I am in now. I got more than one bullet I think. Tons and tons of love dearie to you and the boys and to Nell and Anna. It was a good fight anyhow. Please deliver this to Nannie O'Rahilly, 40 Herbert Park, Dublin. Goodbye Darling.

* * *

Since Helen had planted the seed of 'nursing properly', Jessie had thought about it a great deal, but without putting any definite date on the possibility. The lethargy of bereavement made it difficult to rouse herself to new action. It was easier to keep doing the same things, which required no thought.

On the Wednesday night of the week after Easter, as she lay in bed drifting off to sleep, she was brought back to wakefulness by Brach, first whining in the darkness, and then pawing at the bed. Jessie reached out a hand and located the rough head.

'What's the matter, girl?' she said sleepily, stroking it. Brach licked the underside of her wrist, then put both paws up on the bed and nudged Jessie's arm. Jessie thought perhaps she wanted to go out, and got up to open the bedroom door. Brach padded after her and stepped out into the corridor, but when Jessie went no further she stopped, looked around uneasily and turned back. Jessie listened for a sound of disturbance, sniffed for a hint of smoke, but there was nothing. Besides, the other dogs were down in the Great Hall and would surely have raised the alarm if there was anything wrong. By the night-light in the passage she looked down at the dog, and Brach looked back, swinging her tail slowly.

'I give it up,' Jessie said, and went back to bed. Brach followed, and after padding round the room a few times, she finally settled, and Jessie fell asleep.

In the morning she woke early with a sense that something was different. It was just beginning to get light, but the maid hadn't been in yet. She sat up, listened, then climbed out of bed and went to draw the curtains on a still, grey before-dawn. She turned back to the room. Brach was lying in her usual place on the hearth-rug, nose tucked into her flank, tail curled round. Sometimes she was very catlike, Jessie thought, in the instant before she realised that it was odd that Brach had not woken as soon as she did.

She knew before she touched her that she was dead. From

her posture she must have died quietly in her sleep. Jessie knelt and stroked the harsh coat and the unexpectedly soft ears. Brach's kind were not long-lived dogs, and because of their size and weight it was often the heart that gave out. She had died naturally and suddenly, and in her own place, and that was what one would always wish for one's faithful friend. But it was hard to part with her all the same. She had been Jessie's father's pup, and had chosen Jessie when he died.

Uncle Teddy was a good person to have around at such a time. He took the death of dogs seriously. He asked her if she would like Brach to be buried in the family crypt next to Jerome – she would not be the first dog down there – but Jessie said no. Brach had hardly known him. She had been Jessie's dog. So later that day a hole was dug in the plot up near the Monument where several other dogs had been interred over the years, and Brach was laid reverently to rest.

Afterwards, Teddy said, 'I know you won't want to think about it yet, but the best thing after losing a dog is to get another one. Helle will be whelping in a couple of weeks' time, and you shall have your pick of her litter.'

Jessie thanked him, and put the suggestion aside for another day. They walked home, and Jessie was too aware of the empty place at her heels. She saddled Hotspur and went for a solitary ride. A gallop did them both good, and dried the tears on her face; then she rode up to Cromwell's Plump and stood looking out over the land. It came to her that now there was no reason not to go to London. Brach would have pined for her, and she could not have taken the dog with her, but there was nothing else to keep her here. She would miss Hotspur, but the horse would not miss her. Polly could exercise him, and it wouldn't hurt him to be turned out most of the time. She had nothing left now. Brach's absence made her feel empty and light, like a head of thistledown waiting for the wind to carry it away. Well, let the winds carry her to London, to a new vocation, to serious work, where she could make her proper contribution to the cause that had taken her husband and left her adrift.

The family took the announcement quite well. Henrietta was sad, but she knew from Jessie's face that her mind was made up, that there was no point in arguing. Teddy accepted the wish to nurse properly, understood the desire to 'do one's bit' for the brave boys at the Front. What he did not accept was the need to go to London.

'Why can't you join a local VAD and nurse here?'

Ethel, Robbie and Alice agreed, with different degrees of vehemence, that it was silly to give up the comforts of home and go all that way to do something she could equally well do in York. Even Nanny Emma, when she brought the children down to the drawing-room that day, told Jessie that London was not a nice place for a lone female and she'd much better stay at home with those who loved her.

But Polly was on Jessie's side. She was young enough to understand restlessness and longing for change. Of *course* Jessie should go to London – what sensible person *wouldn't* want to go there? Her only quibble was that Jessie should choose something as dull as nursing. 'Dressing people's wounds and so on – horrid! I'm sure there's something else you could do.'

'But I want to nurse,' Jessie said simply, and Polly shrugged and left it at that.

So in the last days of April Jessie went up to London to initiate her plan. The first step was to join a VAD. At the railway station her taxi-driver directed her to one in Paddington, the London 128, because he had a niece who had joined it. It made no difference to Jessie which she joined, so she took his recommendation. After a short interview, and the showing of her First Aid and Home Nursing certificates, she was enrolled as a full member of the British Red Cross.

Her interviewer, a pleasant, grey-haired woman in her sixties, with a committee member's voice and manner, expressed approval of Jessie's age, her widowed and childless state, and her experience at Clifton, and asked if she was ready to start nursing at once.

'The sooner the better,' Jessie said.

'Then would you like me to arrange an interview for you? The matron of the Number One London General is my god-daughter, and I know she is anxious to take on new nurses. You wouldn't mind nursing in an army hospital, rather than a Red Cross one?'

'It's what I'd prefer,' Jessie said. 'Where is it?

'The Number One London General is in Camberwell. That's in south London. You can get there on the Underground. It's the military wing of Bart's – St Bartholomew's.'

Jessie nodded, knowing nothing about the ancient hospital, though she knew roughly where Camberwell was – her father had sometimes gone to watch cricket at the Oval when she was a child in London.

The woman made a telephone call, and after a lengthy wait while someone was brought to the instrument, Jessie heard herself described and the enquiry put. The woman looked at her and said, 'Can you go for an interview tomorrow?'

Jessie had meant to go back home that night, but the thought of getting everything settled quickly was too tempting. She would find somewhere to stay. 'Yes,' she said.

A few more words were spoken, then the receiver was hung up and the woman said, 'Tomorrow at ten o'clock, then. Take your certificates, and don't be late. Matron is very particular about punctuality.' She smiled suddenly, and said, 'Good luck. I think you are doing absolutely the right thing. Much better than sitting at home feeling sorry for yourself.'

* * *

Now she had the rest of the day to fill, and a lodging to find for the night. She had never stayed in London alone before, and did not know how to go about finding a respectable hotel that would accept a woman on her own. She ran her mind over her acquaintances in London. She meant to visit Maria but, knowing how small her house was, did not want to impose on her. She would call on Maud, but would not dream of asking to stay there.

And then there was Manchester Square. Cousin Venetia would not hesitate to offer her a bed, and her presence would not impose a burden on such a household. But Jessie knew that Violet was staying there, and it would be awkward meeting her for the first time. In the end, her sense of duty towards Cousin Venetia decided her that she must call. She stopped first at a telegraph office to send a wire to Morland Place that she was staying another day and then, not being one to put off an evil, bent her steps to Manchester Square.

She found neither Violet nor Venetia at home, but was received by Oliver, who had a few hours off and was delighted to have someone to talk to. 'The difficulty with irregular hours,' he said, 'is that one can't easily arrange one's company. I was just feeling bored and fancying I had better go and eat at the club, but now you're here we can have luncheon together. Unless,' the thought struck him, 'you've eaten already? Oh, do say you haven't!'

'I haven't,' she said. 'And I'm hungry.'

'Excellent woman. Sit down there, let me get you a glass of sherry, and I'll ring for Burton. Or would you rather go out?'

'I'm not dressed for it.'

'You look very nice to me. That's a smart coat and skirt.'

'This? It's my interview suit – plain and respectable.'

He laughed. 'But there is a war on, you know. Plain and respectable is what we all admire, these days. It's all you'll find at the Ritz.'

Jessie doubted it. 'Thank you, but I'd sooner stay in, if you don't mind.'

'Not at all,' said Oliver.

When luncheon had been ordered, he sat beside her on the sofa and said, 'Now, what's this about an interview?' She told him how she had spent her morning. 'Well, it's taken us a long time, but we've got you here at last,' he said.

'Us?'

'I remember Mark Darroway urging this course of action on you years ago.'

'I've been nursing for some time,' she pointed out.

'Yes, but not proper nursing. You have so much more to give, and I think you are doing exactly the right thing.'

'The family thought I should do it at home.'

'You're more needed here,' he said, 'and . . .' he surveyed her face sympathetically '. . . I think it will do you good to get away from home for a while. Morland Place must be full of memories, and I don't suppose your uncle – with all due respect to him – makes it easier to bear.'

'Uncle Teddy's a dear,' Jessie said, 'but – yes, you're right. I want to be somewhere where nobody knew Ned and won't talk about him. I want to be where nobody knows *me*, and where I can do something useful.'

'You'll be useful at the Number One General all right,' Oliver said. 'And when the big push comes, you'll be worked off your feet.'

'When will that be?'

'It was supposed to be in the autumn, but my father says the French are taking such punishment at Verdun there is great pressure on us to bring the date forward so as to distract the Germans and give them some relief. He wouldn't be surprised if it didn't happen in August instead.'

'Our volunteers – the York Commercials – went out to France earlier this month.'

'Yes, they're bringing out the Kitchener units as fast as they can, to get them trained before the push comes.

Nothing's being left to chance. But big battles mean a big aftermath. Medical services will be stretched to the limit.'

She heard a note of frustration in his voice and said, 'Didn't you want to be out there yourself? I thought you'd planned to go this year.'

He explained. 'Of course, the work I'm doing at Number Two General has to be done by someone, but I can't help wanting to be in the thick of it. Like you,' he said, with a smile, 'I want to use my abilities to the best effect.'

'But they've promised to send you later?'

'Yes. Whatever "later" means.' He shook off the worry. 'But, look, here we both are in London, working at sister hospitals—'

'I haven't been accepted yet,' Jessie pointed out.

'Oh, but you will be. In that coat and skirt? How could they turn you away?'

'Fool!'

He grinned. 'That's better. You've hardly insulted me at all since you arrived. I was beginning to think you'd forgotten how. Anyway, as I was saying, here we both are, and I should take it very kindly if, when our off-duty hours coincide, you would let me take you out to dinner, lunch or tea, as appropriate. It's quite acceptable these days for a man and woman of our advanced years to eat together in a public place,' he added.

'I should take it very kindly too,' said Jessie, 'if you don't think it would cause a scandal for a nurse to be seen eating with a doctor. At Clifton we weren't even allowed to address the doctors directly – though I'm sure most of the nurses had awful crushes on them.'

'We'll go where no nurse ever comes, so no-one will ever know,' he said reassuringly.

Luncheon was served in the small dining-room – soup, fish, an omelette, and fruit and cheese – and over it they talked of more general subjects. Jessie was aware that neither of them had mentioned Violet, and even while it was obviously odd that they should not, Jessie was glad, and suspected that Oliver – always acute – had guessed something of her state of mind. In the end, however, she felt obliged to ask after the rest of the family.

'Oh, my father's busy at the War Office as usual,' Oliver said. 'The mater has got a whole new area of activity. I suppose you heard that she's been made Director of Mobile Radiological Services?'

'Yes, she wrote to my mother about it.'

'Poor Mum!' Oliver laughed. 'She thought having an official title would make all doors fly open, like the magic word, and that all her troubles would be over. They've given her an office and a staff of two and even some money, but she's discovered, poor thing, that she has no turn for administration, and that's what nine-tenths of the job now consists of. It's terribly frustrating for her, because as soon as she became a department, people started writing to it and she hasn't been able to work out a system for dealing with all the correspondence. Of course, as a surgeon, all she had to do at a hospital was tell someone to do something and it got done. She never had to bother with the demn'd details. Now she's getting inky herself, sinking day by day in a morass of paperwork, and whenever she has to dash off and operate, the problems multiply in her absence.'

'Oh dear, it sounds terrible. She must be wishing she'd never started it.'

'I'm afraid it looks to be taking her over, and that was never what she intended,' said Oliver. 'She's a surgeon first and foremost, and the charity things were only supposed to be a sideline.'

And now she had to ask, 'How is Violet? Has she gone back to St James's Square?'

'No, she's still living here,' he said. 'She's gone out to luncheon today with Lady Verney.' He seemed about to add more, but then did not. Jessie supposed Lady Verney was one of the few people in London Violet could safely lunch with, being the friend who first introduced her and Laidislaw and, from the little Jessie knew, rather Bohemian in outlook. Jessie tried to think of something else to say, but at that moment Oliver looked at the clock and gave an exclamation.

'I didn't realise it was so late! I have to be on duty in half an hour. I shall have to go.' He rose, looking down at her. 'I'm so sorry to have to dash away. What will you do? Won't you stay here and have some coffee? I expect Violet will be back soon.' He remembered suddenly. 'You said you have an interview tomorrow – you aren't going back to York tonight?'

'No, I mean to stay in Town.'

'You'll stay here, then? Do. I can safely invite you on my mother's behalf. She wouldn't have you go anywhere else.'

Jessie accepted, with thanks, and then began to say that she would not take coffee, but leave to spend the rest of the afternoon paying visits; but she hadn't got more than the first few words out when Violet came in, back from her luncheon.

'Oh, good!' Oliver said. 'I needn't feel bad about leaving you alone. Forgive me for dashing off.' He bent and kissed her cheek. 'I probably shan't see you later because I shall be working late, but good luck with your interview tomorrow, and be sure to tell me how it comes out. I'll leave you two girls to chat.' He kissed Violet on his way out, and was gone, leaving them to stare uncomfortably at each other.

Violet put the dogs down, and they ran to Jessie, smiling and waving their feathery tails, breaking the awkwardness.

'What a wonderful surprise to see you,' Violet said. She led the way through to the drawing-room next door and sat down. 'I'm sorry I wasn't here when you arrived. What brings you to London?'

So Jessie told her story a second time. Violet listened at first with a doubtful look, not understanding how anyone could *want* to nurse, and afraid therefore that Jessie must be very unhappy; but finally understanding that it was her genuine wish, she smiled. 'I'm glad for you, if it's what you really want; but I'm afraid it will be very hard work.'

'It can't be harder than what I've been doing – and I hope it will be much more interesting.'

A silence fell. Jessie looked at her hands; Violet bit her lip anxiously; the dogs sat gazing at their mistress, wondering if it was time for tea. Then Violet could bear it no longer. She cried, 'Oh, Jessie, don't condemn me!'

Jessie looked up, startled, and then coloured. 'I don't.'

'Ah, but you *do*! You think I did wrong. But I love him so much – you can't think how much! I couldn't help it, truly. And it's different for me, with Holkam – it always was.'

Jessie said nothing. It was all too personal and painful to speak of.

Violet paused a moment, and then said in a small voice, 'There's more.'

'More?'

Violet blushed, but she held Jessie's eyes bravely as she said, 'I'm going to have a baby.'

A torrent of feelings and thoughts rushed through Jessie as the words sank in. A baby! *Another* baby. How could one person be so rich and another so poor? Violet had her comfortable marriage and three children, and now had her lover and would have his child, too; while she, Jessie, had nothing, no husband, no child, and the man she loved separated for ever from her. Violet had said, *You can't think how much I love him*. Jessie wanted to cry, *Yes, I can!* But Violet knew nothing about Jessie's love for Bertie. She had always kept it secret. She wondered now bitterly why she had suffered such guilt over nothing but feelings, when Violet had acted without, it seemed, a trace of conscience.

At last Violet said, 'I'm sorry it makes you angry. But, Jessie, I wish you could forgive me. I do so need my friends. Everything is very difficult for me. I don't know what will happen to me or the baby. Holkam – he's not an easy man. I don't know what he thinks about all this. And now Octavian – Laidislaw – has been sent to the Front, and I don't know w-when I shall see him again.'

The last words came out in a little rush, and tears sprang to Violet's eyes. Jessie thought of Ned, dead in battle, and of Bertie, Lennie and Frank, all in France, and Jack who soon would be. She didn't know when she would see any of them. Why should Violet think her sorrows any greater? But the tears were slipping over Violet's dark eyelashes, and she was fumbling for her handkerchief, looking more beautiful than ever even when weeping, which somehow made it harder to bear. Jessie went and sat beside her, found her more serviceable handkerchief and pressed it into Violet's hand.

'I'm sorry,' Violet said, after a moment. 'It must be my condition making me cry so much, because really I'm very h-happy.'

'Are you?'

'Yes, only of course worried, and missing Octavian and, oh, afraid of the scandal and what Holkam will do and what people will say. I hardly dare go out as it is, and it will be much worse when I start to show. It's all so complicated and horrid. Why can't things be simple? If people love each other, and they're not doing anyone else any harm, why can't they just be left alone?'

Jessie could resist her no longer. There had always been Violet: they had been suckled together by their mothers, who had always meant them to be best friends. It was impossible to go on feeling resentful when she was distressed and needed her. It was not for her to judge the rightness or wrongness of Violet's actions. She put the cause of the difference between them into a separate room in her mind and firmly locked the door. She simply would not think about it, that was all.

* * *

The next morning she went by Underground train to Oval, the nearest station to Camberwell, and, having asked directions, set off to walk to the hospital. It was housed in a teachers' training college, which had been commandeered at the beginning of the war – a grand, red-brick building with gables and sandstone copings and a fine Virginia creeper scrambling across its face. In its grounds and on the open space opposite, huts had been put up for extra accommodation, in the way she was familiar with from Clifton. Inside, the 'school smell' of polish and shoes had long been replaced by disinfectant and that underlying, unpleasantly sweet odour that every nurse could identify as 'hospital smell'.

A porter directed her to the matron's room. The interview was brief and businesslike. Miss Colefax was a small woman, unexpectedly young, and perhaps for that reason she had adopted a grave and dignified manner beyond her years, which precluded any smiles or friendliness, as if they might attract impertinence. She did not invite Jessie to sit down. Remaining standing throughout the interview, Jessie discovered the age-old problem of what to do with her hands, and disposed of it at last by clasping them behind her back. She remembered interviewing maids and cooks, and how they had done the same – though the fatter cooks had clasped them in front, not being able to reach round themselves. It impressed on her what her status here would be – not that she needed reminding, after her time at Clifton.

The matron asked Jessie's age, queried her marital status, glanced at her certificates, and then asked about her experience. She asked one or two sharp questions, and said, 'Very well. I shall apply for you. When can you start?'

'At once – ma'am.' Jessie remembered the honorific just in time to prevent a frown from this woman who was not so very much older than her.

'The formalities will take a week or so. You will receive a letter confirming it, but you may expect to join us here on . . .' she consulted a calendar '. . . on the fifteenth of May. Here is a list of the uniform you will require. Here is a list of what you may bring with you. Do not exceed it. You will live in the nurses' hostel and there is a limited amount of room for personal belongings. Other information will be sent to you with the letter of confirmation.'

She handed Jessie two typed sheets that she had ready on the desk. As the interview seemed to be over – for Miss Colefax had gone back to reading some papers – Jessie said thank you and good morning, received no reply to either, and took herself away. It was as well she had seen with how little gratitude she was received at Clifton, or she might have felt hurt by this studied coldness. But she had learned the hard lesson that no-one liked VADs, and was prepared to do her duty without thanks or praise. She supposed the Tommies at the Front didn't get thanked very often, either.

The uniform list recommended several shops where it could be purchased, and she thought she might as well get that part of it over, and went to a place in the Buckingham Palace Road. By the time she was done, she was tired and longing for a cup of tea, and seeing how much luggage she had accumulated, she gave in to an impulse and desired the packages to be sent to Manchester Square. The sales assistant looked surprised and queried the address. 'I believe that's Lord Overton's house, madam.'

'That's right. How do you know it?'

'We've supplied servants' uniforms there sometimes.' The assistant smiled suddenly and said, 'A lot of high-up ladies are joining VADs these days.'

Is that what I am, Jessie thought, as she left the shop, a high-up lady? Well, soon I shall be a low-down nurse. And the thought cheered her. She had a sense of absolute freedom, of casting off her past and starting out completely afresh.

The feeling lasted only until she remembered she had visits to pay. As Pont Street was nearer, she decided to call on Maud first. Perhaps she might get a cup of tea there at least. But Maud was not at home, and the house was in a state of turmoil, with every sign of a grand spring-cleaning going on – dust sheets, buckets, ladders, orphaned furniture, the front door standing open with workmen going in and out, and a penetrating smell of turpentine and linseed.

'Lady Parke is not expected back until late,' the maid said, and then confided, in a more natural accent, 'She stays out, mostly, while this lot's going on.'

'I'll leave her a note, if I might step inside and write one,' Jessie said.

It took time to locate paper and pencil, and to find a flat surface on which to lean. The maid, who was young and imperfectly trained, hovered about all the time, evidently longing to talk about the upheaval. 'You never saw such a carry-on, mum. Not just cleaning, but painting, too, and new wallpaper in the drawing-room, all the carpets up, and the curtains gone to be cleaned special. And a new boiler being fitted in the kitchen, which Cook says it's driving her mad, all the dirt and tramp-tramp-tramp all day long, and the workmen wanting tea that often, the kettle's never off the stove. It's a good job there's not much cooking to be done, Cook says, or they'd be taking her off to Friern Barnet. But that'll all change when his lordship comes. Special dishes, it'll be then all right. Cook's reading up all her receipt-books now to get ahead of herself, because it'll be nothing but the best for his lordship.'

'His lordship?' Jessie had not been listening, as she tried to pen a proper and sympathetic note to Maud, but those words caught her attention. Did this idiotic girl think Bertie was a lord?

'Lord Manvers, miss – mum,' the girl said. 'He's coming to England on a visit next week, and all this has got to be finished before he arrives, my lady says.'

Jessie put the note into an envelope, sealed and addressed it, and handed it to the girl. 'See Lady Parke gets this, please, with my compliments.' She took her leave, thinking about Lord Manvers, whom she had met on his last visit – a fine and handsome man of the most attractive character, with whom she had had a long and satisfying talk about horses. He had been Maud's father's friend and business associate. He bred horses in India, and came to England from time to time to buy saddlery, clothes and books, and to arrange his finances. Probably this would be a visit of condolence, Jessie thought, and wondered if he would be surprised to find the house so newly done-up, only weeks after Richard's death, when it should be in mourning. But perhaps that was just Maud's way of dealing with bereavement. She had certainly loved her father, as Lord Manvers was bound to know.

After the long walk in Camberwell, the standing, the shopping and the visit to Pont Street, Jessie's feet were hot and aching and she longed to sit down and take her shoes off. It was a little after twelve. She thought she had better pay her visit to Maria – and if she happened to arrive there just at lunchtime, Maria was not the woman to turn her away. One might with impunity call on family unannounced and at mealtimes. Besides, there was a better chance of finding her at home at that time.

The journey on the Underground brought it home to her how far out Brook Green was, and what a sprawling place London had become. Brook Green had once been a fashionable country retreat for wealthy Londoners, and there were some handsome eighteenth- and early-nineteenth-century houses, as well as some countrymen's cottages left over from the original village. But most of it had been filled in with the outward creep of terraces for the working and lower-middle classes. In deference to her feet, Jessie took a taxi-cab from the station, and the driver found the place easily enough. Jessie liked the look of the little house at once, and was prejudiced in its favour when she found Maria at home and lunch not yet on the table.

Maria greeted her with great warmth, and said several times how glad she was to see her. 'You will stay to lunch?'

'If it's not inconvenient.'

'No, no, not at all! I'll just run and tell Sara to put some more potatoes on. Oh, here's my mother.'

Mrs Stanhope came into the sitting-room with an enquiring look. In such a tiny house there was no keeping anything from anyone, and she had come to see who Maria was talking to. Maria introduced them, and there was just time to exchange a few commonplaces while Maria ran to the kitchen and back. Then Maria insisted on showing Jessie every inch of her tiny kingdom, explaining as they went what she had done and planned to do to make it more comfortable and more her own.

Out in the garden they stood under the fruit trees – 'I mean to have a garden seat just here, where it catches the sunshine' – and admired her newly dug vegetable patch. 'Of course, after the war, when Frank is home, we may find it too small. I expect he may want to move,' she said, perhaps a little wistfully, for it was her first house, and Jessie could see she loved it out of all proportion to its merits. 'I don't know,' she added candidly, 'how much money there will be – what Frank will earn or whether he'll have any other income. It was so kind of your uncle to pay for this place for us.'

'Your uncle too, now,' Jessie pointed out.

'It was kind of him, anyway.'

Jessie said hesitantly, 'I don't suppose Frank will ever be rich – but I expect you knew that. What I mean is, I wouldn't want you to think he's likely to be grand in his expectations. I'm sure he'll love this house as much as you do.'

'I hope so,' Maria said. She turned to face Jessie, and her cheeks were warm. 'But it may be too small, later on if not at first, because there are only two bedrooms and, well, I'm going to have a baby.'

It hit Jessie with a delightful shock. Foolishly, she had

still been thinking about Frank as her brother, forgetting he was a married man now. Frank, a father! But it was wonderful! She clasped Maria's hand and said, 'Oh, congratulations! I'm so pleased for you! Have you written to Frank? What did he say?'

'I haven't heard from him yet. I only found out for sure yesterday, and of course I wrote to him at once, but he won't have received the letter yet. Do you think he'll be glad?'

'Of course he will! What a question! What man isn't delighted when he knows he's going to have a son?'

'How do you know it will be a son?'

'It's bound to be – and, goodness, how clever he'll be, with you two for his parents! He'll probably discover some wonderful new thing and be famous. Compton will be in all the history books, like Newton and – and—' Her invention – or at least her education – failed her at that point. 'People like him,' she finished vaguely.

'Compton on photoelectric process,' Maria laughed. 'Compton's diffusion theory. Compton's hypothesis of quanta.'

Jessie had once had quanta explained to her by Frank, and though she didn't remember anything of what he had said, she had at least heard the word, which made her feel better. 'Why not?' she said. 'My cousin Bertie says there are always leaps forward in knowledge after a war. Your son will be part of it.'

The servant came out into the garden to say that lunch was ready, and they walked in together, feeling very much in harmony.

'I'm so glad you came today,' Maria said. 'I was longing for someone to tell.'

'I'm glad I came too,' said Jessie. In some odd way, Maria's baby balanced out Violet's in her mind, and made her easier about it. 'Will you tell them at Morland Place, or would you like me to? I shall be going home tonight.'

'I'll write a letter, but you'll get there before it, so you can tell too, if you like.'

'It will make everyone very happy. Your only problem will be that Uncle Teddy will be determined to take you back to Morland Place for the duration of the war, so you can be properly looked after.'

'I shall be staying here,' Maria said, with such confidence that Jessie was sure she was a match for her uncle. 'But,' she added, 'it might be nice to come for a holiday now and then, if the war goes on much longer.'

Talking equably, they went in to luncheon.

The action at Verdun, which had begun in February and ground on through March and April, continued into May, with the hills and ridges to the north of the town changing hands, always under heavy bombardment. Pétain's new second-in-command, the half-English General Robert Nivelle, was a more aggressive commander, and the German advance was slowed under his repeated counter-attacks; but the cost in casualties was high.

One of Pétain's primary concerns was to keep open the forty-five miles of road between Bar-le-Duc and Verdun, so that vital supplies and reinforcements could continue to feed the massive effort. Despite constant German shelling, trucks moved along it day and night, one every fourteen seconds, causing such wear that repair details from labour battalions had to be kept on hand all the time, along with crews to deal immediately with broken-down lorries, so that they should not block the way. The road's importance was such that it was soon known as La Voie Sacrée – the Sacred Way. Without it, the action would have failed within weeks.

For the British, who were holding the line from Ypres down as far as Albert in Picardy, it was a quiet spring. There were some minor actions at Ypres and near Loos, but so much of the German effort was going into the attack at Verdun that for the British it was mainly a matter of holding the line and preparing for the planned joint offensive with the French in the autumn. But the terrible losses at Verdun, and the desperate French determination that it must not fall, meant that more and more French troops were withdrawn from Picardy, and the British were forced to take over more of the line.

The troops from the Dardanelles, including the Anzacs, were in France now and, together with the New Army battalions coming out, would give General Haig one and a half million men by summer, organised into the First, Second, Third and Fourth Armies, commanded by Monro, Plumer, Allenby and Rawlinson, plus the Reserve under Gough. With so many men available, and with plenty of time for detailed preparation, there was no doubt the coming action would be a success. This was to be the year the Germans were defeated.

CHAPTER TWELVE

On the 15th of May, Jessie presented herself at the No. 1 London General. She left her trunk at the porter's lodge and went up to the matron's room. Waiting outside was another young woman, in a navy coat and skirt and a soft hat, looking rather nervous. She turned to Jessie eagerly as she approached. 'Are you a VAD too? I've come to report but there's no-one here. I was afraid I'd come to the wrong place, or on the wrong day.'

'Have you knocked?'

'Yes, and looked inside, but the room's empty. Did your letter say four o'clock? It seems a strange time.' She smiled suddenly. 'I say, here I am rattling on and we've haven't been introduced. I'm Lilian Proctor.' She held out her hand. She seemed very young: slight and dark and rather pretty, with fine hair drawn into a chignon, from which wisps were escaping in a manner Jessie guessed was incorrigible.

Jessie liked the look of her at once. Besides, it was always pleasant not to be the only 'new girl'. 'Jessie Morland,' she said, shaking hands.

'Don't worry that I talk like this all the time,' the other said frankly. 'It's only when I'm nervous.'

Jessie smiled. 'I don't mind,' she said. 'At my last hospital no-one talked to me at all.'

'At your last hospital? I expect you've got a lot of nursing experience.'

'Hardly any. I was never allowed to do anything but scrub. The ward sister hated VADs so she'd never let me near the patients. I lived in the sluice room.'

'You poor thing! But at least it was a proper hospital. Everyone was very nice to me at the Devonshire in Aylesbury, but it was only for convalescents, and I did so want to do something for the war effort – something that *mattered.*'

A rapid clicking of footsteps interrupted them, and the matron came into view along the corridor. The interview was very brief, hardly more than an acknowledgement of their presence. Matron told them they would be on probation for a month, after which, if they proved satisfactory, they would be invited to 'sign on' for a six-month term, the contract renewable at the end of that time. Their duties would begin the following morning. Now they might take their belongings to the hostel and settle in.

The hostel, they were told by the porter, was a good distance away, nearly two miles.

'But how will we get there, with our trunks?' Jessie asked.

'Avter take a taxi, won't you?' he said indifferently.

It was an unexpected outlay, and Jessie was glad she had brought money with her, especially when she saw the dismay on her companion's face. 'If we share, it won't be much,' she said.

'I didn't expect to have to spend anything just yet,' Proctor admitted. 'I've used nearly all my allowance on things I needed to come here, and my father said, since I'll be getting board and lodging, he wouldn't give me any more. There's a lot of us at home, you see,' she added apologetically, 'and Dad's not all that well off.'

It made Jessie realise again how lucky she was. She had hardly even considered what expenses she might encounter. She must be careful never to flaunt her comparative wealth.

Though her companion chatted on the journey, Jessie barely listened, looking out of the window at what would be her new home. It could hardly have been more different from the surroundings of Morland Place. The taxi drove them through grey and squalid streets. The pavements were strewn with rubbish; paper and cabbage leaves blew along the gutters; everything was black with soot. The terraces of houses and little shops were meanly built and falling into decay; the glimpsed side-streets narrow and gloomy. It had clouded over and was beginning to rain, which made everything look even more drab. The people on the street were poorly dressed, many of them old and bent, the rest mostly women with dirty-faced children – very few young men, as one would expect. The trams rattled and swayed, holding up the traffic; motor-vans and buses belched out fumes; sad horses seemed to hang weakly in the shafts of traders' carts, and a large number of bicycles was weaving in and out, ridden by middle-aged men in flat caps – a factory nearby had just changed shift.

After what seemed like a long journey they came to an area of larger, detached houses, though they, too, were in a state of disrepair, the stucco peeling off them, their front hedges overgrown, with cracked pillars and missing gates. But at least there were trees here, planted along the sides of the street and growing to vast height in the front gardens, tall London planes, elms, and chestnuts just coming into flower. The sight of them did Jessie good. There seemed little else in the landscape that would be green.

At one of these houses the taxi deposited them and their trunks. The driver declined to help them carry them in, with a look that said he knew nurses were no good for a tip. The face of the house was peeling and streaked with soot, and the many windows were uncurtained, which alone gave it a run-down appearance. It was three storeys high, with a half-basement whose windows peeped up from the mossy gloom down a sort of ditch, which was bridged by a flight of shallow steps with the iron handrails missing.

Proctor, looking up at it, said, 'It's not very welcoming.'

She seemed close to tears, so Jessie said cheerfully, 'I expect it's better inside than out. Shall we go in? I think we can manage the trunks if we carry them together, one at a time.'

The front hall was empty of life and of furniture. A single electric lamp hung nakedly from the ceiling on a cord. As they stood wondering what to do next, glancing at the many typed and hand-written messages on a large notice-board – most of them seemed to be forbidding things – the housekeeper appeared from the basement, a very old and bent woman who made alarming noises as she breathed. 'You the new nusses?' she gasped.

'Yes. I'm Jessie Morland and this is Lilian Proctor,' Jessie answered. She was about to add more, but the woman waved away the information with a skinny hand – or perhaps she was fanning air into her mouth.

'My name's Mrs 'Erbert,' she wheezed. 'Me an' 'Erbert lives down atheer. We takes keer o' the place. You two's on the fust floor. Second door you comes to. Can't miss it. I can't be doing with them stairs. One o' the nusses'll come and tell you what's what.'

She went away again, leaving Jessie to wonder how much housekeeping she could possibly do without climbing the stairs.

Proctor was stifling a fit of nervous giggles. 'Oh dear, it's not a bit like I expected,' she said.

'I don't think I had any particular expectations,' Jessie said. There was linoleum on the hall floor, but the stairs were bare, the edges painted maroon, with a pale strip up the centre where once there had been a stair carpet. 'But I wouldn't have imagined this.'

It took two trips to struggle upstairs with their trunks. Their quarters, when they found them, were Spartan. A large, long room, which might once have been grand – the drawing-room, perhaps, for it had a high ceiling with mouldings and a marble fireplace – had been divided into four cubicles down its long side by curtains that hung from rails screwed to the ceiling. A narrow strip down the fireplace side was left bare for access. The two cubicles furthest from the window were empty. Each contained an iron bedstead, a chest of drawers, a small upright chair and a washstand. The floorboards were bare, the fawn-patterned wallpaper faded and rubbed. On each bed was a single pillow covered in striped ticking, and a little pile of folded bedclothes – two grey blankets, two sheets and one pillowcase.

'Well,' said Jessie, 'this is home. I don't mind which I have – do you?' Proctor shook her head rather glumly. Jessie chose, at random, the one nearer the door, and began to unpack her belongings. She was glad that she had put her washing-things in a housewife that her mother had made for her, for now she could hang it on the nail conveniently driven into the wall beside the washstand. The book she was reading, *Nicholas Nickleby*, and her own candlestick, the one that stood on her bedside table at home, went on top of the chest of drawers, making the little space hers. The instructions had said they might display one photograph – which, if the subject was male, must be of a close relative or fiancé – and after some thought she had brought a studio portrait of her mother, which she thought she would find most comforting at times when she was tired and homesick. She folded her clothes carefully in the drawers, put her writing-case beside the photograph, and reflected that everything else she had brought would have to stay in the trunk. She hoped it would not have to be stored too inaccessibly.

Proctor meanwhile was sitting hunched on her bed, apparently incapable of moving. 'Oh dear,' she said, when Jessie looked in enquiringly at her, 'it isn't nice here, not a bit. It's cold, and it smells funny.'

It did smell damp, Jessie thought; and it would probably be cold, for there was no sign that the marble fireplace was ever used: all it was good for was to add a hint of soot to the prevailing dank smell, brought down the chimney by the rain. On the wall over the mantelpiece was another notice-board bearing two messages, one on what to do in case of fire, while the other, ruled into squares, seemed to be some kind of rota.

'I thought someone would welcome us,' Proctor went on mournfully. 'Everyone at home was so proud of me for wanting to come to London and nurse, but here no-one seems to care that we've arrived. I do feel so homesick. I've never been away from home before, and I miss them all already.'

'Put your photograph out,' Jessie said. 'That will make you feel better. You did bring a photograph?'

'I brought lots,' she said, brightening up. 'I thought if I was only allowed to show one, I could change it each week so I can have them all in turn. Would you like to see?'

So she opened her trunk and got out a number of framed photographs, and showed them to Jessie, with voluble descriptions. She was the eldest, she explained, and these were Mummy and Dad, and her sisters Rosie and Marjorie and Ellie, and her brothers Peter and Johnnie and little Phil, and the baby Dickie, and this was a picture of their house, though it wasn't very good because it had been a windy day and the tripod had wobbled so it was a bit blurred, and this was their darling dog Blackie. As she took the last photograph, of a grinning black mongrel with a good deal of Alsatian in him, Jessie felt a pang of sadness for her dear, lost Brach, and through that chink washed in a wave of homesickness of her own, for all at Morland Place, and those away at the war.

The two of them might have fallen into a melancholy, except that they were interrupted just then by the arrival in the doorway of a tall, heavily built young woman in a dressing-gown. Her hair was tousled, her florid face rather cross. She had heavy black brows and the hint of a moustache, and her hands were large and red and seemed all knuckle.

'What's all this noise?' she complained. 'Can't you keep your voices down? Some of us are trying to sleep.'

'I'm sorry,' Jessie said. 'We didn't know there was anyone else here. We've just arrived.'

'Oh, Lord, you must be the new VADs. Has anyone shown you around?'

Jessie shook her head. 'The housekeeper just told us to come up here. Are these the right beds?'

'I suppose so,' said the nurse, grumpily, and then sighed and said, 'Oh, well, now I'm awake, I suppose I'd better see to you. What are your names?'

'I'm Lilian and this is Jessie,' said Proctor, confidingly.

The nurse shook her head pityingly. 'We don't use Christian names here. Lord, you *are* green!'

'I'm Morland,' Jessie corrected, 'and she's Proctor.'

'I'm Rampton. I'm in the room above.' She explained that the two other beds belonged to VADs, and that there was another similar room at the back of the house – the original dining-room – which accommodated four more. On the floor above were four bedrooms, each divided into two, where 'us proper nurses' lived, while on the top floor lived three ward sisters, each of whom had her own room. There was one bathroom, on the next floor up, which all nineteen of them shared – 'The bath rota's over there,' Rampton said, gesturing towards the notice-board over the fireplace, 'but if the sisters want it out of turn they get it. You'd best try and get your names in somewhere while you can.' There was a water-closet on this floor, and another upstairs – 'But you'd better not be caught using *that* one.'

They were to keep their own cubicle clean and tidy and make their bed in the morning before leaving. 'You'll get fined if you don't. The Assistant Matron comes round to check about once a week and you never know when. And don't let her catch you sitting on the bed – it's forbidden.' They could keep a suitcase under the bed but their trunks had to be stored, though Jessie was glad to discover they were kept in a small room on the same floor – it had been a serving-closet to the dining-room in the old days – so they were accessible.

They would go on duty for the first time tomorrow at seven thirty, Rampton told them, but they had to be at breakfast at the hospital at seven, when they would be told which ward to go to. Changes were always read out at breakfast. 'You'll need to get there in time to change into uniform, and the VADs' cloakroom's on the top floor, so leave plenty of time. You'll get an awful rating if you're late for breakfast.'

She told them one or two other minor rules, and warned them to 'watch out for Sister Bates', who was the senior in the house and therefore in nominal charge of them all. 'She's a Tartar.' And then she seemed prepared to leave.

'But what do we do now?' Proctor appealed.

Rampton raised her eyebrows. 'You'd better unpack and make your beds. After that, you can suit yourselves. I'd sleep if I were you – that's what I'm going to do, if you two will kindly keep quiet.'

'Um, what do we do about food?' Proctor went on. 'I'm awfully hungry.'

'All our meals are taken at the hospital,' Rampton said. 'You'll have to find for yourselves tonight.' She looked from one to the other and took pity. 'There's a café down the road that's not too bad. We go there sometimes on our time off. Turn right out of the house, down to the end and turn right again, and it's on the left.' With that she pulled her dressing gown tightly round her, strangled her bulky waist with the cord, and stumped away.

Proctor looked at Jessie, half alarmed, half excited. 'Go to a *café*? Do we dare?'

'It doesn't seem that we have any choice,' said Jessie.

'But I've never eaten in a café before, not without Mummy. You don't think it would be *fast*?'

Jessie smiled. 'It seems to me that it will be part of our

new life here. Perhaps we ought to start getting used to it.'

'Gosh, how exciting!' Proctor said, and then her face fell. 'But I don't think I've enough money.'

'Don't worry, I've got plenty.'

'Oh, but I can't let you pay for me. That wouldn't be right.'

'Just this once,' Jessie said. 'You can pay me back when we get our wages.'

It didn't take much to persuade Proctor – she was too eager for the treat.

They put on their coats and hats and went out into the wet evening. The clouds were bringing on early darkness, and the street-lamps were showing dimly, while the trams rattling by on the main road were like illuminated glass cases with people displayed inside. Jessie had a moment of qualm as they reached the café – Sam's, its name was painted above – because though she had often eaten out, this was something new and different. Inside, through the window, she could see poor people in drab clothes hunched over their tables in silence, stout, middle-aged women in shapeless hats, old men smoking or reading newspapers – none of the smart, chattery people she had eaten in company with on other occasions. She felt the irrational fear of being out of her place – would they look coldly at two young women, or sneer at them, or even refuse to serve them? Would she and Proctor do or say the wrong thing and make fools of themselves? She shook away the thoughts and went in.

No-one looked up at the ping of the bell over the door, but the man behind the counter, beside the shining tea-urn, nodded and gestured to an empty table. They scurried to it gratefully. When they were settled he strolled over, dusted some crumbs off the stained tablecloth, and said, 'Nurses?'

'Yes,' Jessie said, feeling it unnecessary to add they were VADS. 'We've just come.'

He nodded again – a middle-aged man, burly, brown-skinned, large-featured, with a head of thick, curling black hair, well greased. His sleeves were rolled up and his long white apron was plentifully streaked with food and coffee stains. ''Spect I'll be seeing a bit of you, then,' he said. 'Lot of the nurses come here. Sam's my name. What'll it be, ladies? Egg and chips?'

If there was a menu, Jessie could not see it. For ease she said, 'Yes, please,' and then discovered that it was in fact just what she fancied. Proctor, round-eyed with the new experience, could only nod. 'Tea and a slice with it?' Sam suggested.

The tea came in cups, not a pot – large, thick white cups, holding almost half a pint, of strong orange-brown tea with the milk already in. The tannin made Jessie's mouth shrivel at the first sip, and by the end of the cup she was almost light-headed, but she supposed she'd get used to it. The 'slice' turned out to be a round of bread-and-butter, not cake as she had expected. The fried eggs and fried potatoes were piping hot and delicious, but what Jessie had liked most of all was the acceptance of them, both by Sam, who had made it easy for them, and by the other customers, all of whom politely ignored them, except for the old man at the next table who, in rising to leave, caught her eye and gave her a civil nod. The bill, when she came to pay it, seemed very low, and she almost queried it, until she remembered that Proctor was having to pay her back out of her small wages.

Warmed inside and greatly comforted, they walked back in the wet dark to the hostel, and spent the evening settling in, chatting to each other and exchanging their histories. Tomorrow, Jessie thought, they would begin nursing – real nursing, important nursing. When Proctor had quieted down a little at last, she excused herself from more conversation, took up her writing-case and began a letter to Bertie.

Venetia's office in the tall building in St James's Square had originally been someone's bedroom – a good-sized room with faded Chinese wallpaper, a handsome fireplace, fancy mouldings round the ceiling, and a redundant servants' bell by the chimney. It made her think that if Violet was not going to live in her house across the square, the government might well requisition it for the duration.

The clerk, Miss Voysey, proved a real treasure, having worked in the civil service for eight years, and knowing her way round the labyrinth. It was she who, on the first day, manoeuvred around the problem, intractable to Venetia, that they had no stationery supplies, which meant they had nothing on which to indent for them. She disappeared for some time, and came back armed with writing-paper, notepads, pens, ink and some other useful items like paper-clips, and also a number of blank requisition forms. 'The thing to do now, you see, ma'am, is to put in a retrospective order to Stores for all these things. And if we order more than we need, we can "pay back" what we've borrowed to the other departments, so their inventories will be correct.'

'It sounds terribly complicated,' Venetia complained.

'Oh, we do it all the time,' Miss Voysey said. 'I couldn't get any envelopes, though. For some reason they're hard to come by and no-one was willing to part with any.'

To cut through the problem, Venetia gave the young woman some money from her own purse and let her leave early to buy some at the nearest stationer's.

The form-filling and other procedural intricacies annoyed and perplexed her, taking her away, she felt, from what was important work. Miss Kay, the typewriter, and Miss Voysey tried to teach her something of the system, while Venetia taught them the technical and medical terms they would need to know. They did their best to deal with the post every day, but there was more than they could manage, and Venetia came in for her share. Much of it related to the formalities that she wished she could escape; a considerable amount more related to matters that were nothing to do with her.

Miss Voysey was not surprised by that, either. 'It always

happens,' she said. 'When a new department opens everyone knows about it, so they send over all the awkward things that don't fit in anywhere, or that they don't want to deal with themselves.'

Venetia stared at a letter, written in green ink, from a madman who claimed to have invented a new kind of bomb that used nothing but plain water and asking to be allowed to come and demonstrate it. There was another from a lady in Shropshire who felt that all government offices ought to have works of art in them to prevent the employees becoming narrow-minded, and offered to lend her collection of Nollekens busts, left by her late husband – 'but only one to each office, please, as there would not otherwise be enough for all to benefit'.

'And what do we do with them?' Venetia asked.

Miss Voysey permitted herself a small smile. 'We send them on to someone else.'

A week or two later, on the 16th of May, a new department moved into some more of the empty rooms in Winchester House. Venetia was interested to hear that it was the Graves Registration Commission, because she had met its principal, Fabian Ware, at dinner with the Asquiths in early April, and had had a long and interesting conversation with him. He was newly arrived from the Front with his staff in the form of two clerks and one officer.

He had been out in France since September 1914. When the war began, he had discovered that at forty-five he was too old to be accepted as a soldier. Longing, like so many others, to do his bit, he had obtained command of a mobile Red Cross unit. Once in France he had been struck by the lack of any system of recording the graves of servicemen. His unit – a miscellaneous collection of private cars and drivers, all volunteers – was dashing back and forth across north-eastern France in the wake of the retreat from Mons, picking up wounded soldiers and stragglers. But in the course of this they also began to collect notes about the

British dead, their names and the exact place they were buried. With such a fluid situation it was obviously important information: when co-ordinated with Red Cross lists of prisoners-of-war, it meant that missing men could be properly accounted for.

As time went on, Ware began actively to seek out graves to add to his unofficial register, talking to local army commanders, French officials, churchmen and villagers. Sooner or later, grieving relatives would want to know where their loved ones lay. They should not have to depend on the memory of a comrade caught up in the heat of battle, who himself might not survive. Sometimes Ware would come across an impromptu cemetery with a number of British graves, each carefully marked with a neatly made cross, but find no evidence that its position and contents had been officially recorded; on other occasions he would find graves with no markers, or marked with a piece of soap-box with an inscription in pencil that was rapidly being washed away. There were fallen soldiers buried in village churchyards among the locals, in woods and fields, even in private gardens. Somebody ought to know where they all were; and it was important that the graves should be marked with a cross that would not quickly rot away, and an inscription that would survive the weather.

Ware and his men took careful notes, including map references and sketches, of the graves and all the details possible about the occupants. At the end of the year when the Front settled down, he built up a string of contacts who would send him information. The listing of graves became an expanding part of the unit's work, to which in the first winter was added the proper marking of them, by sturdy crosses with painted inscriptions, for which the Red Cross paid.

In March 1915 the unit's work was officially recognised by the War Office, perhaps because of the stir caused by a letter to *The Times*, which described the distress of a lady who had travelled to France to see the grave of her brother, having had its location described to her by his comrades, only to find all trace of it had disappeared. The War Office acknowledged that it was important to the morale not only of the civilian population but of the soldiers themselves to know that if they fell their graves would be properly marked.

The government was determined to prevent any of the war dead from being exhumed after the war and brought back to England for reburial. It would cause resentment if the few families who could afford it were allowed to bring back their sons and erect fine monuments: the rest would feel their sons' contribution to the cause undervalued. When the prohibition on repatriation was issued, it became all the more important that the graves were properly registered. So Ware's unit was given the task exclusively, and received the title of Graves Registration Commission. Ware was given a commission in the General List, with the rank of lieutenant-colonel.

'And now you're back in England,' Venetia said, when she went along to his office to renew acquaintance.

Ware was a quietly spoken man with deep-set, thoughtful eyes and a sensitive mouth below his small moustache. Yet this mild appearance belied an energetic and adventurous soul, with a formidable intelligence that allowed him to grasp and order the vast quantity of detail, which might have defeated a lesser man.

'Yes, we were finding it too difficult to deal with the administration without a settled headquarters,' he said. He came originally from Bristol, and despite his long years in South Africa he still had the faint roundness to some of his vowels. 'So I had to give up my buccaneering and come and be a meek and civil clerk.' His eyes gleamed as he said it, and she did not suppose he would ever be very meek. 'Also,' he added, 'coming to London means I shall be able to employ female clerks, and there is such a tremendous lot of paperwork now, my male staff over there was being overwhelmed.'

He described how the work had expanded. Hundreds of enquiries were coming in from the public, wanting to know the whereabouts of a particular grave. Now, when they sent the information, they tried to send a photograph too – another reason for coming to London, where there were far more firms to do the developing and printing. Meanwhile the registration itself went on. Details of official interments came in; army officers in France passed on information about graves they had come across. In the course of military actions, bodies were often unearthed and then reburied, and Ware's unit correlated information about both sites. Sometimes whole pits full of hastily buried corpses were discovered, and had to be identified by their discs or other personal belongings. All this information ended up on his desk.

'We also have to think ahead, about what's to happen when the war is over,' he said. 'There will be a tremendous surge of people wanting to visit graves. Not only must they know where they are, but they must find them well tended. It mustn't be said that we neglected our dead. And who is to maintain the graves? The French won't care to have it dropped on their plate.'

'We're saving them from being overrun by the Germans,' Venetia pointed out.

He smiled. 'That's not an argument that will appeal to the French. No, there must be some arrangement between the two governments about the cost, and an official structure set up to see that the graves are cared for properly – preferably in a uniform manner. We can't have Jimmy's mother saying her boy's grave isn't as nice as Billy's. The difficulty will be deciding on a standard appearance that suits everyone. Then there are the graves in Mesopotamia and Gallipoli – and who knows what future theatres of war? I can't see the Commission's work ever coming to an end.'

'You make my concerns seem very small,' she said.

He would not allow that, and asked her about her work

in such a way that she found herself telling him everything. She described the units she wanted to send to France. 'I thought each car should have a driver – who would also have to be a mechanic in case of breaking down – a radiologic technician to operate the machine, and a general assistant to take care of administration and so on. I thought three was the minimum number for a unit – two leaves people too vulnerable to accident.'

'Quite right,' said Ware. 'And if I might offer some advice . . . ?'

'Please do. Your experience in the field will be invaluable to me.'

'Then I would suggest that your general assistant should be an active, independent sort of man, because if my experience is anything to go by, your units will have to forage for themselves and find their own lodgings. That takes a certain sort of character – restless, inventive, resourceful. You might do worse than look among the men who volunteered for the army but were turned down because of some minor reason – for being too short, having flat feet, and so on.'

Venetia smiled. 'A good thought – but how would I find them?'

'Advertise,' he said. 'You might also enquire at the recruitment offices – they often have the same people coming back several times, and that sort of persistence marks out your man. How do you mean to train your technicians?'

'Send them to Paris,' Venetia said promptly. 'I've already arranged that with Madame Curie. The difficulty for me is actually getting on with the work. I seem to be swamped all the time with pieces of paper, and I have only one clerk and one typewriter.'

'I sympathise entirely,' he said. 'I told them exactly what I needed before I came here, and I can see at a glance that half of it hasn't appeared. I've only a fifth of the typists I asked for. You must complain, my dear ma'am. It's the

Treasury, more than likely, refusing to sanction the outlay. The Treasury always thinks it ought to control everything.'

'I know that only too well,' Venetia said.

'You must have much better channels for complaining than I have,' he said, eyeing her curiously. 'You know everyone. After all, I first met you at dinner with the prime minister!'

Venetia felt awkward at this near-criticism. 'It's true, I do know many of the people in the government, but I've never had to complain before. I don't know how to go about it.'

'Then might I suggest that we join forces? I will share my experience, such as it is, with you, if you will share your influence with me. Together we ought to be able to solve most of our problems.'

She held out her hand. 'A bargain!'

They talked a little more, and then she took herself away to let him get on with his work. 'By the way,' he said, as he opened the door for her, 'have you thought how you will get your technicians exempted from conscription? It will be an expensive business if you send them all the way to Paris, and then they're called up just when they're trained and ready.'

Venetia said, 'I was ahead of you on that score. I shan't be sending any young men to Paris. I shall be using girls.'

His eyes widened slightly as he looked at her, she thought, with a hint of respect. 'You have quite an adventurous spirit yourself, I see,' he remarked.

The first weeks at the military hospital passed in a daze of exhaustion for Jessie and her new friend. Their hours were from seven thirty in the morning until eight p.m., with three hours off-duty time each day. These hours were never allocated in advance, which made it difficult to arrange to do anything with them. It was best when they fell at the end of the day, so that there was no going back on duty afterwards, or at the beginning so that one could sleep late.

When they fell in the middle of the day, the distance back to the hostel took a large piece out of them, and Jessie sometimes just found somewhere to sit and read or, better still, sleep.

The journey to and from the hostel was a major aggravation. There was a workmen's tram, but it was almost always full, and generally they had to walk. The two miles took half an hour going to the hospital, and rather longer back, up the steep hill. Such a walk would have been nothing to Jessie at Morland Place, across the fields; but to plod the hard, dirty pavements, especially at the end of the day, when her feet were swollen, hot and sore, was a trial. All the nurses complained bitterly about it, and it added seriously to the physical strain of the day.

All their meals were provided at the hospital, and the food was plentiful, if dull. Breakfast at seven was porage, bacon and bread, washed down with quantities of strong orange tea. Jessie soon got used to the strength of it and found it a useful stimulant for getting her on her feet in the morning. At nine thirty there was a meal called 'lunch', which was bread-and-butter and tea, and at twelve came the main meal of the day, called 'dinner', usually a stew, with potatoes, followed by a milk pudding – or sometimes, always popular, a suet pudding with sultanas in it, which the nurses called 'bugs in the bolster'. At four they had 'tea' – bread and jam, and sometimes cake, donated by commercial companies like J. Lyons & Co., as part of their war effort. Supper was at eight when they came off duty: sausages, perhaps, pasties or bully-beef, with the left-over cold rice pudding or blanc-mange from dinner, served with jam. The jam was decanted from enormous tins, and was almost always plum or plum-and-apple, varied occasionally by gooseberry. It was rumoured that the sisters – who ate at a different table and usually at a different time – had blackcurrant or even strawberry, but the story was never verified.

The nurses complained about the monotony of the diet,

but the food was always ample, and some of them had come from homes where they had never fared as well. Jessie was always ravenous and ate everything that was put before her, though inwardly lamenting the absence of fruit and the paucity of vegetables – potatoes, carrots, swede were all they saw.

The greatest trial, apart from the walk home, was the lack of bathing facilities. The hot-water geyser in the bathroom roared and stank and occasionally made alarming explosive noises, but the hot water came out in such a reluctant trickle that it took half an hour for one person to have a bath. At night they were not home before nine, and the lights were turned out at ten; and the sisters in the house claimed priority no matter who was on the rota. Jessie longed to wash off the hospital stink at the end of the day, to soak and ease her aching back and swollen, burning feet; but she had to make do with cold water at the washstand in her cubicle. She sometimes thought about bathing in the night by the light of her candle, but the geyser made such a noise she did not dare risk it. The VADs rarely managed to get a bath at all, unless they walked home during their off-duty time to snatch one.

Once a week they had a half-day off, and at first they were too exhausted by the unfamiliar labour and strain to do more than sleep, eat, bathe, write letters and do a little essential mending. Jessie and Proctor were not often off at the same time, but they had made friends with the other VADs in the hostel, and towards the end of the month, when they had got more used to the work, started to go out with one or another of them.

One evening Jessie went to the kinema with a VAD called Molly West; and on another occasion she had a trip to the theatre with Elizabeth 'Beta' Wallace, a quietly droll girl from Hertfordshire, to see *The Bing Boys Are Here* at the Alhambra, with George Robey and Violet Lorraine. It was rather exciting to go to the theatre with another girl. She felt a little odd at first, and looked about her uneasily as if she expected to be stared at or frowned upon. But the war was changing things. She remembered the strict rules under which poor Maria had suffered when she first knew her – though, of course, it would still be different for a single girl wanting to meet a man. But everywhere now one saw young women together, and even eating in restaurants seemed to be all right, at least during the daytime.

One day when their hours off coincided and were the first three of the day, Jessie, Proctor and Wallace went together to Sam's café for breakfast: fried eggs, bacon, sausages, toast and jam – 'anything but plum', Beta had stipulated, and Sam had come up with some raspberry, rather pippy but heaven to the bored palate. Jessie had asked for coffee instead of the eternal tea, and though it was made with syrup out of a bottle, she enjoyed every drop.

'I wouldn't have believed one could get so much pleasure out of a cup of inferior coffee,' she said.

'When one's horizon is narrowed, everything takes on greater significance,' Wallace said wisely. 'I shall be due for leave soon, and I've found myself planning to spend most of it in the bath.' The others laughed, but she said, 'I'm quite serious. I shall bathe every day, for a couple of hours at a time. I shan't get out until my fingers are wrinkled. All my wildest fantasies now revolve about hot water.'

'I dream about fruit,' Jessie said. 'Strawberries and cherries and apricots. And apples. We have the most marvellous old tree in the orchard at home – I don't know what variety it is, but it has small hard apples streaked with red, and when you bite into them, the juice runs down your chin. They're always the first to ripen.'

Proctor sighed. 'I'd just like to see my mother and the children and dear old Blackie,' she said. She still suffered dreadfully from homesickness, and sometimes Jessie heard her crying quietly at night. 'But I can't imagine doing anything else now, can you?' she went on, sounding a little surprised at the discovery.

Wallace nodded. 'I've been here four months, and I haven't read a newspaper since I came.'

Jessie realised that Camberwell, the hospital and the hostel, had become her whole life. The details and concerns of it had driven everything else out of her, and packed her so tightly that there was no room in her for anything but being a nurse.

Violet's life had narrowed to an even smaller compass. She felt too visibly pregnant to go out any more, and spent her days drifting from bedroom to drawing-room sofa, where she sometimes read a little, but more often daydreamed, reliving the times she had been with Laidislaw, imagining their future together after the war. She took the dogs out into the garden for their exercise, and when the weather was fine she sat out there for an hour or two, for her mother had told her sternly that she needed fresh air. Sometimes she did a little sewing – it was soothing, and did not interfere with her reverie. She made several baby-shirts, and enjoyed embroidering them.

She wrote to Laidislaw every day, growing more fluent at putting down her feelings. His letters to her were more infrequent, but always passionate. She still had not told him about the baby. The situation with Holkam was difficult, and in the languor of her pregnancy she was disinclined to stir up trouble. When the baby arrived, when Holkam came home, when she next saw Laidislaw, when the war was over – all these seemed more suitable times for 'sorting things out'. She preferred not even to think about it. If she kept her mind from unpleasantness she could drift in a blissful limbo, a sunlit place where she and her lover were together.

She received, and replied to, a letter from Jessie, but Oliver had told her what a nurse's schedule was like, and she did not expect to see her. She didn't mind. She wanted no-one but her mother and father and Oliver. She did not even want to go and see her children, and though she said it was because she did not want to have to answer their questions about the new baby that was on its way, the real reason was indolence. She didn't want anything to interrupt the peace of these gentle days.

Letters from Laidislaw were what she fed on now. He felt the same way.

> Your letters, by the way, are vital to me, in the true sense of the word – they give me life. Please don't think that, because I don't reply to every one, I don't treasure them all and think of you constantly. It is the lack of opportunity only that stays my pen.
>
> We are going next week on a special training course, held in the grounds of a château where, the rumour is, the terrain closely resembles that over which we will fight when the expected Big Push comes. We are to practise manoeuvres and certain techniques. I salute our leaders for leaving nothing to chance. We are all looking forward to a change of scene – and rumour also has it that the food is much better there, and that we will be served wine!
>
> The news of the course is welcome after a disappointment – my application to join officer training was turned down. The CO was kind enough to seem puzzled about it when he called me in to tell me personally about the rejection, and murmured something about my lack of experience. We shall put it down to that for now, and say no more.
>
> But by way of softening the blow, hc has given me a special job. I am to be the Battalion Artist, making a series of paintings about the battalion's activities, both in the trenches and out. The Old Man made this up out of his head, but I believe he has certainly hit on something – a record of that sort will be invaluable. One day, when the war is over, people will want to see what it was really like.

He says he is going to pursue it upwards and try to have the War Office make the appointment official, which he thinks will produce a commission for me, but in the mean time his authority is all I need to begin. That, and the materials. I must trouble you again, my beloved, to go shopping for me. I told the Old Man that I thought watercolour the best medium, so I append a list of what I shall need. Please send them as soon as possible, as I'm longing to begin.

She was thrilled for him, and felt that his commanding officer had struck on something really valuable. It *was* odd that Laidislaw had been refused for officer training – she had expected it to be more or less automatic, given that he was a gentleman – but in a way it was a good thing because, as an officer, he would not have time for all this drawing and painting. It was more important for him to exercise his art, both for his own sake and for posterity. Any gentleman could be an officer, but only he was Laidislaw.

CHAPTER THIRTEEN

Jessie had been sent to a ward of Tommies in one of the huts erected in the grounds. Beta Wallace, who was on the same ward, told her that pretty nurses were never sent to officers' wards in case they fell in love, got married and left. Jessie didn't know whether to laugh at the idea of calling her pretty, or to wonder that those in authority thought it impossible for a nurse to love a private. Now they were working together, she and Wallace became very friendly, and even called each other by their first names.

The ward was more than twice as large as the one in Clifton, with thirty beds a side instead of thirteen. They were acute surgical beds, and from the first day she was faced with the sort of wounds that assured her she was doing important nursing. The sister in charge, Sister Fitton, was a young woman, efficient and practical – too practical to allow something as irrational as dislike of VADs to come between her and her patients' good. When Jessie arrived on the first day she quizzed her sharply on her experience, and on learning that Jessie had been taught how to prepare dressing-trays, put her straight to work on that. Jessie progressed rapidly to assisting at dressings – holding the tray, passing bandages and forceps, holding flinching limbs.

Naturally, as the junior, she had plenty of the old, menial work, but she didn't mind it, now that it was not *all* she was allowed to do. It was wonderful to be trusted, and to be judged by what she could do, rather than who she was. All the nurses worked together at times of mass activity such as washing, bedmaking and taking temperatures, and it made Jessie feel she was a part of the team, rather than an adjunct who had to be found work to do.

Proctor was on a medical ward, where there were fewer gruesome sights. They met at mealtimes and exchanged news. Proctor confided that she thought she had been sent to an 'easier' ward because Matron knew she was under age. Girls had to be twenty-three to nurse in a military hospital, and Proctor was only nineteen. 'Though I lied about it, of course,' she said, 'but I'm sure Matron knew all along. She looked at me in *such* a way. You won't tell anyone, will you?'

'Of course not,' said Jessie.

Her experience on the medical ward was not like Jessie's under Sister Fitton. Sister Baddely, a large, grey-haired woman in her fifties, did not have a great opinion of VADs. While not precisely hating them, she still used them to release 'her nurses' for more important work. So Proctor and Leeson, the other VAD assigned with her, spent much of the time cleaning, dusting, oiling bed-wheels, tidying linen cupboards and the like. They did most of the bedmaking and washing, while the 'real nurses' took temperatures and pulses, filled in charts, administered drugs, changed dressings and measured out feeds for those on restricted diets.

Proctor, however, had no conceit of herself and was grateful to be allowed to do anything for the men. The medical ward nursed soldiers with conditions like heart disease, emphysema and diabetes, but they also had gas victims. Proctor was wide-eyed and a little tremulous when talking about them. 'How can people do such a thing to each other?' she asked.

Jessie wondered the same thing every day at the sight of the grotesque mutilations that passed through her ward. The raw and bleeding flesh, the mangled, the ripped and the shattered were hard to bear, and though she did not faint, she often felt her stomach rise. Two things sustained her. One was that the male orderlies were much more squeamish than the nurses, and would do anything to avoid seeing wounds uncovered; pride dictated she must not let her sex down. The other was that many of the patients, though stoical to an amazing degree, could not bear the sight of their own wounds. In turning their faces away they would be looking, instead, at her. She felt she must not show them by her reaction what a horror some part of their body had become. So she schooled herself to show nothing; and she found that concentration, plus a technique of flexing her toes and calf muscles, prevented her from fainting.

The men tolerated the most bitter pain – and, in most cases, faced a future of disability – with such gallantry that, when she reflected on it in the few quiet moments in her days, it affected her deeply. She would weep in the sluice for some young man's perfect body, hideously maimed, for the boy with no face gazing with his remaining eye at a photograph of his fiancée, for the middle-aged family man, now legless, who still tried to joke about it, though his face was blue-white with blood loss and the lines of agony drawn sharply in it, as though with a stylus in wax.

She wrote to Bertie:

> I know now without a shadow of doubt that I am doing the finest work a woman could do in these times, and that nothing less than incapacity must prevent me from carrying on with it. Seeing the world from this side of the hospital divide, I wonder that any strong and healthy girl can hold back. Those of us who cannot go to the Front must do what we can at home, and that means more than committees and flag days and knitting khaki scarves. How can perfectly able girls 'stay at home with Mother'?

Bertie replied:

I am glad you are at last able to do what you have so long wanted, and you can be sure that you *are* making a difference. Don't be too hard on those who don't follow your example. Old habits take time to change. Even I am shocked at the fragile-seeming girls who come into our orbit as nurses, drivers or 'comforts' workers. If I had not grown used to the idea of your active character, I think I might be one of those who think 'a woman's place is in the home'. War will change ideas, but it will be a slow process. And we must be careful not to throw out the valuable along with what is not, just now, convenient. When the war is over and the men come home, women will have to make room for them by becoming womanly again, or I fear for society.

She wrote:

After the war – if that is not just a mythical heaven we dream of – it will be hard for all of us to adjust. You say women must become women again – but soldiers will have to become men. Will that be possible? You must all have hardened yourselves to a terrible degree to do what you have to do. Can you break out of that shell when the time comes?

He wrote:

I hope so – God, I hope so! I *do* feel hardened, but the fact that I can look at myself and see it is surely a good sign? There was the most wonderful sunset yesterday, a thing of flaming banners, gold, purple and crimson. I was watching it from the trench with awe, and wondered if some German officer across no man's land was watching too, and asking himself what he was doing there, living down in a ditch. I think that must prove there is humanity left in me. This grim soldier is not really me, but the shape I assume for the job I have to do. I believe I shall be able to step out of it when it's no longer needed. Aren't your patients men rather than soldiers? You speak of them as though they are.

Their correspondence was more frequent than it had ever been; and now that no-one but her need see the letters, they opened their minds more freely to each other. She got into the habit of writing a little every night in bed before she fell into the dead sleep of exhaustion. Bertie said it was what he did too. Perhaps that was why a more philosophical tone took over their correspondence. She rarely wrote about the hospital and the injured. The blood, the pus, the pain, the smells; the butcher's-slab look of raw flesh, the dull gleam of exposed bone in a mangled wound, the anguished quivering of a newly amputated stump – these were her work. To do it properly she had to concentrate on the single square of injury that required her attention, and then at the end of the day put it all from her mind.

But she did write to him about her fellow nurses, the hostel and its privations, her dreams of food (with which he sympathised), her constantly sore feet, and what she did with her leisure.

We often have to give up our off-time when new patients come in, and we are glad to do it. I have never heard anyone complain. But when I can get away, I like to go and sit in a park I have discovered only ten minutes from the hospital. I buy a bun at a shop I pass on the way, and I take a book with me, but often I do nothing but stare at the trees and smell the grass and earth. That's real refreshment. Sometimes Beta comes with me. I enjoy her company. She is not a 'chatterer' but has an original outlook and often makes me laugh. I can never coax Proctor to come. She says nothing could induce her to walk one step more than she has to.

I like to imagine you [Bertie wrote] in your new surroundings. I can't see you gliding soft-footed about the ward in your angelic headdress – I'm quite persuaded that you *do* glide, but it is too strange to me to imagine. But I can see you sitting on the grass with a bun and a book. That seems like you. You do not mention seeing anyone from your old life, though London is on your doorstep. I am expecting to have some leave soon – is there a hope that I can see you? Fenniman is mourning the fact that Miss Emma is incarcerated in Scotland and therefore out of his reach. Shall I also be disappointed?

She replied,

It will be difficult, because our off-time is not arranged beforehand, but not impossible. If you let me know when you are coming I can put in a request for my half-day to coincide. I have not yet had the promised dinner with Oliver, mainly because I am afraid of being seen. Nurses and doctors are *not* encouraged to notice each other, and for nurses even to speak to a doctor unless directly addressed is a grave offence. There was a scandal about six months ago – still talked about in the dining-room – when a nurse and doctor were caught kissing in the sluice-room on night duty. The nurse was dismissed with ignominy. But a cousin – especially a soldier – ought to be a different matter.

* * *

Russia's fortunes in the war had been mixed. They had started off with a flourish in 1914, advancing rapidly into

East Prussia, and by dividing German attention between two fronts had probably saved Paris. But the Russian Army, though massive, was poorly equipped, with rifles for only two-thirds of the men in uniform. There was a lack of modern equipment and a shortage of shells and ammunition, and the desperate poverty back home meant that desertion was always a problem: men slipped away in the dark to go and attend to their fields and feed their families.

The vast number of largely untrained peasants was no match for the German 'war machine', and through 1915, fighting desperately and with terrible losses, the Russians retreated before its relentless advance. By the middle of July, the Front ran from the southern border of Moldavia almost directly north to Riga. Poland and Lithuania, with a population of 23 million, along with most of Latvia, had been lost to Russia, and she had suffered two million casualties, with another million missing or taken prisoner.

In September the Tsar had replaced his cousin Grand Duke Nikolai as supreme commander – a move that was alarming, Venetia's son Thomas had said to her, because it meant any future failures of the army would be attributed directly to him. Though the people still loved the 'Little Father', who was almost a god to the peasantry, he was not popular in the other social circles because of his blind devotion to his wife, the Tsaritsa Alexandra. This adoration prevented his curbing or even recognising her destructive behaviour. She seemed to be infatuated with the pseudo-priest Rasputin. His venal reputation was well known to all but the imperial family, and he infuriated courtiers and civil servants alike by using his power with the Tsaritsa to secure positions in government for his favourites, and even to influence policy.

Since no-one outside the closest circle to the imperial couple understood why they tolerated such a creature – even that closest circle did not dare tell Nicholas what Rasputin was really like – it was widely believed that the priest was the Tsaritsa's lover. Salacious stories and obscene cartoons were freely circulated in the streets and taverns. What was even more damaging was that, because of her German birth, many peasants believed the Tsaritsa was a spy, and Rasputin her go-between with the German government. Military setbacks began to be attributed to the pair, and added to the growing unrest. The troubles were fuelled by hunger: with so many peasants in uniform, agriculture had collapsed, and there were constant food crises.

Russia had long been a melting-pot of new ideas. Before the war it had boasted the most wide-ranging and brilliant culture in Europe, and had been a natural home for the avant-garde. Thomas had written in great excitement during his early days in St Petersburg about the restless brilliance of the new painters, such as Kandinsky, Bakst, Malevich and Chagall, composers like Stravinsky and Rubinstein, innovators like Diaghilev in the ballet and Stanislavsky in the theatre. Primitivism, neo-classicism, cubism, fauvism, impressionism, abstracticism, geometricism – the energy of new ideas seemed limitless, and with a large population of wealthy young men who had nothing to do, it naturally spilled over into politics.

Venetia had, among his letters, one that dealt amusingly with this aspect of society.

> A young man with any claim to be fashionable has to have his regiment, his club and his revolutionary organisation. We call them armchair revolutionaries, because – perhaps fortunately – they have no desire to act on their mad theories, only to discuss them endlessly in comfort after dinner over a cigar. Revolution and tobacco seem to have a necessary connection! Some of the societies are quite serious about working for political reform: the Socialist Revolutionary Party, whose leading light, Kerensky, is quite a sensible fellow, has modest aims of increasing democracy. Others run the

> gamut between the staunchly pro-Tsarist and the out-and-out anarchist. Without half trying I can think of the Constitutional Democrats, the Socialist Democrats, the Popular Socialists, the Revolutionary Socialists, and the People's Socialist Democratic Party. There are also the Kadets, who are very pro-Tsarist, and to confuse matters further, the Socialist Democrats are divided into the Mensheviks, who tend to be conciliatory, and the Bolsheviks, who hate everyone and everything – even themselves! With all these different groups in the Duma, nothing is likely ever to happen, which is perhaps a good thing, given the combustible nature of idle young men.

In another, later letter he regretted the fragmentation of the parties wanting constitutional change.

> From time to time Kerensky suggests they would get on better if they merged into one, but they all have slightly different demands and no-one is willing to give up anything. It's a pity, as there's no denying that much needs improving. Food production is so primitive and wasteful here, compared with our methods at home. Much of the hunger could be avoided, but the peasants are devoted to their inefficient 'communes'. And if the armchair revolutionaries agree on one thing, it is that the peasant is the heart and soul of Russia, and the commune is the expression of his prelapsarian purity. That's one reform none of them will think of.

Over time, his letters had become more grave and more guarded. On his last visit home on leave he had spoken about the increasing political tensions, the poverty and unrest in the streets, the middle-class disaffection with the war, and the upper-class loathing of Rasputin and, by association, the Tsaritsa.

'Leaving her in charge while the Tsar went to Stavka was a bad mistake,' he complained wearily. 'Good men get dismissed and scoundrels replace them because Rasputin tells her to do it. The intellectual classes see the misgovernment and they can't do anything about it. Grand Duke Nikolai tried to urge the Tsar to a measure of constitutional reform, but he wouldn't have it. Now the Duma is trying to get him to agree to Duma government. He won't agree to that, either. I'm afraid unless something is done to defuse the situation, it may end in revolution.'

The terrible word had made Venetia blench. 'Surely it won't come to that? I thought you said the peasantry adored the Tsar?'

'They do, but of course it won't be they who create revolution. They'll be the blunt instrument wielded by the middle classes – the lawyers and the intelligentsia – to get what they want. They'll offer the peasants land, and if they're hungry enough, they'll listen. With the endless food and fuel crises, and the losses at the Front, I'm afraid that time is coming nearer.'

Venetia had gazed at her firstborn, and grieved at the change in him. He was still well set-up, a tall and broad-shouldered man with the controlled grace of movement of the athlete; but he was almost thirty, and looked it, his face set into grave lines, the first few grey hairs appearing in his dark head. There was little trace now of the light-hearted, gay and eager young man who had first gone to Russia; still less of the popular sporting hero of Eton and Oxford – her laughing, teasing boy. It hurt her to see him so weighted with responsibility.

'Can't you come home?' she had asked. 'You've done more than your time over there. I know you volunteered for the extension of your tour, but I'm sure they would not object if you asked to be moved somewhere else.'

He had looked at her sadly. 'I dare say I could get myself moved, but the thing is, Mama, I can't leave them. They've been good to me. They're like my family now. And it's not even so much the Tsar and Tsaritsa, but the grand duchesses and the boy. I have to do what I can to protect them. If there should be a revolution, they will need someone to speak for them.'

'But that isn't your job,' she had cried.

'It is now.'

'There must be Russians at court who could do it.'

'Not really. It's hard to explain to someone who hasn't been there, but there's a sort of fragility about the whole structure. If things start to disintegrate, I'm afraid it may be every man for himself, and who knows what the Russian courtiers will do? I wouldn't count on them not to save their own skins first. I can't abandon the family. I hope it will never come to it, but if things look bad, it may be necessary to get them out. That's something I can do better than a Russian.'

'If things look bad, you must get *yourself* out,' Venetia had said sternly.

'Yes, Mama,' he had said, with a tired smile. Later that same leave he had talked to her, as if idly, about a system of code-writing that was simple to decipher if you had the key, but almost impossible without. 'It would be useful, for instance,' he said, 'if one thought one's letters were being intercepted.' And he had written out an example for her, using a certain key. She had half expected since then to receive coded letters from him, but he had gone on writing in the usual way, and she put it from her mind as having been merely an interesting topic to discuss.

When Jessie reached the hostel one evening she found a telegram waiting for her, which had been delivered after she had left that morning. It was from Bertie, announcing that he would arrive home on leave the following day, and hoping that he could see her during the week.

The arrangements proved unexpectedly easy to make,

involving only a brief telephone call, preceded by an application, hands behind back and eyes modestly lowered, to the ward sister. Sister Fitton seemed to be in a particularly good mood, for she not only agreed to fix Jessie's half-day in advance, but even suggested herself that Jessie should have it in the afternoon rather than the morning, and said that, as they were not busy, she could go off at noon. When Jessie stammered her surprised thanks, she smiled and said, 'We all want to do what we can for our heroes.'

On the day, Jessie changed in the VADs' cloakroom, washed her feet and stockings in the handbasin, and walked out of the front gate at half past twelve to find Bertie waiting for her, looking handsome, glamorous and somehow *taller* in his major's uniform. A pair of nurses coming in arm in arm couldn't help staring at him as they passed, then put their heads together to whisper as they hurried on towards the entrance door, looking back several times to see who he belonged to.

'It's a pity I don't know them,' Jessie said. 'It would enhance my reputation no end for it to be known I was meeting a major obviously back from the Front.'

'Obviously?' Bertie queried. 'Do I look so travel-stained and shabby?'

'No, foolish! But you're no Hyde Park soldier.' His broad shoulders and air of authority might belong to any officer. It was the long stare, and a certain reserved grimness, that marked out the man who had been in the trenches and in battle, who had seen things that he would never be able to talk about. 'It's in the eyes, and the set of the mouth,' she said. 'Responsibility. Experience.'

He looked down at her tenderly. 'You've changed, too. Responsibility. Experience. You look tired.'

'Nurses are always tired.'

'But no less beautiful.'

She moved her eyes away. She wanted so much to touch

him that she was afraid she might lose control. 'Nurses are always hungry, too,' she added.

He took the cue. 'And I expect you were up at the crack of dawn. When did you breakfast?'

'Seven o'clock – but we have bread-and-butter in the middle of the morning.'

'Nevertheless,' he said, 'you've been toiling hard and deserve the finest luncheon money can buy. If we can find a taxi in this benighted place, I'll take you to the Ritz.'

'I'm not dressed for it.'

He eyed her plain blue costume. 'You look perfectly neat to me. Besides, it's wartime – didn't you know? Everyone understands these things.'

'And I'm with a major in uniform – the ticket of entry, these days, to all places, however exclusive.'

He smiled. 'I'm glad you're learning to appreciate me. Lord, don't they *have* taxis south of the river?'

'Imagine, there are people who actually *choose* to live on the wrong bank,' she teased.

'Poor things. One should feel sorry, really – ah, here's one!' It halted to his masterful gesture, and soon they were safe in its leathern cocoon, rattling towards Vauxhall Bridge, the north bank and civilisation.

As soon as they were settled, Bertie said, 'Let me look at you,' which licensed them both to do what they longed to, and feast their eyes. He looked tired, too, she thought, though he had assured her in his letters that it was quiet on the Front and almost like a holiday. The pleasant chalk downland of Picardy, with its wide, reedy, tree-lined rivers and comfortable little towns, was delightful in the clement summer weather. He claimed to have had time for fishing, and to eat excellent meals of local produce in a variety of small, family restaurants.

Yet he looked worn. 'Is it bad out there?' she asked.

He did not ask her what she meant. He said, 'No, not at the moment – except for the fact of having to be there at all. And the men, the new intake, are splendid fellows, so lively and full of fun. There's the usual number of bad hats, I suppose – or, no, perhaps there really are fewer, after all,' he added thoughtfully, 'because they're volunteers and doing it from the heart. There's a particular spirit among them that makes them a pleasure to command.'

She didn't ask, then, what it was that made him look so strained. Their time together was too short for sad subjects. Instead she said, 'Did Major Fenniman come back with you?'

'No, he has his leave next week, but since Miss Emma is out of reach in Scotland, he's decided to spend it in the fleshpots of Paris. Oh!' He caught himself up. 'I didn't mean fleshpots, of course. You shouldn't say that to her when you write.'

She laughed. 'As if I would!'

'Shows and restaurants and clean sheets are the height of his ambition. He has no eyes for any other female.'

'How are Maud and the boy?' she asked, since it had to be done some time.

'They're well,' he said. 'Richard is a real delight – a proper boy, now, not a baby any longer. I'd like to teach him to fish. Maud has arranged to take him to visit a cousin of hers in Ireland next week, and there'll be good fishing there for a boy who knows how to do it.'

'I didn't know she had cousins in Ireland,' Jessie said carefully.

Bertie did not look at her. 'They're cousins of Richard's, really – her father's. Her second cousins. He had quite a lot of family over there. I didn't realise she'd got so close to them, but apparently they started writing when Richard died, and expressed a wish to see the boy.'

She heard from his voice that there was more to it than that, but she could not ask what. Maud was an impossible subject between them. She sought for a neutral topic and they talked about the war a little. She congratulated him on his 'mention', and asked about Pennyfather, who had come back and was fully fit. He asked about Emma, and Violet, and she spoke of Maria and the family back home. It lasted them well until they were seated in the dining-room at the Ritz, and then a silence fell between them. It was not awkwardness, but the ease of two people long acquainted and very close, who could be silent together.

They lunched on cutlets and gooseberry fool, and when they had finished eating he offered her coffee. She declined and said that she would prefer to walk a little in the park. 'I don't get out of doors as often as I'd like, and it's a fine day.'

Under the great plane trees of Green Park he offered his arm and she took it without hesitation, so natural was the gesture. They strolled in silence for a while, looking at the other people enjoying the day, and the busy pigeons pecking around, the sparrows dust-bathing, the occasional dog trotting importantly by, taking his human for a walk. There was a feeling of relaxation and pleasure in the air, despite the fact that such men as were visible were mostly in uniform. Jessie remembered the last time they had walked in the park thus, and her fingers closed unconsciously on his arm. He glanced down at her, then led the way to a bench, where they sat, side by side and close.

'Jessie,' he said, 'we don't have very long, not long enough to be reserved with each other.'

'But what is there to say?' she asked. The situation was what it was and there was nothing to be done about it.

'Tell me how you are. You seem – more settled.'

She thought. 'Yes, I think I am. I have a place to belong to, work to do, a purpose to my life.'

'You have friends?'

'Not that, really. Just – people to make noises around me and stop me thinking. But I'm not lonely. I think of you a lot, and read your letters, and you seem close to me – closer here in London, in the hospital, than anywhere else. Sometimes I couldn't find you in Yorkshire, but here the war seems nearer, and you with it – as if you're just across the water, and the water is nothing.'

He nodded. 'I feel the same way about you. There's so much I can't say to – to people at home. They don't understand what it's like. I have to mouth platitudes to them. England seems like another planet. But it's different with you. You've seen the results of it. You *know*. It's as if there's a cord between us, stopping us drifting away from each other.'

'Like tethered balloons,' she said, smiling.

They were silent a moment. She felt the regular tide of his breathing close beside her, and felt just then that she would never ask more than this, simply to be near him, near enough to breathe the same air.

'Do you think about Ned?' he asked.

'Not often,' she answered. 'There's too much sadness in it.'

'You can be proud of him. His death was a fine and brave one.'

'I know,' she said. 'I am. But—'

'But?'

She looked up into his serious eyes. 'On his last leave, the last before Loos, he said to me that perhaps we shouldn't have married. I've wondered and wondered what he meant. I don't think I made him happy, though I tried – I did try. It seems such a waste now. I can never put it right. I should have said no when he asked me to marry him, but my father wanted it so much. And it seemed right at the time. Now it all seems just – sad. So I try not to think about it.'

He nodded, and they sat in silence, while the declining sun sparkled through the moving leaves of the trees, scattering them with coins of shadow, of light.

'How long have we?' she asked suddenly. 'When are you expected back?'

'We've all evening,' he said. 'Maud has to go to a meeting tonight. What would you like to do?'

The world seemed so full of possibilities that she could not choose. She felt suddenly gay. She had thought he would have to go soon, and now here was a reprieve. She wanted not to feel sad, not to waste this time together with introspection or regret. But what to do?

'Would you like to go to a dance?' he asked.

Her heart lifted. 'Yes,' she said. 'Yes, that's exactly what I'd like to do. What made you think of it?'

He smiled. 'I'm a soldier home on leave. It's what soldiers on leave do. We could go to the Grosvenor, if you like. There's a dinner-dance on there. I heard some fellows talk about it on the train. They said the band is awfully good.'

She laughed aloud at such an absurd consideration. 'But I'm not dressed,' she said.

'Don't I tell you there's a war on? Nobody will be dressed.'

'Let's go there, then,' she said, standing up. He stood too and looked down at her, and her stomach was suddenly hollow, her breath caught with desire for him. She saw the same thing darken his eyes. 'At least,' he said huskily, 'I can hold you if we dance.'

It had occurred to her, too. They began to walk again, and he reached for her hand and held it a moment before drawing it through his arm. She asked him about the big push that was coming, and he spoke about it matter-of-factly. Preparations were detailed and extensive; nothing was being left to chance. Everyone was confident of success. He talked of his men, the terrain, what would happen afterwards, if the German line was broken – where the enemy would be driven to. She felt the slight roughness of his sleeve under her fingers and the warmth of his body against the back of her hand, and thought what battle meant, what he would face, how many of his men had been killed before, in other actions. He was unlikely to have more leave now before the autumn. This might be the last time she was ever with him. She might never hear his voice again after tonight, never smell the particular scent of him, never see the face she cherished so much. In a few weeks he might be gone, out of the world, leaving her to face it all alone.

As if he heard her thoughts, he paused, and then said in a different voice, 'There's nothing to be done about it, Jess. Nothing at all. You know—'

'Yes, I know.'

'We can only hope, and do our best. If death comes, it comes. But we've had *this*. We've found our perfect match. So many people never do, even in a long life.'

She nodded, her throat too tight for words. Yes, she had found her perfect match – but she wanted more, so much more! She could not be philosophical about losing the one thing she had. And then she thought about Maud, and felt a pang of guilt and pity and sadness. Maud did not even have that.

She had to ask: 'Does Maud know where you are today?'

'Oh, yes,' he said neutrally. 'She knows I'm seeing you. She sent her regards, but she was busy all day, so she couldn't have joined us, even if she'd wanted.'

They had come to the road and he stopped talking while he got them across, through the mass of moving traffic. He had given her something else to wonder about, now. Why did Maud not cancel her engagements while Bertie was home? Why did she prefer him to go alone to luncheon with Jessie, rather than accompany him, or invite Jessie to the house? She was inexpressibly glad to have him to herself, but that could not have been Maud's design.

Later, much later, he took her back to the hostel in a taxi. She was so tired that she fell asleep on the journey, and woke as the cab laboured up Denmark Hill, finding her head resting on Bertie's quiet shoulder.

'What a terrible waste,' she said.

'Do you think so? I rather enjoyed it.' His voice came back out of the darkness. Most of the street-lamps were out

– an air-raid precaution – and they seemed alone on the sea of night. 'You weren't asleep long.'

She didn't feel it necessary to change her position. It was so comfortable, and they had so little time. 'I surprised myself,' she said, 'dancing so much. It must have been the champagne.'

'I always find that at the Front,' he said solemnly. 'A glass of champagne gets one over the top, even when one's really tired.'

'Foolish!' she said. And then, 'Isn't it nice to have time to talk nonsense?'

'God, yes! You may have hit on the very thing that marks out war from peace. One can't imagine the German imperial commanders talking nonsense.'

'And yet they are *ridiculous*,' Jessie said wonderingly. 'When one thinks of the uniform, the moustaches, the strutting – the cartoonists capture it so well. How can something so ridiculous have such terrible effects?'

'Because they take themselves seriously. If they had ever been able to laugh at themselves, we might not be in the situation we are now. When the war's over, let's make a vow never to be serious again.'

The taxi turned into her street. 'Let's not talk about "when the war's over",' she said quietly.

'No,' he said. 'Perhaps we shouldn't.' The taxi stopped, and the driver gave them a prompting glance over his shoulder. 'I shan't be able to see you again before I go back,' he said. 'I have to go down to Beaumont to see to things. I thought I'd take Richard with me. There a nice little stream that runs across my property that would be just right for his first fishing lesson.' He stopped talking abruptly, and in the darkness took her hand. It was time to say goodbye, and he didn't want to speak the word.

She returned the pressure of his hand. 'Bertie, don't get hurt. I've seen what it means. Don't get—' It was absurd to ask him the impossible.

'I'll be careful,' he said. 'I'm always careful.'

Perhaps he was, she thought; but he was also brave. She withdrew her hand from his, and he got out and held the door for her.

'Goodnight. Thank you for a lovely day,' she said.

'Goodnight, my love,' he said softly, and for an instant he pressed her hand again, so that as she walked away and up to the door of the hostel, the warm impression of his fingers remained even as the sound of the taxi faded away, taking him with it.

The British government's main concern about Russia was whether it was going to pull out of the war. If Russia made peace with Germany, all Germany's might would be brought to bear on the Western Front. It was essential to keep German effort divided; but since the retreat in 1915 and the stabilisation of the new front on the wrong side of Lithuania, Russia had accomplished nothing, and there were definite signals that she was losing enthusiasm for the struggle.

So at the end of May 1916 the government welcomed the invitation from the Tsar to send a diplomatic mission to St Petersburg, to discuss troop dispositions and the supply of armaments. It would be an opportunity to encourage him to keep fighting. Lord Kitchener and Lloyd George were to go; but at the last moment Lloyd George announced that he was too busy at the Ministry of Munitions and was pulling out of the trip. Kitchener was to manage alone, sailing for Archangel with his staff of six on the 5th of June.

Lord Overton's busy life had lately been complicated by the return to Westminster of his old nemesis, Winston Churchill. Churchill had left in disgust when the coalition reorganisation had ousted him from the Admiralty, and offered him nothing better than the Duchy of Lancaster. Overton had not been sorry to see him go. He was a natural meddler and was always putting people's backs up with his abrasive tactlessness. The whole Gallipoli mess could be largely traced back to him. Venetia disliked him, too, because of his attitude to the Suffragettes when he had been home secretary. Churchill had gone back into the army, where he proved a good soldier. He had been given command of an infantry battalion, and had done rather well at Plug Street.

But his primary interest was always politics, and at the beginning of May he had handed in his commission and returned to London. In the House, he had caused consternation by demanding the return of his friend Lord Fisher as first sea lord, much to the fury of Balfour, who was first lord of the Admiralty and whose appointment it was.

'Why does he think he can tell everyone what to do?' Venetia asked, when Overton told her about it.

'From what I've heard in the corridors,' Overton said, 'he has an ambition to be prime minister.'

'Well, surely all MPs want that,' Venetia said.

'Most of them, perhaps – but he really believes he has a chance. He sees Asquith's weakness, decides it's only a matter of time before he's toppled, and thinks he can succeed him.'

'He's reckoning without Lloyd George,' said Venetia. 'The Welshman wants to be PM too. Those two may have pretended to be friends in the past, but neither would back the other for leadership.'

'Of course not,' said Overton, impatiently. 'And Churchill has few friends. The best he might hope for, if Lloyd George or Bonar Law should lead a government, is to get the Admiralty back – though I'm not sure the navy would be happy with that. He annoyed the senior officers too much when he was last there.' He sighed. 'It was all pleasantly quiet while he was at the Front. What a pity he didn't stay there.'

Another trouble for Lord Overton was the select committee that was investigating the handling of munitions supply at the beginning of the war. Two million rifles had been ordered from American suppliers, but to date less than five hundred had been delivered; and the abysmal shortage of shells had been widely publicised after the battle of Loos. Sir George Arthur had introduced a vote of censure against Kitchener's management of the War Department, and although the vote had failed, interest in the subject was intense. Matters came to a head, stirred up by Churchill and Lloyd George behind the scenes, when Lord Kitchener was summoned to appear before the committee on the 4th of June, the day before he was due to sail to Archangel. Kitchener had always relied considerably on Lord Overton for advice, and Overton was engaged for days in looking up figures and trying to prepare answers for every possible question.

On the day, two hundred MPs packed the chamber to hear what K would say in his own defence.

'He spoke so well, and so candidly,' Overton told Venetia, when he arrived home afterwards, 'explaining all his efforts to secure supplies, that at the end they gave him a vote of thanks. It was unanimously carried – and the proposer, I might add, was Sir George Arthur!'

'Did you ever meet an MP who knew his own mind from one week to the next?' Venetia asked. 'But I'm glad it came out well. Strangely, I've grown fond of K, for all his faults.' She stifled a yawn. 'Lord, I'm tired! This new scheme of mine wears me out far more than surgery. I hope you don't have to get up early tomorrow, because I should dearly like to sleep late – perhaps until eight, if I'm to be really self-indulgent.'

'Ah,' said Overton, apologetically, and she looked at him sharply. 'The thing is, my love, as I was about to tell you, my plans for the next week or so have suddenly changed. Kitchener wants me to go to Russia with him.'

'Oh, Beauty, no!'

'I know it's rather sudden, but Cunningham has been taken ill – a mild heart-attack, it seems – and K wants me to take his place.'

'I thought you were done with all that after the Dardanelles!'

'We all have to do our duty, dear, when and where it arises.'

'I know,' she said, 'and I don't begrudge you to the War Office, but I don't like you going away. I miss you too much.'

'You'll be too busy in your new office to miss me.' He tried to jolly her along.

'I shall miss you in the evenings and at night – especially at night. I don't sleep well unless you're beside me.'

He took her in his arms. 'I hate to be away from you, too. But needs must.' He kissed her and held her close, and then said lightly, 'And you are forgetting the positive side.'

'*Is* there a positive side?' she said mutinously.

'Russia? St Petersburg? What an unnatural mother she is, to be sure! We have a son there, or had you forgotten?'

She pushed herself back from him and saw him smiling. 'You'll get to see Thomas?'

'Of course I will. In fact, I dare say he will be an essential part of the negotiations. We shall probably be together every day, and dine together every night.'

'Oh, Beauty, I'm glad! You can find out from him if he really is all right. Find out *everything*. Have I got time to write a letter for you to take? I wonder if there's anything he'd like sent over with you – not that there's time to *get* anything . . . I don't know why you're grinning at me like that. A husband in the hand is still worth two sons in the bush, but if you *must* go—'

'Indeed I *must*. But I'm sure if Thomas wanted anything he'd have told us long ago. There's the diplomatic bag, you know. And there's a wonderful shop on the Nevsky Prospekt that sells English goods, everything right down to Pears' soap.'

'How can you know that?' she wondered.

'I take an interest,' he said. 'And now, my darling, if you'll forgive me, I shall have to go and talk to Ash about packing for me.'

'Will you take him with you?'

'No, we'll be sharing servants – three between the six of us. I'll be sharing Macpherson's man.'

'I expect Ash will be pleased. When do you leave?'

'We'll be taking the sleeper to Thurso tonight.'

'Tonight?' she cried sharply. 'But you can't go tonight!'

'Darling, you know the delegation sails tomorrow from Scapa, and we have to *get* there first. It's a long way to the Orkneys. We're catching the eight o'clock train from King's Cross. They're putting on two sleeper-carriages for us.'

'What about dinner?'

'Nothing was said about that,' Overton said. 'I suppose we might have something on the train.'

Venetia pulled herself together. 'Better not take the risk. I can have dinner here brought forward, if you like.'

'A good thought. I should like to sit down with you – it will be our last dinner together for a while.' He smiled at her. 'At least I can be sure of a dinner of *some* sort during the voyage – unlike poor K, who is the world's worst sailor. I dare say he'll be as empty as a drum by the time we get to Archangel.'

Later, after dinner, she went upstairs with him and watched him moving about his dressing-room, picking up the last few things he would need. She said, 'Will you go to Stavka?'

'Probably. Since we were invited by His Imperial Majesty himself, I expect he'll want to talk to us in person.'

'Perhaps you can talk some sense into him about reform. He always liked you.'

'Darling!' His back was turned, but she could hear the smile in his voice. 'He won't even remember me.'

'He'll remember you. He remembers everyone. It's his gift – perhaps his only gift.'

'Well, he wouldn't heed me, anyway. Why should he, when he doesn't listen to his own advisers?'

'Because it's always easier to listen to the outsider. And because he's grateful to you.'

'Grateful?'

'For giving him Thomas.'

She walked over to the window, and looked out at the treetops, dark against the pale evening sky. 'That silly woman!' she said suddenly, thinking of the Tsaritsa, who was endangering her son along with everyone else through her obsession with the mad *starits* Rasputin. 'I always thought her a silly woman. Too religious by half – and the wrong *sort* of religious.'

'You should come with me,' he said, closing his holdall and looking round to see if he had left anything. 'Perhaps *you* could talk sense into *her*.'

She walked up close to him. 'Talk to Thomas as much as you can,' she said. 'Make sure he's really all right. He might tell you things he can't put in his letters. Talk to *everyone*. Find out as much as you can about the situation. If it really is dangerous, try to make him see sense and come home.'

Overton drew her into his arms. 'I'll try,' he said. 'But Thomas is a grown man.'

'He's my son.'

'He'll decide his own future.'

'If I could be sure of that, I wouldn't worry. But I'm afraid other people will decide it for him.'

He kissed her brow. 'People have been talking about revolution in Russia for decades – centuries, even – but nothing much really happens. It blows up for a while and then dies down again. Try not to worry.'

'I need something to worry about,' she pointed out, 'otherwise I shall worry about you.'

'I don't get seasick.'

She turned her lips up to his. 'Oh, Beauty, I do love you so much.'

'After all this time?' he teased, kissing her lightly.

'More than ever.'

'I love you, too. More than ever. Though it does strike

me as rather indecent for a man to love his wife of thirty-one years as much as this.'

She saw he wouldn't be serious, and knew that he did not at all want to go, and would miss her as much as she missed him – more, perhaps. She must let him go easily. She smiled. 'That's a very nineteenth-century attitude,' she said. 'You sound like Lord Melbourne.'

'But I'm much handsomer,' said Overton, and kissed her with his heart on his lips.

CHAPTER FOURTEEN

The train rattled northwards through the long midsummer dusk; by Edinburgh, where they stopped briefly at four in the morning, it was fully light again. Overton woke, wondering where he was, heard the sighing of the train and the station sounds outside, and remembered. He thought of Venetia warmly asleep in their own bed at home, or perhaps stirring, disturbed by the dawn chorus, and smiled to himself. It was a grey dawn here in Scotland, the skies heavy with rain. He turned over and slept again until Macpherson's man came to rouse him with tea and buttered toast at six thirty.

They went on through progressively emptier country, grey and green, haunt only of the stag and the crow, veiled in constant, relentless rain. By the time they reached Thurso, it was lashing the carriage windows, and a fiercely gusty wind was rocking the train. The party gathered protectively around Kitchener in the carriage and talked of anything but the weather: it was going to be a rough crossing, and worrying about his notorious weakness kept their minds off the possibility of their own. But he was as calm as ever, even when, at the port of Scrabster, boarding HMS *Oak*, they followed him up the gangplank and it jerked about under their feet, while the damp, salty wind plastered their great-coats to their legs.

It was more sheltered inside Scapa Flow, where the Grand

Fleet, recently returned from the battle at Jutland, lay at anchor – a mass of grey shipping on grey water, moving restlessly like horses stamping in the stable. They went aboard the flagship, HMS *Iron Duke*, where they were greeted by Admiral Sir John Jellicoe and his staff and senior captains, and taken down to his stateroom for luncheon. An admiral of the fleet in the Royal Navy is not expected to stint himself, and they found every luxury, a panelled room, a table set with the best linen, silver and crystal, a host of white-gloved servants, delicious food and fine wines. The movement of the sea was less felt in this large ship, and everyone was able to relax and enjoy what was put before him: pea and ham soup, turbot, roast chicken and a raspberry blancmange. Only the swinging of the silver lamps and the lapping of the claret in the glasses reminded them of where they were.

Jellicoe was an attentive and genial host, and the conversation flourished. It was general at first, but eventually it came round to the mission before them.

'The whole fleet is seething with rumour,' Jellicoe said, 'about where *Hampshire* is going and why. Somehow it is known that an Eminent Person is to be taken on board, and I believe betting is brisk about your identity, my lord.'

The flag captain said, 'I warrant that by the time you go on board *Hampshire* her whole crew will know everything about it.' He caught Kitchener's slight frown and said apologetically, 'I don't know how it is, but sailors always seem to know everything.'

'That's true,' said Jellicoe. 'But you can trust them. They're no talking fools. And *Hampshire* is a fine ship.'

'She's an armed cruiser of the Devonshire class, and the fastest vessel of her size in the navy,' the flag captain said. 'You couldn't want a better ship for the job.'

During the meal, the movement of the ship around them had been growing more noticeable, and Overton, in the pauses in conversation, could hear the shrill whine of the wind in the rigging somewhere above them. It did not bode well. Though it was June, their journey had always been likely to be a rough one: from Scapa through the northern reaches of the Atlantic, and round the north cape of Norway to Archangel – two thousand miles of cold, rough water. But if a storm was getting up, it would be that much worse. While the table was being cleared for dessert, a young officer came in with a murmured message for the admiral, and when the cheese and fruit had been put on he leaned across to Kitchener and said, 'I wonder if you would not be wise to postpone your departure, my lord. It's blowing up outside – quite a gale developing. We don't feel it so much here in Scapa where it's sheltered, but I assure you, when you reach the open sea you will be facing some difficult conditions.'

Kitchener said, with his customary calm, 'It is not in my power to delay even for a day, Sir John. We must take the rough with the smooth, I'm afraid.'

Overton saw that Jellicoe was quite concerned. 'It's blowing force seven already, and the glass is still falling.'

'Is the ship – the *Hampshire* – unable to withstand the conditions?' Kitchener asked.

'She can stand them,' said Jellicoe, 'but it will not be pleasant for any of you.'

'We must all do our duty,' Kitchener said, 'pleasant or not. I cannot delay my mission. We must sail unless you tell me it is completely impossible.'

Jellicoe hesitated, and then said, 'It is not completely impossible, but I strongly advise you to remain in port until the wind moderates.'

Kitchener smiled under his large moustache. 'Thank you for your advice, Sir John. I think we must sail, however.'

Jellicoe shook his head slightly, thought a moment, and said, 'Then may I suggest that you sail by the western route, rather than the eastern? With the wind in the present quarter, it will be more sheltered, and it will not take a great deal longer. I strongly recommend it.'

'I am happy to accept your recommendation,' said Kitchener.

When luncheon was over, a steam pinnace came alongside to take them to the *Hampshire*. Kitchener's party went up on deck and some of them staggered in the sudden onslaught of the wind. The sky was low, grey, and torn with racing clouds; the wide expanse of Scapa Flow was choppy with white horses. The wind shrieked in the rigging above them, and the warship snubbed herself uneasily at her moorings. It was a day, Overton thought ruefully, on which any sensible man would retire indoors – on dry land – shut all the doors and windows and take up a good book. Kitchener looked impervious as he shook Jellicoe's hand and went down into the pinnace; but the short crossing in the small vessel was enough to have him pale and thoughtful by the time they climbed aboard *Hampshire* and were invited below by the captain to his cabin.

They set sail at four forty-five p.m. and, following the admiral's suggestion, headed for Hoy Sound, the western exit from Scapa. Their escort of two destroyers, HMS *Unity* and HMS *Victor*, upped anchor and followed them. When they rounded Stromness into the open sea, the full force of the wind hit them. It had increased to force eight, and had veered to the north-west, so they were heading straight into it. The cruiser put her sharply raked bows into the oncoming seas, and torrents of water cascaded over her decks in foaming sheets. The captain ordered all hatches battened except the aftermost, and steered a course as close as he dared to the vicious, rocky western coast of Orkney. Though it would be full daylight for hours more, the low skies and the driven spray made it seem almost like dusk. A few lights showed as yellow pinpoints on the crags over to starboard, where crofters in their cottages had found it too dark to work.

Their headway was desperately slow against sea and wind; and soon, astonishingly, the wind increased. The captain, coming down into the cabin to report, said it was now gale-force nine. He had taken off his oilskins to come in, but his face shone wet and the ends of his hair dripped under his cap.

'Is there danger?' Kitchener asked.

'No, my lord. We can ride this out, all right. But we aren't making much headway. I'm afraid there will be a good few hours of this to endure before she blows herself out and we can get on.'

Kitchener nodded and thanked him in an unconcerned way; but *Hampshire* was tilting down and up like a seesaw as the huge waves raced under her, and rising and dropping like a lift into the bargain. Bracing oneself to the constant movement was exhausting: even Overton, who was a good sailor, longed for it to be over. But he chatted cheerfully to Kitchener, who was in a worse way, and suggested a few hands of bridge later, hoping that way to keep his mind off things.

Slow though *Hampshire*'s progress was, she was more seaworthy than the destroyers, *Unity* and *Victor*, who were sagging further and further behind, and struggling not to be driven to leeward. By six twenty it was obvious that they could not be any kind of an escort to the faster ship in these conditions, and the captain came down to report to Lord Kitchener that he was ordering them to turn back. Kitchener's reply was civil but monosyllabic. Overton guessed that he felt it safer to keep his mouth shut as far as possible.

The cabin was stuffy, with so many of them smoking; but with the seas running so high, there was no possibility of opening a porthole. Overton excused himself and went to his own cabin for a breather, and pressed his face to the glass to look out of his porthole. *Hampshire* rose on her tail as the humped back of a tearing wave raced under her, and he caught a glimpse of the two destroyers, well behind, as they turned their sterns to the wind and headed back to

Scapa. Lucky devils! he thought. Their lights quickly disappeared in the grey murk of driven spray, and alone the *Hampshire* ploughed on into the face of the gale, with the seas smashing over her from stem to stern, and the rigging shrieking above like tormented souls.

At least, Overton thought, comforting himself with a little brandy from his flask, the gale would keep them safe from attack by German torpedoes. No submarine would dare venture out in weather like this, nor could survive in such seas, on such a shore.

It was at around eleven that night that Venetia, who had retired to her room and was about to get ready for bed, was called to the telephone. It was Christopher Addison, Lloyd George's number two at Munitions, and her old friend.

'Venetia, my dear,' he began, and at his words, and the tone of his voice, a chill ran down her back, and she felt the hair on her scalp rise.

'What is it?' she said. 'What's happened?'

'It's the *Hampshire*,' he said wretchedly.

A cold, sick weight filled her stomach, and she knew even before she *could* know that this was the moment she would remember for the rest of her life as the ending of joy. She stared at a tiny crack in the paintwork of the dado rail, and Addison's voice went on, relentless, clear – Lachesis and Atropos together, measuring and cutting off her portion of happiness.

'There was an explosion at about half past seven.'

'An explosion? A torpedo?'

'Or a mine. We don't know yet. One of the Orkney territorials at a watching-post saw it. *Hampshire* was only about a mile and a half out, so he could see her clearly. An explosion, and smoke and flame from behind the bridge, he said. He sent a runner to the post office and a telegraph was sent off to Headquarters at Stromness that there was a battle cruiser in distress between Marwick Head and the brough of Birsay. Twenty minutes later there was a second telegraph saying the vessel had sunk. There's no doubt it was *Hampshire*. I'm so very sorry.'

'There might be survivors? The lifeboats?' But she knew the answer. The cold weight in her stomach told her. She had said goodbye to him, and he would not be coming home.

'Admiral Jellicoe sent out ships to the area of the sinking, and land parties to search the shore. He's ordered the whole island population to be on the alert. Everything will be done that can be done. But there was a force-nine gale blowing, and the seas are mountainous. There's little chance the lifeboats could make it – even if they managed to launch them. She went down very quickly. And even with a life-jacket, no-one could survive more than a few minutes in that sea.'

'No,' Venetia heard herself say. 'Even in June it must be very cold.'

'Jellicoe wired the Admiralty, of course, and they informed Asquith and Lloyd George. They asked me if I would break the news to you.'

'Thank you,' Venetia said. 'It was kind of you. It was not a job you could have relished.'

'I'm so desperately sorry,' he said. 'I wish I could hold out hope to you, but your own intelligence will tell you there's almost none. It would be wrong of me to say otherwise.'

'I know,' she said. 'Thank you for being the one to tell me, Christopher. Will you keep me informed of any developments?'

'Of course.'

'I'd like to know everything – whatever you hear.'

'I will pass everything on to you, I promise.'

She replaced the receiver, and then just stood, still staring at the dado rail. She discovered that she was able to sustain two opposing states of mind at the same time:

she knew that Beauty was dead, and yet she did not believe that he could be. She understood, with the intellectual part of her brain, that this was just a neurological state, like the after-image of light on the retina when you close your eyes. He lived on in her mind, which made it impossible to believe he was not still in the world. Even so, it was not something she was capable of making sense of now.

She was aware of Burton coming into the corridor, looking at her enquiringly. She did not know how to cope with him yet. She did not want to speak. She did not know how to move. She was afraid if she did anything, anything at all, something essential inside her would break.

Venetia woke because the telephone was ringing. She heard it, far away in the house, as she struggled up through veils of sleep like cobweb clinging to her mind and limbs. Something had happened, something bad; a weight of oppression was on her even before she remembered. But memory came all too soon, in a sickening downward swoop of her stomach. Beauty was dead. *No, please, no, let it not be!* A lifetime of rational, scientific thought fled before the atavism of entreaty to God, the Fates, any magical power that might intervene. *Let it not be true.* The telephone message would be to say he had been found – hurt, perhaps, but alive. He would come back to her. *Please, God!*

But she had got up automatically and put on her wrapper, and by the time her maid Carless came in – 'A gentleman on the telephone for you, my lady, Mr Addison' – she was alert, brisk, ready.

The clock in the side hall said that it was past eight. She had dozed fitfully through the night, then fallen into deep sleep at her usual rising time. Someone had decided to let her lie. Burton held out the telephone receiver to her, his face blank but an awful awareness in his eyes. She took the instrument and turned her back on him so as not to see it.

Addison was there, passing on Admiral Jellicoe's latest report. There was little chance now of more survivors being found, as the whole shore had been searched. A few men had somehow reached a farmhouse up on the cliffs; others had been found half dead on the rocks below, too weak to climb. A handful had been rescued from two Carley rafts. No lifeboats had been found, only some wreckage of one, and no-one had been taken alive from the sea. All the survivors were ratings: there were no officers and no passengers among them.

Through that long, numb day, the 6th of June, news came in little by little. There were only twelve survivors, out of the crew of 655, plus the passengers. One of them, a stoker, taken to the hospital ship in Scapa, had been able to talk, and gave the information that after the explosion it had proved impossible to lower the boats because the winches were operated by electricity, which had failed when a boiler exploded. The sailors on one boat had tried to save themselves by cutting the ropes, but the boat had been smashed to matchwood against the side of the ship by the force of the waves. That was the only wreckage that had been found, Jellicoe reported – the other boats had gone down with the ship, still in the davits.

She had sunk very quickly, within fifteen minutes, said the stoker, listing heavily to starboard from the moment of the explosion and then going down by the head. About two hundred, he estimated, had got away on Carley rafts. These were enormous cork ovals, from which a grating was slung on which the men would stand, waist deep in water. They were capable of taking fifty to sixty men each, and were unsinkable; but many of those on them were injured, others were overwhelmed by the seas and washed away, and the cold and exposure had killed most of the remainder before they could get to land. The stoker had been one of only four survivors on his raft.

He said that the last time he had seen Lord Kitchener, he had been standing on the bridge, a familiar figure in his greatcoat and cap, with the captain and some of his staff – Lord Overton among them. He had been very calm, talking to the captain, and he had made no attempt to join the scramble for the boats. Venetia could see the scene in her mind's eye: he had decided, unemotionally like a soldier, that there was no hope of survival, and had declined to abandon his dignity. And Beauty had stayed with him, of course. To die like gentlemen.

Later in the day Addison reported, in confidence, that Admiral Jellicoe blamed himself for the disaster, because though he had recommended Kitchener to delay his departure on account of the gale, he had not insisted. But how could the accident have been foreseen? It was not the bad weather that had destroyed the ship. Nor yet was it a U-boat torpedo – no submarine could have operated in those conditions. It must have been a mine – yet they had not anticipated any mines on the western side of the island, since it was thought too far away from the U-boat base in Germany. It was the eastern side that was the known 'lurking ground' of the U-boats, and the eastern side was regularly swept for mines. But Jellicoe had recommended the western route because of the weather.

By the evening of that day, only a hundred bodies had been recovered, and the admiral thought there was not much likelihood of more being found. In such an accident, in such seas, it was not unusual for most of the bodies to be lost for ever. Lord Kitchener's body was not among those recovered – nor, Addison said, with terrible gentleness, was Lord Overton's.

Oliver had obtained immediate compassionate leave from his duties at the hospital, and he had stayed at home with Venetia, for which she was deeply grateful. He answered the telephone, intercepted enquiries, saw off callers, began to make such arrangements as were possible. Without a body there would be no funeral, but people would have to be told, notices placed in newspapers. He was white and shocked, but he was able to function. Venetia did not seem able to act or think. She took Addison's calls, but could not speak to any of the other friends and acquaintances who telephoned or came to the house that June day. She appreciated their kindness, but her mind was blank and her tongue numbed in shock. She wished she could have the luxury, like Violet, of crying. Her pregnant daughter wept on and off all day, and it gave the stunned servants something to do in comforting her. The mistress, sitting at her desk in her private sitting-room, staring at nothing, offered them no scope for action. She did not come down to luncheon, and the tray Carless took up to her was removed, untouched, at teatime.

Venetia sat alone, thinking. There had always been Beauty, from the time of her come-out, from the time she and Olivia, the duke's daughters, had been the leading young ladies of the *ton*, and a bright, gay company of pretty girls and handsome youths had hung about Southport House all Season. Venetia, impatient of the demands of fashion, had frightened away many of her would-be beaux with her sharp tongue. She wanted more in her life than a Season and a 'good' marriage. But she had been inclined to favour young John Winchmore because he handled her lightly and made her laugh. She could remember just how he had looked, leaning against the chimneypiece with his tight cavalry overalls outlining his figure – the handsomest of them all, with that sidelong, faintly self-mocking smile, the exquisite appearance and endless good humour for which equally he was famed in the Blues.

He had not been a good enough match for her in her father's eyes, being only a viscount's son, and not a wealthy one at that. Later, when Venetia had driven away all the competition, and disgraced herself, the duke had looked more favourably on him: it was better than having his daughter remain unwed, at any rate. But she had rejected him and gone her own way, pursuing her career; busy, but lonely – until in the end they had met again, and found a love that had matured with greater age and understanding. They had married at last as independent adults, and for thirty-one years no distance had ever marred their strong and sustaining love.

And now he was dead and gone, and she was no different from hundreds upon hundreds of other women, who had lost their husbands to the war. She thought briefly of poor little Jessie. Jessie had had no body to bury either. She would never know exactly what had happened in her husband's last moments – but, unlike Venetia, she had no child to comfort her. From Venetia and Beauty's love there had sprung three children, and three (no, four!) grandchildren. What they had been, the two of them together, would not die: their love would live on in the flesh they had created.

She remembered him as he had looked when they said goodbye – smiling down at her, grey-haired but still, to her, the handsomest man in the world, the one against whose heart she warmed her own. In their long marriage they had wasted no moment in coldness, quarrel or misunderstanding. They had parted in love; she had said goodbye. There was nothing to regret but the parting itself.

Well, she was no tender maiden, doomed to despair and die of a broken heart. She was a mature woman, of intellect and resource: she would survive this and live out her span. She was sixty-six years old, and she might live another ten or fifteen years – oh, but without him, without the daily sight of him, the sound and smell and touch of him, they would be cold and lonely years!

In the evening Oliver came to beg her to come to dinner – he and Violet needed her, he said, and for once there was no tease in his eyes. He looked like a lost boy. He had been the closest to his father in late years, and they had shared a man's converse on many an evening when Venetia had gone up to bed. She tried to smile and said she would come, but first she asked him to call the servants together in the hall. She stood, with him and Violet, a little way up the stairs where they could all see her, and told them officially what they had known by rumour and whisper all day, that the master was dead. He had been well loved, both for his charm and the small kindnesses he had quietly done to each of them at some time or another. The maids cried, the boot-boy gulped painfully, even the remaining footman swallowed and rubbed his face to hide his emotion. Only Burton kept his trained impassivity, and Venetia kept her eyes on his, to maintain her own as she spoke.

When it was over, Oliver helped her up the stairs, and she was surprised to find she needed his help – her legs were trembling. It had been harder to do than she had expected, to pronounce his death so finally before witnesses. Now he would never come back. She had an instant of agonised yearning for him, and felt Oliver grip her arm more firmly, sensing her collapse. But she pulled herself back from the abyss and walked on, straightening her back.

The next morning every newspaper was full of the story. Huge black headlines blared 'KITCHENER DROWNED', and 'LORD KITCHENER LOST AT SEA'. Photographs of him were on every page, from formal portraits to news pictures taken as he entered or left buildings, or spoke to soldiers at the Front, or sat his horse at reviews. There was one that made Venetia's heart jump painfully as she turned the page and came on it: it had been taken in the Dardanelles, and showed him walking in conversation with General Birdwood. Behind them came members of their respective suites and, seen clearly over Birdie's shoulder, Lord Overton was smiling at something the aide beside him had said.

The day before she had barely thought of Kitchener, had

certainly not taken in what his death would mean. Now there was no escaping it. The nation mourned, hugely, extravagantly. Kitchener of Khartoum was dead: what would they do without him? He was the country's war leader, the figurehead, their good-luck charm. Soldiers mourned as if for a father; people feared that without him the war was lost. Venetia remembered the man who had dealt fairly with her in South Africa, who had asked her to act as his hostess in France; the upright, honourable, professional soldier. She remembered, too, how he had irritated Beauty and others around him by his limitations, his refusal to work in committee, his insistence on certain inconvenient old-fashioned conventions. Those in power had had to find ways round him when he could not do the job, because he could not be left out either. K of K, a giant in his own field, could be a stubborn old man out of it.

But the nation didn't know those things, and they mourned him wholeheartedly; and close upon grief came anger. Who was responsible? It was impossible to believe that their leader had been lost to them by an accident while he was in the charge of the Royal Navy. There must have been foul play somewhere, by someone. The theories began to spring up. A bomb had been planted in the ship; it was the Germans, it was the Irish rebels. U-boats had been seen in the area immediately before the sinking, having been told exactly when and where K would be so they could torpedo him. There had been a traitor in the fleet; Admiral Jellicoe had ordered it; a German had been living in the Orkneys disguised as a crofter for years, waiting for this moment.

Those of more subtle mind whispered that the government had had a hand in it, wanting to be rid of him because he held things back, because he was in the way, because they blamed him for the failure at Gallipoli. Government agents had planted the bomb, knowing it would be blamed on the U-boats.

No theory was too fantastic to be aired. Because his body had not been found, there were those who said he had never been on the *Hampshire*, and one story was that he had shot himself in his office and the 'sinking' had been arranged to cover up the shame of suicide. There were even those who said he had not died at all: rumours abounded that he had been sighted in St Petersburg, in Norway, in the United States, in Australia, in Edinburgh, walking down Pall Mall as bold as you like. Some said he had been kidnapped by order of Lloyd George, who was jealous of him, and was being held in a remote Irish castle by nationalist rebels in the Welshman's pay. Many believed that he had spirited himself away to punish an ungrateful government and would return to save the country when it was at its greatest need. Like King Arthur, and Bonnie Prince Charlie, Kitchener would come again . . .

Maria had left a standing invitation for Jessie to come to tea. She knew the problem her sister-in-law had with finding out her free time in advance, and said, 'I am always here at teatime, and we shall always be pleased to see you, so just come, and don't mind about it.'

The newspapers were still full of discussion of the Scapa tragedy one hot June day when Jessie was toiling in the ward, changing the dressings for a young soldier who was going to die. She could feel the starch in her collar melting and the sweat running down her body under her dress, and a wisp of hair had come loose and kept sticking to her damp cheek, forcing her to push it away with her wrist every few seconds. Her patient, white-faced and hollow-eyed from massive blood loss, did not complain, though she knew he was in pain, but the man in the next bed was feverish from a mixture of the heat and a reaction to morphine, and she could hear him through the screens moaning, sometimes calling out, 'Mary! Mary!' in the toneless voice of delirium. Furthermore, dinner that day had been mutton hot-pot and potatoes followed by plum duff – one of the hospital kitchen's better meals, but making no nod towards the temperature. Jessie felt as though it had formed a concrete mass under her ribs that was impeding her breathing. It was one of those moments when character was needed to continue to feel that nursing was a noble calling.

Sister Tudor put her head round the screens. She was the temporary replacement for Sister Fitton, who was taking her half-yearly leave, and unlike Fitton she despised VADs and did what she could to make them uncomfortable.

'Haven't you finished that dressing yet, Nurse?' she said, looking down her nose and under her eyelids at Jessie by tilting her head back. Her disapproving mouth made a perfect downward curve, like a mask-of-tragedy – or like a fish, Jessie thought: she did bear a startling resemblance to a cod. She was extremely genteel, and the rumour among the nurses was that Tudor was not her real name, but that she had adopted it to give herself cachet. Her real name, they said, was Tubby. It helped them to bear with her ways.

'Not quite, Sister,' Jessie said patiently.

'Well, when you *have* finished it, you can go off duty, take your afternoon off,' Tudor snapped. 'But be sure you leave everything tidy, and re-lay that dressing-tray before you go.' She vanished with a rattle of curtain rings.

It was sheer meanness, Jessie thought, because the half-day was supposed to start at two and it was already twenty past. Tudor could just as well have told her at two o'clock and had someone else do this dressing – they were not busy at the moment – but, of course, *that* would have been no fun for her. Jessie met the eyes of her patient, and he tried to smile, though it was not much more than a twitch of his pale lips. 'I'm sorry, Nurse,' he said. 'I'm a nuisance, keeping you from your time off.'

Jessie was jerked out of her self-pity, shocked to find she was frowning. She hastily adjusted her face and said, 'Not at all. You're not to think that. I'm glad to do this for you. I don't mind how long it takes.'

'That sister has it in for you, hasn't she?' he said. Talking tired him and his voice was weak, but he was making an effort to entertain her, which touched her desperately.

'It isn't me. She doesn't like VADs, that's all.'

'I've heard the others call her "the old trout". She does look like a fish, doesn't she?'

Jessie laughed. 'You'll get me into trouble, talking like that. Suppose she hears? There, now, you're done. Is there anything I can get you? Would you like to sit up a bit more?'

'No, thanks, I think I'll sleep a bit until tea. But could I have a drink of water?'

She helped him sip some water, then made him as comfortable as possible, to show she was not in a hurry; so by the time she had gone up to the VADs' cloakroom and changed, it was three o'clock. But at least there was no coming back on duty: everyone liked afternoon time off best – which was probably why Tudor had tried to delay her, not wanting a VAD ever to have anything nice. A surge of energy passed through her at the thought, and she decided to make the most of the afternoon and go and see Maria.

There was a Polish bakery right next door to the Underground station at Hammersmith, and she stopped to buy half a dozen of their little cheesecakes as a present for Maria before, in deference to her throbbing feet, taking a taxi-cab to Brook Green. And there she found that in this case, virtue – seizing the day – had been its own reward. Maria already had a visitor for tea: Jessie's darling brother Jack.

Helen's fears for Jack had been realised: he had been chosen to join the Home Defence section, and for a time he had been stationed with another pilot-tutor at Northolt. The dispersal around nine airfields had soon been reconsidered as inefficient, and within weeks the force had been concentrated on three airfields, with six pilots and six aircraft at each. Jack had been posted to Hounslow; and from Hounslow that day he been sent into London to take a sensitive package to the War Office.

'It was supposed to be my day off,' he explained, 'but there's no use grumbling. Apparently only I would do! And they kept me waiting ages, though I did have a nice chat with a fellow in an ante-room – seemed very interested in everything I had to say. Of course, you can't be too careful these days, and I didn't tell him too much about Hounslow or our various ops.'

'Do you think he was a spy, then?' Jessie asked, in surprise.

'He seemed as English as can be, and perfectly genuine – but, then, a spy would be no use if he had a heavy German accent and looked dangerous and sinister, would he? I don't *think* he was a spy but, as I say, you have to be careful. Anyway, we chatted about this and that, and finally I delivered my package to Lieutenant Colonel Holt, and then dashed if *he* didn't want to chat too! But he seemed to know a lot about me – asked about my ankle and Helen and how I liked defence duties. Finally I got away, and heading back to Hounslow I realised I wasn't far from Hammersmith so I came to see Maria. And now here *you* are!'

'Here I am,' Jessie agreed. 'Which is what I'd call a very handsome coincidence. What luck I bought six cakes.'

Mrs Stanhope was not there, having gone to take tea with her cousin Mrs Wilberforce, so the three young people were able to relax and please themselves – and have two cakes each. Maria's tea, otherwise, was limited to bread-and-butter and digestive biscuits, so the addition was welcome. Maria, Jessie thought, was looking very well. Her pregnancy was just beginning to show, but she carried it gracefully and didn't seem to mind being 'seen', unlike those daintier females who felt it shameful for anyone to know they were in a delicate condition. She was at the stage when morning sickness was over and her body was filled with health and well-being. Her eyes and hair shone, her cheeks were rosy, and she was brimming with energy. Jessie could see why Frank had thought her beautiful. She was good company, too. She chatted and laughed and kept them entertained with her wit and invention, while she wielded the teapot and jumped up to fetch things, refusing Jessie's offers to go for her.

'You rest your feet,' she said firmly.

'How are Helen and the boy?' Jessie asked Jack, passing the bread-and-butter.

'Very well. Blooming. Helen says he can sit up now, if you support him, and he takes an interest in everything. Of course, everything goes straight into his mouth. He somehow got hold of Helen's bookmark, which is leather, and sucked all the gold tooling off it.' He talked on about the minutiae of babydom, and Jessie listened with affectionate indulgence, thinking how nice it was for a man to take so much interest.

When Jack had run himself down, Jessie asked, 'Is Helen going to go back to flying? She said she would start when Basil was six months, and that's next month, isn't it?'

'She's still talking about it, but – well, I suppose there's no harm in telling you – it might not come off after all. You see, she suspects she might be pregnant again. I got a letter from her yesterday. It's very early days yet, and even she's not sure, but if she *is*, then it will pretty well put flying out of the question for the next year.'

'How wonderful! Congratulations, Jackie darling,' Jessie said, delighted. 'The nation's loss is our gain.'

'Well, I said something like that when I wrote back last night. She was upset about letting the war effort down, but I said to her that we need women to have babies just as much, if not more. Anyone can fly an aeroplane, but only women can have babies. Sorry, Jess.'

'It's all right.'

'I expect she'll see the sense of it. She's a sensible person. But of course it's not a sure thing yet, so don't talk of it to anyone, will you? Not until it's official.'

'Of course not,' said Jessie. 'But you must be glad that you're stationed in England where you can be on hand.'

He shook his head. 'Nothing about being in the defence squadron is good. If I'm going to be in Hounslow, miles from Helen, I might just as well be in France where I can be some use. This whole idea is foolish. It doesn't work. We can't possibly tutor all day and do night flying duties as well. One or other has to be skimped or let go entirely. And I think the brass have realised it, too. They're talking now about forming a separate Home Defence Wing, and taking training out of it entirely.'

'Well, that sounds like a good idea,' Maria said, observing that Jack did not seem very happy about it.

'Yes, it's a good idea,' he said gloomily, 'except that I shall probably be posted to it, and spend the rest of the war pointlessly chasing Zeppelins, just because of this damned ankle of mine. And the irony is that there's absolutely nothing wrong with it now – it's as sound as the other one. I thought when they let me start flying again that it was all forgotten. But the army's like that. If you once put up a black, it follows you for the rest of your life.'

'Poor Jackie. It's a shame,' said Jessie, 'when you *so* want to go to France and kill Germans.'

'You can tease,' he said, 'but every man feels the same. Even old bookworm Frank.'

'It's true,' said Maria. 'All his letters say how important he feels it is to be over there.'

'Has he written recently?' asked Jessie.

'Twice a week, regularly,' Maria said, 'and sometimes more often. He sends me pretty postcards when he finds them, too, and little presents.'

They took a turn about the garden and discussed Lord Kitchener's death and the bizarre theories that were flying about. 'I heard one chap say that a German spy has actually confessed to having planted a bomb,' Jack said. 'He wrote about it in some German magazine. It's all bunkum, of course.'

'I suppose so,' Jessie said. 'Why would the Germans go to such trouble to kill Lord Kitchener, rather than General Haig, say, or Mr Asquith or the King? Though the soldiers are all mourning him, Bertie says.'

'Frank said that, too,' said Maria. 'He said everyone remembers exactly where they were and what they were doing when they heard the news.'

'Here's an odd thing, though,' Jack said. 'I got it from that chap at the War Office this morning. The mine *Hampshire* struck was a moored mine, the sort laid by submarines, and there was a U-boat seen in the vicinity some days before the battle of Jutland. Since the sinking they've swept the area and found twelve more mines. But why didn't they sweep it before? Apparently a drifter hit one of the mines only three days before *Hampshire*. Yet they did nothing about it.'

Jessie said, 'Jackie, dear, this sounds like more bunkum.'

'A fellow at the War Office swore it was true.'

'Everyone always swears their story is true – that's how these mad rumours get about. If there was anything in it, it would have been in the newspapers.'

'It's all being kept secret for political reasons.'

'But *he* told *you*,' said Maria, 'and here you are telling *us*. I agree with Jessie – it's nonsense.'

Jack changed the subject. 'Did you write to Cousin Venetia?'

'Yes, straight away,' said Jessie. 'Did you?'

'Of course. She *is* my godmother. It will be a hard loss for her. How's Violet taking it? She adored her father.'

'I haven't seen her,' Jessie said. 'I wrote her a separate letter, but her reply was only formal.' It would be hard for her to lose her adored father, more especially at a time like this, and Jessie guessed that her mourning would be tinged with guilt that she had caused him pain in his last months. When things had settled down a little, she would propose a visit. She would write to Oliver and ask him to tell her when it would be a comfort and not a bother.

She had not told anyone about Violet's being pregnant so now she could not share these thoughts with her companions. She asked Maria about her plans for the garden, and the other two allowed the subject to be changed.

CHAPTER FIFTEEN

Just a few days later, Jessie received a letter from Helen, with the news that Jack was going to France after all.

> He's terribly excited about it, and so I have to be too, though a shameful part of me gloated at the thought of his being posted to the comparative safety of this new Home Defence Wing. But apparently it was his visit to the War Office that did the trick. The officer he met there, Lt Col. Holt, is to be head of the new wing, and he was considering Jack for his headquarters staff, which is being set up in De Keyser's Hotel on the Victoria Embankment (we should have had to live in London, think of that!). Jack's wing co thought it would be a shocking waste of his talents, so he made an excuse to send Jack to Holt in person, hoping Holt would think the same. Fortunately he did, and nobly decided to give him up to the Greater Good. And the 'nice young fellow' Jack talked to in the ante-room turned out to be a junior minister, and he thought Jack was exactly what was needed at the Front too, and cursed the army's bureaucratic constipation in keeping him so long at home. Between them they hurried through the posting, with the result that Jack is now at home on a short embarkation leave, and will be off to the Front tomorrow. He has been promoted to captain and will be a flight

commander, which makes me very proud. It also involved a rise in salary, which will be most welcome – I gather he told you about my suspicions. They are still only suspicions, but quite strong ones. You can imagine my feelings about not being able to fly! I was quite prepared to go back for a few months, but the doctor flung up his hands in horror at the idea and pointed out my great age, and Jack decided for once to put his foot down with a heavy hand, so if I am increasing, I shall be grounded for something like eighteen months. It is likely the baby, if there is one, will be born with his father still overseas, for though the coming Big Push is meant to be the deciding factor, Jack says there will still be 'mopping up' to do, which might take anything up to a year. He wants me to go and live with my mother while he's away, but I intend to stay here, at least for the time being. I love our funny little house so much, and don't want to leave it. And we have good friends at the school and the factory and in the neighbourhood, who will 'keep an eye on me' – a phrase that means different things to Jack than to me! Keeping an eye is thought necessary since he is taking Rug with him, though what Rug could have done in an emergency is not clear – carried a message to someone in his teeth like a storybook dog, perhaps. Jack begs you to excuse his not writing himself but there is so much to do before he leaves. He sends his love, of course. And now I must close this long letter, dearest Jessie, because I have to write it all over again to Morland Place, and then my mother. Do write when you have a moment and tell me about the nursing. Does it answer the purpose? Has your restlessness eased? Do you feel less wasted and isolated? I do hope so.

Jessie was delighted that her brother was going to get what he wanted at last, though it meant adding him to the list of people she had to worry about. Worrying was a background part of life now and, like other long burdens, could be carried if not with ease, at least routinely. Now Bertie, Jack, Frank and Lennie would all be in France. She wondered if they might ever meet each other. Jack and Bertie had met once at the railway station in St Omer, and Bertie had seen Ned at a distance before Loos, though he had not spoken to him.

That reminded her that she did not think of Ned all the time, as she had done at first. One can get used to anything, she thought, even sadness and loss. Time and life itself were drawing her onward from the place where Ned had been, while he retreated into the past. It was the same for all of them who had lost someone. She thought of Cousin Venetia, and the women at home in Yorkshire she had visited with her mother when they had lost a son or husband. They had empty places in their lives, and nothing to put into them but their work and dedication. The war must be won, at all costs; only when it was would they find out what those empty spaces really meant to them.

Thomas was able to get leave to come home for the memorial service for Lord Kitchener and the others, which was held on Tuesday, the 13th of June, at St Paul's Cathedral. He was granted permission by the Tsar himself, who wished Thomas to represent him at the occasion, both in memory of Lord Kitchener, who had perished on a mission to Russia, and Lord Overton, whom the Tsar had known and admired in his youth. Thomas was due for leave in any case; and the Tsar had secret letters he wished to have carried to the King. Young Lord Hazelmere – now, of course, the new Earl of Overton – was one of the few people around him the emperor trusted completely.

Thomas arrived on the Monday after a long and exhausting journey, but before he could go home to see his mother and family he had to present himself at

Buckingham Palace, where he was kindly received, and spent over an hour closeted with the King, with no-one else present but the personal secretary, Lord Stamfordham. Afterwards, at the King's request, the weary traveller went to Downing Street where his meeting with Mr Asquith was shorter and covered not nearly as much ground. Between a king and an emperor who were cousins there might well be family secrets that a mere, transient politician might not share.

So it was late when Thomas finally arrived at Manchester Square, and was warmly embraced by his mother with the practical words, 'Darling, you must simply long for a bath. The water's hot. Why don't you go up and let Ash look after you? He's been pining for something to do to take his mind off things. We can talk at dinner.'

The only thing he had to ask was, 'Are we dressing?'

'It's only family, so we needn't. But it would be a kindness to the servants – the new lord coming home for the first time, and so on – so we will, if you don't mind very much.'

Thomas smiled faintly. 'With Ash to do the hard work, I don't mind at all. After Tsarskoye Selo, English formality holds no fears for me.'

When he went downstairs, his mind on a stiff drink before dinner, he found a little ceremony preparing in the hall, and he stood on the same step his mother had used a few days earlier, while Burton begged leave to offer the condolences of the servants' hall, and to introduce the staff to the new earl. Thomas went through the ceremony patiently, watched from the drawing-room door by his mother, sister and brother, then pleased everyone by shaking Burton's hand and saying he was glad to be home, and didn't expect to be making any changes.

'You did that very nicely,' Venetia said, when the family was alone in the drawing-room. 'I'm sorry to have sprung it on you, but you know how the servants set store by these things. You struck just the right tone, my love. The earldom will be safe in your hands.'

Thomas only laughed and shook his head ruefully, and was glad to be interrupted by Oliver asking what he would like to drink.

Over dinner they discussed the sinking of *Hampshire* – for Thomas had not heard all the details – and the strange stories of conspiracy that had grown up around the incident and showed no sign of abating.

'We have them on our side of the water, too,' he said. 'We hear that the ship was loaded with gold that Kitchener was bringing to the emperor for the war effort, and they say the Tsaritsa, who is in league with the Germans, heard about it and had the ship sunk to prevent its reaching us. Naturally Rasputin was the agent – he's German too, in case you didn't know it, and they knew each other in her girlhood before she came to Russia.' His mother made a disgusted face, and he said, 'I assure you that's only the mildest and most sensible of the stories. It would break your heart to see how hard she and the grand duchesses work at the hospitals – and not dainty work, either, but proper nursing, sparing themselves nothing. But it does no good with the people, as long as she keeps that filthy *starits* by her. But let's not talk about that,' he went on. 'Tell me, is Aunt Olivia coming up tomorrow?'

'No, she's not well enough. I spoke on the telephone to Charlie. You know her health hasn't been too good for some time, and she was quite shocked by the news. It's set her back. I said we might go and visit her later on, when the fuss is over. It will be as well to get out of London for a few days before the war starts up again.'

They did not sit long that night, in deference to Thomas's weariness, and Venetia restrained herself from asking the questions about his intentions that were burning her tongue. After the memorial service it would be time enough.

★ ★ ★

It was a state occasion, and everyone was in full uniform, with decorations. On the morning, the King and Queen and Queen Alexandra drove in an open carriage with full escort by way of the Mall, Charing Cross, the Strand, Fleet Street and Ludgate Hill, and the streets were lined with oddly silent crowds, many of them in black or wearing mourning ribbons. The tradesmen who usually made hay on such occasions confined themselves to selling commemorative items and memorial cards. The latter were particularly popular, and as well as a picture of the earl, frequently bore a verse. One such said:

> Dear lofty Soul, thy strong and ordered Brain
> Shall not be wasted, though thou art slain!
> Soldier, no bullet pierced thee, no burst shell
> Took thee from us, whom thousands loved so well!

On the front was a tasteful depiction of lilies and the words 'In Loving Memory'; and on the back, under the heading 'Kitchener's Staff who Perished with Him', were listed the names:

Lt-Col. Fitzgerald	Brig.-Gen. Ellershaw	Lord Overton
Lt Macpherson	Sir H. F. Donaldson	Mr H. J. O'Beirne
Mr L. S. Robertson	Detective Maclaughlin	Mr L. C. Rix
W. Gurney	D. C. Brown	

Oliver had collected a number of these, which he was putting away, with the vague thought that Violet's children might like them one day. Despite the appalling verse, or perhaps because of it, they moved him absurdly.

Arriving at the cathedral at noon, Their Majesties were met at the west door by the Archbishop and the Bishop of London, the dean and clergy of the cathedral, the Lord Mayor in his black and gold robes, and the sheriffs with their ceremonial officers. The City mace was draped and carried before them as they were escorted to their seats directly in front of the choir. The immediate families were already in their seats, just behind the royal party, and other dignitaries filled the space behind. The hymns, lessons, psalms and prayers followed their usual form, and all was dignified, solemn and reverent.

Venetia had no difficulty in displaying the expected brave face, right up until the last hymn, chosen by Kitchener's family. It was 'For All the Saints Who From Their Labours Rest', and it had always been a favourite of Beauty's. Violet began to cry during it, and Venetia's throat closed up so that she could not sing. But it was the playing of the Last Post that finally overcame her. She was glad of her veil, for nothing could stop the tears seeping out then. When it was all over, the royal party led the procession out, and Queen Alexandra paused a moment at the end of the row to nod to Venetia kindly, with a look that remembered the many ways in which they had been connected over the years.

Going home afterwards was hard, entering the house the hardest thing, because they were coming home without him, and he would never be coming home at all. Ash, looking old and grey, and Carless were waiting with Burton and Violet's maid in the hall to take their wraps. Venetia took off her hat and gave it to Carless, and murmured that she should help Sanders take Violet upstairs. Though she longed to go to her own room and be alone, she could not abandon poor Oliver, who was looking lost and forlorn, or Thomas, who had come so far to be here.

The boys walked off towards the drawing-room, and Violet got as far as the foot of the stairs, but then stopped, came back to her mother, and looked up at her earnestly.

'Mama, I hope you don't think this wrong but I've decided something. The service made me decide. I'm going to tell him. I'm going to tell Octavian about the baby.' She searched Venetia's face for reaction. 'It made me realise, you see, that no-one is safe. Who would have thought that Papa—' She couldn't complete the sentence. 'If anything happened to him, and I hadn't told him . . .'

Venetia took her daughter's hands and squeezed them. What Violet had done still troubled her, but the loss of Overton put everything into a different perspective. 'I think you are right,' she said. 'You should tell him.'

In the face of death, new life became all the more important, and questions of propriety and the like paled beside it. She *had* the children of her love; and now she wanted Violet to have hers. If there was trouble about it afterwards, they would have to face it together.

The days of Thomas's brief leave were all too soon over; and, frustratingly for Venetia, who had wanted to have time with her eldest boy, he was called away several times for long talks, once with Grey and Asquith, but for the rest with Lord Stamfordham.

'What does Arthur Bigge *want* with you?' she said peevishly. She had known him when he was under-secretary in Queen Victoria's household. 'I've a mind to tell him pretty sharply that you're *my* son, not his.'

'Mostly the meetings are about doing what I can to persuade the Tsar to stay in the war,' Thomas said.

'They think you have influence with him?'

'Perhaps more than I really have. I don't think anyone can persuade Nicholas to do anything he doesn't want to. But of course I will do all I can. The trick is to talk to him *before* he has made up his mind, then let him think that he thought of it for himself.'

'I always knew you would turn out a diplomat,' Venetia said, with a smile, thinking how handsome and mature he looked – statesmanlike, really. 'But you said "mostly"?'

Now he grew grave, and looked at her levelly; and it seemed to her there was sadness in him that she knew nothing about. 'The rest I can't tell you about. I'm sorry, Mama, but I'm sworn to secrecy.'

She felt pain that it should be so, but she nodded and said, 'Then, my son, I shan't ask you anything more. But you will always tell me what you can?'

'Always,' he said, and bent to kiss her brow. She wanted to take hold of him and press him to her closely, sensing that sadness again; but he was a grown man – and an earl now – and she could not treat him as a child.

They had a meeting together with Maxton Greaves, the Overtons' man of business. Venetia knew the terms of Beauty's will, of course, but he asked her to be present when he spoke to Thomas as there were matters she needed to know.

'You will understand, my lord,' Greaves said, when they were comfortably settled in the library, 'that most of the money comes from the Chelmsford estate, which was your late grandmother's in her own right. Your father's means were quite small, though wise investment has improved them considerably in the past twenty years. There was no land in either case, which was a good thing as it turned out – agricultural land and its income having been much depressed for two decades. All the value of the estate is in stocks and shares and other investments, including some Town property, and a good deal overseas.'

Thomas nodded. 'I understood that there was quite a lot in Russia?'

'Yes, my lord. The Chelmsford estate acquired considerable holdings in Siberia and the Urals – mining and industry – and in the Russian railways.'

'And in Germany?' Venetia interposed.

'Yes, you are right,' said Greaves. 'We have taken some losses in Germany, although fortunately Lord Overton's – I should say the *late* Lord Overton's – knowledge of international affairs enabled us considerably to lighten the investment there ahead of time. We transferred the forestry interest to Norway, and the mineral and industrial interest to the United States and Brazil, but I'm afraid the coal mine in the Ruhr valley has been lost to us. I doubt whether, even after the war, it will be possible to reacquire what the present German government has seized.'

'I understand,' said Thomas. 'So how does that leave us?'

'Overall, the transfer out of Germany and the loss of the coal mine has reduced the value of the estate by about fifteen per cent, but what remains is a very considerable amount. You will be, if I may venture to put it that way, one of the wealthier members of the House of Lords, when you take up your seat.'

'I see.'

'I will show you the figures in detail afterwards, if you care to see them.'

'Thank you. But does the whole estate come to me?' He looked worried by the prospect.

'The titles, of course, were yours from the moment of your father's sad demise. Nothing is entailed on the earldom. Half of his estate comes to you at once and unconditionally. The other half goes to your mother –' he bowed to Venetia '– for her lifetime, and on her death is divided equally between you, your brother and your sister. There are a few small legacies and pensions to be observed, but they represent a very small charge on what is, at present, a substantial estate.'

'At present?' Thomas asked, picking up on a slight emphasis in Greaves's tone.

'There is,' Greaves said cautiously, 'still the question of how the estate should continue to be invested. Given what has happened in Germany, I have some misgivings about such a heavy investment in Russia, though it has served us well in the past.'

'But Russia is our ally,' said Venetia.

'Indeed,' said Greaves, 'but who can say whether she will always remain so? One must also consider the volatility of the Russian state itself. I imagine you, my lord, have more intimate knowledge of that than I, but I have sources of my own who are expressing some concern about what might happen if there should be a breakdown of the ruling order.'

Venetia shot a look at Thomas, but he only nodded gravely, and said, 'What do you recommend?'

'That we should lighten our interests there, and perhaps diversify our portfolio. Into South America, for instance: rubber, bauxite and copper, I believe, will yield substantial gains in years to come. And Australia, some think, will be a fertile field for investment.'

Thomas nodded again. 'Let me have your proposals in more detail and I will consider them. I presume you are recommending the same action over my mother's half of the estate?'

'Under his late lordship's instructions, the matter is already in hand – though, of course, my lady, you can now countermand the instructions if you so wish.'

'I'm sure you know better than I about such things, Mr Greaves,' said Venetia. 'Please do what you think right.' She sounded distracted and, indeed, her mind was on other things. She left Thomas to a private conversation with Greaves and the scrutiny of his detailed figures; but when the solicitor had gone, she sought her son again, and said, 'If Greaves is worried about Russia, then I think we should all be. *Is* there trouble coming? What is it he fears – revolution?'

'Everyone fears that,' said Thomas, lightly.

'Don't toy with me. Your father would not have done so.'

'I'm sorry, Mama. The fact is that I really don't know what will happen. There have been subversive elements in Russian society for as long as anyone remembers, but whether any of them is dangerous it's impossible to know. Few tsars die naturally in their beds, but palace revolutions settle down quite quickly with the new tsar and nothing much changes. It's the war which is the unknown element. But don't worry about me,' he concluded, with a smile that did not touch his eyes. 'I'm a British subject. I can't be harmed.'

She looked at him thoughtfully for a moment, then said, 'You did not reply when Greaves spoke about your taking up your seat.'

'He didn't ask a question, so no reply was necessary.'

'But you *will* take it up? You are needed more than ever now, and your father's work, his influence—'

'I am going back to Russia, Mama,' said Thomas, firmly. 'One day in the future I might be able to take my seat, but for the moment I must go back.'

Her heart sank at his words. She did not know what it was she feared for him, but she knew there was danger, and that he knew it too. 'You ought to marry and secure the line,' she said. 'You're thirty years old, you ought to have a wife and an heir.' He smiled at her without responding, and she said impatiently, 'Very well, if you are so taken with Russia that you cannot fancy English girls any more, find yourself a Russian girl. You can do that, can't you?'

'I already have,' he said. 'But I cannot marry her.'

'Don't tease me, Tom.'

'It's not a tease. I gave my heart some time ago, but she can never be mine.'

'She's not married already?' Venetia asked, with a sinking heart.

'No, dearest, she's not married, but I would never be considered a match for her.'

'But you're an earl – and a rich one. Why is she so high? What's her name?'

'Olga,' he said, after a hesitation.

'Not Olga Narishkina? The girl you were pursuing all that time ago? I thought that was long over. You said she'd married someone else, and you didn't seem much upset by it.'

'I wasn't – I'm not. I wished her well. I was quite relieved, if truth be told, when she married Prince Surinin. She and I wouldn't have suited.'

'Well, then?' Venetia asked, a little impatiently. He seemed reluctant to talk about it, yet she felt she must know. 'If not Narishkina, who?'

'She's twenty, and she's beautiful, virtuous, gentle, well-read, thoughtful, quietly valiant – who could fail to love her? But her father would never in any circumstance consider me as a suitor, even though I think he quite likes me.'

A terrible thought came to Venetia. 'Oh, Thomas,' she said, 'not the Tsar's daughter, not *that* Olga? Tell me you haven't given your heart away to a princess.'

He looked away. 'I couldn't help it. Proximity, you know – and one needs must love the best when one sees it. So you see why I have to go back.'

'If it's hopeless, then the best thing to do is to walk away.'

'Perhaps. But I can be of service to her – and if there is trouble coming, I must be there to do what I can to protect her.'

'Does she – does she care for you?' Venetia asked, hardly wanting to know, and yet driven to ask.

'I think so,' he said quietly, looking at nothing. 'I know she likes me, and sometimes when we are talking, there is a look in her eyes, a feeling in the air between us. If she were not Grand Duchess Olga, I think perhaps . . . But she would never do or say anything improper. And it may be my imagination.'

'Oh, Thomas!'

'Don't despair, Mama,' he said, trying for a smile. 'You still have Oliver. Make *him* do his duty.'

'It isn't *his* duty, as you well know,' Venetia said. 'And he has no estate.'

'He's a doctor. Doctors get married. Otherwise, how would all the little doctors come into the world?'

He had made her smile, but she shook her head. 'Oh, Thomas, please think carefully about it. You could still find a nice girl and marry. A hopeless love is a fairy tale, not reality, and it shouldn't guide your life.'

But though he humoured her, she saw she had not changed his mind. She could only hope that when the war ended he would find nothing else to do out there. When the Grand Duchess was married, surely he would come home. Nicholas ought to marry her off quickly, she thought impatiently. Very well, many of the princes he might once have considered were German, but there were others – their own Prince of Wales, for instance. Let Nicholas arrange something for his eldest daughter as soon as possible, and let *her* have her son back!

On the night before his departure, Thomas sat up late in the drawing-room with Oliver, talking quietly, seriously. Venetia woke when they came up to bed and, looking at her clock, saw it was after two.

The next morning he left. It was early, a lovely June morning, full of birdsong and pale, clear sunshine. Venetia held her tall, broad-shouldered son close to her for a moment, and wondered what it was she feared for him. As a mother, she ought to be glad he was not going to the Front: at least she hadn't *that* to worry about.

'Take care of yourself,' she said, looking urgently up into his face. 'Don't—' But she didn't know what to warn him against.

'Don't worry about me,' he said, smiling. And then, though the smile did not fade, his eyes grew serious. 'You remember the code I showed you that time? Do you still remember the key word?'

She stared. 'Yes,' she said, after a moment. 'Yes, I do. But—'

He bent his head and kissed her cheek. 'God bless you, Mama,' he said. And then he was gone.

Violet waited in trembling for Laidislaw's reply to her letter. As soon as she had sent it, her overwrought state made her fear she had done the wrong thing, and she would have called it back if she could. Suppose he was angry that she had not told him before? Or indifferent to her condition? Or felt driven to confront Holkam in some way? She emphasised in her letter the need to tell no-one at present, but wondered afterwards if that would annoy him. Would he be insulted that she was allowing Holkam to assume fatherhood, or relieved that he would not have to bear responsibility, or deeply hurt that she would not face down the world for his sake? Every reaction she imagined seemed more likely than the last, and as the days passed she fretted herself into an attack of colic so severe she thought she was losing the baby. Her maid sent a frightened message to Venetia, who hurried home and received her weeping daughter in her arms, trying to decipher the tear-clotted exclamations about its being judgement on her. She examined her carefully, asked a few questions, dosed her with kaolin and morphia, and sat with her, holding her hand and talking reassuringly, until she fell asleep.

Later, Oliver tiptoed in, home from his shift at the hospital, to find his mother still at the bedside, not so much keeping watch over the sleeping Violet, but staring at nothing, lost in a reverie.

'Is she all right?' he asked, having heard a confused account from the servants when he arrived.

Venetia jerked back to the present. 'Hmm? Oh, yes – just an attack of nerves. She'll be fine in the morning.'

'But you don't look fine, my poor old mater,' said Oliver, tenderly. 'You look tired to death – and I'll wager you haven't had anything to eat since breakfast.'

'Of course I— No, now you come to mention it, I don't think I have. I don't seem to have much appetite these days.'

'Come and have a little supper with me,' he said coaxingly, drawing her to her feet and slipping her arm through his. 'Poor Mum! But come for my sake. I'm lonely too, you know. I miss him so much.'

'I know you do. Oh, Oliver, what will I do without him?

Every day seems so long, and then, at the end of it, he's still not there, and there's the whole night ahead as well.'

'I don't know,' he said. 'I don't know how one gets through what you have to bear. When I think of my own sadness, the very thought of yours appals me. But I'm here, for what use that is. Anything I can do to comfort you, I will do.'

'I know, my son. You are my good boy,' she said, as they walked down the stairs together. He coaxed and petted her, ordered a light supper for them both, and busied himself getting her a glass of wine and arranging the cushions on the sofa until she was forced to laugh and protest that she was not an invalid. 'You'll have me with my feet on a foot-stool next.'

'It helps me to fuss you,' he admitted.

'In that case, fuss away,' she said. 'I wouldn't refuse anything that consoles you. Come and sit beside me and tell me about your day.'

So he told her about the cases he had attended in hospital, and they discussed treatments and techniques until Burton announced that supper was served. They sat down to water-cress soup, a cheese omelette – cooked the way Venetia liked them, nicely runny in the middle – with early peas, and a lemon soufflé. 'Eggs and eggs, dreadful planning,' Venetia said. The chef must be really upset. But the food and wine restored strength to her body, and she was able to be properly enthused when Oliver told her that Kit Westhoven was coming home on leave and would be arriving the following day. 'I assumed you would be agreeable to having him here, but of course he can go to his club if you feel it's too much for you.'

'Too much for me? I shan't be making his bed and fetching his hot water myself.'

Oliver was glad she was recovered enough to be satirical. 'You don't mind, then,' he concluded.

'Of course not. I'm very fond of him – and where else

should he go, poor orphan boy? The servants will be glad of something to do. Are you able to get time off to spend with him?'

'I'm afraid not. I've used up all my favours this last week or so.'

'I suppose you have. Then what will he do all day?'

'He means to come with me to the hospital.'

'Something of a busman's holiday for him, poor fellow.'

'But he says he will like it,' Oliver said, 'working in a proper building with proper equipment, and without fear of a shell dropping on his head. And at least that way we can spend some time together. And we'll be able to do something in the evenings when I'm finished, take in a show, perhaps. Not that he cares overmuch – we'd as soon stay home in the evening with you, in comfort.'

'You must both do as you please, of course,' Venetia said, 'but for a young man not to want to go out pleasuring when he's on leave . . .'

'But you forget, dearest, that he's in mourning too. We should be little pools of silence in a sea of noise if we went to the music hall.'

'Well, stay home, and welcome,' she said. 'I shall be glad of your company, and poor Violet will certainly enjoy having Kit around. She hasn't enough to keep her mind off things, now she can't leave the house.'

When they retired to the drawing-room, Oliver went to the piano and began to play a Bach fugue, which was lying on the stand. Burton brought the coffee, and Venetia poured Oliver's and took it to him at the instrument. He looked up for a moment. 'Light me a cigarette, will you? I need both hands for John Sebastian.'

She lit it and put it between his lips, and speaking round it, he said, 'When were you planning on telling me about your own problems?'

'Mine?' she said. 'You know mine.'

'I don't mean Dad. There's something else, isn't there? I

haven't been your son all these years without knowing when you're avoiding telling me something.'

'When did you become so sensitive to the nuances of others' behaviour?' she countered.

'You see,' he said, moving his head towards her, as a signal that he wished her to take the cigarette away. She laid it in the ashtray. 'You see,' he said, more distinctly, 'how you're not answering again.' He looked down at his hands as he negotiated a difficult passage, and then up at her again. 'You cancelled your list at the Southport.'

'How do you know that?'

'Kenton, the ear-nose-and-throat man, was at the Number Two General today, and he mentioned it.'

Venetia sighed, realising she could not hide it for ever; and who better to confess to than Oliver, who of anyone in the world now ought to understand?

'I had to cancel. It wasn't about Papa. You see—' She stretched out her hands and braced the fingers straight – strong hands, veined with age now, but with no hint of crookedness or arthritis, hands of skill and power, that knew their work almost without her thinking. And as she extended them to her son's gaze, they began to tremble.

Oliver fumbled a note, breaking a link in the endlessly generating chain of perfection, and the music fell apart like a column of water breaking into bright, separate drops. He looked from her hands to her face. He took his cigarette, drew on it, put it down again, picked up the fugue a few bars back and played on. 'How long has it been like that?' he asked softly.

'Since Papa died, I suppose. I didn't notice it until I went in to do my postponed list at the New. I managed to get through the first few cases – they were straightforward – and I don't think anyone noticed anything. But then it got so bad I dropped an instrument, and the theatre sister looked at me strangely, and I felt I had to call off the rest. I thought it was just going back to work too soon, and that it would be better after a rest. But when I went into the Southport, it began again, only worse.'

'I didn't notice anything at supper,' he said.

'I can control it here at home, enough for eating, drinking, dressing and so on. But as soon as I approach the theatre, it comes on.'

He stopped playing. 'It may be the shock of it all. Shock can do strange things.'

'I know,' she said bleakly.

'It will probably pass off after a while. You'll get over it. You're the strongest person I know, and the best surgeon. Give yourself time. Rest, don't think about operating for a while, take a holiday, and everything will be all right.'

'And if it isn't?' she said. Her eyes met his nakedly, and he felt her pain and confusion like a hot wire in his mind. 'What if it never goes away? I've lost your father, but I thought I could get through, following my old routines. If I lose my work as well, I'm not sure I shall be able to cope.'

He took her hands in his – they were icy – and pressed them. 'If you can't operate any more, it will be hard for you, but there are still things you can do. You can go back to your research. You can be a medical doctor. And don't forget your war work, your ambulances. You know that's important.'

'I'm a surgeon,' she said. 'That's who I am.'

'But that isn't all there is to you.' He tried to smile into her weary, suffering eyes. 'You always knew you'd have to retire some time, but you would never have let that be the end.'

'You little know me,' she said drily. 'Retirement was always a fairy story. I fully intended to drop dead in the theatre one day, having just completed a list.'

'God disposes,' Oliver said, 'and He loves to laugh at us. My advice to you—'

'As my doctor?'

'As *a* doctor, at any rate – my advice is to tell your hospitals you will be taking a month or six weeks off, do something else entirely, and stop thinking about it. If you put it from your mind, ten to one you'll find the problem will solve itself. Come, Mother dear, you know that's sound.'

'Yes, you're right,' she said. 'And I really ought to get back to my office. Fabian Ware has been keeping an eye on things for me, but he has too much work of his own to go on doing that.' She freed one of her hands and stroked his hair. 'You are a dear boy, Oliver. I don't know what I should have done without you these last two weeks.'

'I expect you're glad, now, that I didn't "find a nice girl and get married", as everyone's always telling me to. You're sorry you ever urged it on me, aren't you?'

'Not a bit,' she said briskly, taking both her hands from him. 'You *ought* to marry, for your own sake and for the family's. Goodness, if a doctor can't find a willing girl, who can? You're surrounded by nurses all day, half of them sighing over you and making up romantic stories about you in bed at night, if I know anything about nurses. And now you've all the well-born VADs to pick from as well.'

He narrowed his eyes at her, and began playing again. 'Or if all else fails, there's always Cousin Jessie,' he suggested.

'I never said that,' Venetia began to protest, then realised he was roasting her. 'Oh, you are a villain! Suck on your cigarette and be quiet!'

She put it back between his lips, and he grinned round it, and let Bach modulate through an atrocious series of arpeggios and discords into a ragtime tune, 'Adelina, the Boola Girl'. When she protested, he sang the words, vigorously, through his clenched teeth, thumping out the bass with his left hand until the chandelier tinkled.

Laidislaw's letter came the next morning, and was taken up to Violet in bed, with her breakfast tray. When she saw the handwriting on the envelope she turned pale. Her maid busied herself unobtrusively in the wardrobe in case a faint should come on, and watched sidelong as Violet opened it.

> My dearest love, my inspiration – more my own now than ever, my own utterly and completely! I am overwhelmed with joy, I cannot begin to express to you the awe and wonder that I feel when I think of you carrying our child! Oh, my very dearest, if only the war would end tomorrow so that I could come home and be with you! When it does, I swear I shall never leave your side again. You cannot now think that you could remain with H – though I understand that, in the present emergency, when I cannot be with you, you have to keep up the pretence. Things are as they are, until we mend them – as we shall, my darling, never doubt it. Oh, my love, my heart is full of you all day long! My companions are amazed at how gay I seem in our drab and dirty surroundings. It invests my art – did I not say you were my inspiration? The CO is deeply struck with my work and compliments me in terms so fervent they are almost embarrassing. He repeats that he is amazed I have not been given a commission – and then praises his own luck in keeping me. I have done a portrait of him, which he has sent home to his wife, and now all the other officers are clamouring for the same. I cannot oblige them all, of course, but I am taking the time to do a self-portrait, which I shall send to you, and hope that it helps to keep me in your mind's eye – for I know I am still in your heart. How I wish I could be with you! But I hope I may be able to come home around the time of the birth. The others tell me we are eligible for leave after six months, which would be in August. I am pinning my hopes to that, though nothing definite has been said. Many of the officers are going home on leave now, in advance of the 'big push' we are all anticipating. I don't know if our battalion will be in the forefront of battle.

I am as eager as anyone for the fray, not from any blood-thirsty desire to kill, but so that I can prove myself worthy of you, as the knights of old did, through feats of arms. My beloved, I must stop now from lack of any more writing-paper, or I could go on until dawn pouring out my heart to you. Know that it pours anyway, with or without words, that I love you more every moment.

Your own, your very own,
Octavian

The blood came back to her cheeks as she read. Sanders, glancing over her shoulder at her mistress, was reassured. She was glad He had written the right thing – she never thought of him by name, torn as she was between romantic sentiment and disapproval. But she was glad her mistress was happy again. 'Shall I put out the mauve jaconet, my lady?' she said.

CHAPTER SIXTEEN

Kit Westhoven looked older, Oliver thought; but that might be the effect of a new and over-enthusiastic haircut.

'I hadn't time to go to my usual man in Poperinghe, so foolishly I let the battalion barber loose on my head,' he said, running a hand through what was left.

'But you *are* tired,' Oliver insisted. 'You ought to spend your leave resting. Take a book into the garden and sit under the trees. You don't need to come to the hospital with me.'

'The change will be rest enough,' he said. 'If I lie under a tree with a book I shall be prey to my thoughts. I'd much sooner be busy. Is it all right with the hospital that I come in with you?'

'Oh, yes – the medical chief is hoping to get his money's worth out of you, not that he's going to pay you, of course! But be warned – my mother thinks it very odd of both of us to want to use your leave in this way. She means to feed you up—'

'I shan't object to that,' Westhoven grinned. 'I don't know what sort of cow bully-beef comes from, but when the war's over I hope never to see the poor animal again.'

'Don't worry. The conscription hasn't taken our chef yet, and he'd rather die than allow anything in a tin to enter his kitchen. But I was saying – the mater feels you ought to be going out on the Town while you're here, seeing shows, dancing and meeting girls. You'll be hard put to it to convince her you really prefer hospital smells and suppurating wounds.'

'I don't relish them, but it's a case of the dinner of herbs, isn't it?' said Westhoven. 'I want to spend as much time with you as I can, and my leave is short. I don't know when I shall be able to get away again.'

'Don't you get leave every six months?'

'In theory – but in practice it depends on what's going on and whether any of us can be spared. It's quiet all along the Front at the moment, and they're trying to make sure all the officers get a few days, because once things heat up there's no knowing how long it will last.'

'And I'm stuck here at home,' Oliver fretted. 'Why did I let Keogh talk me into it?'

'My dear chap, you're in uniform now. If you hadn't succumbed gracefully you'd have had to do it anyway. We all go where we're sent.'

'He made it sound like a choice.'

'That was just his politeness. Brass can do it harsh or do it smooth, but brass is brass either way.'

Oliver was struck by how much older Westhoven had sounded in the last two exchanges. His experiences at the Front had turned him from a shy boy into a man in a matter of weeks.

'I suppose,' Oliver said, 'if there was a great need at the Front, I'd be sent over.'

'Who's to do the doctoring at home, if all the good men go to France? Who do we send our boys back to?'

'The married doctors,' said Oliver.

On his first evening home they had one of their long talks far into the night. Venetia sat up with them at first, but had to drag herself reluctantly away to bed, though the conversation was fascinating. 'I always prided myself on my stamina, but I don't have your vitality. I must get some sleep or I shall be useless tomorrow.'

When they were alone, Westhoven told Oliver the regiment

was moving. 'We are going to Picardy. I suppose you've heard that a big push is coming? Well, that's where the action is supposed to come off.'

'So you'll be in the heart of it?'

He looked thoughtful. 'I can't pretend I'm not excited at the thought. There's an exhilaration in being there, faced with challenges the ordinary doctor never sees in a lifetime.'

'Thank God for that.'

'Yes, the suffering is terrible. But one finds oneself braced for the onslaught, not only with trepidation but a sort of pleasure. Do you think that vile of me?'

'Not at all. I understand perfectly.'

'I hate the war. But, given that I can't stop it, I want to be in the centre of it, on my mettle, testing my skills against the worst the Huns can do.'

Oliver said, 'I know exactly what you mean. I've felt it when faced with an emergency – too many cases coming in all at once, terrible suffering, more than one can cope with. Adrenaline rushes through the bloodstream. You can become addicted to the feeling, just like cocaine.'

'I'm glad you *do* understand,' Westhoven said. 'You must be so disappointed about having to stay in England. But when the push comes, there'll be convoys coming home, thousands of casualties all arriving together. *That* ought to challenge you.'

'A good attempt,' Oliver commended him, 'but I'd still sooner be out there with you.'

When Jessie had been at the hospital for just under six weeks, she was called to the matron's office.

'I have good reports of you, Nurse,' the matron said. 'You seem to be shaping quite nicely, and I am happy to invite you to sign on.'

'Signing on' had been much discussed at the probationers' tables in the dining-room. It was said that because of the war no-one was ever dismissed, unless they did something very dreadful, like being caught *in flagrante* with a doctor – or a patient. But some who were deemed not up to scratch had to repeat their probationary period. Being asked to sign on was the symbol of approval, and was supposed to happen after a month. Jessie had worried for the past week that she had failed in some way.

As if divining this, the matron said, 'I should have asked you before, Nurse, but with Sister Fitton away on leave I did not have your report to hand. It wasn't because you have not given satisfaction. Sign here, please.' She pushed the contract across the desk, and Jessie signed. 'You are accepted for six months' service. If you continue as you have begun, you will be invited to sign on again at the end of it for a further period. I'm sure you won't disappoint me.'

Jessie returned to the ward, feeling oddly braced, now she was committed to her course of action. She could not leave now without notice given and accepted. She was an official part of the hospital.

When she came out of the gates at twenty past five, she found Oliver lounging against the gatepost, smoking a cigarette and looking furtive. He cast away his cigarette and straightened as she came towards him. 'Are you waiting for me?' she said in surprise. 'I hope you haven't been there all day.'

'No, of course not. Only since five.'

'But how did you know what time I'd come out? I was only told this morning when my off-time would be.'

'I asked a medical colleague of mine, Cuffington, who works here, to enquire discreetly of one of the nurses on your ward. The rest was done by the magic of the telephone.' He noted her expression of alarm. 'Don't worry! He was to explain that a cousin of yours wanted to meet you. All perfectly above board.'

Jessie's mouth quirked as she saw the humour of it. 'I hope it doesn't get back to Sister. Only last month I asked for a particular half-day off so that I could meet a cousin. She'll never believe the same thing twice.'

'But I *am* your cousin,' Oliver said indignantly. 'I must say, I think it's a bit off for you to use *my* perfectly good excuse to go seeing other fellows, especially when you promised weeks ago that you would meet me as soon as you were settled. Who was the wretch, anyway?'

'Bertie. He was home on leave.'

'Oh. Well, I suppose that's all right, then,' he said, pretending a huff. 'But these fellows who are lucky enough to be at the Front carry all before them. We chaps left at home get short shrift from you hard-hearted females.'

He drew her hand through his arm to walk her away. She resisted. 'Oliver, what *are* you doing here?'

He looked surprised. 'I thought I'd told you. I grew tired of waiting for you to contact me, as you promised, and decided to take the initiative. You and I are going out to dinner.'

'Oh dear!'

He gave her a hurt look. 'Why "oh dear"? You're not ashamed to be seen with me?'

'Don't be silly. But I'm not dressed. And I'm very tired.'

'And you'd sooner go back to your horrid hostel than come and frivol with me? I don't believe it. Cuffington *knows* something of that hostel – we won't ask how or why – and he's described it to me. I don't understand why the medical authorities think it necessary to house nurses in such Spartan conditions, but I can't believe that anything except a fierce aversion to my company would make you want to go back there when there's something better on offer.'

She laughed. 'I'm too tired to argue with you. But the thought of going up to Town, with all those crowds, and the noise . . .'

'Ah!' he said. 'I thought of that! I have a motor-car, borrowed from a chap at the Number Two General – by the name of Luttrell, but he doesn't come into the story after this so there's no need to remember it – and I know of a charming place, on the river at Chertsey, a country hotel with a decent restaurant and nice views of some very soothing water.'

'A hotel on the river? People will think—'

'No, dear, that's Henley. You look too respectable, anyway.'

'They'll know I'm a nurse,' she said, showing him her swollen red hands. 'And they'll know you're a doctor by your insignia.'

'They'll think what they think. What do you care? No-one there will know us.' He dropped his fooling air. '*Please* come. It would be an act of kindness. My state of mind is too fragile to bear a refusal. I've reserved a table by the window.'

She let him lead her forward. 'I hope I don't fall asleep and disgrace you.'

'You can doze in the motor on the way.'

The motor-car was a rather dashing little Buick Model 32 roadster, painted cherry red with cream leather upholstery and a highly polished brass klaxon horn. 'It's only five years old, so I hope I don't crash it. Luttrell's father gave it to him for his twenty-first birthday and he wouldn't take kindly. I know I said he wouldn't come into the story again, so forgive the mention. It won't happen again.'

There was little chance of Jessie's falling asleep in it, since it had no doors, so with the hood down there was nothing to stop her falling out of the side if she nodded off. Oliver drove fast and flamboyantly, with full use of the horn at corners and over humpback bridges. The air rushing past her face refreshed her, while the speed exhilarated her, as it always did. Next to riding a good horse, driving in an open motor was the thing she liked best. She looked at Oliver's capable doctor's hands on the wheel, and at his distinguished profile, and thought he was a man any woman could be proud to be seen with. He had grown into his looks with maturity, having been very much in Thomas's shadow as a youngster – less brilliant, less tall, less handsome, less popular. There was always something attractive about a man driving, she thought, and settled back to enjoy it, holding the side of the motor with one hand, and her hat with the other.

The hotel was Victorian mock-Tudor and rather shabby, but inside there was polished wood, crystal chandeliers and a deal of red plush to make up for it. A waiter showed them to a table in a bay window overlooking the river, which gave them a measure of privacy, and brought champagne, which Oliver had ordered for their arrival. Something in the way the waiter handled the bottle and filled the glasses suggested he took it for a preliminary to seduction. Though Jessie still wore a wedding-ring, it would be only natural, as they were obviously doctor and nurse, to suppose the worst.

'I feel like a shop-girl who's going to have to fight for her virtue,' she said, as Oliver raised his glass to her.

'No, do you? How interesting. How do you know what that feels like?' He touched his glass to hers and they drank. 'I thought you'd enjoy champagne, but I can have them bring you sherry or Madeira if you prefer.'

'I am enjoying it. I'm amused that you went to all this trouble for me, though – or did you?' She narrowed her eyes. 'Perhaps you arranged this evening for another girl, and she "chucked".'

'What a dreadful suggestion,' Oliver said, looking rather cross. 'It was all for you, but if you mean to be horrid about it, I shall wish I'd never thought of it.'

She put her hand on his across the table. 'Oh, Oliver, I'm sorry. I didn't mean to be ungracious. This is really very nice and I'm grateful to you. I'm tired, that's all, and a little glum.'

'I'm glum too, which is partly why I asked you. I thought we could cheer each other up.'

'I'm so sorry about your father,' Jessie said. 'It must have been a dreadful shock – so unexpected. He was a wonderful person.'

'I'm only now realising *how* wonderful, now it's too late. One takes one's father for granted, somehow, when he's around – as if he's always going to be.'

'I had a long time to get used to losing my father,' Jessie said. 'He was ill for years, and at the end we knew he was failing. But it didn't make it any easier. I loved him so, and I still miss him, even after all this time.'

'And then you lost poor Ned as well. He was a splendid fellow, old Ned. Everyone liked him at Eton – he was a great sportsman, and he was always standing up for the little fellow. I wasn't at all surprised that he won the MC. I dare say it would have been the first of many decorations if he'd lived.' The waiter laid the menus down before them. 'Look here,' Oliver said, 'let's not think about sad things tonight. Let's make a pact to be as gay as possible. And let's have a good dinner. I don't suppose you often get one, eating in the hospital dining-room – and I seem to be missing all too many meals, these days. You are hungry, aren't you?'

'I could eat a horse.'

'I hope it won't come to that! Though I know nothing about the grub here. Luttrell said it was all right, but I've never eaten with him, so I don't know what sort of places he frequents. I'm sorry, that really *is* the last time I'll mention him.'

Jessie had nothing to do but eat, drink and appreciate Oliver as he sparkled for her, by turns witty, absurd and informative. She saw that he was taking pains to be charming and amuse her, and she was touched. He made her laugh, and it felt good to laugh again. The oppression of the hospital lifted, the war was forgotten, and she hoped he forgot his own loss, too. She felt the affection she had always had for him warm in her, like cherry brandy on a cold hunting morning.

The simile, as it came to her, opened a window on another world, one so remote from the scene she was a part of that it checked her. Would they ever hunt again? Would England ever go back to normal? The war was only two years old, but already it felt as though there had never been anything else. It had become normality.

He saw the change in her expression and said, 'What is it?'

'I suddenly thought of how things used to be, before the war, and it seemed so far-off and strange.'

The buoyancy of performance left him, and he sank a little in his chair. 'Nothing seems stranger to me than the sight of myself in uniform,' he said. 'Not even you masquerading as a nurse.'

'I'm a very good nurse,' she said robustly, but he didn't smile. 'I'm sorry. I didn't mean to spoil your mood.'

'It's not your fault. Everything's gloomy at home – Mama being so stoical it terrifies me, poor Violet in floods all the time, the servants either drooping like scolded dogs or being abominably tactful. This has been a lovely change for me, to be with you and be happy.'

'I've had a lovely time too,' Jessie said warmly.

'I'm glad,' he said. He reached across for her hand. 'We always did get on well together, didn't we? Remember that time on the Isle of Wight, when I confessed to you that I wanted to be a doctor and you didn't laugh at me? I hadn't dared tell anyone else, but I always felt I could tell you anything,'

'You can. And I feel that way about you.' She pressed his hand affectionately.

He closed his other hand over hers, and across the table gave her a serious, questioning look. 'Jessie, we've had fun together, haven't we? And it seems to me that we could be more than good friends – don't you think?'

Jessie stared, puzzled. 'I'm very fond of you,' she said. 'I always have been.'

'It was rotten luck, losing poor old Ned, but that needn't stop you trying again. We could comfort each other. It seems to me a good idea – no, that's not the right word. What I mean to say is – Jessie, will you marry me?'

Her surprise was complete; but much was now explained. His sudden appearance outside the hospital, the borrowed motor, the champagne: he had been building up to this, entertaining her with every exercise of charm at his disposal. This offer was not made on the spur of the moment – he had planned it. She tried to pull her hand back, but he kept it fast, searching her face.

'But, Oliver,' she said, puzzled and unhappy, 'you don't love me.'

'I *do*.'

'Yes, like a cousin or a brother,' she said. 'You're not *in love* with me. And you must know I'm not with you.'

'But does that matter? There's too much emphasis on this "being in love" business, these days. Affection, understanding, sharing ideas, getting on together – they are much more important. We've known each other all our lives – doesn't that count for something?'

These were things she had thought when she had married Ned; but it had not been enough – no, not even when physical desire came to keep them company. Could she desire Oliver? She looked at him in that light, and knew that, in a normal, animal way, she could. He was handsome, attractive; his hands holding hers were strong and capable. She looked at them and shivered, both interested and repelled by the thoughts they engendered.

'Of course it counts,' she said at last. 'But it isn't why people get married.'

'People get married for the wrong reasons all the time. Look at Violet – she married for love. She was mad for Holkam, but what a beast he turned out to be!'

'Your mother and father married for love. Don't you want something as good as that for yourself?'

He looked gloomy. 'I sometimes think the mater and pater did us a shabby turn, being so much in love. Who can live up to them? The children of lovers have a thin time of it, in my opinion. Oh, Jessie, please don't say no out of hand. We could be happy together. We're both alone, both sad – why shouldn't we comfort each other? After the war I shall make a decent income, enough to keep us in good style. And think how happy it would make our families!'

Just for a moment it seemed attractive. He was a handsome, witty, educated man; she liked him, enjoyed his company, was easy with him; and she was lonely. She could never have Bertie. Why shouldn't she settle for as much happiness as she could get?

But she couldn't do that to him. 'You deserve better than that,' she said. She managed to draw her hand away. 'Being comfortable together isn't enough. I know, because I've tried it.'

He stared, interested. 'You mean—You and Ned? I always assumed it was a case between you. He was certainly mad about you – I know *that* for a fact.'

'I thought I was in love with him once, but I wasn't. Now I'm old enough to know the difference, I know I never was. I won't make the same mistake twice. And it would be worse this time because you're not in love with me, either. The first time I did something you didn't like, we'd quarrel, and you'd wish you'd never married me.'

He laughed. 'My dear girl, *I* shouldn't mind what you did! Why on earth should I? Oh, go on, marry me – do! It would be fun. I promise I'll never come the heavy with you. You're a nurse, I'm a doctor – we'd understand each other.'

'Oliver, do stop. I'm flattered that you would think of me, but I can't marry you.'

'Well, I shan't give up hope,' he said. 'The offer still stands, so why don't you take some time to think about it? The idea might grow on you.'

'If it will make you happy – all right, I'll think about it.'

'Good girl.' He smiled at her in the old, wicked, Oliver manner. 'At least now I can tell my mother that I tried. She's always nagging me to get married, rates me shockingly for not "doing my duty", as she calls it. Well, I've cast my line and it's not my fault if the fish won't bite. I've cleared myself with her.'

Her eyes widened. 'Is *that* what all this was about? You dreadful creature! You only asked me because you knew I'd say no! And I thought you actually meant it. It was a horrid, ungentlemanly thing to do, and I shall never forgive you!'

'No, no! That last bit was a tease. I *did* mean it. I said the offer still stands and it does. I think we could be comfortable together – and I certainly don't want to marry anyone else. If you change your mind, I shall be very happy, I promise you.'

'Hmm. Well, I shan't change my mind, so you can rest easy.'

'Oh, Jess,' he said, looking hurt, 'you still don't believe me. And after I borrowed a motor-car and everything, just to impress you.'

'I think you'd better have the motor-car brought round again and drive me home. It's getting late and I have to be up horribly early.' She studied him as he called for the waiter and the bill. 'You really are an odd creature, you know. I'm half inclined to think—'

He leaned across the table, pressed her hand, and said with the utmost sincerity, 'I meant it, every word. Just promise me you'll think about it.'

She sighed, not knowing where she was with him. 'All right, I promise,' she said. 'But the answer will still be no.'

He straightened, gave a satisfied smile, and said, 'We'll see.'

In June 1916 the Germans proposed peace negotiations. It was not a thing generally known, and was kept from the newspapers, but Venetia had enough friends in high places to hear about it. There had been rumours among those in the know since the end of May – Overton himself had mentioned as much to her before the end of that month – but it was from the King's secretary Arthur Bigge, Lord Stamfordham, that Venetia had confirmation of the truth.

He was making a call of condolence, and though they had known each other for many years, the conversation began stilted and awkward. Venetia was not at ease discussing her feelings, even with an old friend. Searching about for a change of subject, she hit on something she was sure would distract him.

'What's this I hear about peace negotiations, Arthur? Surely the French aren't really going to settle?'

'Good heavens! How did you hear about that?' said Stamfordham.

'You forget,' she said, with a faint smile, 'that I know everyone. So there *is* something to it?'

'It's supposed to be the darkest secret,' he grumbled.

'I dare say it is. And you needn't worry that I shall mention it elsewhere. I only ask because you are bound to know. The King could hardly keep you in the dark.'

'Well, since you know so much, I might as well admit that there *has* been an approach, but no-one beyond the prime minister and the chiefs of staff is meant to know, so I trust you not to speak of it to *anyone*.' He was looking at her curiously, obviously wanting to know where the leak had sprung. In fact, she had heard it from Asquith, who, despite his early training as a lawyer, had a well-known weakness when it came to women. Venetia supposed Stamfordham would work it out for himself in due course.

'The German high command did send an emissary to the French government suggesting a discussion of terms,' he told her. 'Of course, the French situation at Verdun is very grave – their losses are appalling, and mounting daily. The Germans must think they are in a strong position: the French are being bled white, and *we* have made no progress against them since last autumn. I suppose they assume they would have the upper hand in any negotiations, so they would be able to secure terms advantageous to themselves.'

'What was the French reply?' Venetia asked.

'They said that before they would even consider the possibility of talking, the Germans must release all the French, British and Russian prisoners they are holding.'

Venetia smiled. 'A typical piece of Gallic arrogance. I don't suppose the Germans will want to comply with *that*.'

'And give up one of their main bargaining counters? Of course not,' said Stamfordham. 'That was just a stalling tactic by the French.' He hesitated. 'I suppose if you know about the peace proposal, you know about our intended action to relieve the French?'

'The coming Big Push?' Venetia said drily. 'My dear Arthur, my milkman's horse knows about that. It's the worst-kept secret of the war.'

'I suppose it is,' he sighed. 'We are managing to keep one or two things back, like the precise date. Again I must enjoin you to secrecy. Our generals wanted to wait until the autumn, but the French have said now they can't hold out beyond the end of the month without relief from us. It's been agreed there's to be an attack on the twenty-ninth of June. So nothing on earth could persuade the French to negotiate before then.'

'Nor our own generals, I imagine?'

'Our chaps wouldn't think of it. They assure us we are going to win a decisive victory. If there are to be peace talks, they must take place *after* that, when we have the upper hand.'

'Victory talks rather than peace talks,' said Venetia.

'Quite so. Frankly, I doubt whether the prime minister could persuade the people to accept peace on any other terms.'

'The war does remain astonishingly popular,' Venetia mused.

'Except among the socialists and conscientious objectors.'

'Well, no-one cares about their opinion. I suppose you're right – the nation would refuse to consider a peace that smacked of compromise.'

'However, it may be a good ploy for us to attack the Germans while they still think we are considering negotiating,' said Stamfordham.

'But, Arthur, if I know about the Big Push, I'm sure the German high command does. The preparations must be obvious to their spotters.'

'But they don't know the precise date,' said Stamfordham. 'Or so I'm assured,' he added, less confidently.

'Well, it doesn't matter too much if they do know when we're going to attack, as long as we win. And you think we will?'

He smiled. 'I'm not a soldier. But the generals are sure of it.'

'Thank heaven for that. Then perhaps we can be done with this wretched war.'

The bleakness of her tone brought him back to the reason for his visit. 'Venetia, my dear, I'm so very sorry. He is a great loss, to the country as well as to you.'

'It was such a pointless death,' she said. 'If he had died in battle – but I suppose he was a victim of the war just the same. And I am no different from any other war widow. There are hundreds of us, and no doubt will be hundreds more. Let us not talk about it.'

'Very well. Tell me about your war work – your X-ray ambulances.'

'The funds are coming in very nicely. And I have a new scheme to coax money out of rich women through their vanity. Fabian Ware suggested it: if they give me the money for a mobile unit, I will name it after them. Few people can resist having things named after them.'

'I believe you're right – but why restrict it to the rich? I dare say those who can afford to buy a whole vehicle are few enough, but a middling sort of person may be able to buy part of one. And the middle classes yearn to do their bit for the war effort.'

'But how can I name an X-ray unit after more than one person?'

'Give the proposed vehicle a popular name – Maud, say, or Hilda – and invite all the women with that name to contribute to it. You could advertise in the women's journals.'

'Arthur, I think you may have hit on something!'

'It's rather traditional, after all, to ascribe a female personality to ships and motor-cars.'

'Yes, and it will give just that touch of humanity to the whole project – the good vessel *Margaret* coming to the soldiers' rescue, bearing the practical goodwill of all the Peggys in Penge, Purley and Pemberton!'

'You could even have a launching ceremony, let them come and smash a bottle on the bonnet. Make sure they provide their own champagne, though!'

Venetia laughed. 'You are a genius, Arthur! I salute you.'

He smiled modestly. 'Perhaps when you have done with the women of England, you may start on the men. I will gladly pledge you ten pounds for the good vessel *Arthur*. So when do you expect your first unit to go to the Front?'

'I'm hoping to get one away this month – I rather shamelessly poached an X-ray operator from the East London, to get the thing going, otherwise I was afraid I'd have nothing to show the sponsors for their trouble. But after that I have to wait for the girls to be trained.'

'Girls?'

'I can't compete with the Army for young men, so I am recruiting girls to go to the Curie Institute in Paris to train to operate X-ray machines. The first three are there now, and another batch will be on the way by the end of the month.'

Stamfordham looked a little concerned. 'Won't it be, well, rather too *rough* for girls out there?'

'It's rough for everyone out there.'

'Yes, but – war is a man's business.'

'This war is everyone's business. We already have women working in armament factories, and there's nothing dainty and feminine about that. And as more men go to the Front, the women will have to do their jobs back home.'

'Then I pray this new action will settle matters so that we won't have to send more men.'

'I have no quarrel with you there, Arthur,' Venetia said.

Since their wet and muddy arrival in February, Frank and his Rifles had found life steadily improving. After two weeks of being shouted at by the training sergeants in the 'bull ring' in Étaples, they were moved up to billets near Fruges, for further training under their own officers: company drill, Swedish exercises, bayonet fighting, rapid loading, trench craft. There were regular route marches to get them fit. They had had plenty of marching in Malta, but now they had their first experience of the reviled French cobbles. And on one memorable day they were issued with anti-gas helmets and had a gas parade, which caused some thoughtfulness.

But spirits remained high. They had been told they would soon be going into the trenches for the first time, near Armentières. Meanwhile, they could use their free time to visit the local *estaminets*, where they could get a pork chop and chips or a gristly local sausage, to vary the monotony of bully-and-biscuit. They were keen to try out the French words and phrases they had picked up. These forays into a foreign tongue sometimes caused much amusement to the French, as when Pratt said to a young woman in a tiny dark shop, '*Je suis un fromage, êtes vous?*' instead of '*Je veux du fromage, s'il vous plaît.*' The girl and her small brother, who were helping in the family shop, collapsed into giggles. Pratt began to get annoyed, while his companions were mystified and a little insulted. It was only when Frank came along that it was all sorted out. Pratt's companions roared with laughter when they knew what he had said, and ever after that he was known as 'Cheesy' Pratt.

There was six inches of snow on the ground on the morning the battalion was to move; and at company orders the officers were told that there was no transport. The Rifles would have to march the sixty-odd miles to the Front. 'I'll keep trying,' said the colonel, 'but we may have to resign ourselves to Shanks's mare, I'm afraid.'

The first day they marched to Thérouanne, about ten miles, and as they had made good time they were allowed out in the town until eight p.m. Frank went with Prendergast and Mascall to find a restaurant, where they ate very tough steak – which Mascall said was horse – followed by tinned sardines. There was no wine, only Dubonnet, which made strange drinking with a meal.

'It's makes a change, at least,' said Frank, at the end. 'I say, Prendy, do you think they might have any Cognac hidden away?'

But the waiter with infinite regret, and an explanation none of them could understand, said all they had was Dubonnet. Mascall suggested it would be cheaper to buy the bottle, and so it proved, so they bought two and washed it down with coffee.

On the last day of the march they came near enough to the line to hear the gunfire and see the flashes in the sky. Because of the danger of artillery fire, they marched without the usual stops, so that by the time they got into billets they were exhausted, and spent the evening quietly, listening to the sound of the war as they had never heard it before, and going early to bed.

And so on the next night they marched up and took over a section of the front-line trenches for the first time. They started off from the village at seven p.m. and after a couple of miles were met by guides from the unit they were relieving, the London Irish. The sky all around seemed to be filled with lights as flares went up and star shells burst; the ground under their feet trembled now and then with an extra large concussion. The clear whirring sound of snipers' bullets was unnerving: Frank reckoned if you could hear them, they must be close.

A thousand yards from the front line they passed through a ruined village, and the guides warned that they would have to get past 'dead man's corner'. A shell fell quite close as they went by, but fortunately no-one was hurt. They were all glad when they reached the head of the communication trench and were able to get underground at last. As they moved forward towards the front-line trench the firing became heavier and there seemed to be bullets whizzing overhead constantly like a swarm of hornets, but they felt perfectly safe down in the trench. It was no worse than being in the marking-pit on the rifle range.

It began to snow while they were taking up position, and the ground underfoot soon became slippery and cloying; but the relief was completed by half past nine without incident, and the men had their first chance to peep over the parapet into no man's land, which revealed nothing but a seemingly endless tangle of barbed wire. They had been told it was a quiet sector, but it was anything but a quiet night: to jittery men who had never been in a trench before, every mound of earth, fence post or scrap of cloth caught on the wire looked like an approaching German, and rounds were being let off up and down the trench all night. The Irish guides, who were staying on for twenty-four hours to help and advise, rolled their eyes. Now, they said, the Boche would have no doubt they had new tenants opposite.

But the men soon settled down, with the famous adaptability of the Tommy. At least they knew that it would be short: they only had to do six days a month in the trenches, and not more than two or three in the front line. And there was always plenty of food, hot tea and a tot of rum every day. They learned the routines, got to discharge their weapons at the enemy, even if they couldn't see him, and experienced what it was like to be under fire. The noise of the shells was shocking, but they got used to it – the regular 'hymn of hate', as they called it, at stand-to night and morning.

Snipers were different. At the beginning of April, during their second stint in the front-line trench, they suffered their first casualty. There was one particularly 'unhealthy' corner the Irish had warned them about, but young Pember thoughtlessly stood up to stretch, and at the same time took off his tin hat to scratch his head. At once there was a whine and a horrid wet smacking noise, and he was dead, lying on the trench floor looking, more than anything, very surprised. Mason, who had been beside him, was cursing in fear and disgust, his face and chest spattered with blood and bits of brain and bone. The others gathered silently around their fallen comrade, lying in the slush – the weather was still bitter and it had been snowing again – with his head in a pool of slow blood, dark as oil. They remained staring in mingled shock and curiosity, until Sergeant Hopper arrived, red-faced, to break up the group.

'Let that be a bloody lesson to you bloody amateurs to keep your bloody heads down and keep your bloody hats on!' he bellowed – only he didn't say 'bloody'.

Afterwards, the men made up a song about it, which they called 'Pember's Lament'. They sang it softly and mournfully to the tune of 'Keep the Home Fires Burning' when they were cleaning equipment.

Keep your bloody heads down. Keep your bloody hats on.
Though the sniper's far away, he can still see you.
Snipers give no warning. Pember won't see morning.
Just remember how he died, and you might get home.

On the night after Pember's death Frank led a work party that spent a good four hours of strenuous labour strengthening what they now called 'Pember's Corner'. As the grey light of before-dawn came, Frank noticed what seemed to be movement in a large shell-hole, and guessed it was the sniper, and that he would be annoyed at having his sport curtailed. He told off Ratliffe, who was the best marksman in his platoon, to take up a position and keep a sharp eye on that shell-hole, in case annoyance made the sniper incautious. Sure enough, soon afterwards a head was lifted over the rim of the hole. Ratliffe's rifle spoke, and Pember was avenged.

There was one other casualty that month, when Goggins slipped in the mud, fell, and gashed his leg badly on a hidden object, which, when dragged out into the daylight, turned out to be a massive piece of shrapnel the size of a dustbin lid. The incident was more notable for the fact that as they hauled it out something else came to light – a human arm, still in its uniform sleeve, which perhaps had been sheared off by the shrapnel and lost in the mud during some previous action. They dug a hole in the trench wall and reinterred it, hoping it would stay put.

At the beginning of May the battalion was moved up to Picardy, part of the force for the coming Big Push. Now there was very specific training. An area of land had been chosen for its similarity to the battlefield, and tapes and signposts marked out the German trenches, redoubts, villages and any other notable buildings and landmarks. Over this ground the men formed up, advanced, captured the German positions, consolidated, advanced – over and over again, sweating as the summer weather warmed up, sworn at by sergeants and watched with critical frowns by senior officers – sometimes even Headquarters observers – sitting at a distance on their horses. Frank was pretty sure he had got his first glimpse of General Haig, and wrote to Maria that he thought the stout old fellow with him must have been General Joffre. 'So we've been inspected by the best!'

The battalion worked harder than it ever had before, but

the men remained in high spirits. This was what they had volunteered for, and everyone said it would be the last battle of the war, so they were glad they weren't going to miss it. Nobody minded that there would be no leave before the day. They would be home in any case – everyone said so – for the August bank holiday.

Frank was enjoying life as an officer. As a little boy he had dreamed of being a soldier, and though there had been rather more of gallantry, gorgeous uniforms and victory parades about his games, and much less of mud and sweat, he still relished the realisation of his dream. There was something thrilling, to his mathematical mind, in the movement of hundreds of men as one. He liked the orderliness of battle plans, the satisfying succession of intention, execution and outcome. Some of his fellow officers complained about the rigid hierarchy of the army, the long-established rules, the pointless-seeming practices that encrusted the soldier's life like barnacles. But Frank revelled in it. It was restful to subordinate his intellect to the ancient, gaudy, mad and mighty machine of the army. The problems he was presented with daily seemed tiny and unimportant compared with the intellectual problems he had wrestled with in his career at home.

With so many troops concentrating in the area, individual units had to spend less time manning the trenches. Aside from rehearsing and training, there was the usual digging and labouring to be done. Miles of assembly trenches had to be dug at night for the troops to pack into before the battle, and the chalky spoil had to be carted away so that the German observers wouldn't see it showing white against the ground. Tons of food, ammunition, and fodder for the horses had to be brought up to dumps close behind the line. Extra roads had to be built, because the area had very few, and suitable stone had to be brought in from as far away as Cornwall, because the local chalk was too soft. There was little water, either, and miles of pipelines had to be laid in, which meant more digging. In cheerful confidence, barbed-wire enclosures were erected to house German prisoners; in sober acceptance, mass graves were dug for the expected fallen.

But there was time for relaxation. The usual football matches and concerts were got up – Mills and Lauder of Frank's platoon brought the house down with their duet version of 'If You Were the Only Girl in the World', with Lauder a convincing female in a blonde wig made of straw and two half-grapefruit under his borrowed dress. Albert, the town nearest the battlefront, was a sad place, having been shelled extensively by the Germans. Most of the inhabitants had left, but in the villages behind it there were still *estaminets* and restaurants to visit, where the businesslike French would remain as long as there was money to be gathered in.

Albert had a magnificent, ornate church called the Basilica, with a lofty tower surmounted by a golden statue of the Virgin holding up her Son towards heaven. In January 1915 a German shell had struck and partly demolished the Basilica, and the blast had toppled the Golden Virgin and left her hanging bizarrely at right angles to the tower. Local engineers had hastened to secure her with chains, and there she hung still, leaning out over the square below, parallel to the ground. Legend had grown up among the soldiers that the war would end when the Virgin fell. Perhaps the Germans had the same legend, for they still tried intermittently to shell the building, as if they wanted to get the business over with.

BOOK THREE

Safety

War knows no power. Safe shall be my going,
Secretly armed against all death's endeavour;
Safe though all safety's lost; safe where men fall;
And, if these poor limbs die, safest of all.

Rupert Brooke, 'Safety'

CHAPTER SEVENTEEN

On his arrival in France, Jack was put onto photographic reconnaissance duties. In advance of the expected action in Picardy, every square inch of the German front line and its hinterland had to be photographed – and not just once, but regularly, so that any changes could be noted. One of the new skills he had had to learn at the flying school back in England was to work a camera, and it wasn't easy. The instrument was strapped onto the outside of the aeroplane, a great square mahogany box with a leather concertina pull-out, and a big lens pointing straight down and focused on infinity. It was loaded with a magazine of twelve glass plates, and as each was exposed a sliding handle on the top of the box moved it into a second, storage magazine and reset the shutter. The shutter was operated by a cord with a ring on the end of it, which was supposed to be easier for the pilot to manage with his thick-gloved hand. Even so, it took considerable practice, as Jack found, to lean over the side of the cockpit and look down the sight, grasp the string – which would be skittering about in the wind – pull it, operate the resetting handle, and repeat, all while flying the aeroplane with the left hand.

He also had to learn to judge the distance between exposures, because the photographs were meant to form a continuous picture. It was wonderful, though, what could be seen on them. The trenches stood out clearly as a crenulated pattern across the fields, and from the shadows it was possible to tell how deep they were, whether they had water in them, where the entrances to the dugouts were, even how many rows of barbed wire they had in front of them.

The enemy went to great lengths to camouflage their gun positions, but an aerial photograph could often see the gun-muzzle sticking out, and the limber tracks leading up to it. And on railway sidings it was possible actually to count the trucks in a train, and sometimes to tell from their position whether they were empty or laden. All this was invaluable to the 'intelligence wallahs'.

It was one thing, of course, to take photographs unopposed over an English field or village, quite another to do it over the German front line, with the Huns resenting it for all they were worth. They put up huge quantities of Archie whenever an RFC kite went over. German anti-aircraft fire was nicknamed Archie, after a popular music-hall song with the repeated line 'Archibald, certainly not!' One verse went:

> A lady named Miss Hewitt was on friendly terms with me.
> She fell in love with me at once and then fell in the sea.
> My wife came on the scene as I threw coat and vest aside;
> As other garments I slipped off to save the girl, she cried,
> 'Archibald, certainly not!
> Desist at once disrobing on the spot!
> You may show your pluck and save Miss Hewitt,
> But if you've got to strip to do it,
> Archibald, certainly not!

There was nothing amusing, however, about the real Archie: it was a serious menace. Photographs had to be taken from comparatively low altitude, around six thousand feet, while flying in a straight line, which gave the Germans ample opportunity to take aim. Jack had to learn the tricks of dodging: banking, sideslipping, climbing or descending to throw out the range. The most valuable lesson he learned was from an old hand, who told him it took a shell about twenty seconds from the time it was fired to reach six thousand feet and explode. So if you actually saw the flash of the gun, you had twenty seconds to change course, and then have the pleasure of watching the shell explode in the place where you would have been.

As well as Archie, there was the danger from German 'fighter' aeroplanes. The usual reconnaissance machine, the BE2C, was not very nimble. Carrying as it did thirty gallons of petrol, two officers, two Lewis guns, four hundred rounds of ammunition, two twenty-pound bombs, a wireless with its accumulator, and a huge camera fitted just where it hit all the air resistance, it was a wonder it got off the ground at all. Once airborne it was all the pilot could do to get it along. The BE's defence, moreover, was the fixed Lewis gun, which could only fire to the sides. This made it very vulnerable to the German Fokker, which could fire straight ahead through the propellors with its interrupter gear. Many good men went down, as everyone in the RFC was well aware, even in England.

By the time Jack arrived in France, the balance was being restored by the arrival of the De Havilland FE2B. Jack almost laughed the first time he saw it, because the 'FE' of its name stood for Farman Experimental, and it bore a strong resemblance to the old Farman in which he had had his first ever taste of flying, all those years ago. It was simplicity itself: a pusher aeroplane with a two-man nacelle slung between a pair of planes, and a long openwork tail boom behind, looking as fragile as a child's toy. But because it carried the engine behind the nacelle, the observer in the front seat could fire straight ahead and all round; and though it was not capable of great speed, it could turn quickly and was quite capable of taking care both of itself and the observation BEs it escorted.

Because of the Fokker habit of flying up directly behind – especially dangerous to a pusher – the FEs had a second machine-gun on a telescopic mount between the two cockpits. The observer operated this by standing up and firing backwards over the top of the upper plane. It was a desperately precarious position for him, with only his feet and ankles inside the cockpit: a sudden movement of the aeroplane could send him falling to his death. It was necessary for pilot and spotter to have complete trust in each other and know at any moment what the other would do. But with its ability to turn more quickly than the Fokker, and its greater field of fire, it was turning the tables on the Germans, who'd had things their own way for too long.

The other new 'fighter' in the RFC's armoury was the DH2, to which Jack was transferred – to his relief – after a couple of weeks on photography. 'I wanted you to learn what the problems were before putting you on defence,' said the squadron commander, 'but now you know what to look out for, I need someone with your flying experience to organise the escort.'

The DH2 was a single-seater pusher with a Lewis gun fixed facing forward. It was not as fast as a Fokker, and could not climb as quickly, but with a 100 H.P. rotary engine it could turn more quickly than anything else in the sky. Indeed, because of the torque of the propellor and the gyroscopic effect of the rotary engine, it was all too prone to go into a spin, and took a skilled hand to operate. After one horrible crash early on, it had been nicknamed 'the Spinning Incinerator'.

But Jack had cut his teeth on Sopwith machines with rotary engines, and felt quite at home in the DH2. When new pilots came out, he was often asked to demonstrate to them, putting one into a series of spins, then explaining afterwards how he had got out of it safely. Most pilots, once they had learned how to handle it, loved it for being able to out-turn anything they were likely to meet. And on the

18th of June, the great German air ace, Max Immelman – the Eagle of Lille – was actually shot down near Lens by a DH2, an incident that was taken up and down the line to mark the end of the Fokker reign of terror

Jack was glad to have been moved to escort duty. He had disliked photography very much: spending an hour and a half toddling along at six thousand feet, presenting a perfect target to the enemy, was not his idea of fun. Not that escort duty was without risk, or the DH2 the perfect machine. With the engine behind you, there was always the danger that in a crash landing it could fall forward and crush you; and the tail boom was exposed and fragile. One day this was revealed to him quite graphically.

He was escorting a BE2C when he was attacked from above and behind by a Fokker. He turned quickly and started to climb. The Fokker turned too, but could not manoeuvre as quickly as the DH2, and though he got his shots in, Jack was able to spiral up to the enemy's height and get in behind him. Then it was a matter of emptying a drum into him: no matter how the Fokker twisted and turned, he could not shake off the nimbler aircraft. Eventually the Fokker banked sharply and sideslipped about five hundred feet, and went into a nose-dive. It looked like an uncontrolled fall, but at the last minute it pulled out, and headed away back over its own line.

Jack turned back to pick up his BE again, and went over the details of the fight in his mind. He thought about the shots the Fokker had got in. He had felt the thud of a bullet hitting something behind; two at least had passed through the nacelle harmlessly, and one had pinged off the Lewis mounting, whizzed past him, almost taking off his ear, and made a clanging noise behind him. He listened anxiously to the engine, wondering if that one had done any damage, but everything sounded all right. He was at about four thousand feet, and spotted his BE to the west, about fifteen hundred feet above him. He started to climb, and then without warning there was a tremendous bang and crash behind him, and the whole machine started to shake wildly.

He glanced back, and the damage made him gulp. One of the engine cylinders had blown clean out, ripped off one of the propellor blades, and smashed through one of the main spars of the top plane. Jack switched off the engine at once, before it could racket the craft to pieces; but the propellor continued to revolve, turned by the air pressure as he began to descend. All aeroplanes were good gliders, by their very nature, and putting down without an engine was something they had all done many times; but now, with the engine minus a cylinder and a propellor minus a blade, the DH2 was desperately unstable. The mad shaking and vibration made it hard to hold her steady. He didn't dare descend quickly, because that would have made the vibration worse; but he was desperate to get lower, afraid the machine would shake itself to pieces. It was all he could do to hold her direction.

Two more struts snapped, and now he was being thrown about, while the Lewis was jerking from side to side and the ammunition drums were leaping like hot chestnuts on a shovel. One came loose and shot past him, making a hole in the lower plane. He was being shaken so much he could not see straight, and it was impossible to choose a landing place. He heard an ominous crack from somewhere in the tail boom – he was sure it had been hit in the 'dog fight'. If it broke off he was done for. Some trees dashed past underneath him; he saw what looked like an open space of grass, and put her down.

It was how he had smashed his ankle: crash-landing in a field – which had turned out to have a ditch in the middle. It was impossible to tell anything about this one – he couldn't even see the damn field through the violent shaking. The wheels touched, he bounced, they touched again – and he was bumping and bucketing over the rough ground. There was a tremendous crack as the tail boom went, and she slewed wildly; but by then the impetus was almost spent, and in a moment he was at a standstill, and climbing shakily out to inspect the damage, dizzy but in one piece.

The BE pilot had turned back to the airfield as soon as he saw Jack was in trouble and raised the alarm, so it was not long before he was rescued. Fortunately his sense of direction had survived the incident and he had put down only a couple of miles from home. A Crossley arrived an hour after he had landed, and found him calmly smoking a cigarette, having quite recovered from his shaking. His squadron commander was not best pleased at losing an aeroplane, but it was plainly not Jack's fault – the bullet damage was quite obvious, though whether it was the first strike or the ricochet that had smashed the engine it was impossible to tell.

Though it had been terrifying at the time, he had got down safely, and the incident only underlined how well even a damaged machine would glide. One of the young pilots in his flight said afterwards, 'I'm beginning to think you can't be killed in an ordinary aeroplane smash. I've seen so many since I've been here, and no-one ever gets killed. You have to have bad luck even to get hurt. It's much safer than motoring.'

'I agree with that,' Jack said. 'With motoring there's always the other idiot to run into you. But don't start getting careless. That landing I saw you do yesterday was a disgrace. I'm going to make you practise with a dummy passenger in the front seat – a hundred-and-twelve-pound bomb! If it doesn't go off, you'll know you've made a good landing.'

The incident faded quickly into the background of his mind, and when he wrote to Helen all he said was that he had been forced to put down after engine damage. This wasn't tact or even good British phlegm, it was simply that the matter had passed out of importance in his life.

* * *

Laidislaw's unit was out of the trenches at Hédeauville when they were told that they were to have the honour of being inspected by the commander-in-chief himself. But it was not to be a formal parade. General Haig wanted to see them about their normal daily tasks – which, of course, took far more organising than a nice, simple parade would have done. The 'normal daily tasks' had to be orchestrated so as to give the brass the best overview, while doing the battalion the most credit possible. Some men had to be doing fatigues, some attending lectures, some drilling, and some, it was decided, ought to be having an 'impromptu' game of football to signify that they were at leisure.

There was much argument as to whether the chosen squad should be playing football or cricket – the adjutant was adamant that football would look 'contrived', given that it was June and the weather was warm. But the CO pointed out that the men never did play cricket unless they were organised into doing it – for an inter-company match, for instance – while they played football at all times and in all weathers, whether they had a ball or not.

So football was decided on, a ball was borrowed from a neighbouring unit – with some resistance, since they were afraid they wouldn't get it back. Footballs were so precious along the Front they were practically currency. The teams were chosen and instructed on how they should behave when the commander-in-chief came by. And the colonel said to Laidislaw, 'I think we should have you sitting on the touchline painting the scene. That would give a nice, natural look to it.'

'Not *on* the touchline, sir,' said the adjutant, who was the sporting type.

'Well, just behind it, then. Don't quibble, Freddie, Laidislaw here knows what I mean, don't you?'

' I think so, sir,' said Laidislaw.

The colonel had a distinctly visionary look to his face. He could see it all in his mind's eye – the corner flags blowing bravely, the friendly rough-and-tumble, the artist capturing it all for posterity . . . Perhaps the painting would one day hang in the mess back home, and be the kicking-off point for the tales of the 39th's daring feats, which had led to victory in the battle of Picardy. In that case, he reasoned, it ought to be done in oils. 'You can do oils, can't you, Laidislaw?'

'I can, sir, but I don't have oil paints with me. They're back in England. And I haven't a canvas, only paper.'

For a moment the colonel thought of having someone go out and buy the necessary stuff, but the look in the adjutant's eye made him think better. 'It'll have to be water-colours, then,' he said, disappointed. 'But you ought to have a proper easel to work from.' That was definitely in his mental picture. The Battalion Artist ought not to have to work on his knee – as the colonel had seen him doing so often – when Haig himself was coming round. 'Our own carpenters can knock you something up. Tell the adj here what you want and he'll see to it.'

So on the great day, when various groups were doing bayonet practice, rifle practice, digging latrines, peeling potatoes, sitting in unnaturally straight rows listening to a lecture on trench hygiene, or sweating under the June sun at Swedish drill, Laidislaw found himself sitting at his newly contrived easel, with a scene sketched out and paints at the ready, waiting for the signal that the Great Man was on his way, so as to have the right amount of paint on the paper when Haig actually reached him.

Laidislaw would have felt annoyed at having his genius controlled and used in this paltry way, but he was feeling particularly good that day. They had had sausages for breakfast – always a high point in army life – and he had had a letter from Violet the day before, which he looked forward to reading again before supper. It was a fine day, with high, fat white clouds in the blue sky that would make a very good background; and there had been an aeroplane buzzing about a little while before, which he intended to put into the picture. He, as much as the colonel, could see this painting, in years to come, becoming part of the battalion's history. As he waited, he even planned another piece, which he intended to do from memory, of General Haig *watching* the football match. A photograph of the general would serve to supplement memory, and it could pass into regimental legend, become an icon of the war. It really *ought* to be in oils. He could paint it in watercolour, then copy it in oils when he got home. One day it would be the centrepiece on a wall in the National Gallery – Laidislaw's *Football at the Front*. Whenever the great victory of 1916 was discussed it would be that image which leaped to everyone's mind: the soon-to-be successful general taking the time before the battle to watch a football match. Laidislaw, as much as Haig, would have made history.

He was so deep in his thoughts that he missed the signal to start painting, until the lieutenant doing the signalling had become almost frantic, hopping up and down on the opposite touchline, wildly flapping the handkerchief with which he had been supposed merely to feign blowing his nose. Laidislaw began hastily to paint. A while later the processional knot of brass arrived and the CO and the general were right beside him.

'And what have we here? No, no, don't get up,' said an educated Scottish voice. Laidislaw half rose and sat again, and looked up at the biggest brass of them all. A little grey old man, he saw, with a handsome nose, big white moustaches over a sharp chin, and tired, far-focused eyes. 'Oh, yes, now that's very good,' Haig said, leaning a little forward to see. 'You've quite a talent.'

The comment annoyed Laidislaw for many reasons – that a mere soldier should think of passing judgement on his work; that Haig should be so ignorant as to say it was 'very good' when it was obviously barely started; that he was stuck here, performing for the army, when he should have been furthering his meteoric career. But even against his will, he had absorbed a little of the awe felt for the top man at the Front.

'This is Private Laidislaw, General,' said the CO. 'We think a lot of his skill with the pencil and brush.'

Haig nodded, evidently not recognising the name at all. 'Yes, very good. I should like to see it when it's finished,' he said politely. 'It has . . .' He paused, considering, and Laidislaw braced himself for some dull, Philistine conclusion to the sentence. 'So much *movement*,' the general completed, leaving Laidislaw to wonder whether it was, after all, the most banal of comments on a painting of a football game, or indeed a valid compliment on his technique.

The little party was moving on; the incident was over. Laidislaw relaxed and muttered to himself, 'So much *movement*!' still undecided whether to take umbrage or not. One of the figures in the ceremonial party detached itself and turned back. They had been standing behind Laidislaw – he had seen no-one but the general and the CO – but now as this man stalked towards him he saw a tall figure with a dark, handsome, frowning face. A little ripple of apprehension stirred him, like a cold breeze on his neck. Military discipline made him begin to rise, and this man did not tell him to stay seated. He was not interested in the picture. His eyes were fixed on Laidislaw's face, and they were eyes of cold contempt.

'So,' he said, looking Laidislaw up and down, 'this is the creature who dares to dishonour my family name. I must say I expected something more than a mere dancing-master.' Laidislaw stared in silence, and he added, 'You haven't an idea who I am, have you?'

'Lord Holkam?' Laidislaw managed to say at last.

'Stand to attention when a superior officer addresses you,' Holkam barked.

Laidislaw came unwillingly to attention, the evils of his situation occurring to him. They were in the army. Holkam was his senior, and he must obey his orders. He was helpless before Holkam's rank. Yet he could not stop himself replying. 'I thought from your comments we were to talk man to man, as equals, not soldier to soldier,' he said.

'Speak when you're spoken to,' snapped Holkam. 'In the first place, I am a soldier, you are not. You are a performing monkey. In the second place, I am a man, you are not. A butcher's dog stealing meat from a basket might be your equal, though I'm not sure about that. Even a butcher's dog can be trained to be useful.' Laidislaw quivered under the requirement to be silent, his throat tight with the words that wanted to spill out, his hands balling themselves into fists despite himself.

Holkam noticed the hands and gave him a sardonic sneer. 'And before you forget yourself, remember that the punishment for striking a superior officer is death.'

'You may be my senior, but you are not my superior,' Laidislaw said between clenched teeth.

Holkam raised an eyebrow. 'Oh, the dog bites, does it? You, my fine fellow, are nothing but an adulterer, the lowest form of life.'

'And if you weren't hiding behind your uniform I would fight you fair and square.'

Laidislaw saw that barb strike home.

Holkam's mouth tightened. But he did not retaliate. Indeed, if they were alone and not in the army, he could have thrashed the painter, beaten him to a pulp with his fists. But it would be lowering his dignity to argue the point. He had turned back on a whim, to see what he looked like, the dog who had seduced Violet, and he wished now he had not. It was worse than he had thought. Laidislaw was an upstart, a counter-jumper, a sneaking mountebank. Well, he would have his revenge – and he would eat it cold, and relish it the more.

He looked from Laidislaw to the painting. 'And is this how you spend your days?' he asked, his voice neutral.

'I am the battalion painter,' Laidislaw replied, unsure whether to be proud of that or not.

'Sir. You address me as "sir" – and that is the last time I shall overlook the omission, Private. Battalion painter, eh?'

'Yes – sir.'

'But I'm sure you would like to play a more active role in the war. When the Big Push comes, for instance, you'd like the chance to prove your courage? I dare say the others think you've landed a cushy job, and dislike you for it.'

Laidislaw didn't know what to answer. Anything he said would invite mockery, and might provoke retaliation. He could take it for himself, but he did not want Holkam to come down on Violet – and there was the baby to consider. He knew that Holkam knew about the baby. He didn't know whether Holkam knew that *he* knew, or whether that would make things worse. So he said nothing.

After a moment Holkam nodded, as though a question had been answered, and turned away. His group had got ahead and he must rejoin it before he was missed. Out of the corner of his eye he saw Laidislaw begin to relax as his attention was taken from him, and on an impulse he turned back. 'By the way – *Private* – when the war is over, if you have survived, I shall make sure that you never see the child. Do you understand?' And he walked away.

Laidislaw stood rigid with emotion until he was sure Holkam was not going to return, then collapsed onto his seat. They had been the most horrible few moments of his life – he had never liked confrontation, which perhaps was why he had always preferred the company of women. It was not that he was afraid, but the the smell of anger, the ozone taste in the air of fist-fights, had always revolted him, right from a boy. He wanted to thrash Holkam, and he hated himself for wanting it.

Amiens, the cathedral city, was sixteen miles behind the line, so it was out of range of artillery and, unlike Albert, had not been pulverised. Every kind of facility was available there, hotels, restaurants, bars, shops, churches; women, too, for those inclined that way. But undamaged civilisation was the greatest lure. Every officer who had free time, and could rustle up the transport, headed there whenever he could for an evening's recreation.

One evening Frank and some friends went into Amiens for dinner. They were strolling along the rue Noyon when an officer running down the steps of the hotel bumped into them. The rough-looking mongrel at his heels barked sharply, and Frank saw the winged badge of a pilot on his breast as he caught the man's arm for balance. Then his eyes went to the face with delighted recognition.

'Jack!'

'Frank!'

The brothers shook hands, laughing with pleasure. 'I heard you were out here, but I never thought we'd bump into each other,' Frank said.

'If not here, where?' said Jack. 'Everyone comes to Amiens sooner or later. But look at you! My little brother, the officer!' he grinned. 'You look every inch the part. All you need is that toy rifle of yours, and the Hussar kepi made of cardboard you used to set such store by. Remember how you howled when Jessie took it and wouldn't let you have it back?'

'If you insist on embarrassing me in front of my friends, I shall be forced to remember things from *your* childhood,' said Frank. 'Fellows, this is my big brother Jack. Jack, my particular friends Bill Prendergast, Freddie Mascall and Jock Langley.'

They shook hands all round. 'A flying man, eh?' said Prendergast. 'I've often wondered what the world looks like from up there.'

'Seen anything of the Germans?' Langley asked.

'We know where they are,' said Jack.

'Pity you can't just shoot them from up there,' said

Mascall, 'and save us all a deal of trouble. Drop bombs on them, or something.'

'Now where would be the fun in that for you?' Jack said.

'Quite right, Freddie,' said Prendergast. 'I want my crack at Fritz, now I've come all this way. Dashed poor show if we went home without firing a shot.'

'Where were you off to?' Frank asked. Jack explained that he had come into Amiens for dinner but couldn't locate which hotel his friends were dining at. 'Dine with us, then,' Frank said at once. 'I should love to have a jaw about home.'

It was decided, after a little wrangling, that the other three would go off on their own and allow the brothers to have a quiet time together. Jack then proposed, instead of a hotel restaurant, a little place he knew on the quai Bélu in the quartier St Leu. 'It's not much to look at,' he said. 'But the food's wonderful.'

The quartier St Leu was one of the older parts of the city, a maze of little canals and bridges like a miniature Venice, with the cathedral high up on its cliff brooding over it. Much of the area was run down and dirty, and other parts were occupied by small studios, garages and *ateliers*: the smell of oil, cheap cigarettes, rotting fishheads and sewage scented the air. Rug had a wonderful time putting his nose into unspeakable things. But one or two of the more open *quais* had taverns and cafés jostling shoulder to shoulder with shops and fish sheds, and the sudden influx of soldiers with money to spend had brought an upsurge of prosperity to them.

Jack led the way to Au Chat Affamé, whose exterior paintwork of garish blue had the virtue, at least, of being newly applied. Inside, it was dark and shabby, but the inevitable smell of French cigarettes and lavatories was overlaid with the cheerful scent of garlic, the checked tablecloths were spotless, and the welcome was warm.

'*Messieurs, messieurs, bonsoir! Soyez les bienvenus! Par ici, s'il vous plaît. Voici votre table – réservée exclusivement pour les officiers de goût et de discernement.'*

'He seems to know you all right, old fellow,' said Frank, amused.

'Can't do. I've only been here once before. I suspect it's flannel.'

The waiter looked back and beamed. 'But I can speak in English if you prefer. We 'ave a very nice table always for our brave allies – the best in 'ouse.'

The food was, as promised, very good. They began with Somme eels, done the local way in a vinegar and egg sauce, followed by saltmarsh lamb, cooked slowly with Picardy beans. By way of savoury they had the house speciality, leek tart, and then a plate of macaroons with a local sweet wine to dip them in. Under the table, Rug did very well out of scraps slipped down to him from both sides.

Frank sighed with pleasure at the end of it and said he had not eaten so well since he left Morland Place. 'It's quite a treasure, this place,' he said. The waiter, hovering, seemed pleased with the praise and proposed coffee and a *digestif* of a locally made apple brandy.

They had talked of home, inevitably.

'What do you think of the news from Morland Place?' Frank said. 'You've heard about Rob and Ethel's new baby?'

'You must have heard more recently than me,' Jack said. 'What was it? Is she all right?'

'You know Ethel – pops 'em out like shelling peas,' said Frank. 'It was another boy. They're calling it John.'

'A nice, plain name. Who was that after? We don't have any Johns in our family.'

'Oh, I think they just took a fancy to it. Anyway, that's one down and two to go.'

Jack grinned. 'Just to think of both of us waiting for babies at the same time!'

'A feast of new Comptons,' Frank agreed. 'When is yours due?'

'Not till next February. You'll have yours first.'

'Yes, in November. I wish I could be there. I wonder if I'll be due leave then.'

'There's not much to it, you know,' Jack reassured him, 'and Maria's young and healthy. Women do that sort of thing all the time.'

'You were there when Helen had her first,' Frank pointed out.

'Yes, and completely in the way, as the various women-folk made no bones about telling me. I had nothing to do but fret and ask foolish questions.'

Frank smiled. 'But, still, you were glad to be there asking them.'

Jack agreed. 'I had a letter from Jessie last week. A short one – she was very busy. But she seems to be liking the nursing well enough.'

'She's stuck it out all right – good old Jessie,' said Frank. 'It's comforting to know that if anything should happen to one, there'd be grand girls like her to take care of us.'

'Not so much of the girl now, though,' Jack said. 'She'll be twenty-six in December.'

'What else did she say?'

'Oh, this and that. She's seen Oliver Winchmore, but not Violet yet – they're all in a state of shock about Lord Overton, of course. Oliver took her out for dinner, which was decent of him. Emma's still in Scotland, and "fretting against the curb", as Jessie says. Her guardians don't mean to let her go until she turns twenty-one in January. They want to get her safely married off while they still hold the reins. Jessie says Emma wrote that she's always having men shoved at her, but because of the war they're getting older and younger – either sixteen or sixty, Emma says, and frightfully unsuitable.'

'Well, she only has to hold out a few months more,' said Frank. 'Then she can go to London and catch a young lord on leave. What else?'

'In the letter? Let me see – oh, yes, she writes that Polly's taking lessons in estate management now. Of course, Uncle Teddy indulges her – but what can she want to know about that for? Little James will inherit the estate, and long before that Uncle Teddy will have found her a rich husband.'

Frank grinned. 'Maybe she wants to manage the rich husband. I can't see her knuckling under to anyone, can you? Even if he was the Duke of Devonshire.'

It was a wonderful, comfortable chat. They spoke about anything but the war, ignoring the khaki everywhere, and the distant rumble of guns coming and going on the breeze like thunder rolling around hills. Only when the coffee and brandy were drained did Jack say, 'I suppose we won't have another dinner like this for a while.'

'Not until after the battle,' Frank agreed. 'Once they start the barrage there'll be no slipping into Amiens for something decent to eat.'

'There'll be four of us in it this time. You, me, Bertie – and Jessie said that Lennie wrote to Polly to say he was somewhere near Serre.'

'Will you be scared?' Frank asked suddenly.

'No,' said Jack. 'Somehow you can't be, up there. Even when you're having a hot time, you're too busy doing things to be scared, and afterwards you just forget it.'

'You're glad to be flying again?'

'I can't tell you how much so. I think it must be the way sailors miss the sea when they're ashore too long. It's like another world – high above the line, on a cool, clear morning, and down below everything on the ground so tiny and sharp you can see the smoke coming from an enemy train like a little thread of grey wool.' He grinned. 'And then a Boche fighter swoops down on you from above because you haven't been paying attention, and a burst of machine-gun fire turns your nacelle into a sieve!'

Frank laughed. 'I hope you don't tell Helen that sort of thing.'

'I tell Helen everything. But what about you? Shall you be scared, do you think?'

'One can't tell, really, until it happens, but I don't think so. I just want to get on with it. I wouldn't be able to live with myself if I hadn't done my duty – but to be honest, I'd hate to have missed out on it.'

'I know what you mean,' said Jack.

General Sir Douglas Haig had been content with the original plan for a joint Anglo-French action on the river Ancre near Albert in the autumn. The presence of the French veterans on the right would steady his untried troops, and attacking on a front of twenty-five miles, the Allies would surely crush the Germans and put them to flight. But the action at Verdun had changed things. By May, the French were asking officially for the offensive to be brought forward to the summer, to distract the Germans and give them some relief. And as they withdrew more and more men to bolster their desperate efforts around Verdun, it began to look as though, rather than being a joint assault, it would be a predominantly British one.

By June, when the French said they could not hold out beyond the end of the month, the plan had changed substantially. Now it was to be an almost wholly British attack, over a mere eight miles of front. There would be few French veterans to stiffen it. Moreover, Haig had had months less of the time he had counted on to train the New Army units. They were still hardly more than civilians with guns.

But Haig, a dour lowland Scottish Presbyterian, knew his duty. He had accepted the French plea for assistance, and since there was no help for it, he got on with his plans without complaint. To those near him, he no longer talked about defeating the Germans that summer in the French department of the Somme. Victory would now come in 1917, he said. The battle in Picardy would have three objects:

to relieve the French at Verdun, to inflict weakening losses on the Germans, and to place the British advantageously for next year's victory.

General Rawlinson – in command of the Fourth Army, which would bear the brunt of the fighting – wanted to take the German defences in stages. He wanted the initial attack limited to taking the German front-line trenches, and consolidating there while the artillery was brought up; then to attack the second line and, after further consolidation, the third.

Haig, however, believed that the initial advantages of Neuve Chapelle and Loos had been wasted by not pressing on at once, giving the Germans time to regroup and bring up artillery of their own. And Haig was a cavalryman, having begun his career in the Hussars, then serving with the Lancers. He had commanded mobile columns in the Boer War, and the static nature of the present conflict was a constant frustration to him. There was his beautiful cavalry, sitting doing nothing – or, worse still, being obliged to fight on foot! If only the infantry could break through the line and put the Germans to flight, the cavalry could pursue and clean them up. The war of movement that would follow was a war he knew how to fight and win.

Moreover, the government had recently threatened to disband the cavalry altogether by the end of the year, saying it was too expensive to keep the five divisions in idleness in France, what with the cost of fodder, and the manpower tied up with feeding and tending the horses. Such a dreadful thing must not be allowed to happen. So he rejected Rawlinson's ideas, and aimed at breaking through the German defences in one massive attack, so as to carry the fight into open country beyond. It was vital to maintain the momentum and keep the Germans on the back foot – and this time he would have sufficient troops to do it.

His front ran from Montauban on the river Somme in the south to the river Ancre in the north. The Fourth Army under General Rawlinson was to attack in the centre, before the town of Albert, take the German trenches and, if possible, press on to Bapaume, up on the Pozières Ridge. Three divisions of cavalry under Gough would be stationed directly behind the Fourth Army, ready to take advantage if there was a breakthrough. Meanwhile, the First and Second Armies, positioned on the flanks, would make constant threatening moves to confuse the Germans as to the real objective, and prevent them concentrating their reserves in the centre. The Third Army, positioned to the north of the action, would mount an all-out attack on Gommecourt, both to eliminate the awkward salient there – an object in itself – and to create a diversionary movement.

To ensure success, the attack would be preceded by the longest and heaviest artillery bombardment ever known – five days of it, using more than fifteen hundred guns – which would so shatter the German trenches that all the infantry would have to do would be to walk over no man's land and take them. The battle would take place on the 29th of June, and even the starting time had been decided long in advance: seven thirty, which was rather late, according to accepted custom, but would give the morning mists time to clear and allow the artillery commanders to see the positions they were shelling in daylight, and make any adjustments necessary. It would rob the infantry of the cover of twilight in their advance, but the French insisted it was worth it.

On Saturday the 24th of June the artillery barrage began, with everything from three-inch trench mortars to heavy howitzers, aimed at cutting the German wire, and pounding the German trenches, strongpoints, support lines and artillery positions. Each battery paused now and then to cool the guns, bring up more ammunition or rest the gun crews, but the firing continued non-stop, day and night. The noise was so tremendous it could be heard as far away as the south coast of England, telling its story: that the big battle everyone had been waiting for was approaching. Perhaps it was a warning to the Germans – if they didn't already know about it – but it was very cheering to the British troops at the Front, and the people back home, too.

CHAPTER EIGHTEEN

Bertie, Fenniman and Pennyfather were returning together from Battalion Headquarters when they saw an officer step down from a transport, heave out a bag, and then stand looking rather helpless as the transport drove away.

'Hullo-ullo,' said Bertie. 'That chap looks familiar. I think I know him.'

'Whether you do or not, he seems lost,' said Fenniman, 'and we can't abandon a fellow officer in distress. Come on.'

They changed direction and walked towards him, and as he turned his head, Bertie said, 'I do know him. It's Oliver Winchmore – you know, Violet Holkam's brother. I'm sure I've mentioned him.'

He called, Oliver turned, and a smile of mingled welcome and relief broke out. 'Bertie! Good heavens! To think of its being you!'

'More of a surprise that it's you,' Bertie countered, as they shook hands. 'My friends Fenniman, Pennyfather.'

'How do you do?' Oliver said cordially; and to Fenniman, 'I've heard a lot about you.'

Fenniman raised an eyebrow. 'Nothing slanderous, I hope?'

'But what are you doing here?' Bertie asked. 'I thought you were stuck in Blighty for a year.'

'So did I, but they relented at the last minute. It seems

an old fellow, an army doctor, hauled himself out of retirement and presented himself to the RAMC, so they remembered their promise to me and sent me over in time for the battle.' He flinched as a particularly heavy concussion shook the air around them and the ground under their feet. 'I say, are we safe here?'

Bertie grinned. 'Do you think I'd stand here talking to you if we weren't? But we might get knocked down – some of these drivers are wild fellows,' he added, as a loaded transport roared by within a whisker of them. 'Where are you headed?'

'The casualty clearing station. I have a friend already there who's going to settle me in. The transport corporal said I "couldn't miss it", damn his hide.'

'Walk along with us, then,' said Bertie. 'We go almost right past it.' They fell in together and lit cigarettes, and Bertie said, 'I was sorry to hear about your father.'

'It was a blow,' said Oliver. 'And when this call came, I did hesitate for a moment, because of leaving the mater and Violet. But Mum was shocked at the idea of not doing one's duty, let alone refusing military orders. She said Dad would turn in his grave.' He paused. 'Not that he has one, of course, but he was a soldier all his life. So we dried our tears, and here I am.'

'Ready to join the jolly fray,' said Fenniman.

'The more the merrier, that's what we say,' said Pennyfather.

'I must say, the noise of these guns convinces me at last that it's going to come off,' Oliver said. 'There's been talk for so long I'd started to discount it.'

'Oh, it's going to come off, all right,' Pennyfather said.

'We've just been having last-minute chats with our CO and staff,' said Fenniman, glancing at Bertie.

Bertie said, 'It's a new strategy. They've told us that instead of going over in our own way, as the circumstances dictate, we're all to attack in extended line at a steady pace.

As our artillery shells the enemy, we advance as close as possible behind the barrage, and the barrage lifts a specific distance at specific intervals.' He demonstrated with his hands. 'Troops and barrage creep along together. Obviously, with that plan, you can't have small groups of men dashing about all over the place and running into their own shell-fire.'

'Obviously!' said Fenniman drily.

'Is it not a good idea?' Oliver asked, reacting to the tone.

'If it works,' said Pennyfather. 'I suspect it's one of those ploys beloved of top brass – it looks so good on paper they can't resist it.'

'Given that so many of our men are green,' said Bertie, 'it's obviously tempting to want to keep them together and make them advance at a steady pace, rather than risk panic and disorder.'

'Sounds sensible.'

'Yes, and this bombardment you can hear . . .' Fenniman said, pausing as a deafening boom obliterated the end of his sentence. 'This bombardment is meant to pulverise the Hun in his trenches, so all we'll have to do anyway is to stroll across and count the bodies.'

'Well and good if it does,' said Bertie. 'But we've been disappointed by the results of the bombardment before. And if the Hun *isn't* pulverised, the extended line makes too good a target for old sweats like us to feel comfortable. We three were just deciding that if there's any resistance, we'd be better off running at them hell for leather and yelling like fury.'

'For one thing,' Fenniman took over, 'it gives Herr Wurst less time to get a shot in at you.'

'And for another,' said Pennyfather, 'it frightens them to fits.'

Oliver frowned. 'But surely the senior officers must know that, if you do?'

'Ah, who knows what senior officers know?' Fenniman said lightly.

Pennyfather said, 'One of the problems is that most of the officers in the field are as green as their men. You can't simply rely on their judgement. So the brass has to issue one order for everyone. One size fits all.'

Bertie grinned. 'But we have been out from the beginning.'

'And the mark of a good officer,' said Fenniman, 'is knowing when to ignore orders.'

Oliver said, 'Well, your secret is safe with me. This uniform sits upon the shoulders of a confirmed civilian. I'm a doctor first, second and third. I hear you were home recently, Bertie?'

'Last month,' said Bertie. 'How did you know?'

'Jessie told me. I took her out for dinner one evening.'

'She told me she was afraid of being seen with you because she's a nurse.'

'Oh, I'd thought of that. I took her to a place far away from any hospital.'

'That was nice of you,' said Bertie.

'Being nice was part of my campaign,' Oliver said. 'I asked her to marry me.'

In the middle of the din there seemed to Bertie to be a small but profound silence. Out of it he said neutrally, 'Did she accept?'

'She said she'd think about it.' He scrutinised Bertie's expression. 'Do you think it was too soon? She didn't seem to be offended.'

'I'm sure she wasn't. But I didn't know you cared for her in that way.'

Oliver didn't answer that. Instead he said to the others, 'I'm afraid this must be boring for you, all this family talk. We're cousins, of a sort, you see. Played together as children.'

'I've often envied Parke his childhood,' said Fenniman, who was an only child.

'It *was* fun,' Oliver admitted. 'Lord, how long ago it seems now! Do you remember that tremendous cricket match we had one year, Bertie? Me and Thomas, you, Jack, Robbie and Frank, poor old Ned, of course. And Ashley Morland was there, over from America, as I remember. And Maud's brother – I've forgotten his name.'

'Raymond.'

'Ray, that's right. He's dead too, of course – out in Africa. But we were all there that day, knocking the ball about, and Jessie and Violet sat watching us – do you remember? – and Jessie was mad as fire because we wouldn't let her play.'

'Yes,' said Bertie. 'I remember.'

'Happy days! And here we all are, at the Front.'

He looked around him with a rather distracted air, and Bertie had sympathy. For someone fresh from England the noise and activity could be bewildering at first.

Have you any tips for a new boy?' Oliver asked, as if following Bertie's thoughts.

'Look after your boots,' Bertie said promptly. 'They're impossible to replace out here.'

Oliver smiled. 'But seriously!'

'He is serious,' said Pennyfather. 'There's nothing worse than uncomfortable feet.'

'You should eat whenever food is offered,' said Fenniman. 'Never turn down a meal, even if you've just had one. And sleep whenever no-one wants you for anything. Food, sleep – and good boots. That's the secret of happiness.'

'I can see I'll get no sense out of you,' Oliver laughed.

'We're talking perfect sense,' said Fenniman, 'and we'll meet you when this is over so you can admit as much to us handsomely—'

'Over a bottle or two of wine,' said Bertie.

'Or three,' Fenniman corrected, after a thought.

'It's a bargain,' said Oliver, shaking hands. 'Here, or in Piccadilly?'

'Either,' said Bertie.

'Both,' said Fenniman and Pennyfather together.

* * *

While the bombardment continued, all the last-minute preparations were gone over. The battalion commanders had to decide who would go into the attack. In some earlier actions whole battalions had been virtually wiped out, which had made rebuilding them difficult. This time the commanders had been ordered to keep back ten per cent of their personnel in order to form the nucleus of a new battalion, should there be that sort of disaster. It was hard for them to choose because everybody wanted to go. Those picked to stay behind felt hard done-by, and were often teased by their companions. In one battalion a private, acting as a clerk in HQ, was told he would not be part of the attack because he was the only man who could write shorthand. He was so upset at being excluded that he cried, 'If I cut off my hands, can I go then?'

Equipment was issued, orders gone over again and again, pay books were made up, last letters home composed, will forms filled in. Battalions were paraded and addressed in inspiring terms by their commanding officers. One told his men that the barrage was doing their work for them: they would be able to stroll over with a walking-stick, smoking a pipe – they would hardly need a rifle.

Meanwhile, night raids had to be continued so that the Germans should not suspect anything unusual was in train. Reports came back from the raiders that in some places the wire had not been cut by the bombardment; or the Germans had crept out again during a pause to repair it. There, the shelling was renewed and increased. During the day the RFC was out in force, spotting for the artillery, reporting on damage, and flying over the German lines, destroying German observation balloons and keeping their spotter aeroplanes back so that the enemy artillery should remain blind.

But the weather was a problem. On the 26th and 27th there had been a series of those summer storms Jack and Bertie remembered from the early days of the war: a sudden massive gathering of clouds, a torrential downpour, and the murkiness afterwards as the lakes of water turned to steam in the sun's warmth. It was bad weather for flying, and with all the water lying about it would be bad underfoot for a battle. In the early hours of the 28th it was still raining heavily, just twenty-four hours from the moment the whistles were due to blow and the British Army was to go over the top. By mid-morning the rain had stopped, the skies cleared and the sun came out; but it would take time for the ground to dry out. The decision came down from Headquarters: the battle was to be delayed by forty-eight hours.

It meant a huge amount of reorganisation. The first wave of men, already settled uncomfortably in the front-line trenches, had to be recalled. Those who had been brought up ready to take their places after the off had to be moved back, and more remote troops told to stay put. The movements of two hundred battalions and their support units had to be redrawn; and the artillery were told they had to go on firing for another two days.

Some of the commanders were not displeased with the idea of two more days to get the German wire cut. Others were annoyed that, having worked their men into a peak of readiness and excitement, they had somehow to get them through forty-eight hours of anticlimax. In the battered farmhouse that was the West Herts officers' mess, Bertie, like all old soldiers, simply shrugged and took the opportunity to relax. It made no difference to him what day they attacked: he would do his duty just the same. And, as he said to Fenniman, 'At least it's an easier date to remember, if it is going to be the great victory – the first of July.'

Late in the afternoon of Friday, the 30th, the front-line troops began to march back to the positions they had evacuated two days ago, and as the night drew on, more and more men filed down into the communication trenches and shuffled their way forward, trying to get to their allotted positions for the off. Not all the trenches had dried out: in some places they had to wade through ankle-deep mud. Behind them, more and more units moved in, and the night was invested with muffled curses and sharp orders, complaints and arguments. In some places the Germans were still shelling, and the advancing troops had to fling themselves face down when a star shell burst over them.

But at last everyone was in the right place. In the trenches the men were packed tight and uncomfortably, unable to lie down. Still, most of them managed to doze on and off, propped against each other or the trench wall. Some talked quietly, others thought of those at home. One or two were sent back down the line at the last minute and were going to miss it, after all: an elderly corporal with violent stomach-cramps, a private who had fallen through a rotten duck-board and broken his leg, a Pal whose rifle had gone off by mistake and injured his foot – and one bemused Northampton, who was told his orders for leave had just come through.

By four o'clock dawn was coming, and there was enough light to see the German lines. It was a windless day, rather grey, misty near the rivers, and with a light drizzle here and there, which soon cleared away. Breakfast arrived – hot food for the lucky ones – and petrol cans full of tea laced with rum, which was known as 'gunfire'. Everyone was stiff and chilled from long inaction, and the hot drink and spirits did them good. By now they had got used to petrol-flavoured tea.

The British guns thundered. They had set up a routine of firing from six twenty-five to seven forty-five a.m. to get the Germans accustomed to it so that this morning when they stopped at seven thirty it might take the Germans by surprise, and keep them in their dugouts while the attack began. The rain had stopped and the sky was cloudless and blue, with the promise of a hot day. At seven twenty the barrage reached a crescendo, with every gun working flat out to pound the German line. The men in the trenches were awed and cheered by the sheer, deafening madness of it – and the rum had worked its magic, too. They were ready to go.

Lennie and his mates were crouched in an assembly trench to the north of Gommecourt, where they would be part of the diversionary attack. The British barrage had provoked heavy German retaliation, and shells were flying over and exploding all too near, so that sometimes they were spattered with earth and debris.

'Bloody 'ell, Yank,' said his nearest neighbour, roaring into his ear, 'Ah thowt our guns were supposed to've beat the buggers already.'

'We're meant to draw fire,' Lennie yelled back. 'That's what a diversion is.' Talking was too much of a strain, but he felt warm and safe, despite the shells, packed close in with his friends; and the thought of the battle to come was like a song in his mind. They had done good work, important work, in Egypt, but this was what he had joined up for, almost two years ago, that day in York. In a few minutes he and Summers and Parker and all the rest of them would be going out at last to show the enemy that he could not get away with what he had done, not while there were good men in the world.

Jack had been out on dawn patrol, but it had been too misty to see much of what was going on on the ground. The mist was like a low cloud layer, white-grey and continuous. Almost like grey water, it lapped at the edges of the uplands that rose above it into the sunlight; and he noticed an odd phenomenon, that it trembled and rippled from below with the force of the barrage going on out of sight to him, as if it were a lake and invisible stones were being lobbed into it.

Bertie and his men were in no man's land, having filed quietly out in the night and through their own wire to spread out in line and lie down to wait for the hour. They would be the first off at seven thirty. The German shells were passing over them but exploding well to their rear. He had spoken to his platoon officers and, whatever the top brass said, they were not going to walk slowly and give the Germans a target. During the night he had seen, through his field-glasses, men moving around in the German trenches, and he was convinced that the barrage had not knocked all the fight out of the enemy. It would not be a walk-over; but he knew from old experience that the Germans did not like being charged. *Take them at a run, and you can take them*, he thought.

He felt the presence of his men around him, the line stretching right and left into the darkness, and it was a good feeling. He thought of his friends Fenniman and Pennyfather – the three of them, together since the beginning, and still here. *'Still here,'* he whispered to the grass under his cheek; and he dozed lightly, and saw his cattle at Beaumont coming down to the brook to drink, slow-moving and peaceful in their own misty dawn. He dreamed he was lying in the long grass, dry after the summer. A golden wind was moving it gently back and forth, now revealing, now hiding the scene, so that he saw it like the glimpses of another world . . .

Frank in his trench checked his watch yet again, then thought that the movement might look nervous to his men, and stuffed his hands into his pockets. He was not at all nervous. They had planned and rehearsed until the whole battle was mapped out in detail in every mind, and now there was nothing left for the generals in their chateau to do: it was all up to them, the privates and sergeants and lieutenants. Frank knew his men and loved them: they were the best, the cream of humanity, brave, modest, self-effacing, humorous. He was proud to be with them. Several of them were looking at him now. One was rather pale and anxious, and Frank felt sorry for him. There was nothing to fear. They were going out to fight for their country and their loved ones at home, and there was nothing nobler a man could do. He met the eyes of the anxious man and, removing his hand from his pocket again, smiled and gave a little 'thumbs-up' sign.

Laidislaw was also in a trench, somewhat to his own surprise. He had been disappointed a week ago to be told he was one of the ten per cent staying behind. 'Your talents are too rare to risk in battle,' the CO had said – flattering, but not what he had hoped for. Then one day a lance-corporal had come round and given him an extra hundred rounds of ammunition. 'You'll need these for when we go over,' he had said. Later the same day an orderly had given him two hand-grenades and an entrenching tool. 'For the attack,' he had said.

'But I'm not going,' Laidislaw had told him.

'No good tellin' me, mate. I just do what I'm bloody told. An' I done it, right?'

So Laidislaw had gone to the adjutant, who had looked, for some reason, rather embarrassed.

'Ah, yes, it seems that you are to be part of the attack, after all,' he had said, avoiding Laidislaw's eyes. 'You'll be attached to A Company and go off in the first wave. Congratulations.'

'Thank you, sir. But may I ask—'

'Not now, there's a good chap. Bags to do. Just go and report to Captain Anderson. He'll tell you what to do.'

So here he was, not only in a trench with the other fighting men, but in the first wave, the honoured place. He was taut with excitement. It was not bloodthirstiness. He didn't even have any particular hatred of the Germans. It was simply that this was the most extraordinary adventure that could ever come a man's way, and he intended to enjoy every minute. It was mixed up with pride, with manhood, with the way Holkam had looked at him and called him a performing monkey; and it was to do with the drawings and paintings he had made over the past weeks, with his growing understanding of the men around him, and the beauty that was in them, in their firm and unwavering purpose. He felt, for the first time in his life, a part of the nation he lived in, intimately bound up with its expression of collective will, blood of its blood; its fate his own. The stern beauty of holiness was on him, on all of them, and though it was a rifle he held in his hands, not a brush, he was painting everything he saw in his mind, and the light in the pictures was exalting.

At seven twenty-eight a.m. the mines painstakingly laid by the sappers were blown. Jack, flying over La Boisselle near the centre of the line, saw the flash, then the earth beneath him seemed to heave like someone under a blanket in bed. The roar of the explosion came a moment later, with a buffet of air that tossed his DH2 up and sideways like a piece of paper. And then from where the earth had convulsed a great brown column of soil rose up, glittering a little where stones and moving particles caught the sun, climbing up and up until it seemed to pause, holding its shape in the air like a great dark Christmas tree four thousand feet high. Then it fell away, its silhouette shortening and widening until it had collapsed in a vast, dusty circle. A second explosion came a moment later, and another dark tree reared up into the sky. Jack circled the site for a minute or two, and as the fog of dust in the air cleared, he could see the craters below him, two staring white eyes in the green chalkland sward.

A sudden strange silence fell. It was seven thirty, and the guns were changing their elevation. Everything seemed still below him, the countryside basking in sunshine under a clear blue sky as though it was any ordinary summer day. He could see birds flying down there and, though he could not hear it over the sound of his engine, a dot hanging in the air that he knew was a skylark.

The barrage began again. It was time.

* * *

Lying out in no man's land, Bertie heard the skylark. Skylarks always made him think of Jessie, and for a precious second he allowed himself to see her face in his mind. Then the guns roared, he checked his watch and scrambled up, blowing his whistle. To either side of him, long lines of men rose in a sort of ripple, each five yards from his neighbour – he saw some adjust their dressing, glancing left and right, as though they were on the parade-ground. Then they advanced. On this land where they walked no man had trodden in daylight for two years, and few at night. It was little damaged so far, with few shell-holes. There were wild flowers growing in the grass, mouse-ear and meadow cranes-bill, sainfoin, vetch and clover; butterflies and small moths went up before them, and a rabbit went dashing away and bolted down a hole. He glanced back at his men, and saw their faces, eager, determined. Whatever apprehensions they may have had through the night had dispersed now they were on their way.

Then the German machine-guns opened up. It was like a sudden summer storm, except that the pelting raindrops were lethal lead: the air was thick with vicious, whizzing death. The barrage had not been as successful as the brass had supposed it would be, Bertie thought grimly. Up and down the line men were being hit, twirling and falling as he had seen so many times before since this war began. The long, steady line-abreast was the perfect target for machine-gunners: they were traversing left and right as though spraying with a fire-hose. Time to get going.

'Come on!' he yelled, stuck up his arm and started to run. He felt something strike his hand a hard blow even as he was dropping it again. He looked, and saw the top of his little finger was gone, though he felt nothing as yet. As he ran, he dragged out his handkerchief and tied it clumsily round his hand, thinking – as one thinks absurd things in the heat of the moment – that he had no time to go back and look for the missing bit. He reached the German wire and found it well cut – it was not difficult to scramble over. The men were advancing now in skirmishing order, presenting a less easy target, but such was the weight of German fire they were still falling in terrible numbers.

At last there was the German trench in front of him. A German officer jumped up onto the parapet and Bertie saw the jerky movement of his hand as he threw something, even as Bertie levelled his pistol and shot him. Something rounded and black flew towards him – a grenade. It landed over to the right of him, and out of the corner of his eye he saw Cooper pick it up automatically and throw it back. His heart clenched in protest but there was no time to shout before the thing was done. It exploded as it went over the parapet. The German machine-guns had fallen silent in the last few seconds and he heard now that his men were yelling as they ran. Rifles were thrown over the parapet in front of them, Germans were standing up with their hands raised, surrendering. '*Kamerad!*' one of them shouted. '*Kamerad!*'

Bertie glanced back, and saw how few of his men were left. Half of them had fallen to the machine-guns. The Germans saw it too, and those who had stepped out of the trench now seemed to change their minds, made a grab for their rifles and were shot for their pains. The West Herts did not falter, still came on yelling. Other Germans standing in the trench seemed in doubt whether to lower their hands or not. One levelled his rifle and fired, and the others began to do the same. It made the decision easy. 'Get 'em, lads!' Bertie yelled. There was a swift fusillade, and then they were jumping down into the trench and fighting hand-to-hand. Bertie shot one big blond lad coming towards him, then grabbed a fallen rifle and used the bayonet and the stock – more effective in the situation.

The fighting was fierce but short, and soon the remaining Germans were scrambling over the parados towards their second line and the village beyond, or running for the dugout entrance. A few who were not quick enough flung up their arms, their eyes wide with fear, screaming, '*Schießen Sie nicht!*'

They were quickly disarmed, and Bertie set about consolidating the trench. There were dead men in grey, and wounded ones, lying about, but there must be others down the dugout. It was important not to let them mount a counter-attack. 'The dugout must be cleared,' he said. He sent his sergeant, Mills, with three men to perform this task. There were two entrances to the dugout. He told Adams to throw a large, rounded stone down the stairs on one side, and it was enough to have the Germans, in terror of a hand grenade, come rushing up the other. Then Mills went down with his men to check there were none lingering.

'Electric light, sir, still on, would you believe it?' Mills said grimly, when he emerged. 'So much for the bloody barrage.'

'It's like Buck'nam bleedin' Palace down there,' one of the men said.

The prisoners seemed cowed and dispirited, and terrified of their captors. Bertie guessed they had been told tales of horror about what the English did to prisoners. When Hutton, out of kindness, offered a cigarette to one of the wounded, he stared at it as though it were an instrument of torture.

There was much to do, clearing the dead out of the way, attending to the wounded, piling the enemy arms, setting a guard at each end of their section of trench, disposing the others to guard the parados in case the Germans came back, and searching out supplies, food and water and any medical kit the Germans had left, in case they should be there long. It seemed likely, Bertie thought, that they would. The battle plan was for the attack to go in in a series of waves. The West Herts had been using a two-company front, with Bertie's A Company alongside B Company. Bertie's orders had been to consolidate when the first objective was taken, and when the mopping-up platoons of C Company

– which Pennyfather had taken over from him when they were both promoted – arrived, they would go on to the second objective.

But now there was a new element: the Germans had been using their artillery to pound British positions and front-line trenches, but now they had changed the elevation and were laying down fire right across no man's land. Because they had started out in no man's land, and because they had run, A Company had crossed ahead of it, but pity the poor fellows who had to get across now. There was certainly no sign of C Company yet, so for the moment Bertie's men were on their own.

Lennie's battalion had sustained casualties during the night from German shelling, and their assembly trenches were still very wet from the recent rain – some of the platoons had spent the night knee deep in water. Lennie was luckier, his part of the trench being only muddy. He and his friends were in the second wave, and when the whistle went they scrambled out, ran forward and jumped down into their own first-line trench. Ahead of them the smokescreen obscured the view, but they could hear the constant tacka-tacka-tack of the German machine-guns through the artillery's roar. Jumping down, Lennie almost landed on a dead man, and twisted his ankle trying to avoid him. A shell must have struck there, because the parapet was smashed flat and there were half a dozen dead Tommies. Lennie's scalp shifted backwards and his stomach tightened at the sight of the bloody wreckage. 'Gee, Christmas!' he whispered. One of his companions retched helplessly; another swore off a repetitive string, 'F—! F—! F—!' as though he would never stop. But there was no time to brood. Their officer was urging them on, up and out. With one thought about the pity of it, that these chaps had died before they ever had a chance even to attack, Lennie scrambled over the broken lip of the trench wall, staggered on a piece of debris, and then, mindful of orders, set off at a steady walk into the smoke.

The German machine-guns chattered their constant hate. Lennie felt and heard the bullets whistling past him, chopping away at the line. He saw Copfield go down, and Bellerby, and Bunter. There were dead men everywhere, men from the first wave, mown down in lines like dominoes. And when they came to the wire, the German wire that seven days of bombardment ought to have cut to shreds, they found it hardly touched, almost intact, barring their way. The reason was not far to seek: lying all around there were hundreds of orange 'toffee-apple' bombs, minus their sticks – duds that had failed to explode. Corporal Gatting, one of the veterans, cursed the armaments factories long and fluently. There were dead men all along the wire barrier, heaped in places. Some had tried to climb over and been shot as they struggled; hung over the wire teeth like washing, they seemed to struggle still as machine-gun bullets constantly struck them in the relentless traversing of the German guns.

'We've got to get through that lot somehow,' Gatting shouted. 'There's got to be a gap.'

Men were running up and down, trying to find a way through. Where there was a break in the wire, the Germans had had time to train their weapons, and shot them like sitting ducks as they struggled through. The fire seemed to intensify – how was that possible? – and Seaton, beside him, dropped flat, dragging Lennie down with him. He was not shot, however. He yelled, 'Get down, Yank, for Chrissake,' as Lennie landed beside him, and for a moment they could do nothing but press themselves flat to the earth and hope. After a while the intensity of fire let up a little, and Lennie cautiously raised his head. There was no-one left standing, though whether they were all dead or only sheltering like him it was impossible to tell.

He nudged Seaton with his elbow. 'I can see where we can get through,' he said.

'Are you mad? Like that lot?' He jerked his head towards the tattered scarecrows.

'No, not like that,' Lennie said. 'Underneath. Over there, there's a kind of dip. We can wriggle under. It'll be okay.'

Seaton raised his head a little and stared. He saw how it was. You couldn't see the dip when you were standing, only lying flat like this. 'Our packs'd catch on it,' he said.

'We'll take 'em off. Come on.' Lennie began wriggling forward on his stomach. Other heads were lifting now – not all dead, then – but no-one was moving yet. Lennie crawled past Corporal Gatting, who was minus most of his head. He had been shot through the eye. The sight only stiffened his resolve. Everyone had liked the corp. It was up to all of them to try to get through. At the wire they struggled out of their packs. 'I'll go first,' Lennie said.

'Face up,' said Seaton, suddenly.

'What's that?'

'Go under face up. That way you can see to unhook yourself.'

'Right it is!' Lennie saw the point. Face down one would be helpless to see where one was snagged. The earth was soft in the dip, and yielded as he pushed himself through with his feet, making the depression deeper. He held the wire carefully off his face, and once through, rolled quickly over onto his front to face Seaton. 'Shove the packs through!'

Seaton shoved and he hauled, and they were through. He stacked them behind him. Seaton was coming through now, and some of the others had seen what they were doing and were crawling in the same direction. Lennie had forgotten the Germans for a moment, until a bullet hit the pack behind him with a thump and a ping off the metal cap of his water-bottle. It was a stray bullet, he realised, but it would not be long before they saw what was happening and trained their guns on this new breach in their defences. 'Quick, quick, hurry up!'

Seaton was through and they struggled into their packs,

got up and started forward again. This time, by tacit consent, they did not walk, but jogged as fast as they could. Lennie glanced back, and saw more of their chaps coming through. With each passage the dip wore deeper and made it easier. Even Tubby Spicer might make it through. Holt and Summers caught them up – they had abandoned their packs and so could move faster – and little Parker was hot on their heels. The gunfire was less now. They had instinctively veered away from the hottest hail.

When they reached the German trench, it was deserted. Some of the first wave must have got this far, because there were signs of a battle, some dead Germans and the body of Lieutenant Vickers, who had been leading the first wave, shot through the neck and, to judge by the blood on his back, through the lung as well. The ladders had been pushed over against the parados – the first wave must have gone on, chasing the retreating Germans.

The five of them stood panting, looking about them nervously. 'What do we do now?' Summers said.

'We go on,' said Lennie. Why did they ask him? And yet it seemed natural for him to decide things for them.

'Hold up, there's old Tubby coming,' said Seaton.

Spicer was running towards them, making surprising speed considering that he was limping heavily. He reached the trench and almost threw himself in, landing half on top of Summers, who was fortunately big and strong enough to take it. Spicer's eyes were so wide they looked as though they might fall out of his head, but though he was sweating heavily he seemed strangely calm. 'By heck, I'm glad to see you fellers,' he panted.

'Any more coming?' Summers asked, massaging his shoulder where Spicer had hit him with his rifle butt.

'I dunno,' said Spicer. 'I saw half a dozen get through before the Germans found the place, but I don't know where they went.'

'How did you get through?' Lennie asked in amazement.

'I shoved me pack through first and they shot that. But they got me in the foot after, the bastards.'

Lennie was surprised, never having heard the peaceable Spicer use a swear word before.

'How bad is it, Tubby, mate?' Seaton asked.

'Dunno. Hurts like hell, but I can get along on it. I'm not taking me boot off to find out.'

In a graphic moment of imagination, Lennie realised Tubby was afraid the whole foot was only held together by his boot, and if he took it off it would fall to pieces.

'We should follow the others,' he said.

At that moment there was a heartfelt moan behind them, and they all jerked round as one of the dead Germans lifted his head. 'Christ, that one's still alive!' Holt shrieked, his voice shooting up to a boyhood tenor in his fright.

Lennie's rifle seemed to have swung itself up to his shoulder by its own volition, but the German did nothing but shake his head pitifully, and raise a trembling hand to his head. Lennie understood he was trying to salute them, and lowered his rifle. The man's face was colourless as whey, and he was lying in a small lake of blood. 'It's all right,' he said. 'He's had it.' And then it seemed a strange and horrible thing to have said about a fellow human being. He went over and crouched beside the man. He spoke no German, so could not ask him if there was anything he could do for him, but he put a kindly hand on the man's shoulder.

The German's eyes locked on his in pitiful appeal. He seemed very young to Lennie. There was a down of golden stubble coming through on his chin. His lips moved.

'What do you say?' Lennie asked him, leaning closer.

'*Wasser*,' the man whispered. '*Wasser*.'

'What's he say, Yank?' Seaton asked.

'I dunno. It's German I guess.'

'*Wasser. Bitte*.'

'Bitter?' said Holt, over-excited in his fear. 'Bastard wants a pint of bitter? So do all of us, mate, and we're more likely to get one than you, you Hun bastard.'

Lennie looked over his shoulder and frowned at Holt. 'Ssh! He's dying.'

'Maybe he just wants a drink,' Parker said. 'Maybe that's it, and he doesn't know how to ask for water.'

Lennie reached round for his water-bottle. It was precious stuff on a battlefield, and they had all been told many times not to waste it. But you couldn't refuse water to a dying man. What would Granny Ruth think of him if he did? The pathetic eyes grew eager. He slipped a hand under his enemy's head to raise it a little and carefully let a few sips trickle into the German boy's mouth. When he let him down again, the boy whispered, '*Danke*,' which Lennie understood well enough.

'We'd best get on, Yank,' said Parker, quietly. 'We can't help him.'

Lennie nodded and was about to rise, when the German grabbed his arm. '*Bitte*,' he said again, but this time he fluttered his fingers against his breast pocket. There was something in there he wanted. Lennie reckoned '*bitte*' couldn't mean beer after all. He undid the button and slipped his fingers in, and brought out the only thing there – a photograph of a woman. It had been done by a professional in a studio, and she was in a smart dress with earrings and beads round her neck, but she was much too old to be this lad's sweetheart: she must have been in her thirties, maybe older. He put the photograph into the trembling fingers, and the boy's eyes changed focus to gaze at it. '*Mutter*,' he whispered, and lifted it to his lips. Tears began to seep from his eyes.

Lennie stood up. 'We've got to go now,' he said, though the boy couldn't understand him. He wasn't listening anyway. He was looking at the photograph, and his neck trembled with the effort of holding his head up enough to do it.

'Come on, Yank,' said Parker.

'Aye, come on, leave that bastard. We need you,' said Holt.

Lennie turned away and became brisk. 'Right. I reckon we keep going in the same direction until we find the others. They must be somewhere,' he said. His companions stepped aside to let him pass, and he saw that he was expected to lead them literally as well as figuratively. He slung his rifle round, scrambled up the ladder and led them forward at a dog-trot towards the sound of firing. He saw the German boy's face clearly in his mind as he went, as if he were a loved one. Must have been his ma in the photograph, he thought. Maybe he didn't have a best girl. And he thought of Polly, and imagined himself kissing her photograph if he were going west – not that he had one. He would have liked to visualise Polly's face just then, but the German boy's was all he could conjure up. He wished he hadn't seen his tears. It must be lonely to die all alone like that. He wished he could have stayed with him to the end.

They found more men of the first wave lying dead in their path, but they didn't find any live ones. The fire they were trotting into became heavier, and soon they were under attack from a German strongpoint set up in the ruins of a farmhouse. They had to scuttle for shelter in a shell-hole, and once inside there was nothing to do except wait for help. Tubby Spicer was white with pain by then, and Summers had been wounded in the thigh, but they couldn't go back now. There was firing all around, and they had no idea where the rest of the British attack was. Lennie had the feeling that they were out there on their own, and he wondered if they would ever get back.

Along the whole length of the battlefield, eighteen miles or so, the waves went in, company following company in remorseless order, in some places battalion following battalion. Where no man's land was wide, there might be anything up to twenty waves in the open at once. They fell like grass before the machine-guns; and where the wire was not properly cut they fell in heaps at the few gaps, or as they tried to struggle through. At one point on the line, the CO saw that it was hopeless and stopped the later waves going out, setting them instead to fire at the Germans opposite, whom they could see standing up on their parapets shooting the wounded in no man's land.

Of those who got through, many found the German trenches almost untouched by the bombardment, and had a fierce battle on their hands before they could take them. Others found the trenches pulverised as promised, and scrambled through towards the second line. Up and down the Front there were pockets of success, trenches captured, footholds gained, scores of prisoners taken; fierce little battles, sometimes hand to hand, brought little local victories. But too many of those who had won through were 'in the air', and their conquests fragile without reinforcements.

And now the German barrage being laid down across the middle of no man's land was killing more than the machine-guns had. It looked hardly possible for reinforcements to get through at all.

CHAPTER NINETEEN

In a captured trench, it was hard to know what was going on elsewhere, even in the next bay. It might be held by one's own side, or the enemy, or be quite empty. Once he had secured his own section, Bertie's next job was to find out who was next door. At a rough guess he had about fifty left of the hundred men he had started off with, of whom two were too badly wounded to be capable of fighting on. He also had sixteen German prisoners to guard, but they did not seem likely to cause any trouble – they appeared only too glad to be out of the fighting and kindly treated by their captors.

With his servant Cooper, who had not strayed more than a couple of feet from him all morning, and a party of five, he went to reconnoitre. To his left he discovered the survivors from B Company. With the varying fortunes of war they had found the wire in front of them largely uncut, and in trying to get through the few gaps they had suffered heavy losses, including their captain and three of their lieutenants. There were only twenty of them, under the remaining lieutenant, Armstrong.

Beyond them Bertie found a handful of New Army men from the Huddersfield Chums under the command of a corporal, who looked so relieved to see a British officer Bertie thought he was going to collapse.

'We got Jerries next door, sir,' he said. 'We 'ad a look that way when we first got in. I dunno how many of 'em. We shot a couple and nipped back sharpish, and they haven't bothered us since, but . . .' He left the sentence eloquently unfinished. 'We thowt it were Jerries both sides. We didn't know what to do.'

'Have you cleared that dugout?' Bertie asked.

'Chucked a couple o' grenades down, sir, an' shouted, but no-one came up.'

'Those dugouts are big and deep. There could still be Germans down there, unhurt. You'll need to clear it properly. I'll send some of my men along to help you. When you're sure there's no-one else down there, get all the supplies together that you can find – especially grenades. We're running short of them. If there's any water, make sure you ration it. We don't know how long we'll be here, and it's going to be a hot day.'

'Yessir. You're right about that, sir,' said the corporal, squinting up at the brazen sky.

'Get some of this debris together and block off the end of the bay, and then lay sandbags up against it. You'll have to take them from the parapet, but we've less to fear from that direction.'

'Right, sir, I'll get on to it.' The corporal hesitated. 'Are the reserves coming, sir? Are we going to get reinforcements?'

'I sincerely hope so,' said Bertie. 'But I don't intend to give up this position without a fight, so if they don't come, we'll hold the Germans off by ourselves.' He glanced at the men within earshot, and added, 'Is there a man here who isn't worth ten Germans?'

They grinned and said, 'No, sir,' and 'Not likely!'

'Then we'll be fine.'

On the right of Bertie's own company, the Germans were still in possession, and Mills had already seen to the blocking of the end bay to prevent a counter-attack. In all, they held about two hundred yards of trench and, after further reconnoitring ahead, discovered a remnant of men from the Ulster

Rifles who had somehow got as far as the second line of German trenches, and were desperately clinging to a foothold there with thirty-eight men under a lieutenant. Bertie was equally determined not to lose this foothold, which would be their jumping-off point if and when reinforcements arrived. He sent some of his own company to join them, and carefully disposed his available force – about a hundred and twenty men in all – through the area he held.

He had done what he could; but they were under constant attack, and they could not hold out as they were for ever. His tiny force was sustaining casualties. If reinforcements didn't get through soon, he would have only two choices – either abandon the position that had been won at such cost, which he didn't mean to do, or go back across no man's land and fetch help. As the hard sun climbed the sky and still no-one came, it looked as though it would have to be the latter for him.

In their shell-hole, Lennie and his friends were in a sticky position. The Germans in the ruined cottage kept firing at them. Holt had been killed, shot through the neck. Seaton had been hit in the chest: they had propped him against the side of the hole and tried to make him comfortable, and at first he had panted and moaned, but he hadn't moved or made a sound for some time, and Lennie suspected he was dead. Tubby Spicer wasn't much use to them now – he kept fainting from the pain of his wounded foot, and they had to prop him out of the way, too. It was left to Lennie, little Parker and the wounded Summers to keep going.

They were running out of ammunition, and Lennie had suggested they did not fire unless a really good target presented itself. Once they stopped firing completely, the Germans would come out and get them, so it was important to make the ammo last as long as possible. 'We've got to hold out until reinforcements come,' he said. So they waited in silence, and every now and then a Hun would wonder if they were finished and look out, and then they'd take a pot at him. Summers reckoned they must have got half a dozen of them by now, but there was no knowing if they were really hits, or how many there had been to start with. And there was no knowing who else was around or who might come along next. If it was more British troops they were all right, but if it was Germans . . .

The bright sun climbed the sky, the booming of the guns went on and on, the air filled with dust and the ground trembled from time to time. They were very thirsty, but Lennie made them ration their water, not knowing how long it would have to last them. Fortunately Spicer was now unconscious, so he didn't need any. They took a drink each from one of the bottles. The Germans seemed to get tired of the situation and sortied from the back of their cottage, trying to creep up against the walls to overcome the little group in the shell-hole. There was a short, sharp exchange of shots, and the three survivors, aiming carefully, made the best use of their ammunition and picked off five of them, three probably dead, and two wounded who managed to make their way back to the cottage, before the enemy decided to give up the frontal assault.

But in the fray, Parker took a shot through the shoulder. While Lennie kept firing at anything that made a target, Summers bound up the wound as best he could, using his bayonet knife to tear a strip from Parker's shirt so as to make a kind of sling, holding the arm against his chest. It was the left arm, and Parker said he could still use his rifle, by propping the muzzle on the edge of the hole – but it would be impossible for him to aim properly, and despite his brave words, he was evidently in terrible pain, and might at any time faint away, like Spicer.

The three of them were silent for a while, watching the German position, firing now and then, and wondering how it would end. Finally Summers said, 'Yank, I reckon you and Nosy ought to make a run for it.'

'What?' said Lennie, startled. 'I'm not leaving you.'

'You've got to. You're not hurt, and Nosy's got both his legs. You two can make it back. I can't walk, and Tubby's out of the game. Sooner or later we're going to run out of ammo, and the Jerries'll come out and get us. No, listen!' He stopped Lennie's protest. 'When you're gone, I'll keep firing until we're out of ammo, and then I'll surrender. I'll wave a hanky or summat. The Jerries'll look after us.'

Would they? It wasn't spoken aloud, but the thought was in both their minds that they didn't know what Germans did in such a situation. If their positions were reversed, of course they would look after wounded Germans who surrendered but, well, after all, they *were* Huns, weren't they?

'I'm not leaving you,' Lennie said again.

Parker now spoke up, quietly: 'Lofty's right, Yank. Look, if we stay, we'll either get shot or taken prisoner, and that's two less to fight the bloody Boche. If we can get back, we can still be soldiers and do some good.'

It was true; but Lennie still felt a desperate indecision. To abandon Summers and Spicer – especially since he had 'taken command' of them – seemed a horrible betrayal. 'But we joined up together, we're friends. We've been together all the way. I can't leave you to save my own skin.'

'Don't be daft. You've got a chance. Take it. I would.' Summers met his eyes steadily. 'I'll be all right.'

Parker said, 'If we're going, we've got to go now.' He was white and his face was grim with pain.

A shot whistled past between them, only narrowly missing. 'Go on, for God's sake!' said Summers.

'Okay,' said Lennie. 'But I'll come back for you. I'll get help and come back for you.'

'Right,' said Summers. 'Go now. I'll cover you.'

Parker left him his rifle, since he could not fire it one-handed. That way he could use his right hand to steady his wounded left arm. He and Lennie eased themselves over the lip of the hole, slithering on their bellies like snakes, and when they heard Summers firing, they sprang to their feet and started to run. Lennie had never sprinted so fast before: the urgency of the situation pumped through his veins and he literally ran for his life. There was a blessed pause of a few seconds as the Germans were taken by surprise, and then they were shooting at the runners, but instead of taking aim they just sprayed the general direction with fire, and though bullets smacked the earth around, nothing touched them. Then they were out of range, safe for the time being. Parker sat down abruptly to rest, and Lennie hunkered beside him. 'Are you all right?'

Parker nodded, and then said tersely, 'I'll manage. Don't worry about me,' and shut his mouth tight to bite off the pain. Lennie looked back, but he couldn't see his friends down in the hole, though he could hear Summers firing still. He looked around. 'We'll go this way,' he said. 'There's more cover if anyone comes.'

Bertie's force was shrinking alarmingly, and there was nothing they could do for the wounded except bind them as best they could with what field bandages they could find, and put them down in a dugout for safety. More seriously, they were running out of ammunition. Still no-one came, the German barrage was still going on, and it was possible no-one knew they were here, or that they needed support. There was nothing for it but to go back and find out what was happening.

When he announced his intention to Armstrong, his servant, Cooper, said something he had never expected to hear. 'Let me go, sir.' Cooper was one of the remaining regulars from 1914, an old sweat, up to all the wangles, whose first priority was always his own comfort. Extreme circumstances certainly had odd effects on people, Bertie thought.

'Thanks, but it has to be me,' he said. 'I don't know what the situation is back there and I might have to pull rank to get anywhere. Armstrong, you're in charge while I'm gone.

Keep your eye on the chaps in the forward trench. Try to hold it if at all possible.'

'Yes, sir.'

Bertie had already gone a hundred yards before he realised Cooper was behind him. 'I'm not leaving you, sir,' he said, before Bertie could open his mouth.

'Then you're a bloody fool,' Bertie said, but he smiled as he said it, and Cooper smiled back – another rare event. Fancy the old devil being this keen on him, Bertie marvelled. 'Our best defence is speed, I think,' he said. 'No use trying to dodge every bullet – we'll get through or we won't. Go as fast as you can, and if I'm hit, you're to go on – that's an order!' He anticipated the objection. 'If I'm hit, you're to go on, make the report to the CO, and try to persuade him to send reinforcements.'

'Yessir,' said Cooper, a trifle sulkily.

It was a hair-raising journey. What saved them was the accuracy of the German bombardment: the shells struck at exact intervals in a dead straight line, the columns of earth thrown up, dark against the sun, like a row of French poplars. Oddly, their closest shave came when passing the British wire, when they came under fire from a jittery Tommy and had to fling themselves down flat. Bertie hoicked a handkerchief out of his pocket and without lifting his head waved it above him. When the firing stopped he rose cautiously to his knees and pointed to his and Cooper's khaki. After a moment an officer climbed up on the parapet and shouted for them to come in.

'Terribly sorry, sir,' he said, as he helped them down. 'The man's an idiot.' It was Lieutenant Allan, from D Company.

'Where is everyone?' Bertie demanded. 'Where's C Company?'

Allan made a helpless little gesture. 'Out there somewhere, sir. They went over on time. I'm afraid they caught it pretty hard.'

Bertie heard the words with no sense of shock. He had seen too many men fall today to be able to feel anything yet. 'And D Company?'

'Brigade orders, sir. They're not to go over. The reserve battalion's being held back, too.'

'Where's the CO?'

'Dead, sir,' said Allan.

'For Christ's sake,' Bertie muttered.

'Shot, sir, through the head, and killed. Major Fenniman's in charge now. He'll be in the HQ dugout.'

Thus Bertie found him, looking grey in the face and anxious, until he caught sight of Bertie and grinned almost fit to split his face. He grasped Bertie's hand, the other gripping his shoulder with painful relief. 'Of all the people I'm glad to see, you must be number one on the list! You're a sight for sore eyes – and not even wounded.'

'You think I ought to have been?'

'It's hardly decent,' Fenniman agreed. 'I don't know what you've been through, old boy, but I tell you it's worse being stuck here, not able to do anything about it.'

'Tell me about the CO.'

'He was almost frantic. Of course, we saw the carnage. It was worse when C Company went out because the German barrage had started then. And no messages came back – nothing. He was fidgeting about, and then suddenly he said, "I've got to go and see it through. I've got to lead my men." The adj tried to dissuade him, but he was determined to go. As soon as he got up on the parapet he was hit. The adj went out to him and managed to get him back, but he was dead – died instantly, I should think – and the adj was shot too, badly wounded.'

'God,' said Bertie, feelingly. What a waste – and no wonder Fenniman looked so strained! 'So you're in charge.'

'As you see.'

Bertie made his report to his friend in form, explaining the situation, and said, 'I've got to have more men. You must send reinforcements. We can't hold out much longer as we are, and I'm damned if I'll let go of those trenches. Let me have D Company.'

'No can do,' Fenniman said unhappily. 'It's orders, from Brigade. They're not to go over in the present circumstances.'

'Then give me *someone*. There must be *someone*.'

'There are a lot of stragglers – mostly B Company, who got stopped by the wire and managed to make their way back. C Company mostly got through or were hit, but there's a few of them around, and one or two of yours.'

'I'll have them,' said Bertie.

'And there are the odds and sods – cooks, stretcher-bearers, clerks.'

'I'll take them all. Anyone who can carry a gun.'

'Right-oh! I'll go and round 'em up. They'll be pretty fed up with having to go out again when they've just managed to get back.'

'Too bad for them!' said Bertie. He looked round. 'Where's Cooper?'

'Your servant? You brought him with you?'

'He insisted on coming – attached to me like a limpet, and now he's disappeared.'

'Scrounging, if I know anything about Cooper,' said Fenniman, who did. He had scrounged for them both on the long retreat from Mons. 'Best let him have his head.'

'You're right. Nothing is ever gained by coming between Cooper and his dispositions. If he makes himself comfortable, chances are he'll make me comfortable, too, in the process.'

Bertie took time, while Fenniman was rounding up the men, to get his wounded hand properly dressed. It made him a little sick to look at it, but the MO said he was pretty lucky, losing only an expendable part of his hand, and the left hand at that. 'And it's a clean wound. Cauterised by the bullet. Hardly any bleeding. Nothing really to do but keep it clean and let it heal.'

The men were assembled, and if they were fed up, they didn't show it. The odds and sods seemed eager to be off, and Bertie heard some of D Company telling them they were lucky blighters to be allowed to go and have a crack at Fritz. Many of those who had been over before had lost their packs, and these he put to carrying ammunition and stores. Cooper appeared at his elbow in the nick of time, with a haversack on his back. 'A few necessaries, sir.' He anticipated the question. 'I took the liberty of pledging your credit with Lowe, sir.' Lowe was the colonel's batman. Cooper shrugged in reply to Bertie's look. 'Well, sir, he don't need 'em no more. I got light stuff – chocolate, Horlicks tablets and the like.'

Fenniman shook his hand hard. 'I wish I was coming with you,' he said, his eyes searching Bertie's face as though to remember it.

'Someone's got to mind the shop. Don't worry, old chap, I'll be back.'

The odds were rather against it, as they both knew. But they were soldiers. This was what they did.

When Lennie and Parker neared the German trench, through which they had passed earlier, Lennie said, 'I wonder if that wounded Jerry I gave water to is dead now. I suppose he must be.' Parker didn't answer. Lennie turned to look, and saw that he had paused again to collect himself. 'Take your time, old man,' he said, and turned back to look at the trench again. People were moving about in it, and for a moment his heart lifted, thinking that reinforcements had come up. Then he saw, with a shock that made his heart clench, that they were wearing the *wrong helmets*. Not the Tommy's tin hat but grey soft caps and here and there an unmistakable *Pickelhaube*. 'Get down!' he hissed, dropping to the ground and pulling Parker down with him. The trench had been retaken. His mouth dried as he realised that if they had taken a few more steps someone must have seen them, and that would have been that. By stopping as he had, Parker had saved their lives.

Fortunately the Germans were all facing the other way, towards the British Front, the direction from which they expected trouble. 'What do we do now, Yank?' Parker whispered.

Lennie stared, racking his brain. Germans in front of him, Germans behind him – what *was* there to do? But he was *damned* if he would give up. Think, damn you, think! There must be a way out of this. Can't stay here, can't go on. He thought about Granny Ruth, who had been through a war worse than this one – the Civil War. What would she do, if she were a man and in his position? Out of his memory came her voice saying, 'If you can't find a way round a problem, you'll just have to ride right over it.' He grinned to himself, in spite of his predicament.

'What are you smiling about?' Parker asked, a little shortly. He couldn't see anything amusing in the situation.

'Thinking about my granny,' Lennie answered. 'A real hellion! Always reckoned to ride right over a fence instead of looking for a gate. She'd jump anything she could see daylight over.'

Then his face felt suddenly hot and then cold in quick succession as the ridiculous thought came to him. 'Nosy,' he whispered, 'we'll jump it.'

'*What?*'

Lennie lifted himself a little to look. He had always been a good athlete. He had long legs and, like Granny, he could jump anything. 'We'll jump right over it.'

Parker's eyes showed white as he turned his face to his friend. 'I don't think I can. Not – not over their heads. I can't.'

'You can!' Lennie said. 'How wide is a trench, anyhow? It's just a little old field ditch, when you come down to it. I bet you've jumped over ditches every day back home in Yorkshire.'

'I – I dunno,' said Parker. Lennie saw he was afraid – afraid of the Germans. He didn't want to go near them. It was a mad plan – exposing them at close quarters to Hun bullets and bayonets. Suppose when they jumped one of them just reached up and grabbed their ankles? That was the worst! Lennie shivered at the thought, and then steeled himself.

'You *can* do it,' he said firmly, 'and you're going to. If we stay here we're done for, and I'm not leaving you behind. Now, take a few deep breaths and follow me. Run like hell, don't think about the Jerries – and don't look down!'

Carefully he stood up. No-one shouted. They were still looking the other way. His heart was pounding and his scalp prickled. *This one's for you, Granny,* he thought. Parker, beside him, was up and taking deep breaths as ordered. 'It's just an old field ditch,' Lennie whispered to him. 'Ready? *Go!*'

They were off. From a standing start Lennie took great tearing strides, his excited eyes searching out the best place for a take-off. Parker, winged with fear, was beside him, matching step for step. Still no-one looked round. They couldn't hear their approach over the continuous bellowing of the guns. Three, two, one – and Lennie took off, feeling his muscles crack with the effort of jumping as fast and far as he could. He saw no glimpse of the men whose heads he cleared, but as he landed he heard their cries of astonishment. He landed clean, but Parker stumbled and gave a little cry, of alarm, perhaps, or pain from his wounded shoulder. Lennie grabbed his right upper arm and jerked him forward, preventing him from falling. Then they were running hard for a gap in the wire, beyond which he could see a wide, shallow dip where thick reeds grew. They would make for that.

The jabbering German voices grew higher with indignation, but their surprise had obviously inhibited them, for there was no rifle crack, no explosion of pain in his back.

Lennie's strides were so long now he was almost leaping; Parker was pounding doggedly beside him. The reeds were before them. Lennie grabbed Parker again, and then he was in the air, like their school football captain back home making a flying touchdown; they were both in the air, diving into the reeds, skidding face down, burrowing further in.

They stopped, and Lennie pressed himself flat, turning his face to the side to gasp for breath. The ground was spongy under him, the reeds were sharp, and the pungent smell of bogland filled his nostrils.

'Are you all right?' he asked. Parker didn't reply. Lennie turned his head to him, and saw he was white with pain, but conscious. 'Keep still,' Lennie said. 'They can't see us if we keep still.' Parker nodded slightly, and closed his eyes.

Now the Germans were firing, a positive fusillade, but the shots passed over or ranged wide. It was a perilous safety, but better than nothing. Well, what now? Lennie thought, when his breathing had returned to normal. They were on the right side of the German trench, but they still had no man's land to cross, and as soon as they left these reeds the Germans would see them and shoot them. They needed to hold on until dark, when they could slip away; but they were too close to the German line: sooner or later, some of their shots would find them.

The firing stopped, and after a moment he heard a German voice shouting in English: 'Tommee! Tommee! Are you there? Why don't you come in?' And then, 'Give up, Tommee! Come in to us. We won't shoot if you come in.'

Lennie laid a warning hand on Parker's arm and kept absolutely still, hoping that their breathing was not shaking the reeds. Perhaps if they kept still old Fritz might think they had been hit already.

The voice came again, stern now. 'Tommee, if you don't come we get angry. Don't make us fire again. Give up now and we be nice.'

Lennie was not in the least tempted. He would never

surrender – better to die here than be shamed that way. He thought for a moment of his friends back in their shell-hole, and a sharp pain caught his breath, because he realised Summers had felt the same. When he ran out of ammunition and the Germans came, he would not let himself be taken. He would fight with his bayonet and die like a soldier. If for no other reason, Lennie and Parker could never let the others down by surrendering.

The voice that had been haranguing them stopped, and there was silence for a moment; then the next phase began. They were firing rifle grenades. The explosions were strangely muffled by the boggy ground, but either they were bad shots or they didn't know exactly where in the reed bed they were. It must have been the ninth or tenth that sounded different. Its whine came close and the detonation was deafening. Even as he pressed his face into the mud Lennie felt a violent blow and searing pain to his leg. He swore silently, *Not my leg! Not my damn' leg!* The pain was terrible. Hadn't everyone said you didn't feel any pain at first? *God damn!* He rolled over as slowly as he could onto his back, and, panting with pain and the fear of what he would see, he raised his head just a little and looked down his body. His trouser leg was torn to bits and there was a mess of blood. Slowly, slowly he bent his knee towards his chest and reached out, finding his hands were trembling horribly. He felt with flinching fingers, and found blood, slippery exposed flesh, something thin and metallic where it never should have been. He got hold of it, and lost it through the slipperiness of the blood and the shaking of his fingers. *Coward!* he derided himself. *Don't be such a damned coward!* He got hold of the metal again and managed to pull it out through the pain that shrieked in him, then let his leg down and lay panting and cursing, while his whole body trembled like a hurt dog.

'Yank! Yank! Are you all right?' He became aware that Parker had been calling him plaintively for some time.

'All right,' he said. 'Keep still.'

Was he all right, though? Was he done for? There was blood on his face, too, and a stinging pain in his forehead and cheek. He felt them, and found more cuts from the shrapnel. He wiped his hand absently on his trousers. His leg was white-fire agony. Could he still run? Oh, *why* did it have to be his leg? He could have taken a wound in his arm, like Parker, and that wouldn't have mattered. The sound of more grenades – a sound he had simply ceased to notice while he was occupied with his wounds – came to him. They *couldn't* stay here. His leg would damn well have to hold him. But as soon as they broke cover the Boche would see them. They were in range. What were the odds they'd all miss?

Then he smelt it, the sharp, satisfying tang of smoke – not dirty old gunsmoke, but good clean smoke, like at home when Bessie had just lit the fire, the smell of burning kindling – or like when they had a bonfire of leaves out in the yard in fall. He eased himself over again onto his front to look. He understood suddenly, and almost laughed. One of the rifle grenades had set fire to the reeds. They were going to be burned out – but it didn't matter, because the smoke would give them cover, just enough so that they could get out and get moving without being shot at. Now, if only his leg would hold him . . . He could hear the German voices behind him, jabbering about what they had done. The smoke was drifting back and forth over the reeds, swinging like a grey cloth being waved, holding together because there was hardly any air movement. He felt there was enough of it now for him to sit up, get out his handkerchief (he'd used his field bandage on Parker) and tie it round his calf as tightly as he could. There was a chunk of flesh missing, he saw, and hoped it would not affect the muscle too much.

Parker sat up too and watched, and reached over to help with the knot.

'Are you ready?' Lennie said. 'We're going to make a run for it, while the smoke covers us.'

'I'm ready,' said Parker. 'But can you run?'

'I'll have to,' said Lennie. 'Come on.'

He took a couple of deep breaths, eased himself onto his haunches, and then, with a glance at Parker, launched himself out of the reeds. He almost fell the first time his weight came on his injured leg, and he made a couple of long, limping steps before he heard the outcry behind him. They had seen them – or at least seen the movement. 'Run!' he said to Parker. 'Don't worry about me. *Run!*'

Now the fear coursed again through Lennie's blood and he forgot his injury, forgot to limp, simply ran again, as he had run on the other side. There was a long rattle of shots, and then the sound of a machine-gun, but nothing touched him. The Germans must not be able to see them properly through the smoke. Parker pounded along, his breath sobbing now they didn't have to be quiet, holding his injured arm against his chest. Not being able to use his arms for balance made him clumsy, and when he stumbled, Lennie grabbed him and hauled him along, running like a mad thing across no man's land, feeling no pain, determined to live.

Somehow, Bertie and Cooper crossed the hell of fire and were not hit; but the guns and the shells took their toll of the men with them, and the relieving force they had started out with was reduced to thirty by the time they reached the trenches the West Herts were holding. But at least they had got fresh ammunition through, so they could hold out a little longer.

Armstrong seemed more than relieved to see him – evidently, Bertie thought, he had expected to be left in the lurch when Bertie was inevitably killed on the journey. More men had fallen casualty, but they were still holding on to their two positions – just.

'Is anyone else coming, sir?' he asked.

'Not yet,' said Bertie. 'They'll send another battalion

eventually – they must do. For the moment we're on our own, but we must hold on until they get here.'

The morning wore away, stifling hot now; everyone was weary from the noise of the guns, and the constant tension, the constant battle. Bertie's numbers were shrinking. He went across to the second-line trench and saw they could not hold on there any longer. It was a bitter thing to give it up, but the position was untenable, and if they did not come now they might not get back at all. He ordered them back to the first-line trench, and a while later watched angrily as the Germans reoccupied what they had vacated. Apart from other considerations, it gave the enemy a good position to fire at them from.

It was past noon when a messenger finally got through from Fenniman, but it was not about reinforcements. 'Brigade orders: no further attempts are to be made on the German positions today. You are to withdraw as soon as expedient and return to British first line.'

It was both a disappointment and a relief. He hated to give up the little they had achieved, but it could only be a matter of time before they were overrun. 'Mr Armstrong, we are to withdraw. You'll need to tell off a rearguard.'

'Yes, sir,' said Armstrong, whose arm was bound with a piece of torn shirt. Such was discipline that he did not show a flicker of relief, if indeed he felt one.

Now, thought Bertie, I've got to get 'em home.

The wounded were streaming back, in far greater numbers than had been expected. The advanced dressing stations gave the minimum of treatment, and removed and labelled the soldier's rifle before sending him on back. Walking wounded followed a route marked out with white tape, others were taken by motor ambulance, and all converged on the casualty clearing stations where there were better medical facilities. There, the nurses and orderlies sorted and classified them, redressed wounds where necessary, gave the lightly wounded reassurance and a cup of tea. The badly wounded lay on stretchers waiting their turn for the attention of the surgeons.

Inside the operating tent, Oliver felt he was working flat out, though Kit had told him that this was not as busy as it would be later. These were the wounded from the British trenches, and those who had fallen near the line and could be easily retrieved. It would not be until nightfall, probably, that the stretcher-bearers would be able to start bringing in the wounded from no man's land – those who had not bled to death in the mean time. Oliver had no reason to disbelieve him, yet it seemed to him things could not get more frantic than they already were.

The wounded were brought in and placed before him in a frightening stream of desperate wounds. He saw things that he had never seen before, even at the No. 2 back in London. The reason was that so many of the wounds before him were not survivable. He worked desperately to save a life, and failed, and went on to the next one. It was a relief when someone came before him whom he could definitely help. But he felt himself horribly slow and clumsy. He glanced across at Kit sometimes and marvelled at his sheer speed, and the rapidity of his decisions, and his admiration made him feel like the younger of the two. Between patients, Kit threw him a taut smile and a reassuring word. 'I've got quicker out of sheer repetition. You'll soon pick it up. Sometimes you have to turn the really bad ones away and concentrate on the ones you can save.'

'I don't know how you do that,' Oliver confessed.

'You'll work it out,' Kit said, and turned back to his table as another case was dumped before him.

As a doctor and a surgeon Oliver had long since got over any squeamishness, yet some of the mutilations that came before him came close to oversetting him. Exploding metal could do things to the human envelope of flesh that no-one should ever have to see, let alone suffer. He had not thought much about war before, but now he found himself thinking that it was madness, nothing less, to set man against metal in this way. The human body was a miracle of form and function, something that filled him with awe for its strength, complexity and grace. To see it reduced to badly butchered meat was an outrage. Sometimes that day he was close to tears; but the need for concentration and speed, and his growing physical weariness, gradually induced a sort of numbness that was a spiritual relief. He cut and stitched – like a mad tailor, he told himself – and ceased to think of the cases as men at all. It was the only way to get through.

Eighty-four battalions attacked in the first hour of the battle, and with mixed success. On the right wing, all the first objectives had been taken, the German front-line trenches were occupied, and the men were ready to advance towards Montauban. In the centre, where the cavalry waited to follow up the breakthrough, fortunes were mixed. The main road from Albert to Bapaume ran Roman-straight through Pozières and must be taken, but though some progress had been made, the terrain was very difficult there. On the flanks of this central attack some units had got footholds in the German trenches, but the road itself had not been taken and there had been heavy losses. North of Thiepval the Ulstermen had fought hard, advanced and taken the German trenches, but they were in the air, having created a deep salient into the German line, and were in danger of counter-attack from the village itself, which had not been taken. On the left wing, north of the river Ancre, one German strongpoint had been taken and there were a few isolated units holding sections of German trenches, but much of the first attack had failed. And at Gommecourt, one half of the pincer movement, which was meant to encircle the village, had achieved its first objectives and was prepared to push forward, but the other had been completely repulsed and made no advance at all.

For the generals at HQ there was nothing more they could do at this stage but to trust the commanders in the field. Even if reliable reports had come back, to change orders now would cause confusion and do more harm than good. Nearer the line, information coming back with the walking wounded and other stragglers was mixed. Some talked of heavy losses – it was not uncommon to claim to be the only survivor of one's platoon, but it was an old army custom and not necessarily true – while others spoke of enemy trenches taken and not a German left standing. Some Brigade commanders had seen the first waves go over and fall under fire and were wondering whether there was any point in sending the second, who had been supposed to cross no man's land in safety to German trenches already taken. On the other hand, large numbers of German prisoners had been brought back and were being marched off to the barbed-wire cages prepared for them. Not all who had been taken had arrived. Crossing no man's land could be as dangerous for them as for a Tommy. At Gommecourt around three hundred had been sent back, but only around a hundred and seventy had made it.

But whatever the early fortunes and disappointments, the day was still young and there were plenty of men in reserve. The artillery was firing steadily, there was no shortage of shells or ammunition, and no shortage of the will to win.

Only at the casualty clearing stations was there a serious problem. Before the battle General Rawlinson had personally ordered eighteen ambulance trains for the evacuation of the wounded to the base hospitals, but by noon only one had arrived, and half of the men it had taken away had been either the sick or the wounded from the previous day. Now the efficiency of the medical units further forward was bringing the wounded in large numbers to the CCSs, and the system was clogging up. All the tents were full, and men were being laid out in the fields, long lines of them, suffering under the hot sun. The need for the stretchers to be reused meant that the wounded had to be put down on a blanket or more often a makeshift spread of straw. The orderlies struggled to rig up some shade for those left outside, and to get them a drink of water and a cigarette, but more and more were arriving all the time and none was leaving. Oliver told one of the orderlies to run to his sleeping-tent and get a tin of fifty Capstans to distribute among the waiting men, and the RAMC major stormed off to the telephone to find out where the trains were. Oliver and Kit had long since ceased to notice that they were standing in blood. They worked on, pausing only now and then to flex aching fingers and rotate an aching neck, before bending to the task again.

Back in England, the first news of the battle was in the evening papers on the Saturday night. 'GERMAN DEFENCE BROKEN ON 16-MILE FRONT', blared the headline, with the subheading, BRITISH TROOPS' FINE WORK NORTH OF THE SOMME.

> After a steady bombardment of the German line, lasting a week, followed by a concentrated bombardment of special intensity, the British Army attacked the enemy this morning north of the Somme on a front of 16 miles. On the remainder of the British front raiding parties again succeeded in penetrating the enemy's defences at many points, inflicting loss on the enemy and taking many prisoners.

The editorial mentioned that there was a disposition to regard this as the beginning of the 'big advance', but that it was impossible for anyone 'on this side' to read the minds of General Joffre and Sir Douglas Haig. It might be just a raid to test the enemy's defences, or to draw German troops from other parts of the Front, or it might be the prelude to a much bigger attack on a still wider front. The editor warned that, while being prepared for news of great events, it was unwise to draw large conclusions from early reports of such attacks.

Elsewhere a special correspondent reported from British Headquarters that it was too early yet to give more than the barest particulars, as the fighting was still intensifying, but that British troops had already occupied the German front line and taken many prisoners while, as far as could be ascertained, British casualties had not been heavy.

With so little to go on, the newspapers had to fill their columns with the same thing repeated in as many different ways as they could think of, along with reminders of the last main action the previous September, and speculations about what the long bombardment would have meant to the Germans.

Despite the newspapers' warnings, those who had men at the Front in Picardy had gleaned enough hints to be sure that this *was* the start of the big advance. All now waited and longed for news from their own particular men. The York Commercials, it was known, were in the area and would be in the action. There was a particular tense hush in the city and its environs that evening, and few raised voices in the public houses that night; and on Sunday the churches and chapels entertained record congregations.

The Sunday papers brought little but some official reports from Sir Douglas Haig that there had been continued heavy fighting, and some long articles from special correspondents about what it had been like to be with the troops in the hours before the attack. York was pleased that one reporter had been following the fortunes of an unnamed 'North-country regiment', which they chose to believe was their own dear boys.

> How splendid they seemed, like the Heroes of another age, our glorious Youth, as they marched with a smart, swinging pace. I watched them pass, all those tall

Yorkshire men, and something of their spirit seemed to come out of the dark mass of their moving bodies and thrill the air. They were going up to the Line, without faltering, without looking back, and singing as they went!

CHAPTER TWENTY

On Sunday morning, when Jessie went down to the meal they called 'lunch', Beta beckoned her to a place she had saved at the end of a table. She had had her three hours off that morning, and was just coming on duty.

'The postman brought this for you,' she said, passing over an envelope. 'It's from France, so I thought you'd want it as soon as possible. It might be news of your relatives who were in the action yesterday.'

'But how could it get here so soon?' Jessie took the envelope. 'It's from Bertie,' she said. She hadn't expected to hear anything for a long time yet. But when she opened it, she saw at once that the date was Thursday's. As she read, she felt the blood rush to her cheeks. Beta saw it, and tactfully concentrated on her bread-and-butter.

> My love, my love, I met Oliver today, going up to his unit. He'd just arrived in France. He told me that he had seen you, and proposed marriage, and that you said you would think about it. Is it true? Are you going to accept him? He is a fine man, handsome, clever. He will have a good career after the war. Any woman would be proud to have him. I love you too much to be selfish, if it will give you a measure of comfort and happiness. You must consider only yourself in this. I want you to be happy, and if this is what

you want, it's what I want too. But please write soon and tell me your mind. I can't bear the uncertainty. I think of you too much for my own good. We will be going into the line soon. You and I both know what may happen. One can only do one's duty and trust in God. If we are parted, remember the future is only a veil, and beyond it is another Country. Oh, my love, I take you with me in my heart.

Ever your
Bertie

She had not written to him of Oliver's offer, not supposing he would ever hear about it. Now he had gone into battle without knowing how she felt. If he should fall . . . She looked up and saw Beta's expression of concern: her face must have been registering more than she wished. She tried to smile, but it was a poor, thin thing.

Beta spoke. 'It's not – he's not—?'

'This was written before they went into action,' Jessie said.

When they returned to the ward Sister Fitton met them at the door and said, 'Hurry up, Nurses, there's a great deal to do. We've just heard there's a convoy coming in. We have to make room for the wounded. All but the really ill patients will be going down to Embury Ward. Then the beds will have to be made, instruments sterilised, dressing-trays prepared. You won't be taking your time off this afternoon, Morland.'

'No, Sister,' Jessie said. Everyone gave up their free time when a convoy came in. It was expected – but no-one would have dreamed of doing otherwise.

They had, as Sister Fitton said, plenty to do – too much, indeed, but they got it done anyway. When the siren sounded to say that the first ambulance was drawing in, they were ready. Then they were plunged into a maelstrom of work such as Jessie could not have imagined before. These men were fresh from the battlefield, still in their muddy and chalk-smeared uniforms – most of them lousy – few of them with anything more than field bandages, caked in their own blood, over their wounds. And such wounds! Jessie helped the orderly transfer the first soldier from the stretcher to the bed, and was struck with a sort of frozen terror as she contemplated the ruin of a man before her. She was afraid to touch him. She didn't know where to start. For an instant she wanted to burst into tears and run away, and her hands trembled so much she had to clasp them together to stop them. But then experience, and her own sense of duty, took charge. This was her work, and this man was depending on her. The thought of what he had suffered and must be suffering still, which had paralysed her for a moment, now galvanised her. She picked up the scissors, smiled at him, laid a hand for an instant on his to reassure him. 'Don't be afraid. You're in good hands now. We'll take care of you,' she said. She was proud to hear her voice come out calm and steady, and was rewarded by the faintest flicker of relief in the suffering face.

On Monday there was more in the newspapers, though most of the reports were significantly without detail, and not all were accurate. The action of the 1st of July was continuing, they said. The British Army had advanced with great success in some quarters. The villages of Montauban, Serre and Contalmaison had been taken. There were 9500 German prisoners, almost all unwounded, and significant capture of guns and war *matériel*. The fortress of Fricourt had fallen on the 2nd, and La Boisselle would soon be in British hands. Progress would be slow but steady, with the need to consolidate every gain.

To the vague but cheering paragraphs in the newspapers were soon added the accounts of wounded men coming back. Each had his story to tell, and each account was completely personal, minute as to detail but without any idea of the bigger picture. But there were enough who had witnessed the terrible losses of the first advances – and whose stories lost nothing by exaggeration – for rumours to begin to fly about the country.

They hit particularly hard in the towns that had provided Pals units, who were now hearing that entire battalions had been wiped out. In the absence of any real information, crowds gathered in anxious murmuring groups in public houses and on street corners, while others besieged the newspaper offices and the town hall for names, names, names. Now the fatal weakness of the Pals system began to be seen: in a normal battalion, the recruits came from all over the country and the losses were equally spread; but with a Pals battalion, an entire football team, the whole former staff of a small factory, all the young men in a single street might fall at the same time. The local losses were huge, overwhelming.

In the *York Mercury* on Thursday, along with reports that the fifth day of the offensive had been 'wholly favourable', came the headline,

YORKSHIRE'S NOBLE PART IN
GREAT BATTLE

HEROES OF THE SOMME

YORK 'COMMERCIALS' BATTALION LOSES MANY MEN

And now names began to appear: on Thursday those of five officers who had officially been reported as killed, along with a photograph of each and a brief account of who he was and what he had done before enlisting; on Friday more officers and the first of the non-commissioned officers and privates killed, and a long list of the wounded. In the back-streets of York blinds were drawn, men went off to work with black bands hastily sewn to their sleeves. Letters of condolence flooded into the post office, along with a continuing stream of letters from the War Office, each bringing personal grief to a little group of people who had been waiting in agony for news.

At Morland Place, Teddy read out the names. So many were known to him: he had helped bring the battalion into being. Others were personally known to the family: railway employees, men from Ned's factory, farm workers, former servants. Both the Bellerby boys from White House Farm, Joe and Tom, were casualties, Tom, the younger, killed in the first attack, Joe wounded and brought in after lying out in no man's land for twenty-four hours. The big names of York, Bayliss, Pobgee, Havergill, all featured in the lists. James Peckitt, heir to Peckitt's Boots and Shoes, who had joined as a ranker and been given a commission two months ago, was dead, aged nineteen; Captain Richard Canthorpe, elder boy of the owner of Canthorpe's Optical Equipment Company, was dead, aged twenty-seven.

With the names there were photographs. It was the photographs, appearing every day, which were perhaps the hardest to bear. Most of the subjects were in their service caps, the pictures taken with such pride when they had first got their uniforms. The young faces – so young! – looked out with imperishable dignity and sometimes a faint, pleased smile, at the world they were so proud to serve, so eager to offer their life for. And in the midst of their sorrow, the families were proud, too, and their pride, and the respect of their neighbours for the sacrifice, kept their backs straight and their heads high.

The Commercials had been in action at Serre, where the fighting had been bitter. Serre had been the extreme left wing of the main attack, and to the left of them had been a section of line where no attack had been made, the gap between them and the diversionary advance on Gommecourt. The Germans, of course, could see that there was no preparation for action in that section, and had been able to pour all their forces into defending Serre. Wilder reports during the week after the battle said that only seven of the battalion had come back from the field. As the list of names of killed and injured grew longer day by day, it sometimes felt as if the figure must have been true. There *were* families who were receiving letters from their sons who were unhurt, but naturally they did not command much attention in the prevailing shock and grief.

For the family at Morland Place, news of their own particular sons was slow in coming. The first they had was one of those Field Service Post Cards, which had printed phrases on the back to be deleted as applicable (with the stern warning that if anything was added the post card would be destroyed). All the phrases had been crossed out except

I have been admitted into hospital
wounded
and am going on well
Letter follows at first opportunity

It was from Lennie, and it arrived on the Thursday, the 6th. It was postmarked the 5th, and Teddy concluded that it must have been posted in England, which meant the dear boy was in an English hospital somewhere. He hurried off to see what he could do about finding out where he was.

Never before had Maria read the newspapers with such attention as now every day she pored over the columns of report and speculation, while her mother watched her across the breakfast table, nervously sipping her tea. On the Tuesday she found a piece in *The Times* – which was generally regarded as being more accurate than the other papers because it got its information from the German reports of the battle published by newspapers in neutral countries. It was a short account of what the Londons had been doing in the great attack.

It began with general praise of the battalion, saying that they were an outstanding unit whose recruits were mostly intelligent, well-educated men who would have been officers in any other division. It went on to say that they had formed one prong of the two-pronged attack at Gommecourt. The Londons had gone over the top at seven thirty a.m., and attacked with such courage, enthusiasm and verve that they had taken the German front-line trenches at once. By nine a.m. they were reported to have taken all their objectives and to be in possession of the whole south side of the salient, from where they were to link up with the attack coming in from the north. It had been a first-rate piece of work that could not have been done better by regulars – praise indeed!

Mrs Stanhope had Maria read it again to her, slowly, then said, 'So it doesn't mention Frank by name?'

'No, Mother, of course not,' said Maria. 'It's just a general report.'

'And where is this place they attacked, dear?'

Maria leafed through until she came to another report, which showed a rather blurred and indistinct map of the area. Mrs Stanhope peered at it hopefully, as though it might tell her something, and sighed. 'I do think he might have written. He ought to know that anxiety is not good for you in your delicate condition.'

'I don't suppose he's had a chance yet, Mother. It says the fighting is still going on. He won't be able to write until he gets out of the line and back to their billet.'

'I'm sure he could write in the evening,' Mrs Stanhope complained. 'They surely don't fight at night-time, do they?'

'No, Mother, but they'd be on duty as long as they were in the trenches,' Maria said patiently.

'Well, it doesn't take long to dash off a note,' Mrs Stanhope sniffed. 'I do hope, Maria, that he isn't going to prove an *inattentive* husband. I did have my doubts when you decided to marry him, and when I look at this tiny place he's left you in, after all you've told me of Morland Place . . .'

Gratitude, Maria thought, had a short life. She didn't rise to the bait, knowing Mother was still suffering from the loss of Daddy and the shock of finding out she was destitute.

Later that morning, a letter came from Frank. Maria's heart leaped when she saw the writing on the envelope; but it was dated the 30th of June, the day before the battle.

> My own darling wife, we go up to the line tonight. I am absolutely certain I shall come through all right, but just in case I get a knock-out, I want you to know that I have no fear of death, except in the sense that everyone must fear it, as something unknown they must go through. Death is only the gateway through which we must pass into our real Life. Viewed like that, there is nothing to fear from death, and nothing to regret, except the thought of leaving you, and our dear baby. But the years we might spend together in this world are as nothing compared with the eternity we will have together in the world to come. I know what I am doing is right and good. I could not come home to you, or spend the rest of my life with you, as I am certain I shall, if I had failed to do my duty by our country and our people when we were up against it. I kiss this letter. Darling, lay your lips where mine have been, and remember that I shall be loving you as dearly at the moment you are reading this as I do now while writing it.
>
> Ever your devoted husband,
>
> Frank Compton

Maria folded the letter and slipped it into her pocket. At various moments during the day she liked to put her hand in and touch it, and feel that in doing so she was touching the hand that had written it. She felt his confidence, and took comfort from it. He had said he thought he might be wounded but not killed, and though she could not bear the thought of his being hurt in any way, it was a bargain she was prepared to make, if it was what was necessary to have him alive and coming home to her.

At the casualty clearing stations, the work went on unremittingly. Oliver and Kit took no rest the first day. By midnight on the 1st of July only five ambulance trains had run, one in the morning, two in the afternoon and two in the evening. They removed a little more than three thousand casualties. But ten thousand wounded had reached the CCSs in the central part of the line, where the Fourth Army was attacking, and there was only accommodation for nine thousand. When darkness fell, the work of retrieving the wounded from no man's land began in earnest and a further flood descended on the overflowing stations. Ambulance drivers, already exhausted from their day's labours, drove from place to place in the dark, searching for somewhere to deliver their loads. The field ambulances, unable to send the wounded on, had to accommodate them in barns and sheds and fields, where they were still in danger from German shells. And all around the CCSs, wounded men lay on blankets in the open, waiting to be attended to. For many, what had been a simple wound was complicated by the delay, and some paid with their lives. Rations also ran low, and many went hungry.

At ten o'clock on the morning of the 2nd, Oliver was told to stand down for two hours. It was his first break – they were being let off in relays. He had long since gone past any physical awareness of his tiredness, and the major more or less had to prise the scalpel from his fingers. He wandered back to his tent where he washed as best he could, ate some biscuits, then collapsed onto his cot. When he was woken two hours later he wished he had never stopped, because he felt far worse for his short rest. Every bone ached, his head felt full of cotton wool, and his eyes burned in their sockets as if their lubricating fluid had turned to sand. He sat stupidly on the edge of his camp-bed and yawned and yawned, and wondered how he could be of any use to anyone now. But his batman thrust a mug of hot coffee into his hands, brewed so strong you could have trotted a mouse across it, and when he had drunk his way down that he felt a little closer to being alive than he had five minutes ago. He returned to his labours, and noted that, inside the tent, the scene looked exactly as it had when he had left, except that Kit was not there, having gone off in his turn. He took his place at a table, and at once a wounded man was put in front of him. It was, he thought madly, like the service at the best restaurants. Then his mind snapped into position, as though on elastic, and he plunged back into the seemingly endless work.

Frantic telephone calls and outraged complaints during the night had had their effect, and every available train in the British area had been diverted. They came and went constantly, being filled and despatched the moment they arrived, and gradually the backlog of cases was moved out. During that day and the next, non-stop train movements took around thirty thousand casualties away, and by the morning of the 4th, the Director of Medical Services reported that he was satisfied the arrangements were now working smoothly.

Oliver and Kit heard this being spoken of in the background, but for them their focus was minute and unrelenting, fixed on the few square inches of flesh on which they were working at any moment. After that first terrible day, things grew just a little more ordered, and they were sent off duty at regular intervals to get food and to snatch a little sleep, while the flood of wounded eased from a deluge to a heavy flow. At the French ports of Boulogne and Dieppe and Le Havre, the hospital ships took on their loads and crossed in endless succession to Southampton, where a train left every hour taking wounded to hospitals all over the country, wherever there was room.

* * *

At the No. 1 General, there was no off-time, and nurses worked well beyond their normal hours. For the first two nights, as convoys kept coming in, the day nurses stayed on right through the night, and were let off at intervals during the following day to change their aprons and sleep in a cubicle set aside for the purpose. Jessie was kept so busy, she hardly had time to think about Bertie, Jack, Frank or Lennie. They were merely a background anxiety, like the distant rumble of thunder – or of the guns.

On Wednesday she received a hastily scribbled note from Helen to say that Jack had written.

> They have all been flying almost non-stop, mostly artillery spotting, but despite the 'Archie' and several 'dog-fights' he has come to no harm. He writes a great deal about his view of the battle, but I won't trouble you with repeating it. No doubt he will write to you in due course and recount it all. For now, I know you will only want to know he is well.

Then on Thursday evening she received a note from her mother, reporting what they had heard of Lennie, asking if she had heard yet from Bertie, and begging her to pass on immediately any news she had of any of them.

And on Friday she received, like a lifeline, a letter from Bertie. It was dated Wednesday evening.

> We came out of the line in the early hours of this morning. The fighting goes on, though nothing like as intensely as on the first two days. That was a pretty sort of hell! As hot as anything we've seen so far. We had some success, though not as much as we'd have liked, but we've given the Boche a bloody nose. I'm afraid some of the New Army men are disappointed, having believed they would walk over and win the war in one day. They acquitted themselves magnificently, however, with such steadiness

and courage they might have been veterans. My own battalion took quite a hit, and since Saturday night we have had to be reinforced in our trenches by half a bttn of KOYLI – tall, splendid chaps who reminded me painfully of 'home'! We marched back to billets this morning, and at roll-call were down to 380 out of the 720 we started with. We lost a great many officers, including the CO – and Pennyfather was hit, head and knee, I don't know how badly. He's back in England now. I was wounded, but not seriously. Fenniman did not go over, and is now acting CO. I imagine, given the number of casualties, that you have been kept too busy to write. As to what I said in my last – I still mean it, and if being 'engaged' to Winchmore means that you do not feel able to correspond with me, only give me the hint and it will all stop. But please try to send me a line, one way or the other. I hope you have good news of your brothers and cousin. All these menfolk are such trouble to you!

God bless you.

Bertie

He was safe! Oh, but wounded! He said not seriously, but she knew how little he regarded such things. He had taken a terrible wound in the arm in the retreat from Mons, and soldiered on with it. *How* was he wounded? *Where* was he wounded? Had he had it attended to? Was he in pain? When she slept, her fevered dreams had her dressing his wound again and again, and it was different every time (always something she had dealt with in reality in the hours just past), so that she never got to the end of trying to tend him.

But he was alive, and safe for the moment, out of the line. She forewent her sleep at the next break to write to him – though afterwards she was never sure how coherent the letter could have been – and told him that she was *not* engaged to Oliver, and had only told Oliver she would think about it so as not to hurt his feelings. Her love for Bertie was stronger than ever. She loved Oliver like a brother, as she had loved Ned, and she was not going to make the same mistake again.

On Saturday morning she received a further note from her mother, to say that Lennie was in St Bartholomew's hospital in London. When Jessie was next off duty could she go along and see him and find out how bad it was? Jessie shook her head wryly at the idea of being off duty; but when she went on the ward, Sister Fitton said that the worst of the emergency was over, and they would all have their off-time that day. Jessie was given two-to-five. As soon as she was released, she took the tram, changed to another at Vauxhall, and trundled along to the ancient blackened hulk of the hospital, where the east wing had been given over to sick and wounded soldiers.

There were a great many wounded from Picardy there, and it took some enquiry to find Lennie, but she discovered him at last, sitting up in bed in the usual charity-chest striped pyjamas, looking rather pale but remarkably cheerful. He had a bandage round his forehead and a sutured gash in one cheek, and there was a cage under the bedclothes that reminded her uncomfortably of poor Daltry.

But Lennie's face split into a grin when he saw her, so he couldn't be desperately hurt. He received her gifts of cigarettes and chocolate with enthusiastic thanks. 'Though, truth to say, I'm gladdest of all just to see a friendly face! It's good of you to come. You must have been rushed off your feet since Saturday.'

'We have,' she said. 'This is my first time off.'

'And you've given it up to come and see me!' He shook his head, and bit his lip as tears came to his eyes.

Jessie saw he was not as calm and cheerful as he had tried to appear. It was his way, to hide his feelings. But he was young, a long way from home, and hurt. It would be surprising if he weren't in danger of weeping a little. 'Was it very bad?' she asked.

The real pain burst out. 'All the fellows I joined with – all gone west! Seaton, Holt, Spicer. I saw Seaton die, I think. He gave a kind of gasp . . . I got Parker back, but he's got a terrible wound in his shoulder. And Summers – we had to leave him behind, in a shell-hole, with the Jerries firing at him. He'll be dead now, too. I know he wouldn't surrender.'

Jessie nodded. 'It's hard to be the one to survive,' she said. 'It makes you feel guilty that you aren't dead too.'

'You understand,' he said gratefully. 'Guilty – that's just how I feel.'

'But, Lennie, think of all the people who are glad you're alive. They were so happy at Morland Place to hear from you.'

'How's Polly?' he asked eagerly.

'Relieved,' Jessie said. She had no idea, but it hardly mattered what she said, as long as she comforted him. 'She hasn't been able to sleep for worrying. I dare say they'll be coming to visit you soon. But tell me, how bad is your leg?'

'It was a piece of shrapnel in the calf. It took out a chunk of muscle. It's pretty bad, but I'm not going to die of it. It's a good Blighty-one, that's all. Should be worth a few weeks of leave. I got these cuts on my face at the same time. And then when I was waiting to be seen at the ADS, I got hit again, but that was only a flesh wound, in the arm.' He gestured to his right bicep. 'I was pretty lucky because I'd lost my tin hat by then, so it could have been a knock-out for me. A fellow lying nearby got his head nearly taken off. That was pretty bad. The Boche kept on shelling us.'

'Did you have to wait very long to be seen?' Jessie asked.

'Long enough,' he admitted. 'But when they came along at last I made them take little Parker. He was much worse than me, poor old Nosy. I say, I wish you could find out for me what happened to him. I hoped we'd be on the same hospital ship, but he went such a long time before me, I don't even know what hospital he's at.'

'Uncle Teddy's the man for that. He's very good at finding people,' said Jessie, and thought with a pang of Ned. Not Ned, of course. He'd never be able to find Ned. Perhaps it was that failure that made him persevere. 'I'll write and ask him, if you like.'

'Do you really think he'll come and visit me?' Lennie asked shyly.

'I expect so,' Jessie said. 'He comes to London regularly.'

'And Polly?'

That was a trickier question. 'If Uncle Teddy allows it,' she said tactfully; and Lennie, with his old-fashioned ideas of etiquette, thought that a perfectly reasonable answer.

Out at rest, the West Herts were unusually quiet. Those who had not joined the action the first day felt awkward in the presence of the survivors, though it was not their fault or their choice to have been kept back. Everyone was worn out from the spell in the trenches, nerves stretched to the limit by the constant noise of their own artillery, the intolerable shrieking of German shells, the continual alarms. Now, away from it, most of all it was the missing faces haunting them. It seemed impossible to speak a sentence or think a thought without old So-and-so's absence interrupting it. During the nights everyone had done his stint at going out to fetch in the wounded, and later the nearest dead. Even so, they knew they had marched out leaving an unknown number of their companions behind. There were bodies it was impossible to retrieve because of where they lay – and others that had been blown to such shreds they never would be found.

So they settled down to clean their equipment without the usual noisy banter, talking quietly to each other, reminiscing like old men recalling the battles of long ago. And when someone started a song, it wasn't one of the rousing, wry, cynical Tommy songs, like 'Back in Billets' or 'Kiss the Sergeant for me, Mother' or 'Bullets for Breakfast', but the tender, melancholy strain of 'Keep the Home Fires Burning'.

But a couple of days of relative quiet and better food revived their spirits. Some of the lightly wounded came back, and many stragglers. Tales began to be told more boastfully, and even those who had not been in the first day's attack had their stories of near misses from shells and night forays into no man's land. And they gloried in the exploits of their companions, whose honour belonged to all of them. Much talked of was Major Parke's solo crossing of no man's land to fetch reinforcements, and the way he had led them back when they had had to give up the trench. It was thanks to him, they reckoned, that ninety-one of A Company had made it back.

The arrival of several sacks of mail worked its usual medicine too. While mail for missing men was sent back, by custom parcels were not returned, but shared out among the whole company. So there was chocolate and tinned meat and cake and cigarettes in plenty for everyone, biscuits, sardines, and extra sugar in the tea. There were sad moments, too – Harrup's wife had tucked a photograph of the baby between some chocolate bars; and Milcher's parents had sent two tins of sugar, each containing a half-crown, one from Mum and one from Dad. No-one quite liked to spend them. They gave them eventually to Bertie to dispose of. He converted them into a bottle of whisky, and everyone had a dash in his evening tea and toasted Milcher that way.

One thing no-one thought about was the overall plan of battle and whether it had succeeded or failed. That was not their business. It was one thing for the New Army to chatter about strategy; but they were regulars, and they scorned such airy-fairy dispute. All the same, they were pleased when their divisional commander visited them and gave a speech, praising them. They had advanced, he said, 'undismayed by heavy artillery or deadly machine-gun fire. It was a magnificent display of disciplined courage worthy of the best traditions of the British race.'

It was true, and they knew it. They received the praise without smirking or shuffling, as their just meed.

The general went on, 'We had a most difficult part of the line to attack, and faced formidable resistance from the Germans, who kept their best troops for us, but still you gave Jerry a bloody nose! So although we did not do all we hoped to, you more than pulled your weight, and by your splendid courage, determination and discipline, you held the enemy down and enabled our friends in other parts of the line to achieve the brilliant successes that they have. We have got to stick it out and keep on hammering, and next time, God willing, we will pull off a big thing. With splendid troops like you, who are determined to stick it out and do your duty, we are certain of winning through to a glorious victory. I salute every one of you as a comrade-in arms, and rejoice that I have the privilege of commanding such a band of heroes as you have proved yourselves to be. God bless you all.'

After the dismiss, as the men walked away, Bertie overheard a few of their comments.

'T'warn't a bad ol' speech, really.'

'Well, it's no more than the truth.'

'We'll get the bastards next time. Like the Old Man said, we gave old Fritz what-for. He won't forget *that* in a hurry.'

'Did you see that pickle-helmet Jonesy picked up while we was in that trench? I wouldn't mind one o' them for a soovyneer!'

Someone started up one of their ruder songs, 'Stick a Sausage on Your Spike, Kaiser Bill', and the rest joined in, grinning at each other. So Bertie knew everything was all right.

Violet had received a scribbled note from Laidislaw telling her that he was 'going over the top' with the others after all. She had no experience of thinking about what a battle really meant, for Holkam was with Headquarters. So at first she was merely surprised, and then rather pleased and proud

– since that was evidently the way Octavian expected her to feel about it. She knew he was brave and noble and would be splendid in action.

The early accounts of the battle, vague as they were, gave her no material for anxiety. She did little more than glance at the headlines, and feel glad, on a patriotic as well as a personal level, that things were going well. But as the week progressed she began to hear the names of some of the officers who had fallen, names she knew very well. Tommy Draycott – who had married Angela Burnet, one of the girls she had come out with – had been shot as soon as he climbed out of his trench. He had not gone two yards, so it was said, before he was shot in the thigh. They got him back to an aid station, but the bullet had severed some important blood vessel and he died only minutes later. Kind, amusing, genial Tommy – all the girls had liked him, and envied Angela when she got him; Tommy with that little forelock of fair hair that always *would* fall forward, no matter how much oil he used, so that his friends used to call him the Shetland Pony – Tommy was dead. It was so hard to believe. He was just such another man as her father had been when young – handsome, good-natured and popular.

Then, as the week went on, there were others: Billy Wentworth and Tim Westerham were both badly injured, Peter Hargrave was missing – Emma had had a crush on him for a while. And then the word came that Kit Dawnay had been killed. Kit had been one of her beaux, and Lady Dawnay was one of her mother's friends, one of the few who had stood by the Overtons when Violet's scandal had broken. She couldn't bear it that Kit Dawnay should be dead.

So now the fact that she hadn't heard from Laidislaw took on an awful significance. And *why* had he been told at the last minute that he was going, after all? It seemed like a malign action of Fate, as if some inchoate force – Providence, the army, God, even – were conspiring against them. He would have been safe, left behind; now he had gone into terrible danger.

She asked her mother – her only source now that Oliver had gone to the Front – for information. Venetia could do nothing but to try to soothe her. Yes, soldiers did get killed sometimes, but many more of them came through all right. There was nothing to be done about it but pray, and trust to God.

But hadn't Lady Dawnay prayed and trusted? And Kit Dawnay was dead. What were Octavian's chances, if so many of the young men she knew were dead?

Venetia, trying to keep her daughter calm for the baby's sake, had other things to think about. Was it Holkam who had had Laidislaw sent to the Front in the first place? Was it his influence that had changed Laidislaw's orders at the last moment? If he came through this action, how long would Uriah the Hittite last, if someone was determined to keep him in the forefront? She felt helpless and angry; the more helpless and angry because she always remembered Beauty's words, about Laidislaw having to face the same dangers as every other man. Comforting Violet, and bereft now of Oliver's support, she longed and longed for her husband, missed him with such violence that sometimes, lying wakeful in the night, she could hardly breathe with it, and had to sit up, dizzy and alone. Oh, Beauty! Not fair! We were supposed to grow old together. *Not fair!*

Each day brought with it the ominous absence of word from Laidislaw at the Front. Venetia ministered to her daughter, tried to keep her cheerful, persuaded her to take a walk in the garden each day, for the baby's sake. She wondered briefly if Jessie would come and visit if asked, thinking that perhaps she was the one old friend Violet would like to see; but a second thought told her that at the moment there was no chance that Jessie would be able to come. Venetia had heard there were twenty thousand casualties from the first day, which would mean, according to the usual ratio, fourteen thousand wounded. It was not excessive, considering more than half a million men had been involved, but it was still a large number.

And then on Saturday came the letter. The whole household had been waiting for it. It had hardly hit the hall mat before it was being borne up the stairs on a silver salver at the closest Burton had ever come to a run.

Venetia herself took it into Violet's room, where she was still in bed, and was rewarded by seeing the light and joy return to that pale face with its shadowed eyes. Violet fumbled the letter open, tearing the envelope badly in her haste. Then she lifted her eyes to her mother's, and said, 'He's safe.'

'Thank God,' said Venetia.

Sanders came in with the usual tray of coffee and bread-and-butter. Her face betrayed that she had really come to get the news, and Venetia took pity on her and said, 'He's all right.'

The maid had, in a stroke of genius, brought two cups, and Venetia poured for them both and sipped the powerful brew – had the chef supposed they would need it stronger than usual? Violet read her letter. Venetia was glad for her daughter's sake to see it was a long one.

> It was the most extraordinary experience of my life – not one a sane person could possibly wish for – and yet I am glad I have been through it! To live so intensely is not given to ordinary men in ordinary life. The sensation, the excitement, the brilliance of it all was like a fierce light making every colour and outline clear, sharp, important. To place one's life at risk in that way is to own it the more absolutely afterwards. I feel more alive than I have ever been, and every breath has a savour I have never known. The sound of a bird, the sight of a leaf blowing across my path – I have to stop and wonder at them as I never did before. The thing

itself was terrible – blood and dirt and pain and noise – noise most of all, intolerable noise – and yet out of it has come this visionary sensation, a buoyancy, as though my very bones had turned to pure light.

We are out 'at rest' now, and my good CO, dreadfully apologetic that I was made to go 'over the top' at all – though I try to hint that there's no need – excuses me all fatigues so that I can paint. As you can imagine, I am in a frenzy of creation all day and far into the night, trying to get down all I have seen before the inspiration fades. There is a quality to my painting that was not there before, and more than ever I am convinced I was sent here for a purpose. What other painter ever had this chance to capture the essence of war?

All this, fascinating though it was, was not what Violet had wanted from the letter. To know he was safe, yes – but she wanted, *needed*, something more personal to her. She found it in the last paragraph.

In all this, did I forget you? No, my love, you were with me, most of all when shells were bursting around me and death came close, for you are the very reason of life. I think of you constantly, not when I have solitude, for I never do, but when I seek it, for you are my solitude, my place of rest. I am not sorry that the war has called me away – though I regret every moment I am not with you – because it has made me understand more clearly than I ever could at home what you are to me. In a strange way what is here, what I see, is defined by what you are, in absence and yet always present in my mind. How can I explain? The poor human words – I love you – are so inadequate. When I come home I hope to find a way to make you know it. To be with you – can such perfect happiness exist in this sullen world? Oh, so dear and far and near –

too far from me, and yet as close as my heartbeat. I long more than life itself to place a single kiss upon your hair, and hang my love around you like a garland.

Violet finished reading. She didn't say anything, only looked at her mother with a sort of mute gratitude, which told its story. She didn't offer Venetia the letter, and Venetia didn't ask to read it. She had a suspicion that what the young man wrote to her daughter would disturb her even more than the basic fact of their affair. Violet lay back against her pillows, the letter under her hand, which was resting on the swell of her belly, as though she were putting it as close as possible to the child, his child. She closed her eyes, and drew a deep breath, her first for days.

Maria received a letter on Saturday morning, too. It was from France, but it was not in Frank's handwriting, though the hand was educated. Something cold and heavy seemed to settle in her stomach, and she was glad her mother had not come down yet. To guard against interruption, she took it out into the garden to read, sitting on the old kitchen chair with the broken back, which she had placed in the sunny spot under the cherry tree, to represent the bench she hoped to have there one day.

Near Courcelles, France. Thursday, 6th July 1916
Dear Mrs Compton,
It is with the greatest regret that I must inform you of the death of your husband, Lt Frank Compton, on Saturday, 1st July, during the action around Gommecourt. Lt Compton led his men over the top in the first wave, and advanced without flinching into heavy enemy fire. He fell halfway across no man's land. One of my men who was with him tells me he died instantly, shot through the heart, and would have felt nothing. Because of the continuing action it was not

possible to get to him until Tuesday night. The body was interred here yesterday with a short ceremony, and he lies with his men and fellow officers who fell with him. His grave is marked with a cross.

Lt Compton was an exemplary officer, and was much loved both by his men and his fellow officers. He will be very much missed by us all. I beg to extend my most heartfelt sympathies to you at this sad time, and remain,

Yours very sincerely,

J. F. Carlton-Bassett, Lt Col.

Maria sat holding the letter in her lap for a long time. It was a warm day, but windy, and the wind was warm too, like living breath as it stirred the hairs on the top of her head, and the leaves of the tree above her. They rustled, with a whispering noise, and laid their flickering shadows over her, and the little cherries bobbed like the earrings on a dancing girl. They would be ripe soon, but he would never taste them. He would never sit with her on a bench under this tree, and watch the shadows creep across the grass as the sun turned.

She sat still for so long that the striped cat from next door came stalking up without seeing her, hunting flies in the grass, with much crouching and absurd, tigerish leaps. She watched him out of a world of pain. Mrs Stanhope called from the house, and the cat straightened up to look towards the sound, then saw Maria, and came on tiptoe to press against her legs. She reached down automatically to stroke his head, which he butted up under her fingers. It felt surprisingly hard and near under the thin silk of fur. She thought she would remember the touch of the cat's head and the sun-dapple of leaves for ever.

The maid must have told Mother where she was, because she appeared at the back door now, shading her eyes to see. She called something that Maria didn't hear. There seemed to be something wrong with her ears at the moment – they were full of a roaring. And her throat hurt so much, she had to put her hand to it and rub it.

Mrs Stanhope came towards her, concerned at her lack of response. 'Maria, dear, are you all right? I called you twice.'

Maria couldn't answer, with her tight, straining throat. Then Mrs Stanhope saw the letter in her lap.

CHAPTER TWENTY-ONE

Henrietta went to pay a visit of condolence to Mrs Bellerby at White House Farm. She could not drive herself in the pony-phaeton, because Jessie's Bhutias were out on loan to a farmer, and she had never learned to drive a motor-car, so she had Jessie's Hotspur saddled and rode over. She was vaguely pleased to find that her habit, which she had not worn for a long time, still fitted her. It was important, these days, to have little things to be pleased about. Hotspur had not been getting enough exercise lately, but he behaved himself like a gentleman. Even though he danced a little in his pleasure to be out, he laid his feet as delicately as if he were on eggshells, and his bounces were no more unseating than being rocked in a rowing-boat on a lake.

Bellerby was out about his work, and the older children, Christopher, Mary and Rosie, were at school; only the baby, Stephen, who would be two at Christmas, was with his mother. Mrs Bellerby came out from the kitchen when she heard the hoofs, and seeing who it was sent the child away to play in the garden. She came to take Hotspur's head as Henrietta slid down.

She was a hill-woman, from the Yorkshire Dales, and she always moved well, head high and proud. Now in her grief she was almost queenly. 'You'll come in, maistress, and tek a cup o' tea,' she said. It was not a question. Not to take tea would have been as much of an insult as not to offer it.

She gave Henrietta the old title because, though Alice was Teddy's wife, everyone knew it was Henrietta, born and raised at Morland Place, who was its real mistress.

Henrietta tied Hotspur to the gatepost and followed Mrs Bellerby inside. The kitchen was scrubbed and spotless, the range blackleaded to a deep glow, the pewter on the mantelpiece polished; a blue vase of blowsy white roses was on the windowsill, where the window stood open, letting in the soft air and the sound of birdsong. Henrietta glanced around to see what work she had interrupted, and was surprised to see no evidence of food preparation – whether it was making bread, baking cakes, or getting the men's dinner started, it took up most of Mrs Bellerby's time every day. She also had her hens and the kitchen garden to tend, butter and cheese to make for the house, and in their seasons the various picklings and bottlings and preservings – to say nothing of caring for the odd orphan piglet and lamb. But today, for all the kitchen revealed, she might have been sitting doing nothing.

Mrs Bellerby was about to lead the way through to the sitting-room, as befitted such an eminent visitor, but Henrietta stopped her. 'Please don't trouble. I am very happy here in the kitchen. I hope I didn't interrupt your work.'

For a tell-tale instant Mrs Bellerby looked around her with blind, bewildered eyes; and then she said, 'Ah were just going to do a bit o' mending. Nothing that can't wait.' It was a moment's confusion that told how badly she had been hit by what had happened to her sons. There was nothing else to show it. Her face was as smooth as marble.

She moved about, making the tea – getting out the best cups and saucers, spooning the 'good' tea from the brightly coloured tin on the high mantelpiece into the best china pot, filling it from the kettle that sat always steaming on the range. She laid everything out on the table, and Henrietta did not offer to help – that would have been improper – and was glad of her disinclination to chatter. It was a relief to get away from words. There had been so many of them lately – kindly, well meant, but every one an intrusion.

'You'll tek a piece o' my plum cake,' Mrs Bellerby said, fetching the big round tin from the dresser. She served the cake in the traditional manner, with a slice of Wensleydale cheese, and watched impassively as Henrietta tasted.

It was delicious, moist, full of fruit, with a hint of spice. 'It's very good,' Henrietta said. 'Mrs Stark says you make the best plum cake in Yorkshire.'

Mrs Bellerby merely nodded, as though she was listening to something else at the same time. 'Ah were thinking o' sending one to our Joe. Will they let him have it, if Ah do, d'ye think, maistress? Ah knawnt about hospitals. None of us has ever been in one.'

'I'm sure they will,' Henrietta said, and since the subject had come up, 'How is he going along?'

'We've heard na more yet,' she said. 'Just what his mate, that was with him at the time, wrote to us.'

'I'm so sorry about Tom,' Henrietta said.

Mrs Bellerby looked at her, and as their eyes met the mask suddenly dropped and she was there, clear and stark and filled with pain. 'Ay, well, we're both in t'same boat, aren't we?' was all she said. Then she was stone again, asking if Henrietta's tea was to her liking.

They talked a little of farming matters, war shortages, whether there would be any shooting this autumn – the pheasants'd be a blamed nuisance if they weren't picked off. Only on the second cup did Mrs Bellerby get up and fetch from the sitting-room the box in which she kept her letters and treasures, and showed a photograph of Joe and Tom at the Front, taken when they were in billets, standing with their arms around each other's shoulders, grinning at the camera from under their peaked caps. It was hard to tell them apart. There was only a year between them, and they were both tall, well-built, fair and ruddy. Joe was just a little the taller, but there was not much in it. In the box, too, was a fancy French post-card Joe had sent once, with real lace stuck on it, and a St Christopher medal Tom had brought back last leave, oval, with pretty filigree work around it.

'Not that Ah hold with such popish things. Ah couldn't wear it, o' course. But it is pretty. Our Tom said St Christopher is really an English saint, and the French papists don't hold with him at all, but Ah told him, "Don't be soft. Where's there a church called St Christopher's, Ah'd like to knaw?"' She smiled, and then caught herself smiling, and looked for an instant so stricken that Henrietta's own pain welled up in her.

'He was a good boy,' she said.

Mrs Bellerby looked at her with the weariness of suffering, and said abruptly, 'It's like when you get a thorn in your finger. You forget about it for a bit and carry on, and then you try and grasp something, and it hurts.'

Henrietta nodded. They understood each other. It had been hard to lose Ned; but Frank was the child of her body. A mother could never get over losing her child. You learned to live with it, like a deep, unremovable thorn, but you never got over it.

Teddy had gone up to London to see Maria the moment the news of Frank's death was heard. He reassured her, before she had even had time to wonder about it, that he would take care of her and the baby. Their marriage was so recent that Frank had had no opportunity to make provision, other than to arrange for his army pay to be sent to her. When that, and the small insurance that would be payable, were spent, she would have been destitute once again.

His next words she already knew him well enough to anticipate. 'Why don't you come back to Morland Place now? There's no reason to stay here any longer.'

'Thank you – you're very kind – but I can't leave my mother.'

'Bring her with you,' Teddy said, with some generosity, since his few meetings with Mrs Stanhope had engendered no deep admiration for her.

'She would not wish to leave Cousin Sonia – Mrs Wilberforce.'

'Could she not go and live with her again, while you come home with me? It's not as if you couldn't visit.'

Maria said painfully, 'I know that must be the way of it. I know I can't expect you to maintain a separate home for me.'

'That wasn't the point,' Teddy began to protest, but Maria shook her head.

'Please – I do understand, and Mother will too, when I have worked on her a little. She *will* go and live with Cousin Sonia – it was what they always planned, if Daddy died and I . . . and I got married. She just needs time to adjust. And I want to stay here, just for a little while. Will you please let me? You see, this is where – it would have been where we lived together, Frank and I. *Our* home. I just want to be here a little longer,' she ended forlornly.

Teddy pressed her hand. 'Of course,' he said. 'Take your time, and come when you're ready.' A thought struck him, and he added, 'But you will come before the baby's born?'

Maria nodded. The baby was Frank's child, and belonged to them at Morland Place. She understood that. If Uncle Teddy was to take financial responsibility for the child, it was only fair that he should determine the course of its life. Probably it was what Frank would have wanted, too, to have her safe under that roof. There was comfort in the idea.

In York, as in other Pals towns, it was hard, slow work coming to terms with the losses of July the 1st. Old Colonel 'Hound' Bassett said, with tears in his eyes, 'It took two years to make us, and two hours to destroy us.' The Commercials had lost twelve officers and 208 other ranks killed or missing, with an additional eleven officers and 224 wounded. The colonel began to collect for a special commemorative stained-glass window, to be installed in one of the bays in the eastern arm of the Minster. It was the concentration of the casualties that made it hard to bear. The entire Clifton Cycling Club, for instance, which had joined as a group, was either killed or wounded, and the former Railway Arms Darts Team had lost all but one member. Such wholesale local losses made things seem worse than they were. Despite Hound's words, the battalion still existed, was still out in France, was still fighting.

In Picardy the push went on. There were no more great setpieces, like the battle of the 1st of July – which was to be officially called the Battle of Albert – but small-scale attacks went in up and down the line, keeping up the pressure on the Germans, and making gains, a foothold here, a hundred yards there. La Boisselle was taken on the 6th of July, Contalmaison on the 10th, Mametz Wood on the 12th. The newspapers continued to be full of cheering reports of advances and successes, and the war remained as popular as ever.

Some of this popularity was due to a moving picture called *The Battle of the Somme*, which was being shown in kinemas up and down the country. Its fame spread by word of mouth, and huge numbers went to see it. Jessie went with Beta in London, and wrote home about it, so that when it was shown in York all the adults from Morland Place made a point of going to see it. As both Lord Kitchener and General Haig hated the press, there had been very few graphic images from the Front since the war began, so the impact of this moving picture was immense. It had been filmed during the battle on the first day, and there were thrilling scenes of the men actually advancing into fire. Shockingly, there were also images of men being hit and falling dead. Such a thing had never before been shown to the general public, and there were those who disapproved vehemently of making an entertainment out of death. But for most it was a deeply moving experience to see what the men at the Front were going through. In York, it placed the deaths of their own Commercials in context, and only increased pride and stiffened resolve. The same was true nation-wide. Nobody was going to give up now. As the cost mounted, so it became more imperative than ever that those deaths should not have been in vain.

On the night of the 13th/14th of July, there was a daring night advance and dawn attack on a wide front on the right wing, from Delville Wood to Bazentin-le-Petit. The commanders in the field asked for only a five-minute barrage, saying that a longer one would only alert the Germans that an attack was coming; and this time high-explosive shells with delayed-action fuses were used, so that they would explode among the wire and the trench defences, rather than detonating uselessly before reaching their objectives. This proved very successful in cutting the wire and largely destroyed the first-line trenches. The attack went in, taking the front line with little opposition. The advance went on with such speed and dash that by mid-morning the German second line had been broken, 1400 German prisoners taken, a deep salient driven into the German position, and 6000 yards of the vitally important Pozières Ridge was in British hands.

The main road from Albert to Bapaume ran through the village of Pozières, which was at the top of a long slope leading to the main ridge. It had been an important object on the 1st of July, and one that had notably failed to fall. The Germans had invested it heavily, and its eminence made it very hard to capture. The British continued stubbornly to inch forward up the road, with fierce fighting and continuous loss, trying to reach and consolidate a position from which a final assault could be launched.

One of the ways in which the commanders kept morale in the field from flagging was the system of rotating the men, both in and out of the trenches, and in and out of different parts of the line. Bertie's West Herts had been fighting on the left of the road on the 1st of July; on the 14th they were elsewhere, and it was Laidislaw's 39th who were in that position.

A few days later, Venetia received a visit from Lady Sandown, who brought with her a letter from her son Lord Tranley at the Front, which she silently proffered. In the letter, Tranley reported that he had heard from the second-in-command of the 39th, who was a friend of his, that Laidislaw had been killed in the fighting on the 16th, as they were trying to push forward up the road. Tranley had written to his mother, knowing that the army's machine would not inform Violet of the fact, since there was no official relationship between them.

> I don't know whether Laidislaw has made any arrangement to have Lady H informed if anything happens to him. I, of course, can't do anything, not being a particular friend of either and only unofficially knowing about the *affaire*, through you. So I am hoping you will know what to do, dearest, and leave it in your hands. It would be too hard for the poor thing never to be told, don't you think? Or to have a letter of hers sent back marked 'Killed in Action', in that brutal way. I had no particular brief for Laidislaw, never having met the fellow, but Henry tells me his CO says he has been doing wonderful work, recording the war for posterity in paint. It seems a shame such a talent should be lost to the country, even if he and Lady H did rather make exhibitions of themselves. Henry also says apparently L has no relatives. I have no idea what happens to the paintings in that case – perhaps they'll belong to the Army? If so, I dare say they'll get filed away in some basement in Horseguards and never be seen again, which would be a pity . . .

Venetia stopped reading, and Lady Sandown said, 'I'm sorry for the way Tranley expresses himself. Of course, he was writing to *me*, but it seemed easier to let you read it than try and explain.'

Venetia saw there was nothing more about Laidislaw in the letter. 'He doesn't say how he was killed.'

'I suppose you may be able to find out, through your old friends, or Overton's colleagues. But it would be a delicate business. If enquiries were made, Holkam would be bound to find out, don't you think, and that might not be useful for the future? Because sad though this will be for Violet, I can't help thinking – and I know you'll agree – that the right thing now would be for the whole business to be forgotten and for Violet to settle down with Holkam again.'

In a moment, Venetia thought, she will say, 'This is all for the best.' She wished she wouldn't. She knew, now, how much Violet really loved Laidislaw, and for all the propriety and good outcomes in the world, she could not wish her daughter to suffer such pain as this would cause her. She forestalled Lady Sandown's next remark, which was hovering on her lips, by saying quietly, 'She really loves him, Kitty. It wasn't just a casual *affaire*.'

Lady Sandown looked shocked. 'Oh, my dear, I didn't think it was. Violet isn't that sort of girl. But, you know, it's probably all for the best in the end. It couldn't have ended well. And from what "Des" Desborough said, Holkam has publicly acknowledged the child, so it must mean he's willing to let bygones be bygones . . .'

Venetia let her old friend talk herself out, then thanked her and excused herself. She must break the news to Violet. There seemed nothing to be done but simply to tell her.

Violet had been sitting out in the garden for her daily measure of fresh air. Venetia went to find her there, and in the end she didn't have to say anything. Violet looked up as she approached, and saw death in her mother's face.

Venetia sat beside her and took her hand, cold as a stone.

She said, 'You must be brave, for the baby's sake. Darling, the news has come in a roundabout way, but there's no doubt about it.'

'He's dead?' Violet whispered in disbelief. Her eyes searched her mother's face for information, for the truth. 'Not even wounded?'

Venetia shook her head, unable to speak. She longed for Beauty to be there to help her, to comfort his favourite child. She had never felt so alone as she did now, the executioner of her daughter's hopes.

A long time later, up in her bedroom, Violet's tears had eased at last. She lay face down on her wet pillow, while Venetia stroked her hair, and the little dogs sat nearby, uneasy, hoping for things to go back to normal.

After a while, Violet said, her voice muffled, 'I wish I knew what really happened. I can't bear to think of him suffering.'

Venetia hesitated. 'I could make enquiries,' she began doubtfully.

Understanding came to Violet's eyes and, with it, wisdom. 'But if you found out it was bad, you wouldn't tell me, would you? You'd make something up.' Venetia didn't deny it. 'Perhaps,' Violet said, after a moment, 'it would be best not to know.'

There was silence then for a long time. It began to grow dark, but Venetia didn't want to move to put on the light. It was growing chilly, too. Violet had been still for so long, Venetia thought she might have fallen asleep – like the dogs, who had crept up on the bed and were curled like two light brown feathers, side by side.

But then Violet spoke out of the gloaming. 'I don't want to stay here. I don't want to have my baby here. Can't we go away somewhere?'

Venetia's mind was slow, as cold as she was. 'We could go to Chetton,' she began.

Violet spoke quickly. 'No, not there. I couldn't bear it – without him.'

Venetia had already discounted it. Her second thought was better. The idea was like a small candle flame in her mind, the first light in the darkness: a place where they would be safe; a place that spoke of happy childhoods, sunny days, innocent love – and of that hope that every baby ought to come into the world with, whatever happened afterwards.

'There is one place,' she said.

Violet looked enquiring, and then a shadow of warmth came to her expression. Not a smile yet, but it was a start. 'Oh, yes! Oh, Mummy, I'd like that. Oh, yes, let's go there.'

And so Venetia settled her affairs for an absence, and they packed their bags, and fled to Yorkshire.

Part of the estate Venetia had inherited from her mother was Shawes, the beautiful little Vanbrugh house just across the fields from Morland Place. She had stayed there regularly when the children were young, and the Morland Place children and the Winchmores had played together like brothers and sisters. Of late years Venetia and Overton had been too busy to come down to Yorkshire, but Shawes was kept within an hour or two of being habitable by a resident housekeeper. It only needed a telegram – there was no telephone there – to have the dust sheets taken off, the beds made up, and food ordered in.

A second telegram to Morland Place – of courtesy, to say they were coming – elicited an invitation that they stay there instead. Venetia pleaded off, and Henrietta prevented Teddy from pressing any further. All the same, when they arrived at York station they found Simmons waiting for them, with Teddy's big blue-and-silver Benz, to convey them smoothly and silently to Shawes. And when they got to the house, the housekeeper greeted them with the information that a large hamper had come from Morland Place, along with flowers for all the main rooms *and* a maid to arrange them, since the housekeeper was bound to be too busy for such fripperies.

Such thoughtfulness was touching, especially when the verbal message was delivered, that 'Maister Morland said particular that you wasn't to thank him, my lady, and that no-one wouldn't bother you, only when you was feeling up to it, you should send a message, and they'd wait on you, and see if there was anything they could do to make you more comfortable.'

Venetia and Violet remained in seclusion for several days, resting, talking little, rediscovering the house and the lovely, overgrown garden. They sat on the terrace in the sun, or under the shade of the old walnut tree, watching the dogs romp about chasing crickets through the grass. Each had her thoughts to occupy her, and sometimes they would go an hour together without speaking. Once, Violet said, 'It's lovely here. I wish we could stay for ever. Do you suppose Holkam would let me bring the children here? After all, it's not as if *he* was ever here.' *He* meant Laidislaw, of course.

Venetia couldn't answer that. 'Best wait until after the baby's born,' she said. There was no knowing how he would react to that. They could only wait and see.

Violet sighed assent, knowing her mother was right. Then she said, 'We're the same, now, aren't we? Poor Mummy.'

Widows both, Venetia thought – that's what Violet meant. And, oh, she missed Beauty! Shawes might have no Laidislaw memories to haunt Violet, but Overton was here, round every corner, to torment Venetia with happy memories. She wanted so fiercely to see him that sometimes she thought she might make him appear around a corner by the sheer force of her longing.

When five days of solitude had passed, Venetia said that she must invite the Morland Place family to call. 'It's only courtesy,' she said.

Violet said, 'I don't want them to see me like this. I know you must invite them, but I'll stay in my room when they call.' But she spoke calmly. Her advanced pregnancy was cushioning her against reality. Nature had a way of making sure babies got born: Violet was almost in a dream, a cocoon of motherhood.

A note was sent to Morland Place, and the next day Henrietta walked over.

'I'm so glad to see you,' Venetia said, hugging her. 'And I'm glad you came alone.'

'Teddy wanted to come, but I made him see it would be too much all at once.'

'Dear man! But much as I love him, I'm not ready for company yet. *You* don't count as company.'

'I'm not sure anyone would find me good company just now,' said Henrietta.

'Oh, my dear! I'm so sorry about Frank.'

'Your loss is so much greater,' said Henrietta. 'And poor little Violet – Venetia, I know she did wrong, but we've all been sinners in our time. I just want to say how very sorry I am. Is she hiding away?'

'Yes, upstairs. She doesn't want to see anyone. She's *very* pregnant, poor child.'

'When is it due?' Henrietta asked. They walked out into the garden arm in arm, and talked about families and babies and such comfortable subjects, as old friends may, who need not say the obvious or the polite, but merely lean against each other, sadness to sadness, for comfort, and find it there in great measure.

Teddy was disappointed that he could do nothing better for his neighbours than leave them alone, but he swallowed his pride and contented himself with making sure that fresh flowers were taken over – for there was 'nothing worth picking in Shawes' garden' – and the occasional basket of choice fruit, a couple of ducks from his own ponds, a box of Mrs Stark's macaroons – oh, and the newspaper, ironed and sent over daily when he had finished with it, in case Venetia wanted to read it, because she wouldn't want to be bothered with ordering it for herself, but she had a brain, unlike the women of his own household, and was used to keeping up with events.

In mid-August, when Violet went into labour, Venetia sent word to Morland Place, and Henrietta and Nanny Emma came over, and between the three of them they delivered her, quietly and without fuss, of a fine baby boy.

Teddy arranged for Lennie to come to Morland Place for his convalescence. The army was only too glad to have his place made free for another. There was no officially published estimate of the wounded from the battle of Albert, but the numbers were high, and with the fighting going on in Picardy, as well as the normal activities in other parts of the line, there were always more casualties coming in.

So Lennie came back to Morland Place and was installed on the sofa in state, his leg heavily bandaged. The doctors had said that they did not know how he had run at all. The bandage round his head had been reduced to a lint dressing held with sticking-plaster, but, along with the scar on his cheek, it still gave him a romantic air. The maids were engaged in silent struggles with each other over who was to attend him.

Polly's feelings about him were painfully mixed. His being wounded made her feel tender towards him, and she was afraid of that tenderness. Lying on the sofa, interestingly bandaged, he was all too easy to love, especially when she rediscovered what fun he was to talk to, and how alike they thought about so many things. The glow in his eyes when he looked at her told her that he still felt the same. He wanted to marry her; but she had no desire to be tied down yet. She knew her father would not approve, and she had a vague feeling that he was right, that there were great things ahead for Miss Morland of Morland Place, which she could not yet fully imagine, but which would never happen to Mrs Lennox Manning.

Teddy had been enquiring about what had happened to Lennie's friend Parker and there was a sad moment for Polly when the news came that he was dead. He had been taken back to Blighty on a hospital ship and had ended up at the No. 3 London General at Wandsworth. They had amputated his arm at the shoulder, and he had survived the operation, but had died two weeks later of 'complications'. The news had affected Lennie badly and for several days he was silent and withdrawn. Polly tried to comfort him, touched that he had cared so much for a colleague.

And then a letter came to say that Lennie had been cited for the Military Medal, for his courage and initiative in taking command of his group of comrades when they found themselves isolated and without an officer; for leading them to harry the enemy; and for his courage and daring in bringing a wounded colleague back to his own line. Now Lennie was obliged to tell the full story, with more detail about his own role in that day's actions. Everyone's admiration for him grew, both for his exploits and his modesty in not talking about them before. The story, especially the bit about jumping over the trench full of Germans, was such a good one that Polly discovered everyone in York was talking about it, and even the convalescent officers she visited had heard of Lennie. It was difficult for a girl of sixteen to keep her head when the hero of the hour had eyes only for her.

Two days after the birth, Violet was still hiding deep in her protective cocoon from the world and the hurt it contained. She kept the baby with her all the time, and with Nanny Emma's help was learning to feed it herself, something she had not done with her other children. It was an extraordinary sensation – strange, wonderful, and desperately poignant all at once. In those moments she came closest to thinking about Octavian, something she had forbidden herself to do since the day her mother had brought her the news. She knew she could not cope with thinking about him yet.

She did not give a thought to telling Holkam that the child was born – what had it to do with him, in any case? But Venetia had to think of the future on her daughter's behalf. Holkam had acknowledged the child, and if there was ever to be a reconciliation between Violet and her husband, tact must be employed from the beginning. So she sent a carefully worded telegram, announcing the birth, to Holkam at HQ in France.

A reply came back the following day, suggesting that Holkam had been thinking about the event and had his answer ready. There was no word of congratulation or of tenderness for his wife – perhaps it was foolish to have expected it – but he ordered that the child be christened, with the names Henry and Douglas. Henry had been one of Holkam's father's names, so that was a compliment; and Douglas, of course, was the commander-in-chief's name. It was a fashion in some regiments to give a child the commanding officer's name. In any case, it implied an interest in the baby that Venetia thought must be a good thing, in the circumstances.

She told Violet, who looked up at her in surprise and said simply, 'His name is Octavian.'

For all her sympathy with her daughter, she felt a little impatience. What benefit could there be in alienating the man who was, after all, the child's father in the eyes of the law? But Violet, lovely and compliant though she had always been, could be stubborn. It took considerable tact and persuasion to bring her to accept Holkam's choice. Even then, when the moment came and she was asked by the vicar for the names, she said, 'Henry Douglas – Octavian.'

In the middle of September, a further battle was planned, to take the villages of Flers and Courcelette, one on either side of the Bapaume road, and to advance a distance of two and a half miles, on a front of three and a half miles. It was an ambitious plan, but much had been learned in the two and a half months of fighting in Picardy, including how properly to manage a 'creeping barrage', as the new strategy was called, how to cut wire with artillery, and how to consolidate advances and clear trenches and dugouts. The New Army, which had never been lacking in courage and determination, now had experience too.

Also on this occasion there was the possibility of using a new weapon, the armoured fighting vehicle. The RNAS had been using armoured motor-cars from their base in Dunkirk since 1914, to recover shot-down pilots and, with the addition of machine-guns, to harry the enemy's cavalry. In 1915 Churchill, then first lord of the Admiralty, received an idea for a larger, tracked version, called a Landship, which could cross enemy trenches, flatten barbed wire, and destroy enemy strongholds. He set up a Landship Committee to promote the idea, and when he resigned, Lloyd George took it over. Construction of a prototype finally began in August 1915. To maintain secrecy, the tarpaulin-covered objects were labelled 'water tanks', from which the term 'tank' drifted into general usage among those working on it.

Work continued through the winter. On the 2nd of February 1916, it was demonstrated in the park of Hatfield House to the government and senior army officers, and the Army ordered a hundred of them. Now they were ready, and there was much speculation about when they would be used. Above all, secrecy about them must be maintained, which meant they must not be used in 'driblets', but be held back until they could be deployed in large numbers, in a combined operation, so as to maximise the shock and surprise they would cause.

Since the action in Picardy had begun, General Haig had received plenty of conflicting advice about whether or not to use the new weapon, which was still very much in the experimental stage. Still, it had to be tried out some time. Already it was autumn: with rain and constant shelling, the ground could only get worse, and the experts of the

Armoured Car Division of the Machine Gun Corps, who operated the tanks, said the condition of the ground would be a critical factor. Things were not going as well in Picardy as hoped, and advance was slow. Haig decided he had nothing to lose.

From the beginning there had been debate about whether these 'tanks' should be used purely for infantry support or regarded as armoured cavalry. It was decided in the end in favour of the infantry, and such tanks as could be got to the area in time – around forty-eight of them, shipped in in crates, in secret, and assembled behind the lines under heavy camouflage – were shared out among the twelve divisions that took part in the attack on the 15th of September. Preparation for the battle was careful, with a massive three-day bombardment, briefly suspended at regular intervals so that the RFC could report on progress and pinpoint new targets. Then, at zero hour on the 15th, the infantry went over the top.

The tanks were a mixed success. They were prone to mechanical difficulties. The best engine so far developed was barely strong enough to move one, and many of them broke down. Others 'ditched' – became bogged down – or did not manage to cross trenches and shell-holes as well as had been hoped. Some had difficulties with their steering equipment – another weak point – and went off in the wrong direction. Others still shed their tracks. And while they were impervious to rifle and machine-gun fire, they could be, and were, knocked out by shells or a well-aimed grenade.

But they were of tremendous benefit to the morale of the infantryman, who felt reassured by the monster rumbling along before or beside him; and when they loomed up out of the mist, the Germans ran in terror. In the end, only about a dozen of the machines managed to play an active part in the battle, but those dozen had done just what had been wanted of them – shielded the advancing infantry, beaten down the German wire, and attacked and destroyed machine-gun nests and strongpoints. It was a good start. By mid-afternoon, 6000 yards of the German first line and 4000 yards of the second had been taken and consolidated, and the British held High Wood and the Bazentin Ridge. An exultant newspaper report talked of 'a tank walking up the High Street of Flers with the British Army cheering behind it'.

When he came out of the line, Bertie wrote to Jessie:

> My battalion has taken Martinpuich – well on the far side of Pozières, which seemed like a distant objective after the 1st of July. We are making progress, but it seems painfully slow, and very costly in lives. I feel this year's campaign must come to an end soon, as the weather is deteriorating. By the end of the month we shall be bogged down in a sea of mud. At all events, we did what was required of us, and relieved the French – and I hope they are suitably grateful!
>
> I have better news of Pennyfather, whose head injury is no longer causing anxiety, though his knee is still swollen and painful and he cannot walk on it. As soon as I have leave, I must go and visit his family and make sure they are all right. I was sorry to hear about poor Violet's friend, by the by. I understand his CO, Colonel Villiers, is very impressed with his work and has shown it to Gen. Haig, though what the Old Man thought of it rumour does not divulge. I never heard that he cared for paintings. I believe he is quite fond of music, however!

The Prime Minister's son, Raymond Asquith, was killed in the action of the 15th of September. He was a lieutenant with the Grenadier Guards, having asked to be posted to a battalion from a staff position. As he led his men over the top that day at Ginchy, near Delville Wood, he was shot instantly in the chest and died soon afterwards. Venetia reflected that no-one, however powerful, was immune from the effects of this war.

She had left Violet and her new baby in good hands at Shawes and come back to London to attend to her war work, and heard the news on the Sunday, the 17th, in a telephone call from Addison. Raymond Asquith had been an exceptionally brilliant man, an outstanding scholar, handsome, witty, warm-hearted and full of fun. He had been a barrister before he volunteered on the outbreak of war, and had already been accepted as a prospective Member of Parliament for Derby. Given both his tremendous talents and his great personal magnetism, there must have been a fine political career ahead of him: he might have been prime minister one day. It was a great loss to the country, and to his family, his wife and three small children. She knew how much Asquith would mourn him, and was sorry for the beleaguered man.

There was already muttering among the Conservatives that he did not have a proper grip on the war, that his leadership was insufficiently dynamic. The war was costing too much and achieving too little. But the agitation was not all from the opposition parties. After the Cabinet reconstruction following Lord Kitchener's death, when Lloyd George had acquired the War Office, Venetia had heard a furious Margot Asquith mutter that it was only a matter of time before she and her husband would have to leave Downing Street. The Welshman wanted the crown, and Venetia had no doubt he would be busy fomenting dissent. She wondered whether, after such a blow as losing Raymond, Asquith would have sufficient heart to carry on with the fight.

Addison also had some more cheering news: that Major Parke had been put forward for a DSO for his actions on the 1st of July – for pulling together the isolated troops and holding the section of trenches, for crossing no man's land to bring back reinforcements and ammunition, and for getting his men away in good order when the withdrawal was ordered.

'From what I hear it was thoroughly deserved,' Addison

said. 'Four times across no man's land under the heaviest of fire. The fellow must have a charmed life.'

Venetia expressed her pleasure at the news, and later wrote to Henrietta with congratulations, and to Bertie himself inviting him to call when he was next in London.

Towards the end of September, Maria made the move to Morland Place, having finally settled her mother in the flat in Hammersmith. It was not in Mrs Stanhope's nature to come to any decision quickly, or to act on it when she had. It had taken Maria's growing size finally to bring her to the point. She had become a mother late, and had had such a hard time at the birth that she had never wanted another child. The thought of finding herself alone with Maria when the time came made her regard her daughter in the manner of one eyeing a grenade with the pin out. When one day Maria complained of a stomach-ache – brought on, probably, by eating figs – Mrs Stanhope had such a palpitation that shortly afterwards she announced that she was quite ready to remove to Cousin Sonia's.

Maria arrived at Morland Place with a pitifully small collection of belongings – a few clothes, books, one or two childhood treasures, and Frank's letters tied in a slim bundle – and was warmly welcomed by everyone. She found all the talk and bustle tiring, after the months of near seclusion with only her mother for company. The person she found it easiest to cope with was Robert. He had been desperately grieved by the loss of his brother. Frank in particular had been his pet. His earliest memories were of the baby, bandy-legged in his sagging napkins, staggering after him, hands outstretched. Frank's first word, after Dada and Mama, had been Obob, and when control over his speech and limbs had been achieved, his most frequent cry was 'Wait for me, Robbie!' as he tagged along on Rob's every expedition.

When Frank's widow arrived, visibly pregnant with Frank's child, it was all too much for him. For a man who usually had no difficulty in speaking his opinion, he was unexpectedly reduced to silence by Maria. He could only express himself to her in shy glances and smiles – which she found more touching than volumes of words. Sometimes, when he arrived home from work on his bicycle, he would bring her a little paper of toffee from the shop on the corner of Micklegate, and slip it into her hand as he passed, like a criminal passing stolen goods.

Maria was installed in the bachelor room that Frank had used to occupy, conveniently near the nursery and Nanny Emma. She liked the small, plain room, and felt there might be something of Frank's spirit there to comfort her. It was so hard to believe that she would never see him again. Their marriage had been so short. Just five days together, that was all they had had – just long enough to make the new life inside her, before he stepped out of his. Was that what it had all been for? One to live and one to die. It seemed so wasteful – and yet she was so glad of the baby. Without it there would have been nothing left of him, his brilliance, his dazzling promise.

Nanny Emma inveigled her into the nursery as often as possible, and she found comfort there. She liked the idea that her baby would be one of them, and grow up among a noisy, cheerful muddle of cousins. Her own childhood had been isolated and solitary, and though she had not been unhappy, knowing nothing else, she was glad that Frank's child would have something better.

The one thing that worried her was what she was to do with herself. Since she had first gone to school she had been used to an ordered life of activity and the exercise of her intellect.

Now she saw what Ethel, who seemed to want to claim her as her new best friend, expected her to become: another matron just like her, filling her days with knitting and small-talk about children. It horrified her. She must have something to do.

After two weeks, something happened that offered hope. Teddy had already lost his secretary, Baskin, earlier in the year. Now Baskin's unsatisfactory replacement, Protheroe, was also called up.

'What am I going to do?' Teddy said despairingly, at dinner. 'How can I replace him? There's no-one left. I can't compete with the army. And I'd only just got him trained. He wasn't up to much, really, but at least I could leave the routine matters to him.'

'I could help you,' Maria said. Her voice failed in her excitement and she had to repeat it.

Teddy heard only a general expression of sympathy. 'Thank you, my dear, you're very kind,' he said, brushing it aside, and carried on, 'I don't know even where to begin to look. If I take on another lad just out of school, I'll have the same problem – get him trained, and a year later the army'll take him.'

Maria said, more firmly and a little louder, 'What I mean is, I can do the job. I can be your secretary.'

Teddy stopped in mid-breath and looked at her. He frowned. 'But—' he began, and she forestalled him.

'I'm used to working regular hours, and my job as a librarian taught me clerical skills. I can write letters, keep documents in order, answer the telephone. I'm also used to doing research – finding things out, tracking down information, making notes and preparing reports. And I learn quickly.' Her eyes burned with enthusiasm as she willed him to understand, to be flexible and not dismiss her. 'I can do it. Please let me.'

Teddy shook his head. He knew Frank's wife was clever, as Frank had been. And she had been 'going out to work', though that was not something anyone wanted to remember. Of course, many businesses were having to take on female clerks, but the idea seemed to him very *off*. Secretaries were men, always had been. And a lady of the house? His own niece? What would people say? It would look odd. It would feel odd. How could he give her orders, or berate her if she got things wrong?

Then he thought, with a sense of relief, that probably she was worried about 'paying her way'. He admired her spirit, but hastened to reassure her. 'There's no need, my dear, no need at all,' he said. 'You mustn't think of it. You are one of the family, and there's no question of having to earn your living or anything of that sort.'

Henrietta, who had been watching Maria's face, suddenly spoke up. 'It isn't that, Teddy, she said. 'She *wants* to do it – don't you, Maria?' Maria nodded gratefully. 'Think how it must be, to be really clever and not be allowed to use your mind. It would be like keeping a hunter shut in a stable day in and day out.'

The example his sister had chosen made perfect sense to Teddy. A high-bred animal in prime condition would kick its box to pieces if it wasn't exercised. He saw that, of course. But was a mind – and a woman's mind at that – the same? He thought of something else. 'There's your condition to think of.'

'I have six weeks to go,' Maria said quickly. 'I can learn the job as I do it, and carry on afterwards.'

'What about while you are confined? I'd have no-one at all for months.'

'Oh, Ted, women don't confine themselves for months these days,' Henrietta said. 'They're up and about after a fortnight.'

'I'll help while she's in bed,' Polly said, interested in the whole idea.

'And I will,' Henrietta said. 'I used to do the accounts years ago.'

'Well,' said Teddy again, still doubtfully.

'I promise you I *can* do the job,' Maria said, 'and I won't let you down. Please give me the chance to show you.'

He yielded, still unconvinced, but too gallant to disappoint a female if he could help it. 'If it means so much to you, we'll give it a try. But if you get overtired, that will be the end of it, d'ye hear?'

Maria started first thing the next morning – before he could change his mind. Protheroe still had two days before he had to leave, and in that time she passed through the office like a whirlwind. Her orderly mind was shocked at the muddle, at his lack of method. She could see at a glance a dozen better ways of doing things. Teddy's lingering doubts were banished by the energy with which she straightened the mess, snapping questions at poor Protheroe. He was always to be seen trailing after her, clutching a piece of paper and stammering that he didn't know, quite, but he thought it might be thus-and-so, only to have her say firmly, 'Never mind. I think I shall do it this way.'

By the end of a fortnight, Teddy had almost forgotten that there had ever *not* been Maria; and she managed him so tactfully that he never had to feel overcome by her superiority. She allowed him to believe she managed well because he explained things so clearly, so they were both happy.

As soon as she understood the job, Maria began to arrange matters to allow her to leave it while she had the baby. Polly took to dropping in when her father was not around. Seeing Maria happy in her 'job' confirmed Polly's desire to learn to run her father's estate. Maria was much better at explaining things than any of her father's employees, and also went under the flattering assumption that Polly was perfectly capable of running a business. Polly, while not intellectual, had a good brain and learned quickly, and by the time Maria had to retire to confinement, she was confident that Polly could manage things for two weeks.

On the 11th of November she went into labour, and after a long struggle, she gave birth to a boy, a long, dark baby with a beautifully rounded head. She was astonished at the depth of her feeling. She had been prepared to grow gradually to love him, thinking that there was not much, after all, to like about very small babies. But when she looked into the tiny face, she fell instantly and desperately in love. A vast tenderness surged through her, a rapture she had known before only in Frank's arms, on their wedding night.

Nanny Emma immediately proclaimed the baby 'the image of Frank', and everyone decided he would be named after his father. But Maria didn't want her child to live all his life in the shadow of a man he could never meet. He ought to have a name of his own. On the day of his birth, when Nanny Emma was on her way down to evening prayers, she mentioned that it was St Martin's Day. While she was away, Maria mused on that, trying the name in her mind and against the image already burned there of her child's face. When Henrietta came to visit her after chapel, she told her that she had decided to call the baby Martin.

Henrietta showed no disappointment. She said, 'We've had a Martin in the family before. A long time ago, now, but it is a Morland name. I think it suits him very well.'

Maria was so grateful for this generous response that on an impulse she added, 'And Francis, of course. Martin Francis.'

'Both very good saints,' Henrietta assured her.

CHAPTER TWENTY-TWO

General Haig declared the battle in Picardy ended on the 14th of November. Thereafter there would be defensive action only, until the following spring. The weather had deteriorated, and the last few attempts had foundered in the terrible, slimy mud of the Somme and the Ancre. Haig would gladly have halted action many weeks earlier, but General Joffre pressed him with increasing vehemence to continue to attack the Germans. British efforts had taken the weight of the enemy away from the French at Verdun, but Joffre now had another idea – a war of attrition. The Allies must simply kill as many Germans as possible. The mathematics were simple. If more Germans died than French and British, the Germans would lose the war.

It was not a plan Haig could agree with, but he was under political pressure to co-operate with the French, because it was, after all, 'their' war. So in worsening weather, in rain, gales and plummeting temperatures, the British Army struggled on through the mud against heavy German fire to build on the successes of the late summer. The whole of the Thiepval Ridge was taken, and the line was pushed up to within three miles of Bapaume; and at last, on the 13th of November, Beaumont-Hamel fell. Fighting continued sporadically in the Ancre valley for a few more days, but by the 19th all was quiet again.

Since the 1st of July, the army had advanced an impressive

six miles along a front of twenty, and had taken almost all its objectives. The German Army had been dealt a weakening blow, with heavy losses and thousands of prisoners taken – most of them unwounded. But the cost had been high, and the British Army was exhausted as it settled into winter routines. Haig had done what he set out to do, and positioned the army for victory the following year. And among the soldiers, they said that no-one else could have done it. Only Haig could deliver the victory in 1917.

Winter set in hard and early – the last actions were fought partially through snowstorms – and there was a rush to get extra blankets, leather waistcoats, thick gloves and balaclava helmets to the men in the trenches. Bertie's men had been rotated out of Picardy before the end, having done their share, and were wintering near Armentières. He wrote from billets in Le Doulieu.

> We are not badly off here. Even when we are in the line we have decentish trenches that do not flood except in the heaviest rain, and I have a fair-to-middling dugout which a predecessor has furnished with a couple of queer-looking chairs, like deck-chairs with knotted string instead of canvas. Surprisingly comfortable. Our billet here is good, some splendid oak-framed barns for the men, and a rather battered small manor house for us officers. I'm sharing a room with Fenniman, which is pleasant as we don't feel as much like going out in the evenings as before. We lie on our beds and read and smoke, hardly even talking. I believe we must be tired!
>
> My boys are hardened veterans now, adept at making themselves at home. The weather's too bad for football, so they occupy themselves with getting up a Christmas concert. They talk of nothing but Christmas. I hope some of them, at least, will get home. They are tired, but content, feeling they have

done their part. Everyone is sure we will win the victory next year, so that we can all go home. The war seems to have been going on so long, it's hard sometimes to remember that it had a beginning and will have an end. It was the Germans who started it, wasn't it? We all need to feel that we are in the right, or we will lose what little firm ground we stand on. As we get better at fighting this modern kind of war, it becomes harder to see how it can be resolved. After four and a half months in Picardy, the Old Man still never got the breakthrough for his cavalry, or the war of movement we know we could win. Sometimes I'm afraid we shall simply stay here for ever, killing each other ever more efficiently until the last man standing declares himself the winner. Forgive me – I ought not to speak so depressingly. It's just the cold and the rain and the end-of-year tiredness. And the longing to come home, and to see you. I'll be more cheerful come the spring.

Speaking of seeing you, I am certain to have some leave in December, though it's unlikely to be at Christmas. I hope we shall be able to meet. You must be due some leave soon, surely? Will you spend it at Morland Place?

Jessie was called to the matron's office in the third week of November and told she was due for a week's leave, which would begin the following day. She was not surprised that her leave had become so suddenly 'due'. She had been warned by the other VADs that their holidays would be got over early so as to allow the 'real' nurses to have theirs in December, preferably close to Christmas.

'And when you come back, Nurse,' the matron went on, 'you will be going on night duty for three months. You will have to move your things into the VAD night quarters on your return from leave, so make sure to return a few hours early.'

Jessie was not unhappy with the thought of night duty. It would be something different, and one was always ready for a new experience. Also it had the benefit that the night quarters were in huts in the park, which meant no more of that exhausting daily journey to and from the hostel. And it would mean having more free time during the day.

The matron, however, seemed to think that she would be upset at the thought of three months of nights, for she continued, 'It may seem like a long time, but there is every possibility that it may be extended if the war goes on for much longer, so you should do your best to get used to it. And I have one more thing to say, Nurse: you have given satisfaction so far. I can tell you now, before you go on leave, that in December you will be asked to sign on again.' She paused, to give Jessie the opportunity of murmuring her thanks. 'Continue to do your duty as you have done, and we shall be very pleased with you. That is all.'

So Jessie packed her bags and went to Morland Place, to be received rapturously by her family – especially her mother, who had seemed to think she would never see her again. Uncle Teddy at once started planning a large party, persuaded she must be pining for company; Polly wanted her to come out riding, convinced she must have missed horses most of all; and Nanny Emma wanted to drag her off at once to the nursery to see the new inhabitants, little John and even smaller Martin. Only Lennie, leaning heavily on a stick, but walking at last, guessed it right. 'I bet the first thing you want is a long, hot bath.'

Jessie smiled at him. 'With water that comes up to here,' she said, marking the base of her neck with her hand.

And remarkably, within the hour, that was where she was, in her own dear room, in front of the fire, with Tomlinson toasting the towels before the flames and saying, 'I can't believe you're really here. But how thin you've got!'

'Mother will soon remedy that,' Jessie said comfortably.

The week fled all too quickly. She did go riding, despite

inclement weather, for the sheer joy of being on horseback again. Hotspur greeted her with dragon-like snorts and a series of whinnies that shook his whole body. He nudged her so hard he gave her an impressive bruise on her breastbone, then thrust his head under her arm and just stayed there, pressed against her, while she caressed his ears and tried not to cry.

She enjoyed long talks with Lennie, and with Maria, and pretended to enjoy Uncle Teddy's party, though she was really too tired for it. She made a horseback tour of the farms so as to pay her respects to all the tenants, and was given tea and cake at each place in such bounty that she could hardly mount after the last stop. And she went over to Shawes to see Violet, who was still living there in a strange, serene seclusion, refusing invitations to come to Morland Place or be visited. But she received Jessie, though it seemed at first it was only to show off her baby.

It was fortunate that Jessie had been inoculated by handling John and Martin, for otherwise she might have been overcome when Violet's baby was placed in her arms. If what Violet had done was wrong, she had paid for it, God knew. She would not talk about Laidislaw – did not even mention him – but Jessie could see in her face how shocking the loss of him had been. She really had loved him. Jessie could not begrudge her the baby, and since Violet forgot to ask for him back, she found herself holding him until he fell asleep, cradling him in a way that felt natural, and strangely comforting.

When the nurse came in to take him away, Violet said, 'When we were babies, our mothers decided we would be friends always.'

'I know. Mother's often told me about that.'

'And they agreed that they'd be second mothers to each other's children.'

'Yes.'

'I know you don't have a baby yet,' Violet went on, 'but

I'd like us to be like that. Will you be second mother to little Octavian? And when you have a baby, I'll do the same.'

'But I—' Jessie began in protest.

'You'll marry again one day,' Violet said. 'I don't believe God would let you be wasted. And then you'll have a baby. He'll be a little younger than Octavian, but it won't matter. I'd like them to be friends the way we always have been. Will you, Jessie? Please.'

Jessie said, 'Of course.' But she would never marry, or have a child. She knew that now. And Violet's baby was also Lord Holkam's. Violet seemed to have forgotten that. 'What will you be doing at Christmas?' she asked, on the heels of that thought. 'Will you be going to see your other children?'

Violet didn't want to think about that. 'It seems so far ahead. I can't think about it now. I'd like to stay here for ever, just like this.'

Jessie thought she would probably feel the same. But she doubted life would leave her friend alone for ever.

While Jessie was home, a letter came for Henrietta from Emma Weston in Scotland, asking if she could come and stay for Christmas.

> Uncle Bruce has agreed, after being worked on for weeks together by me – and very hard work it was, too! – that I can come for Christmas on condition that I go back to Aberlarich for New Year and for my twenty-first birthday. The Scots always celebrate Hogmanay much more than Christmas, so I don't think it's a great sacrifice on their part. And I suspect they are planning a large celebration for my coming-of-age.
>
> So may I, please? And since I have to go back so soon after Christmas, can I come a good, long time in advance of it? Will Jessie be home? I do so long to see her. Please ask her if you see her to let me have news

of Major Fenniman. I know you won't be shocked by my asking, dear Aunt Hen, because I'm nearly independent, and it's only asking for news, after all. That can't be frowned on in these modern times, can it? Though Uncle Bruce has never realised the times are modern, and would have forty fits if Major F actually wrote to me!

'What a pity you won't be here,' Henrietta said. 'You must write to her, Jessie dear. I expect you've been too busy lately, but you could do it while you're here.'

'Yes, I will. But I wonder what she *will* do when she's twenty-one,' Jessie mused.

'Run away from Scotland, that's for sure,' said Polly, passing by at that moment. 'As far and as fast as she can.'

'She might have fallen in love with a Scotch boy by now,' Jessie pointed out. Polly only gave her a scornful look as she hurried upstairs to see Maria.

'*Have* you any news of Major Fenniman?' Henrietta asked.

'Only that he's all right,' Jessie said. 'I dare say what she really wants to know is where he'll be on the day after her birthday, so that she can actually write to him, if not dash off and see him.'

'You think it's a case between them, then?' Henrietta asked.

'I don't know,' Jessie said, and she sighed without knowing it. 'How can anyone tell about someone they never get to see? This war seems to be going on for ever.'

Henrietta tactfully dropped the subject. Like Violet, she cherished the thought that one day, when the war was over, Jessie would meet someone else and get married again. It would not be natural for a young woman to stay unwed for ever.

Lord Holkam had a few days' leave at the end of November, and was not best pleased to discover from his mother-in-law that his wife was still hiding herself away in Yorkshire with the baby. He was annoyed to have to make the tiresome journey to York. Even though the train service was fast and frequent, he had the habit of thought of his father's generation, that anything further north than the hunting shires was beyond civilisation.

He would have been pleasantly surprised by the comfort of the train, the attentiveness of the service and the lavishness of the dining-car food, if he had been in a mood to give credit to anything connected with the business. As it was, he arrived at York station in a foul mood, took a taxi, and observed the empty countryside into which he was driven with anger and perplexity. What in God's name was she *doing* here? He was aware his wife was no lover of the country. Her visits to Brancaster, his seat near Lincoln, were few and short. Had some profound change come over her? He didn't like to think of that, and his temper gave way to full puzzlement.

The house seemed to him a ruin, though at second glance it was only the garden that was in disarray. He had something of an eye for architecture, and saw at once that the house was beautiful. *Very* beautiful. In fact – he allowed himself to wonder just for a moment if Violet would ever inherit it from her mother, or whether it was entailed on her brother. *That* would be a waste. It ought to belong to someone who could appreciate it.

The servant who opened the door to him did not recognise him, and while there was no reason why she should, it brought the frown back to his brows. Then the damn' fool woman was so stupid as to say that 'her ladyship never sees anyone'.

'I'm her *husband*,' Holkam said, annoyed that he had to remind her. 'Take me to her at once.'

He marched after the woman as she dithered along, mumbling to herself, and was shown into a small parlour overlooking the terrace. A daybed was drawn up to the window, and Violet was reclining on it, looking out at the garden as though it were full of summer flowers. She turned her head as they came in, her face serene and softly enquiring. For a moment Holkam thought, almost wistfully, how beautiful she was.

Then the housekeeper said, in upset tones, 'It's Lord Holkam, my lady. He did insist.'

Violet's eyes widened and a look of sickness came to her face. She seemed suddenly much older, her cheeks hollow and her complexion yellowed.

Holkam could not know that the sight of him had brought the full realisation of Laidislaw's death crushing down on her, the knowledge she had successfully held at bay for so many months. He thought only that she hated him and was afraid of him. He turned and waved the servant away, and when they were alone, he said shortly, 'Well, Violet. Have you nothing to say to me?'

'I was not expecting you,' she said faintly. The blood began to return, so that she was merely pale rather than yellow. But her thin cheeks and shadowed eyes made her seem wraith-like, as though she had been ill, and might still be snatched away on a breath. 'Won't you – won't you sit down?' she managed to say at last. He drew up a chair impatiently and sat. 'Are you on leave?' she said next, at a loss for anything better.

'Yes, and I arrived at home to find you hundreds of miles away in Yorkshire.'

'I have been here ever since . . . ever since.'

'So I understand from your mother. But that will have to change. How can you be so foolish? If we are to salvage this situation you must return to London with me, so that we can be seen together. And you must live at Fitzjames House, at least for part of the Season.'

'I can't,' she said faintly. 'Have pity—'

'Have *pity*? What pity did you have on me when you embarked on this appalling course of action? I am prepared to do my duty and accept the child, but you will have to do yours. Since this – this paramour of yours is no longer a threat to us, we can put the whole unfortunate business behind us.'

'You don't understand,' she faltered.

'I understand perfectly. You lost your head over some Bohemian bounder and made a damn' fool of yourself. But I got you out of it all right, and if you behave properly it will all be forgotten in time. Fortunately, people's memories are short in wartime.'

Her eyes seemed to darken. 'What do you mean, *you got me out of it*?'

He paused a telling moment, avoiding her eyes. 'I mean that I have let it be known that I acknowledge the child. Even named it after the commander-in-chief. Damn it, we wet the baby's head in the mess!'

Then she knew. A sickness settled in her. 'That's not it. That's not what you meant.'

'What are you talking about?' he said impatiently.

'You did it,' she said. 'You had him killed.'

'Don't be such a damned little fool.' There was a spot of colour in his cheeks.

'I always wondered. It seemed so odd that he was called up so soon, and then sent to the Front. And then at the last minute—' She closed her eyes a moment. It was hard to breathe.

'I don't know what you're talking about.'

'At the last minute they told him he was going over the top after all. You got his orders changed, didn't you?'

'Don't talk such rubbish. How on earth do you think I could have had anything to do with it? Thousands of men were killed. He was just one of them.'

She shook her head. A terrible weight in her chest told her that she was right. Somehow, somehow Laidislaw had died because he had been her lover. *Octavian, Octavian! Oh my dear, what did I do to you? I shouldn't have loved you.*

She held her head up and looked at him levelly, like a

man, as she had never done before. She said, 'I don't know what you did. I suppose I shall never know. But it's over now. Nothing can bring him back.'

He thought she was capitulating. He almost smiled in relief. 'That's the sensible attitude to take. Now we must see what we can do to repair the situation. You will come back with me to St James's Square—'

She shook her head impatiently. 'No. That's all over. I cannot live with you, ever again.'

He stared back, searching for weakness. He had always been able to dominate her, and would again. 'I can stop you seeing the children.'

'I know,' she said.

'I can take the brat from you as well,' he said viciously.

'I know.' Her eyes were hard. 'But you will not.'

She was not backing down. He didn't understand. Where had she this sudden strength from? He was almost afraid of her. 'I won't divorce you,' he warned, trying to guess her thoughts, which were suddenly opaque to him.

'I don't want a divorce.' She seemed suddenly tired. 'Holkam, I don't mean to torment you. We are what we are. You have done what you thought best, as I did. I will come to London. Not now, but soon. I will open the house. I will act the part of your wife. I know you want things to appear respectable, and I will do my best. For form's sake, I will be seen with you. But I will not live with you – like before. You know what I mean.'

A sickly sneer crossed his face. 'That, I assure you, I can do without.'

'I know,' she said again, wearily, and with dignity. 'For your part, you must allow me to live where I like. I may often wish to be here, or at Brancaster, or – elsewhere. You will not object.'

'So you can frolic with some other jack-dandy painter you happen to pick up from the gutter?' he said. 'I think not, my lady.'

Her face bleached with anger. 'How dare you speak to me like that?'

'I didn't mean it,' he said hastily. And then, annoyed with himself for having faltered, he snapped, 'Oh, live where you please, so long as you don't shame me or my children.'

'And you,' she replied evenly, 'will not shame my children.'

There was a pause, and then he gathered himself together and said with a nervous laugh, 'Come, my dear, let's behave like civilised creatures. Can't we be friends, after all? We shared so much together – before all this happened.'

'Friends,' she said, bemused; and then she made the effort too, for the children's sake. 'Yes, let's be friends.' She drew a weary breath and said, 'Will you be staying the night? I ought to have a bed made up for you. I don't know what there is for dinner. I don't trouble about it much myself.'

He looked at his watch, in a panic to get away now. 'No, no, don't trouble. I can still get back to Town if I go now. No need to put your servants out. Perhaps you'd have them telephone for a taxi.'

She laughed strangely. 'But there's no telephone here!'

In the end the maid was sent across to Morland Place to telephone for a taxi, and after half an hour of artificial conversation, Holkam was borne away to safety, leaving Violet in peace. I'm glad he didn't ask to see the baby, she thought.

At the beginning of December, Lloyd George's plotting came to a head. Lord Northcliffe's newspapers, especially the *Daily Mail* and *The Times*, stepped up their campaign against Asquith, demanding his resignation. Lloyd George persuaded most of the parliamentary Labour Party to come over to his side, on the promise of more influence; he split the Liberals, and managed to take Asquith's only Conservative friend, Balfour, with him. The Conservatives, left with only Bonar

Law as a potential prime minister, knew they could not form a government, even with Northcliffe's help, without Balfour and his faction, and without Labour's quiescence. They opted to stick with a coalition under Lloyd George.

On Sunday, the 3rd of December, a message was taken to Mr Asquith at Downing Street asking for his resignation. Betrayed by so many colleagues, and weary to death of the fight, Asquith resigned on the 5th, and Lloyd George went to the Palace to kiss hands on the 7th, as the prime minister of a coalition government.

All done in time for Christmas, Venetia thought, when she heard. She had not admired Asquith in the beginning, but she had warmed to him over the years. She was sorry for him, and for the country, too. With such a man as Lloyd George in the principal seat, it would be all intrigue and deceit and newspaper flashiness from now on, she thought.

In accordance with her agreement with Holkam, Violet came to London for a few days in December to let herself be seen and to spread the right words with the right people. Then she took the baby and went down to Brancaster to be with her other children for Christmas. Holkam joined her there – staff officers had no difficulty in getting leave to coincide with Christmas. It was a stiff and uncomfortable time for everyone. Robert, seven, and Richard, nearly six, were old enough to feel the atmosphere. They were rather afraid of their father in any case; their beautiful mother they saw as a divine but infrequent visitor from another world. And they didn't know what to make of the new baby, introduced as their little brother Henry, but with such an icy tension in the air they thought there must be something wrong with him. Charlotte, four, was just old enough to be interested in a baby, which she regarded in the light of a particularly elaborate doll brought specially for her. But it didn't seem to do much of anything but sleep, so she soon grew bored with it.

The weather was beastly and Brancaster was a chilly place, exposed to the Arctic winds, full of draughts that the fires, sulkily smoking, did little to mitigate. The Holkams had some dutiful visits from neighbours, showed their faces in church, and attended a Boxing Day ball at a nearby great house – a haven of warmth, Violet found it. She was delighted to find Freddie Copthall among the guests, and almost flew to him, discovering how much she had missed him. He greeted her calmly as always, and asked, tentatively, after the baby. He had sent a beautiful Carolean silver chalice as a present when he heard of its birth. It was a typical piece of Freddie thoughtfulness.

Holkam departed on the day after Boxing Day, and Violet gathered all her children and fled to Shawes, where Robert, Richard and Charlotte discovered that Christmas could be a delightful thing after all. Venetia was waiting for them there, and a day later Oliver and Kit Westhoven had their leave and joined them. They all felt as if Christmas was only just beginning.

Emma Weston arrived at Morland Place well before Christmas with a mass of luggage and a whole trunk full of wonderful presents for everyone, exquisitely wrapped in coloured paper and ribbon, so different from the neat brown-paper parcels tied with string that were the norm. She flung out her arms and said, 'Oh, it's lovely to be here again! Like coming home!' and proceeded to make Christmas start very early, and go on merrily as long as possible.

Lennie was still with them, though his leg had healed so well he was to be recalled to the regiment after Christmas and put on light duties, and expected to be going out to the Front again when the spring offensive started.

Uncle Teddy did his best with the celebrations, and his best was always good. There was no hunt that year, with the shortage of horses and the hunt servants having been called up. The master and some kennelmaids (*maids!*) kept hounds exercised and hoped for better things, but he was talking of having to knock them on the head in the spring, and had not bred any new puppies. But Teddy organised shooting, and there were parties, dinners, and a ball. Jack, whose squadron had been moved to Merville in November, had his leave at Christmas, and he met Helen and Basil at Morland Place for it – Helen's new baby was due in February. So, much of the family was together. It was a pity Jessie couldn't be with them. And Frank and Ned were in everyone's thoughts.

With the advent of the party at Shawes, the two households joined, to the great advantage of all. Oliver, Kit and Emma together organising games and foolish fun, the two doctors made extra men for Polly and her young female friends to dance with, and Violet, one of a party for the first time in months, found everyone kind and tactful and enjoyed it more than she had expected. Henrietta loved having Venetia there, and welcomed the little Fitzjames children, who seemed to her touchingly grave and so unused to fun they hardly seemed to know how to play. The denizens of the Morland Place nursery soon took care of that, and before the season was over, they had learned to romp – still a little shyly, perhaps, but it was a start.

'You should let them live here all the time,' she said to Violet at one time, watching them play blind man's buff with high shrieks of merriment. 'It would be good for them to have other children to play with.' From what she had heard of Brancaster, it was a fearsome, desolate place for little children.

'Perhaps I will,' said Violet.

Jessie quite enjoyed night duty, once she got used to it. The accommodation was in small individual huts in the park, which was more privacy than she had had since she arrived. The night nurses had their own bathroom, too. The first few times it was rather frightening to be alone on the ward when the Sister had gone down to supper at midnight. With no light but the small, shaded lamp at Sister's desk, the long ward was a place of shadows and odd, muffled noises – rustlings, little groans and snorts from the men, an occasional moan. Sitting at the desk, Jessie had her back to the ward door, far away at the other end, and it was impossible not to imagine people – or *things* – creeping up on her. Twice she was sure she heard footsteps approaching, but when she turned there was no-one there. On another occasion she saw something white moving stealthily in the corner of her vision, and jumped up, stifling a cry, to find it was a light passing across the window from outside.

But once she got used to it, she enjoyed the quiet, and the responsibility. With only two of them on duty, it meant that serious, interesting nursing fell to her part. On one occasion there was an emergency, and she and the night sister, Jenkins, had to work frantically together to save a man's life. It was much more fulfilling than making beds. Jenkins was a young woman, and they got on well together, with less formality than on the day shift. Jenkins even told her about her fiancé at the Front, and showed her his letters.

It was hard at first to stay awake through the night. She spent her first few night duties yawning desperately, wondering how she would ever be of any use, and praying there would not be an emergency. But once she adjusted, she learned to do with very little sleep, which meant she had her days free. Night duty was eight thirty to eight thirty, and officially night nurses were supposed to be in bed by eleven thirty, but no-one ever checked on them. Provided you were not so unlucky as to bump into a sister, you could do as you pleased. Jessie found that after breakfast and a bath she got her 'second wind'. It was fun to be about London on her own, at a time when everyone else was busy.

It also meant that when Bertie had his leave she was able to see him without having to rearrange her off-time. They met at Waterloo Station, under the clock, crossed the river and walked along the Embankment, happy just to be together. It was bitterly cold, the sky lowering grey and threatening snow. 'It must be terrible in the trenches now,' she said.

'Better the cold than the rain,' he said.

Her hand was through the crook of his left arm. She looked at his gloved hand and said, 'Show me.'

He stopped and took off the glove. The little finger ended short, in a shiny knob and a raw scar. Tears filled her eyes at the sight of it. 'Oh, Bertie,' she said.

'My dear,' he said, concerned at her tears. 'It could have been worse. I'm still here.'

'I hate you to be hurt. And it looks so – pathetic. I hate you not to be perfect any more.'

'It didn't really hurt,' he said kindly. 'There was too much going on at the time to notice it. And I never was perfect.'

'You know what I mean.'

'I know what you mean,' he said, and resumed the glove. 'Oddly enough, it's that aspect of it that I disliked the most. I hate to see my hand maimed. But, my God, when I think what's happened to the others—'

'How's Pennyfather?' she asked, after a pause.

'His knee is still swollen like a football. A great deal of pain and he can't walk on it. I went to see his wife and boys – a dear little thing, she is, like a sparrow. Too proud to take any help, though I suspect things are tight for them. Nice boys – longing to be old enough to join the Army.' He paused. 'I suppose that's why we will always have wars. Little boys think it's so glamorous.'

'You did.'

'I know. But war was different then. I wonder if the Germans had known what it would be like whether they would have started it all. It's not like charging on horseback in gorgeous blues and scarlets. It's squalid. Messy and squalid and without dignity.'

She looked quickly at him. 'But – necessary?'

He made an odd little grimace. 'Oh, yes. We will all do

our duty, however unpleasant. You too – it can't be nice tending wounds day and night. And such wounds!'

'I hate what it means to them. But I know I'm helping – doing good. That's what's important.'

'Yes,' he said.

'I know about your DSO,' she said suddenly. 'Why didn't you tell me?'

He looked down, his eyes laughing at her a little. 'It was nothing, really. They have to give them to someone.'

'But I want to be proud of you. I *am* proud of you.'

'Does it need a medal?'

'No, of course not. But I like it that they take notice of you.'

'I wouldn't want to spoil any pleasure of yours. If I get another one, I'll tell you.'

She saw he wouldn't be serious about it, shook her head and laughed, and they walked in silence a while. It began to snow, and they stopped and leaned on the parapet and watched the large flakes falling into the swirling grey-brown river, disappearing as soon as they touched the surface. She shivered, and he put his arm around her shoulders. He seemed to do it without thinking, but she stiffened an instant, wondering if anyone would see them. And then, not wanting to disturb his mood, she made herself relax, and leaned into the big, warm, comfortable bulk of him. She thought of what it would be like to be married to him, to sleep beside him at night, to find him there when she woke and curl up against his sleeping warmth. That simple pleasure – just that. She would have settled for it. Oh, God, why could not such things be? Loving each other with such dearness, they must never have what ordinary, lucky people had.

He spoke, and it seemed as though he had followed her thought. 'I wish we could be married,' he said quietly. 'I wish I had waited for you. I feel so much a part of you that sometimes I have to remember we aren't, and I surprise myself. It's as if I'm reading a book I know really well, and I turn the page to find the ending's wrong. What would I give to rewrite that one little bit? Why can't we go back in life and put things right? Everything seems to go in such straight lines, and how can we know from the beginning where they'll lead, and which is the right one to take? It doesn't seem fair.'

She pressed against him, and had nothing to say. He looked down at her, and smiled, and brought his other hand up to push a thread of hair away from her brow. The gesture was one of such tenderness it almost broke her heart. She looked up into his loved face, and thought she would give all of this world and the next to be married to him for just a day, to put her hands up and cup his face and kiss him as his wife, with the right to do it. Her stomach was hollow with love, her bones felt empty with it; wanting, wanting, and never to be fulfilled.

He said, 'You're cold. And you must be hungry. Come, we'll go and get some luncheon. The Savoy's just along here. That'll do.'

In the restaurant he seemed to set himself to entertain her, and did it well. He was light, amusing, charming, like in the old days, before the war, and she let him see that she was happy. It seemed all she could do for him, all she could give him, to let him please her in the only way allowed.

When Christmas was over and everyone had gone away, Violet went back to London with her mother and the children, meaning to do a little shopping, and give the older ones a last treat before they had to go back to their lessons, perhaps take them to a pantomime or a circus performance, if she could find one.

Fitzjames House seemed gloomy and cold, though she had telegraphed ahead for it to be opened and made ready for her. Her mother, who had come to the house from the train with her, shivered and said, 'Why don't you come home with me until the place has warmed up. I don't believe the servants have lit enough fires.'

'It's always cold for the first week in winter,' Violet said.

'Then come and stay with me for a week,' Venetia said. Violet hesitated, thinking that Holkam wouldn't like it. But then she saw the shadow in her mother's eyes, and thought what it must be like for her to go back to Manchester Square, without Papa, without Oliver, without her. Before Octavian's death, she would never have thought about her mother having feelings. What a selfish creature she had been! She had grown up a little now, she hoped.

'I'll come for tonight,' she said. 'It's too cold here for the children. Just let me give Varden some orders, and see what there is in the post.'

Venetia gathered the children to her, and encouraged them to play with the dogs to keep them occupied while Violet interviewed the butler and sifted through the small heap on the hall table. She saw her lift a large, square, flat parcel with a puzzled look, and drifted closer, wondering what it could be, hoping it was not something unpleasant for her daughter.

Violet opened it, and took out a sheaf of papers, with a letter pinned to the top one. Venetia saw her turn white. They were drawings.

'It's from Colonel Villiers,' Violet said, in a thread of a voice. 'He's sent them to me. He says – he says he understands that I will know how to dispose of them, given that Private Laidislaw had no next-of-kin.'

How kind, Venetia thought dazedly. How very kind. Someone must have explained things to him – Tranley's friend Henry, perhaps. A little, secret, kindly gesture behind Authority's back, which would harm nobody and do good where it mattered most.

Violet unpinned the letter and looked at the drawings, one by one, handing each to her mother as she finished with it. Faces, faces – they leaped out at the eye, some delicately sketched, some dashed in watercolour, some heavily chiaroscuro, but every one so invested with life that though the subjects were none of them famous in any way, Venetia felt curiously as though she knew them. There were soldiers in every pose – sitting dozing on a box in the sun; shaving in shirtsleeves and braces, before a looking-glass lodged in the twigs of a bush; slumped on the firing-step smoking a cigarette, rifle resting against the trench wall; staring over the parapet, squinting into the distance; grinning over a hand of cards. A whole army lay under her hands, in uniform but not uniform, the human reality behind the neatly dressed lines and smartly marching companies. Soldiers all, going about their soldierly routine, looking out, looking up, smiling as they passed, leaping from the paper into her mind before they passed on, back to their trenches and whatever fate had befallen them. How many, she wondered in sudden, vivid pain, were dead now? Laidislaw had captured their essence and put them on paper so that they should live for ever. He had made these doomed men immortal. He had done something so important and so – *gracious*, in the Godly sense, that Venetia found her mouth dry with emotion and could not speak.

Violet looked up at her mother, and there were tears on her cheeks. 'I told you,' she said softly. 'I told you, didn't I, Mama?'

'Yes, darling,' said Venetia. 'You told me.'